TERRY and the Pirates

by MILTON CANIFF

GAL GOT OUR PAL

FLYING BUTTRESS
Classics Library

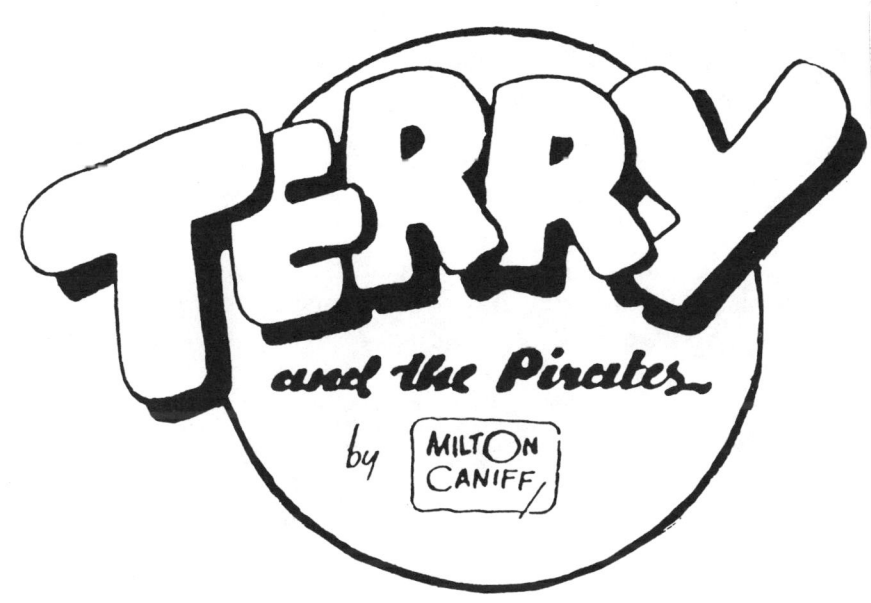

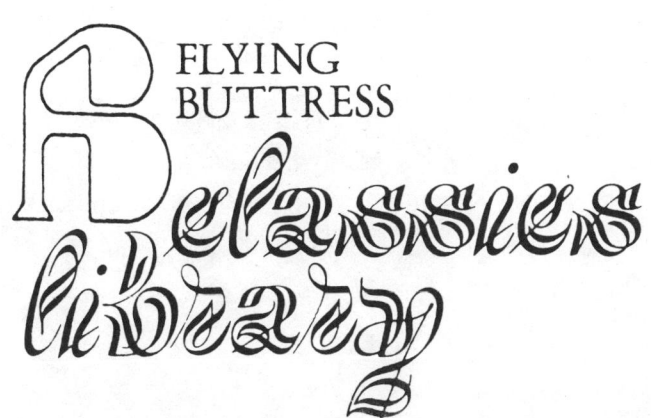

Our Story So Far...

Capt. Blaze's jig is up! Everybody's conspiring against him. Cue-Ball, his assistant, betrays him and steals his gold just as the farcical but dangerous Singh-Singh shows up demanding it. Worse yet, his own vengeful daughter, Miss Cheery, has just managed to put everyone in his fort to sleep with an evil opium brew dropped in the evening stew... on the eve of Singh-Singh's attack! Pat has yet to partake of the tainted meal...

ISBN 0-918348-63-3
© NBM 1989
cover designed and painted by Ray Fehrenbach.

Terry & The Pirates is a registered trademark of the Tribune Media Services, Inc.

THE FLYING BUTTRESS CLASSICS LIBRARY
is an imprint of:

NANTIER · BEALL · MINOUSTCHINE
Publishing co.
new york

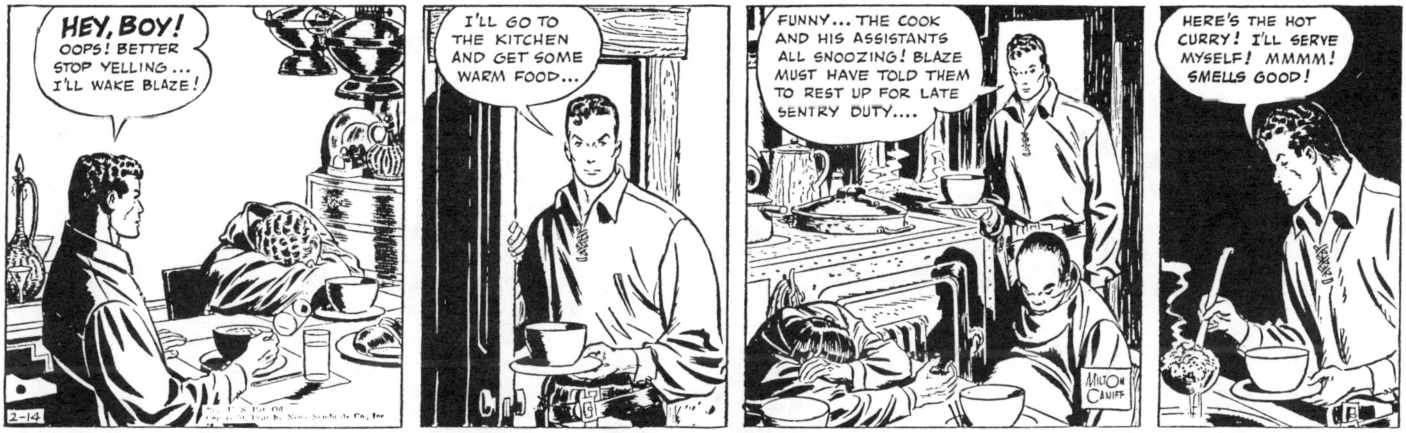
HEY, BOY! OOPS! BETTER STOP YELLING ... I'LL WAKE BLAZE!
I'LL GO TO THE KITCHEN AND GET SOME WARM FOOD...
FUNNY... THE COOK AND HIS ASSISTANTS ALL SNOOZING! BLAZE MUST HAVE TOLD THEM TO REST UP FOR LATE SENTRY DUTY....
HERE'S THE HOT CURRY! I'LL SERVE MYSELF! MMMM! SMELLS GOOD!
MILTON CANIFF
2-14

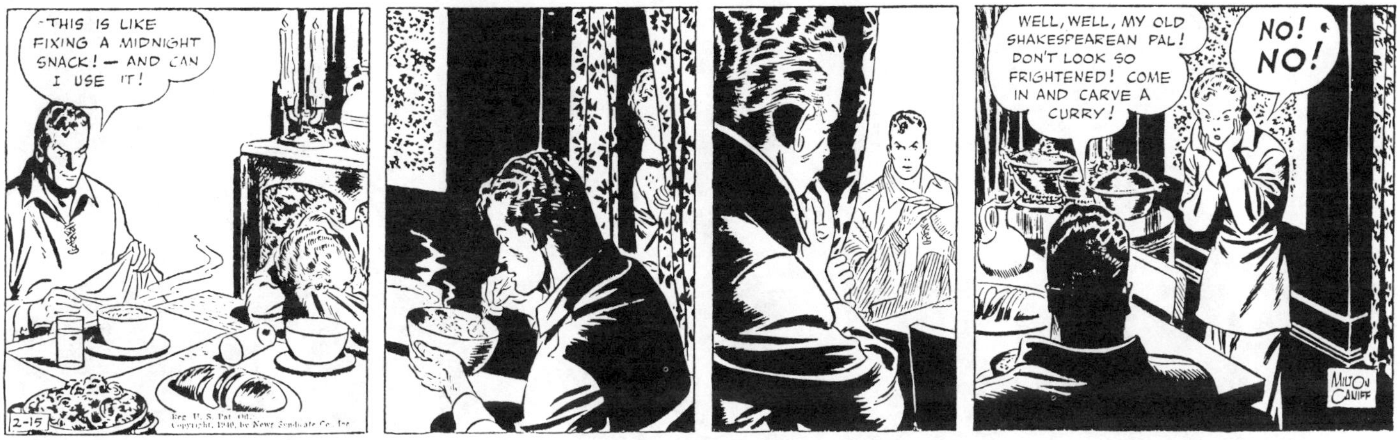
THIS IS LIKE FIXING A MIDNIGHT SNACK! — AND CAN I USE IT!
WELL, WELL, MY OLD SHAKESPEAREAN PAL! DON'T LOOK SO FRIGHTENED! COME IN AND CARVE A CURRY!
NO! NO!
MILTON CANIFF
2-15
Reg. U. S. Pat. Off.
Copyright, 1940, by News Syndicate Co., Inc.

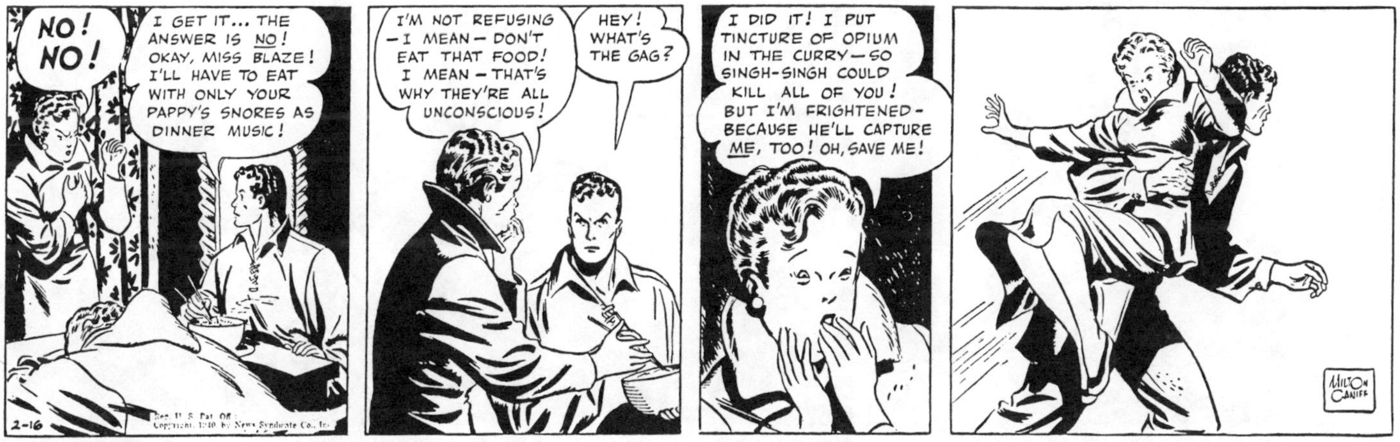
NO! NO!
I GET IT... THE ANSWER IS NO! OKAY, MISS BLAZE! I'LL HAVE TO EAT WITH ONLY YOUR PAPPY'S SNORES AS DINNER MUSIC!
I'M NOT REFUSING — I MEAN — DON'T EAT THAT FOOD! I MEAN — THAT'S WHY THEY'RE ALL UNCONSCIOUS!
HEY! WHAT'S THE GAG?
I DID IT! I PUT TINCTURE OF OPIUM IN THE CURRY — SO SINGH-SINGH COULD KILL ALL OF YOU! BUT I'M FRIGHTENED - BECAUSE HE'LL CAPTURE ME, TOO! OH, SAVE ME!
MILTON CANIFF
2-16
Reg. U. S. Pat. Off.
Copyright, 1940, by News Syndicate Co., Inc.

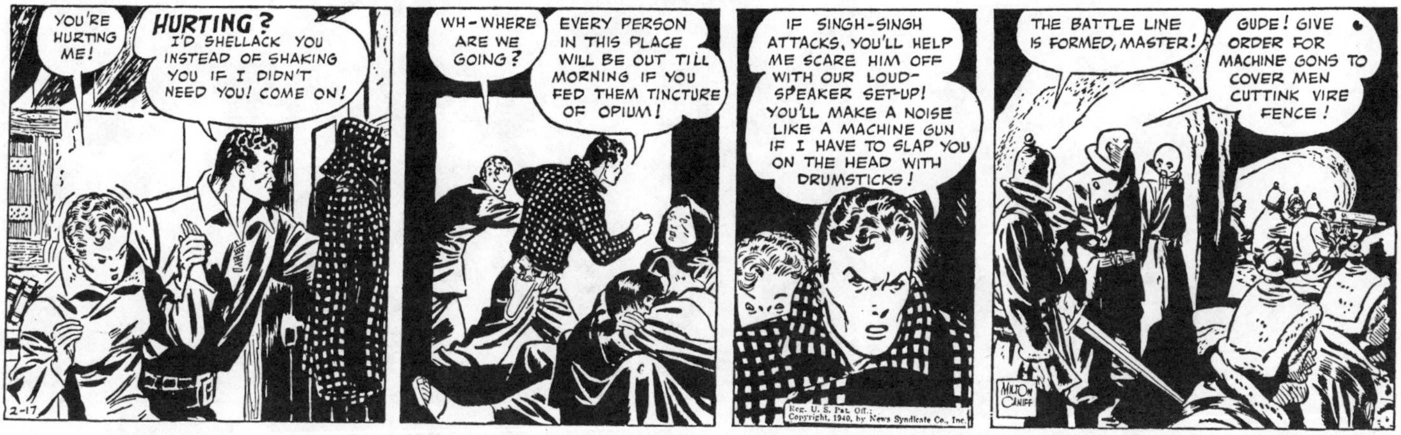
YOU'RE HURTING ME!
HURTING? I'D SHELLACK YOU INSTEAD OF SHAKING YOU IF I DIDN'T NEED YOU! COME ON!
WH-WHERE ARE WE GOING?
EVERY PERSON IN THIS PLACE WILL BE OUT TILL MORNING IF YOU FED THEM TINCTURE OF OPIUM!
IF SINGH-SINGH ATTACKS, YOU'LL HELP ME SCARE HIM OFF WITH OUR LOUD-SPEAKER SET-UP! YOU'LL MAKE A NOISE LIKE A MACHINE GUN IF I HAVE TO SLAP YOU ON THE HEAD WITH DRUMSTICKS!
THE BATTLE LINE IS FORMED, MASTER!
GUDE! GIVE ORDER FOR MACHINE GONS TO COVER MEN CUTTINK VIRE FENCE!
MILTON CANIFF
2-17
Reg. U. S. Pat. Off.
Copyright, 1940, by News Syndicate Co., Inc.

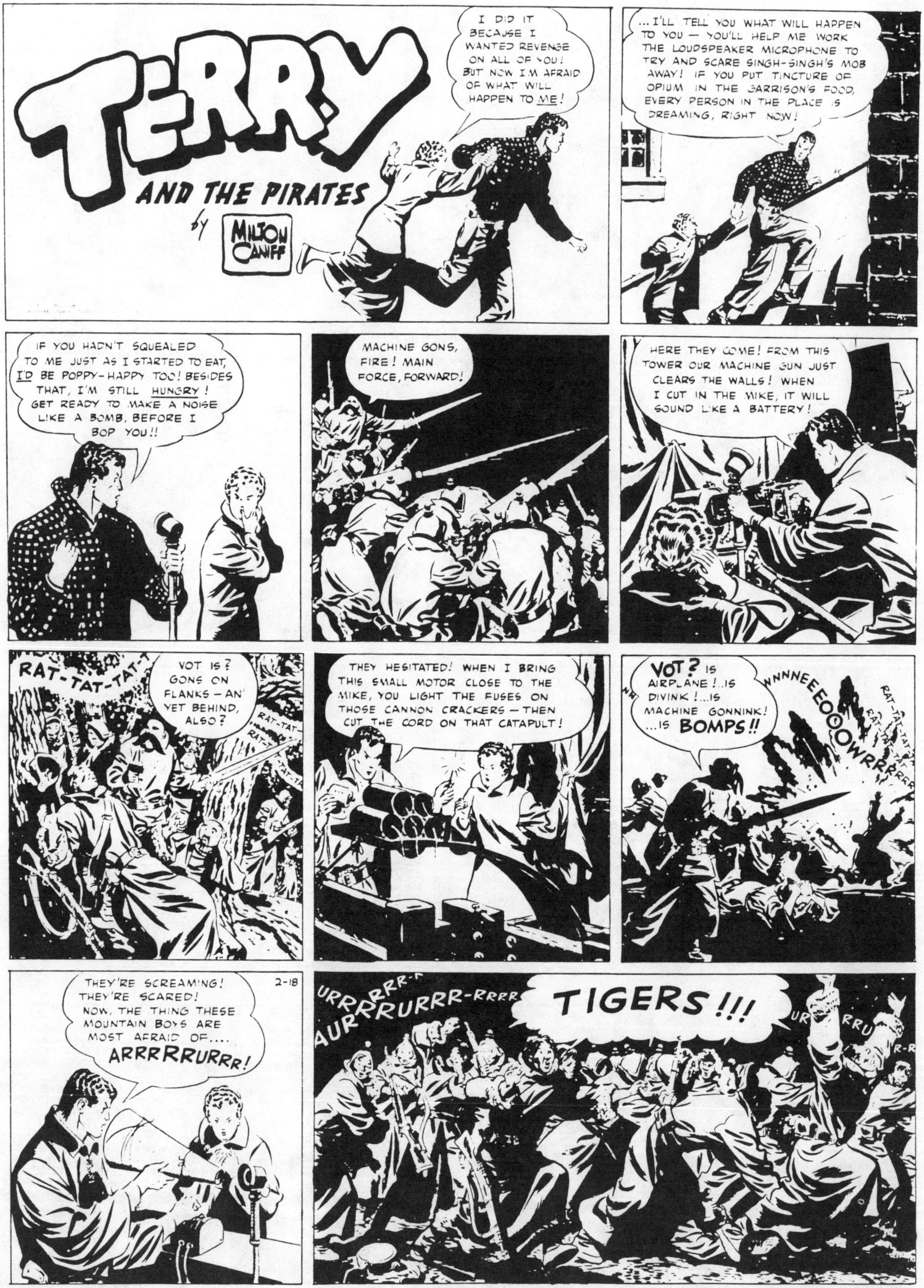
TERRY AND THE PIRATES
by MILTON CANIFF
I DID IT BECAUSE I WANTED REVENGE ON ALL OF YOU! BUT NOW I'M AFRAID OF WHAT WILL HAPPEN TO ME!
... I'LL TELL YOU WHAT WILL HAPPEN TO YOU — YOU'LL HELP ME WORK THE LOUDSPEAKER MICROPHONE TO TRY AND SCARE SINGH-SINGH'S MOB AWAY! IF YOU PUT TINCTURE OF OPIUM IN THE GARRISON'S FOOD, EVERY PERSON IN THE PLACE IS DREAMING, RIGHT NOW!
IF YOU HADN'T SQUEALED TO ME JUST AS I STARTED TO EAT, I'D BE POPPY-HAPPY TOO! BESIDES THAT, I'M STILL HUNGRY! GET READY TO MAKE A NOISE LIKE A BOMB, BEFORE I BOP YOU!!
MACHINE GONS, FIRE! MAIN FORCE, FORWARD!
HERE THEY COME! FROM THIS TOWER OUR MACHINE GUN JUST CLEARS THE WALLS! WHEN I CUT IN THE MIKE, IT WILL SOUND LIKE A BATTERY!
RAT-TAT-TAT-T
VOT IS? GONS ON FLANKS — AN' YET BEHIND, ALSO?
RAT-TAT-
THEY HESITATED! WHEN I BRING THIS SMALL MOTOR CLOSE TO THE MIKE, YOU LIGHT THE FUSES ON THOSE CANNON CRACKERS — THEN CUT THE CORD ON THAT CATAPULT!
VOT? IS AIRPLANE!...IS DIVINK!...IS MACHINE GONNINK! ...IS BOMPS!!
WNNNEEEOOOOWRRR
THEY'RE SCREAMING! THEY'RE SCARED! NOW, THE THING THESE MOUNTAIN BOYS ARE MOST AFRAID OF.... ARRRRRURRR!
2-18
URRRRRR-RURRR-RRRR
AURR
TIGERS!!!

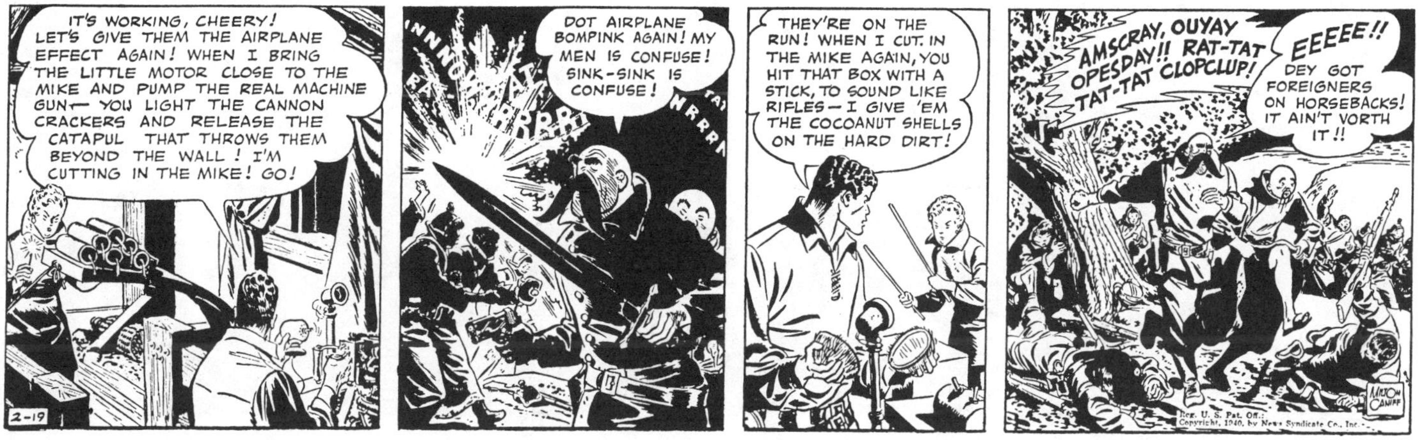
IT'S WORKING, CHEERY! LET'S GIVE THEM THE AIRPLANE EFFECT AGAIN! WHEN I BRING THE LITTLE MOTOR CLOSE TO THE MIKE AND PUMP THE REAL MACHINE GUN— YOU LIGHT THE CANNON CRACKERS AND RELEASE THE CATAPUL THAT THROWS THEM BEYOND THE WALL! I'M CUTTING IN THE MIKE! GO!
2-19
DOT AIRPLANE BOMPINK AGAIN! MY MEN IS CONFUSE! SINK-SINK IS CONFUSE!
THEY'RE ON THE RUN! WHEN I CUT IN THE MIKE AGAIN, YOU HIT THAT BOX WITH A STICK, TO SOUND LIKE RIFLES— I GIVE 'EM THE COCOANUT SHELLS ON THE HARD DIRT!
AMSCRAY, OUYAY OPESDAY!! RAT-TAT TAT-TAT CLOPCLUP!
EEEEE!!
DEY GOT FOREIGNERS ON HORSEBACKS! IT AIN'T VORTH IT!!
MILTON CANIFF
Reg. U. S. Pat. Off.; Copyright, 1940, by News Syndicate Co., Inc.

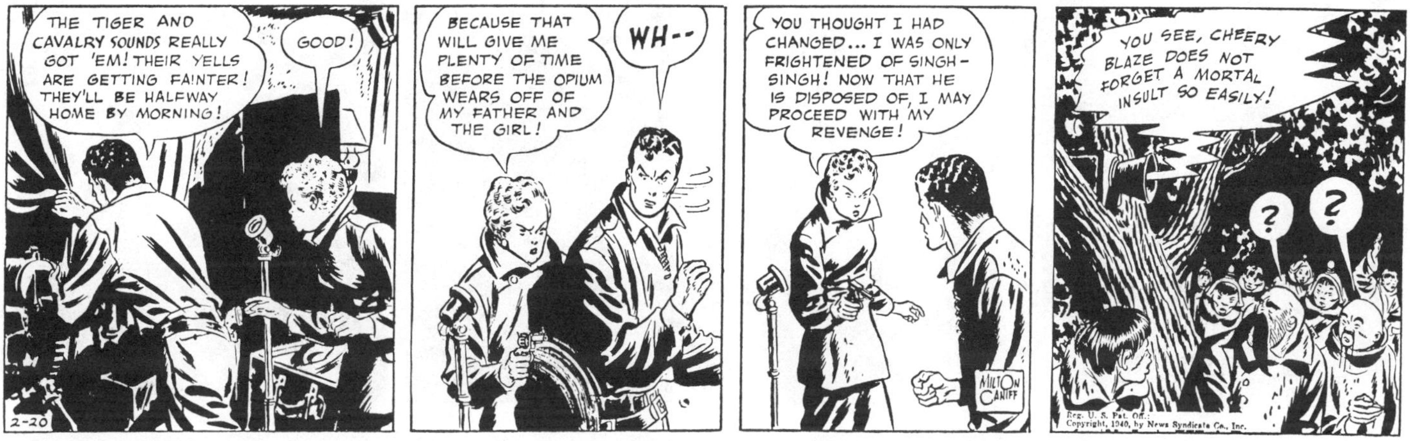
THE TIGER AND CAVALRY SOUNDS REALLY GOT 'EM! THEIR YELLS ARE GETTING FAINTER! THEY'LL BE HALFWAY HOME BY MORNING!
GOOD!
2-20
BECAUSE THAT WILL GIVE ME PLENTY OF TIME BEFORE THE OPIUM WEARS OFF OF MY FATHER AND THE GIRL!
WH--
YOU THOUGHT I HAD CHANGED... I WAS ONLY FRIGHTENED OF SINGH-SINGH! NOW THAT HE IS DISPOSED OF, I MAY PROCEED WITH MY REVENGE!
MILTON CANIFF
YOU SEE, CHEERY BLAZE DOES NOT FORGET A MORTAL INSULT SO EASILY!
?
?
Reg. U. S. Pat. Off.; Copyright, 1940, by News Syndicate Co., Inc.

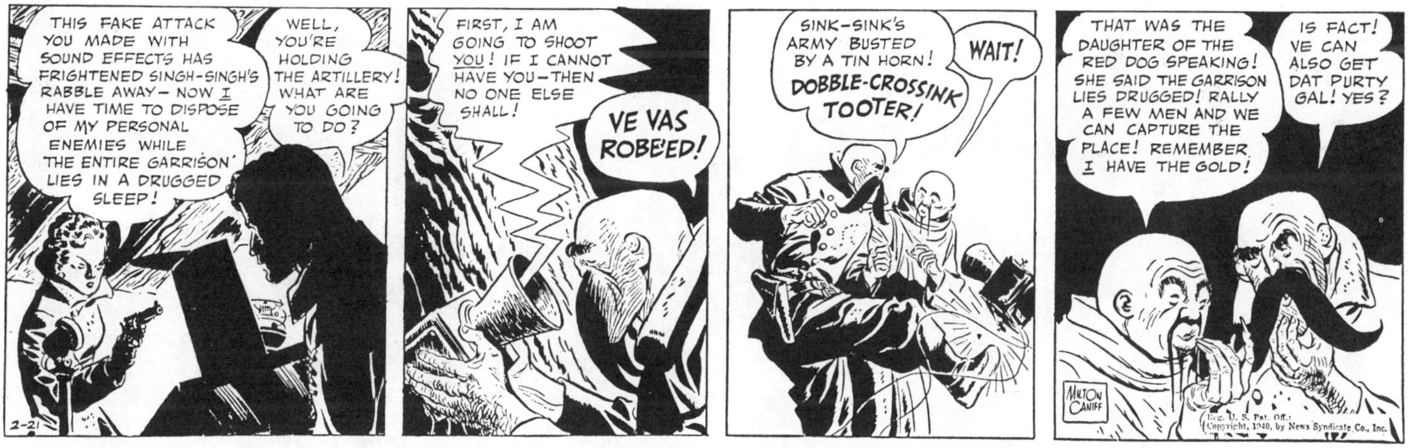
THIS FAKE ATTACK YOU MADE WITH SOUND EFFECTS HAS FRIGHTENED SINGH-SINGH'S RABBLE AWAY— NOW I HAVE TIME TO DISPOSE OF MY PERSONAL ENEMIES WHILE THE ENTIRE GARRISON LIES IN A DRUGGED SLEEP!
WELL, YOU'RE HOLDING THE ARTILLERY! WHAT ARE YOU GOING TO DO?
2-21
FIRST, I AM GOING TO SHOOT YOU! IF I CANNOT HAVE YOU—THEN NO ONE ELSE SHALL!
VE VAS ROBE'ED!
SINK-SINK'S ARMY BUSTED BY A TIN HORN! DOBBLE-CROSSINK TOOTER!
WAIT!
THAT WAS THE DAUGHTER OF THE RED DOG SPEAKING! SHE SAID THE GARRISON LIES DRUGGED! RALLY A FEW MEN AND WE CAN CAPTURE THE PLACE! REMEMBER I HAVE THE GOLD!
IS FACT! VE CAN ALSO GET DAT PURTY GAL! YES?
MILTON CANIFF
Reg. U. S. Pat. Off.; Copyright, 1940, by News Syndicate Co., Inc.

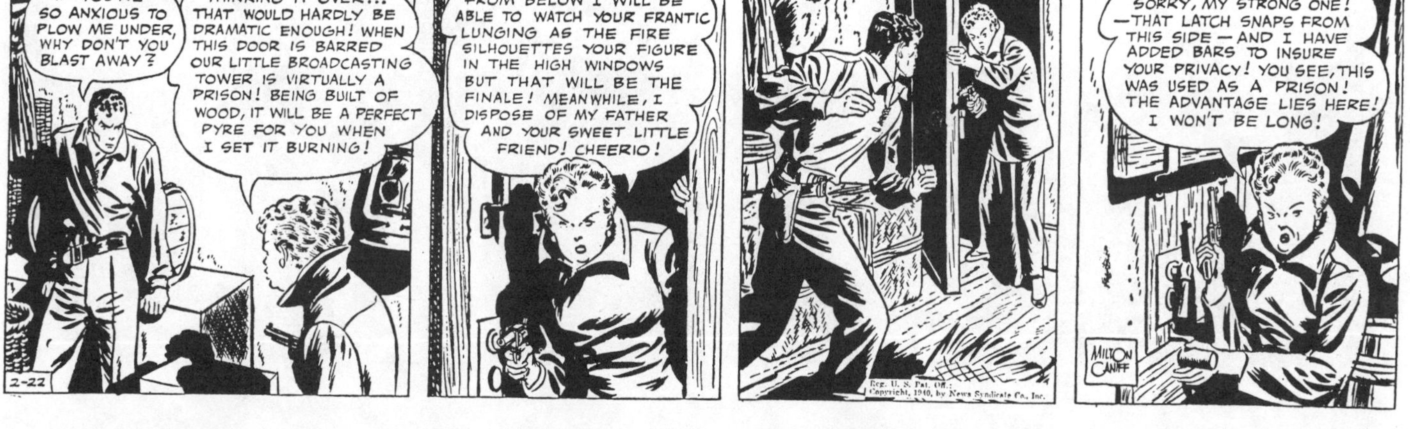
IF YOU'RE SO ANXIOUS TO PLOW ME UNDER, WHY DON'T YOU BLAST AWAY?
THINKING IT OVER... THAT WOULD HARDLY BE DRAMATIC ENOUGH! WHEN THIS DOOR IS BARRED OUR LITTLE BROADCASTING TOWER IS VIRTUALLY A PRISON! BEING BUILT OF WOOD, IT WILL BE A PERFECT PYRE FOR YOU WHEN I SET IT BURNING!
2-22
FROM BELOW I WILL BE ABLE TO WATCH YOUR FRANTIC LUNGING AS THE FIRE SILHOUETTES YOUR FIGURE IN THE HIGH WINDOWS BUT THAT WILL BE THE FINALE! MEANWHILE, I DISPOSE OF MY FATHER AND YOUR SWEET LITTLE FRIEND! CHEERIO!
Reg. U. S. Pat. Off.; Copyright, 1940, by News Syndicate Co., Inc.
SORRY, MY STRONG ONE! —THAT LATCH SNAPS FROM THIS SIDE — AND I HAVE ADDED BARS TO INSURE YOUR PRIVACY! YOU SEE, THIS WAS USED AS A PRISON! THE ADVANTAGE LIES HERE! I WON'T BE LONG!
MILTON CANIFF

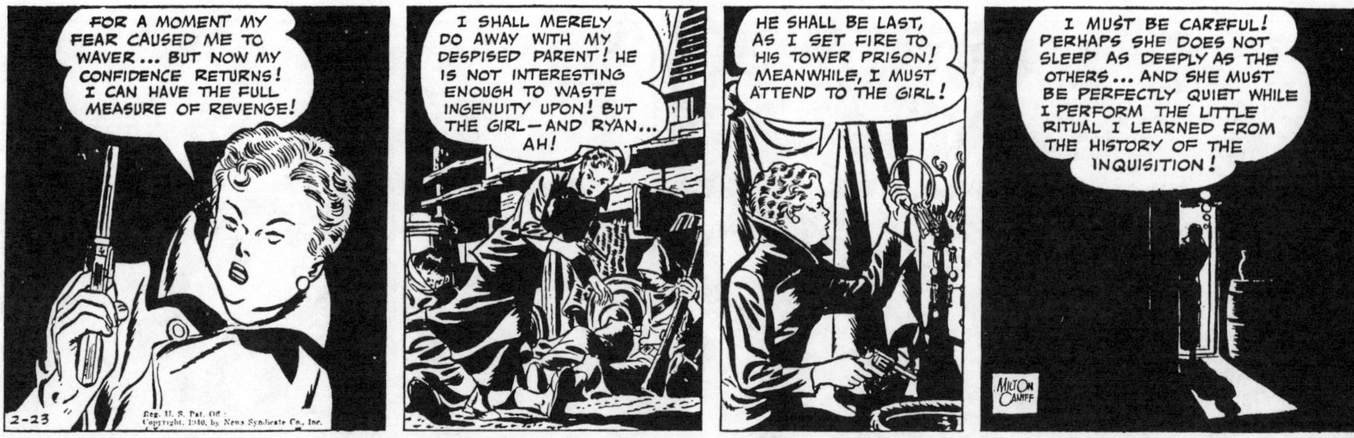
FOR A MOMENT MY FEAR CAUSED ME TO WAVER ... BUT NOW MY CONFIDENCE RETURNS! I CAN HAVE THE FULL MEASURE OF REVENGE!
2-23
Reg. U. S. Pat. Off.: Copyright, 1940, by News Syndicate Co., Inc.
I SHALL MERELY DO AWAY WITH MY DESPISED PARENT! HE IS NOT INTERESTING ENOUGH TO WASTE INGENUITY UPON! BUT THE GIRL—AND RYAN... AH!
HE SHALL BE LAST, AS I SET FIRE TO HIS TOWER PRISON! MEANWHILE, I MUST ATTEND TO THE GIRL!
I MUST BE CAREFUL! PERHAPS SHE DOES NOT SLEEP AS DEEPLY AS THE OTHERS ... AND SHE MUST BE PERFECTLY QUIET WHILE I PERFORM THE LITTLE RITUAL I LEARNED FROM THE HISTORY OF THE INQUISITION!
MILTON CANIFF

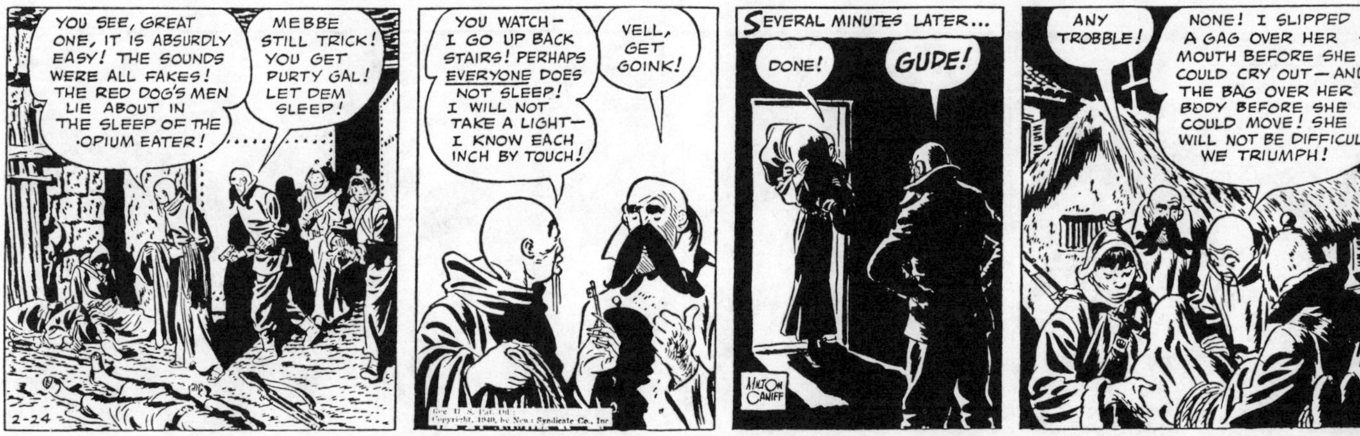
YOU SEE, GREAT ONE, IT IS ABSURDLY EASY! THE SOUNDS WERE ALL FAKES! THE RED DOG'S MEN LIE ABOUT IN THE SLEEP OF THE OPIUM EATER!
MEBBE STILL TRICK! YOU GET PURTY GAL! LET DEM SLEEP!
2-24
YOU WATCH— I GO UP BACK STAIRS! PERHAPS EVERYONE DOES NOT SLEEP! I WILL NOT TAKE A LIGHT— I KNOW EACH INCH BY TOUCH!
VELL, GET GOINK!
Reg. U. S. Pat. Off.: Copyright, 1940, by News Syndicate Co., Inc.
SEVERAL MINUTES LATER...
DONE!
GUDE!
MILTON CANIFF
ANY TROBBLE!
NONE! I SLIPPED A GAG OVER HER MOUTH BEFORE SHE COULD CRY OUT—AND THE BAG OVER HER BODY BEFORE SHE COULD MOVE! SHE WILL NOT BE DIFFICULT! WE TRIUMPH!

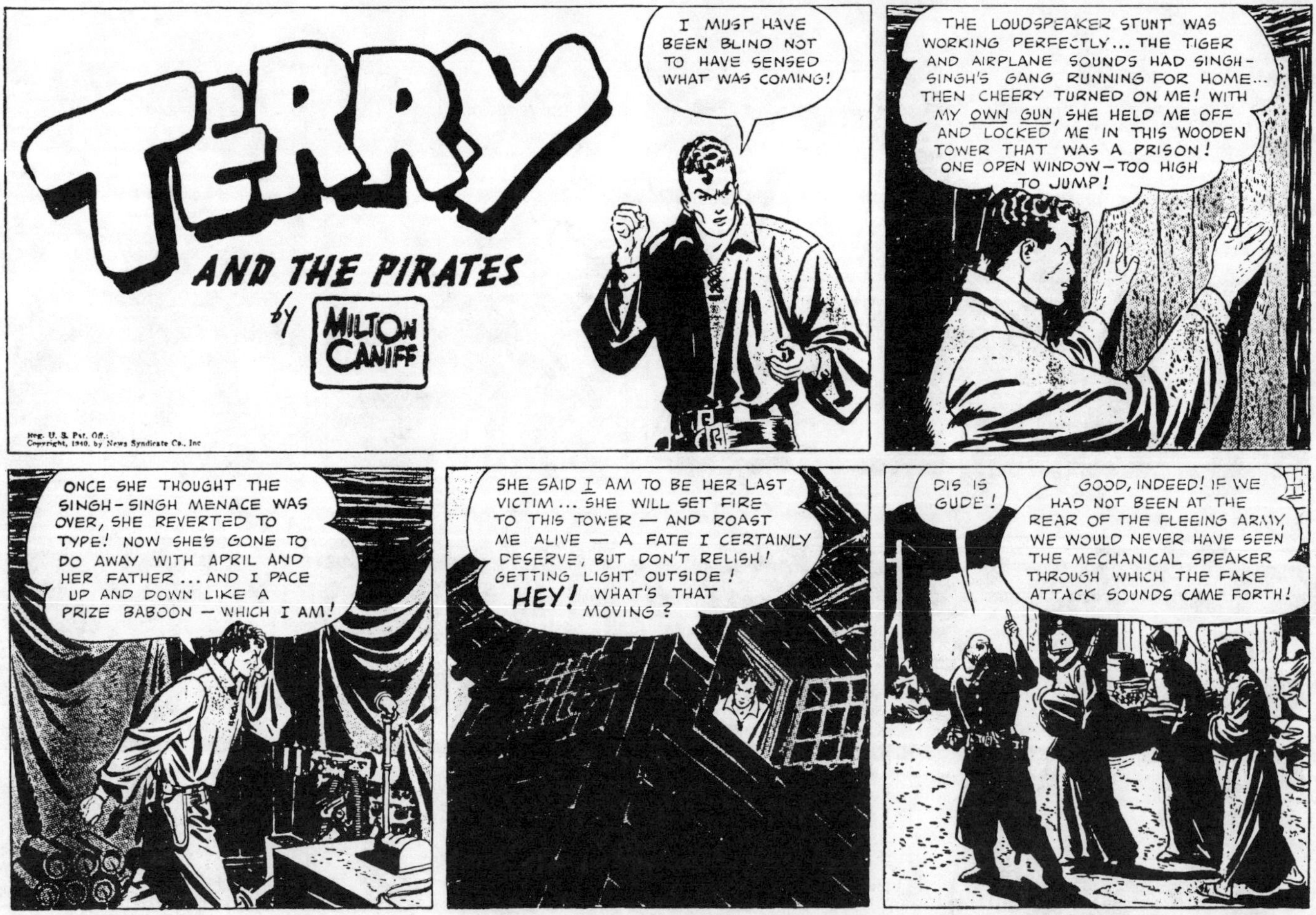
TERRY AND THE PIRATES
by MILTON CANIFF
Reg. U. S. Pat. Off.: Copyright, 1940, by News Syndicate Co., Inc.
I MUST HAVE BEEN BLIND NOT TO HAVE SENSED WHAT WAS COMING!
THE LOUDSPEAKER STUNT WAS WORKING PERFECTLY... THE TIGER AND AIRPLANE SOUNDS HAD SINGH-SINGH'S GANG RUNNING FOR HOME... THEN CHEERY TURNED ON ME! WITH MY OWN GUN, SHE HELD ME OFF AND LOCKED ME IN THIS WOODEN TOWER THAT WAS A PRISON! ONE OPEN WINDOW—TOO HIGH TO JUMP!
ONCE SHE THOUGHT THE SINGH-SINGH MENACE WAS OVER, SHE REVERTED TO TYPE! NOW SHE'S GONE TO DO AWAY WITH APRIL AND HER FATHER ... AND I PACE UP AND DOWN LIKE A PRIZE BABOON — WHICH I AM!
SHE SAID I AM TO BE HER LAST VICTIM ... SHE WILL SET FIRE TO THIS TOWER — AND ROAST ME ALIVE — A FATE I CERTAINLY DESERVE, BUT DON'T RELISH! GETTING LIGHT OUTSIDE! HEY! WHAT'S THAT MOVING?
DIS IS GUDE!
GOOD, INDEED! IF WE HAD NOT BEEN AT THE REAR OF THE FLEEING ARMY, WE WOULD NEVER HAVE SEEN THE MECHANICAL SPEAKER THROUGH WHICH THE FAKE ATTACK SOUNDS CAME FORTH!

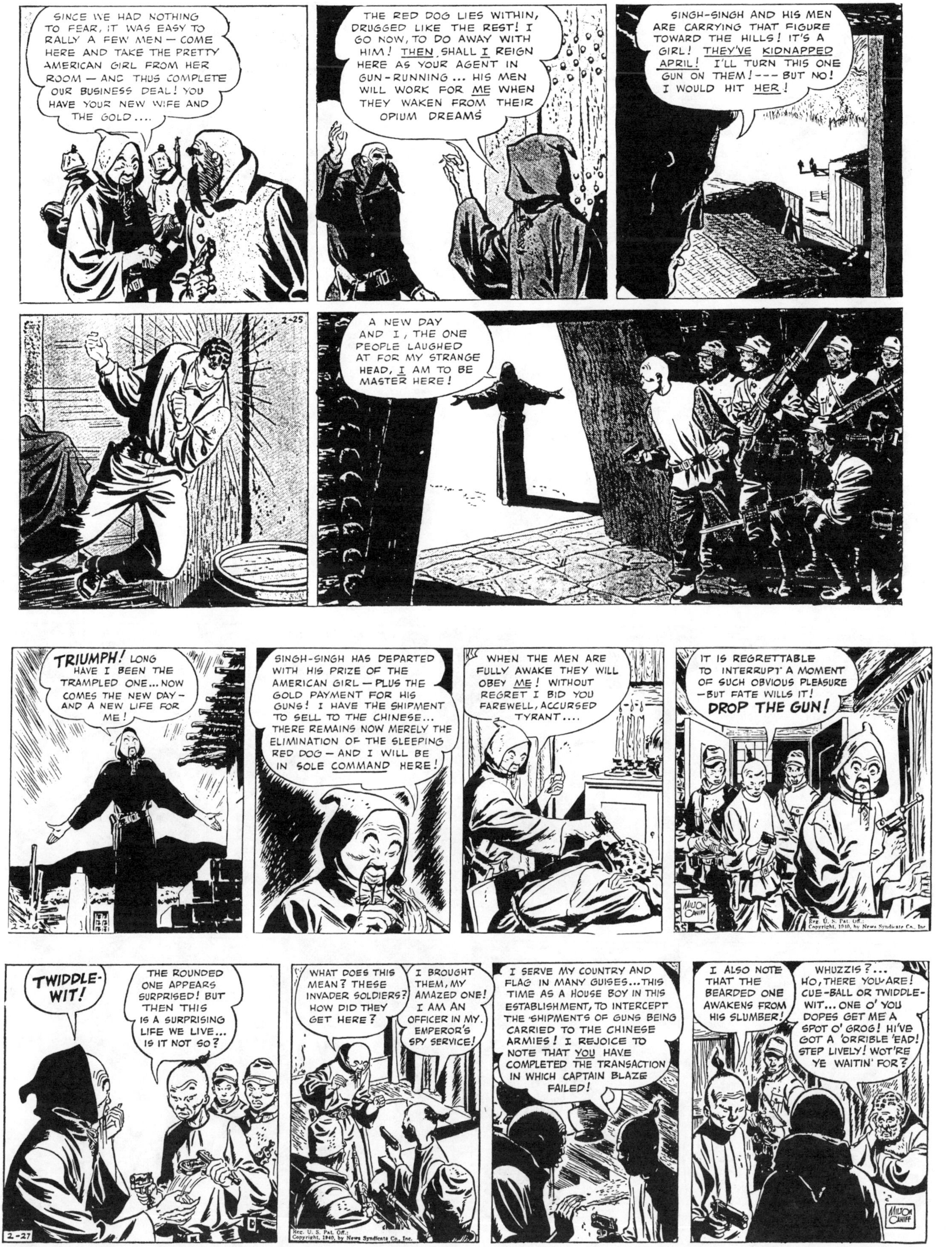
SINCE WE HAD NOTHING TO FEAR, IT WAS EASY TO RALLY A FEW MEN — COME HERE AND TAKE THE PRETTY AMERICAN GIRL FROM HER ROOM — AND THUS COMPLETE OUR BUSINESS DEAL! YOU HAVE YOUR NEW WIFE AND THE GOLD....
THE RED DOG LIES WITHIN, DRUGGED LIKE THE REST! I GO NOW, TO DO AWAY WITH HIM! THEN, SHALL I REIGN HERE AS YOUR AGENT IN GUN-RUNNING ... HIS MEN WILL WORK FOR ME WHEN THEY WAKEN FROM THEIR OPIUM DREAMS
SINGH-SINGH AND HIS MEN ARE CARRYING THAT FIGURE TOWARD THE HILLS! IT'S A GIRL! THEY'VE KIDNAPPED APRIL! I'LL TURN THIS ONE GUN ON THEM! --- BUT NO! I WOULD HIT HER!
2-25
A NEW DAY AND I, THE ONE PEOPLE LAUGHED AT FOR MY STRANGE HEAD, I AM TO BE MASTER HERE!
TRIUMPH! LONG HAVE I BEEN THE TRAMPLED ONE... NOW COMES THE NEW DAY - AND A NEW LIFE FOR ME!
2-26
SINGH-SINGH HAS DEPARTED WITH HIS PRIZE OF THE AMERICAN GIRL — PLUS THE GOLD PAYMENT FOR HIS GUNS! I HAVE THE SHIPMENT TO SELL TO THE CHINESE... THERE REMAINS NOW MERELY THE ELIMINATION OF THE SLEEPING RED DOG — AND I WILL BE IN SOLE COMMAND HERE!
WHEN THE MEN ARE FULLY AWAKE THEY WILL OBEY ME! WITHOUT REGRET I BID YOU FAREWELL, ACCURSED TYRANT....
IT IS REGRETTABLE TO INTERRUPT A MOMENT OF SUCH OBVIOUS PLEASURE —BUT FATE WILLS IT!
DROP THE GUN!
MILTON CANIFF
Reg. U. S. Pat. Off.; Copyright, 1940, by News Syndicate Co., Inc.
TWIDDLE-WIT!
THE ROUNDED ONE APPEARS SURPRISED! BUT THEN THIS IS A SURPRISING LIFE WE LIVE... IS IT NOT SO?
2-27
WHAT DOES THIS MEAN? THESE INVADER SOLDIERS? HOW DID THEY GET HERE?
I BROUGHT THEM, MY AMAZED ONE! I AM AN OFFICER IN MY EMPEROR'S SPY SERVICE!
Reg. U. S. Pat. Off.; Copyright, 1940, by News Syndicate Co., Inc.
I SERVE MY COUNTRY AND FLAG IN MANY GUISES... THIS TIME AS A HOUSE BOY IN THIS ESTABLISHMENT, TO INTERCEPT THE SHIPMENTS OF GUNS BEING CARRIED TO THE CHINESE ARMIES! I REJOICE TO NOTE THAT YOU HAVE COMPLETED THE TRANSACTION IN WHICH CAPTAIN BLAZE FAILED!
I ALSO NOTE THAT THE BEARDED ONE AWAKENS FROM HIS SLUMBER!
WHUZZIS?... H'O, THERE YOU ARE! CUE-BALL OR TWIDDLE-WIT... ONE O' YOU DOPES GET ME A SPOT O' GROG! HI'VE GOT A 'ORRIBLE 'EAD! STEP LIVELY! WOT'RE YE WAITIN' FOR?
MILTON CANIFF

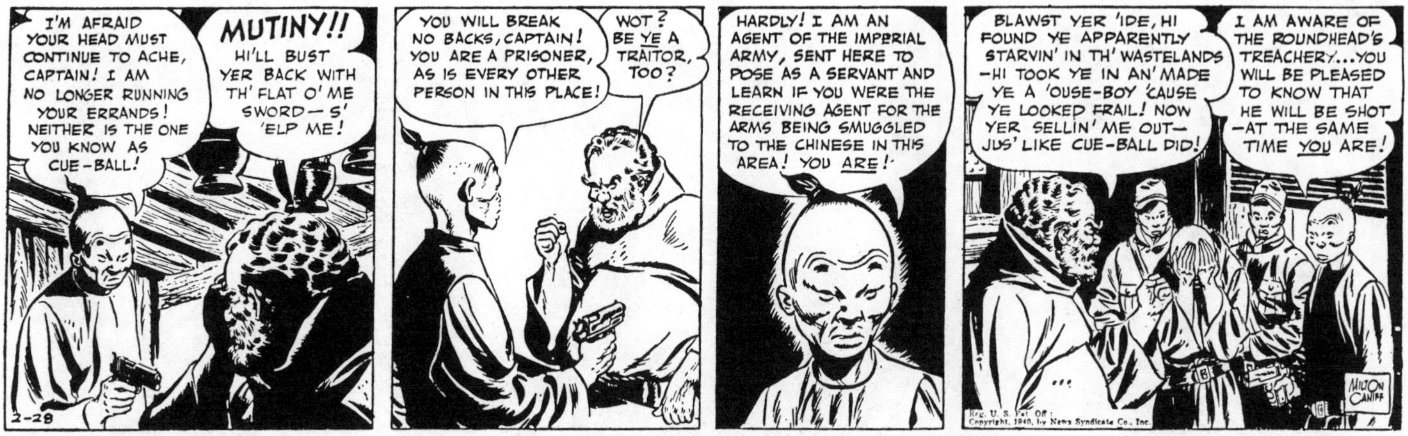
I'M AFRAID YOUR HEAD MUST CONTINUE TO ACHE, CAPTAIN! I AM NO LONGER RUNNING YOUR ERRANDS! NEITHER IS THE ONE YOU KNOW AS CUE-BALL!
MUTINY!! HI'LL BUST YER BACK WITH TH' FLAT O' ME SWORD—S' 'ELP ME!
2-28
YOU WILL BREAK NO BACKS, CAPTAIN! YOU ARE A PRISONER, AS IS EVERY OTHER PERSON IN THIS PLACE!
WOT? BE YE A TRAITOR, TOO?
HARDLY! I AM AN AGENT OF THE IMPERIAL ARMY, SENT HERE TO POSE AS A SERVANT AND LEARN IF YOU WERE THE RECEIVING AGENT FOR THE ARMS BEING SMUGGLED TO THE CHINESE IN THIS AREA! YOU ARE!
...
Reg. U. S. Pat. Off.: Copyright, 1940, by News Syndicate Co., Inc.
BLAWST YER 'IDE, HI FOUND YE APPARENTLY STARVIN' IN TH' WASTELANDS —HI TOOK YE IN AN' MADE YE A 'OUSE-BOY 'CAUSE YE LOOKED FRAIL! NOW YER SELLIN' ME OUT—JUS' LIKE CUE-BALL DID!
I AM AWARE OF THE ROUNDHEAD'S TREACHERY...YOU WILL BE PLEASED TO KNOW THAT HE WILL BE SHOT—AT THE SAME TIME YOU ARE!
MILTON CANIFF

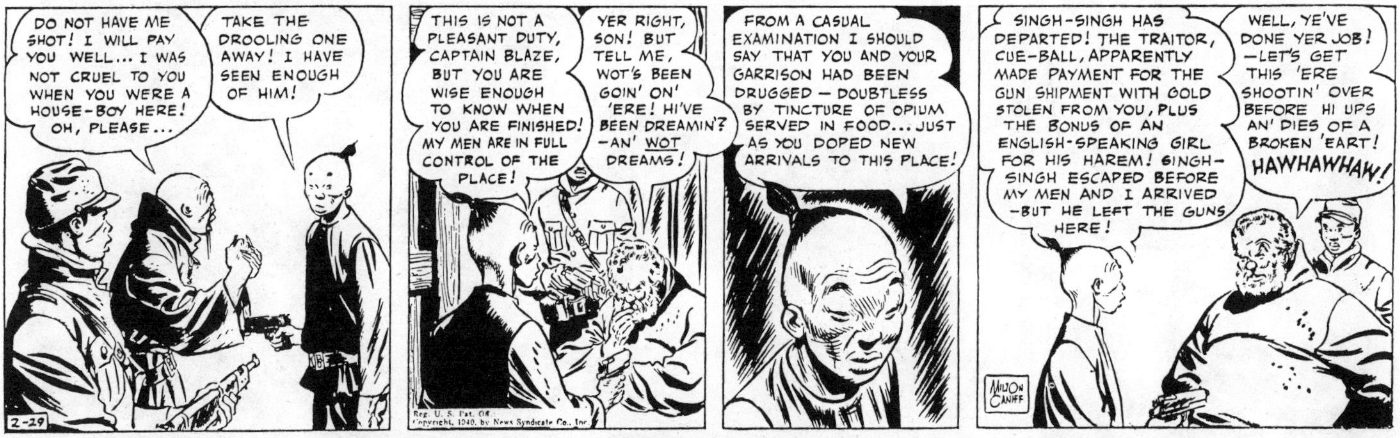
DO NOT HAVE ME SHOT! I WILL PAY YOU WELL... I WAS NOT CRUEL TO YOU WHEN YOU WERE A HOUSE-BOY HERE! OH, PLEASE...
TAKE THE DROOLING ONE AWAY! I HAVE SEEN ENOUGH OF HIM!
2-29
THIS IS NOT A PLEASANT DUTY, CAPTAIN BLAZE, BUT YOU ARE WISE ENOUGH TO KNOW WHEN YOU ARE FINISHED! MY MEN ARE IN FULL CONTROL OF THE PLACE!
YER RIGHT, SON! BUT TELL ME, WOT'S BEEN GOIN' ON 'ERE! HI'VE BEEN DREAMIN'? —AN' WOT DREAMS!
Reg. U. S. Pat. Off.: Copyright, 1940, by News Syndicate Co., Inc.
FROM A CASUAL EXAMINATION I SHOULD SAY THAT YOU AND YOUR GARRISON HAD BEEN DRUGGED—DOUBTLESS BY TINCTURE OF OPIUM SERVED IN FOOD...JUST AS YOU DOPED NEW ARRIVALS TO THIS PLACE!
SINGH-SINGH HAS DEPARTED! THE TRAITOR, CUE-BALL, APPARENTLY MADE PAYMENT FOR THE GUN SHIPMENT WITH GOLD STOLEN FROM YOU, PLUS THE BONUS OF AN ENGLISH-SPEAKING GIRL FOR HIS HAREM! SINGH-SINGH ESCAPED BEFORE MY MEN AND I ARRIVED—BUT HE LEFT THE GUNS HERE!
WELL, YE'VE DONE YER JOB! —LET'S GET THIS 'ERE SHOOTIN' OVER BEFORE HI UPS AN' DIES OF A BROKEN 'EART! HAWHAWHAW!
MILTON CANIFF

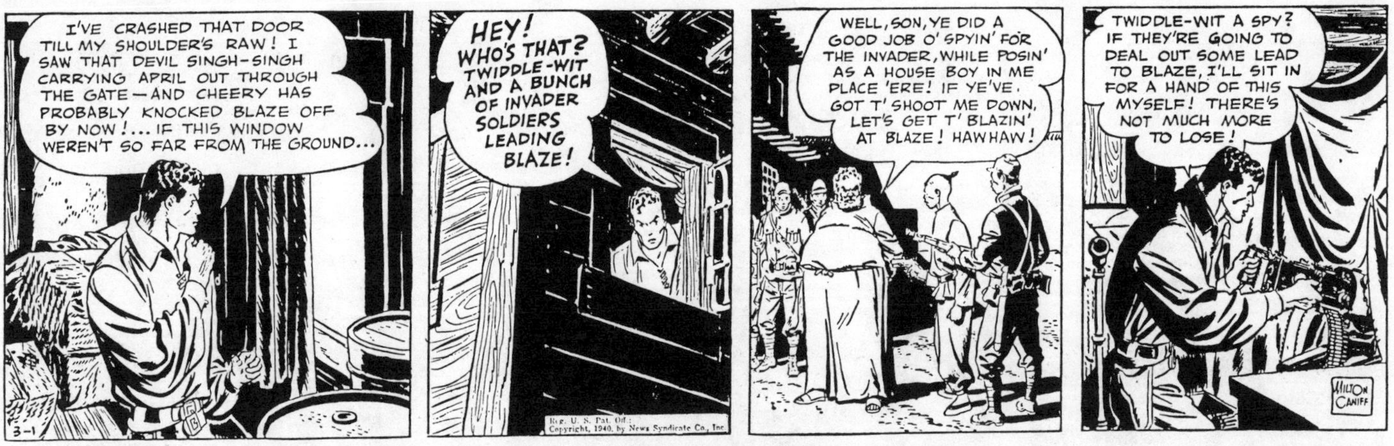
I'VE CRASHED THAT DOOR TILL MY SHOULDER'S RAW! I SAW THAT DEVIL SINGH-SINGH CARRYING APRIL OUT THROUGH THE GATE—AND CHEERY HAS PROBABLY KNOCKED BLAZE OFF BY NOW!...IF THIS WINDOW WEREN'T SO FAR FROM THE GROUND...
3-1
HEY! WHO'S THAT? TWIDDLE-WIT AND A BUNCH OF INVADER SOLDIERS LEADING BLAZE!
Reg. U. S. Pat. Off.: Copyright, 1940, by News Syndicate Co., Inc.
WELL, SON, YE DID A GOOD JOB O' SPYIN' FOR THE INVADER, WHILE POSIN' AS A HOUSE BOY IN ME PLACE 'ERE! IF YE'VE GOT T' SHOOT ME DOWN, LET'S GET T' BLAZIN' AT BLAZE! HAWHAW!
TWIDDLE-WIT A SPY? IF THEY'RE GOING TO DEAL OUT SOME LEAD TO BLAZE, I'LL SIT IN FOR A HAND OF THIS MYSELF! THERE'S NOT MUCH MORE TO LOSE!
MILTON CANIFF

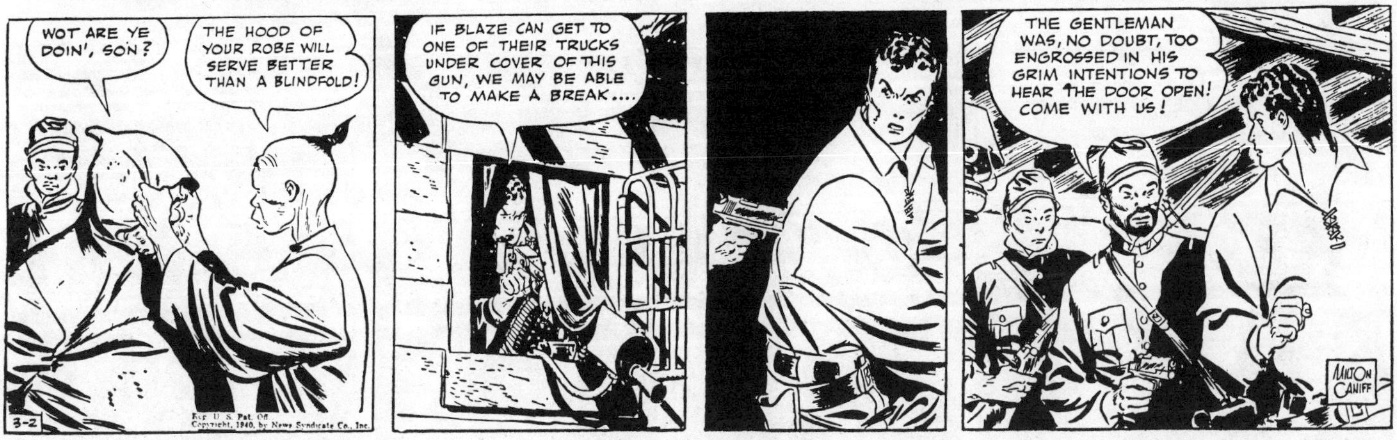
WOT ARE YE DOIN', SON?
THE HOOD OF YOUR ROBE WILL SERVE BETTER THAN A BLINDFOLD!
3-2
Reg. U. S. Pat. Off. Copyright, 1940, by News Syndicate Co., Inc.
IF BLAZE CAN GET TO ONE OF THEIR TRUCKS UNDER COVER OF THIS GUN, WE MAY BE ABLE TO MAKE A BREAK....
THE GENTLEMAN WAS, NO DOUBT, TOO ENGROSSED IN HIS GRIM INTENTIONS TO HEAR THE DOOR OPEN! COME WITH US!
MILTON CANIFF

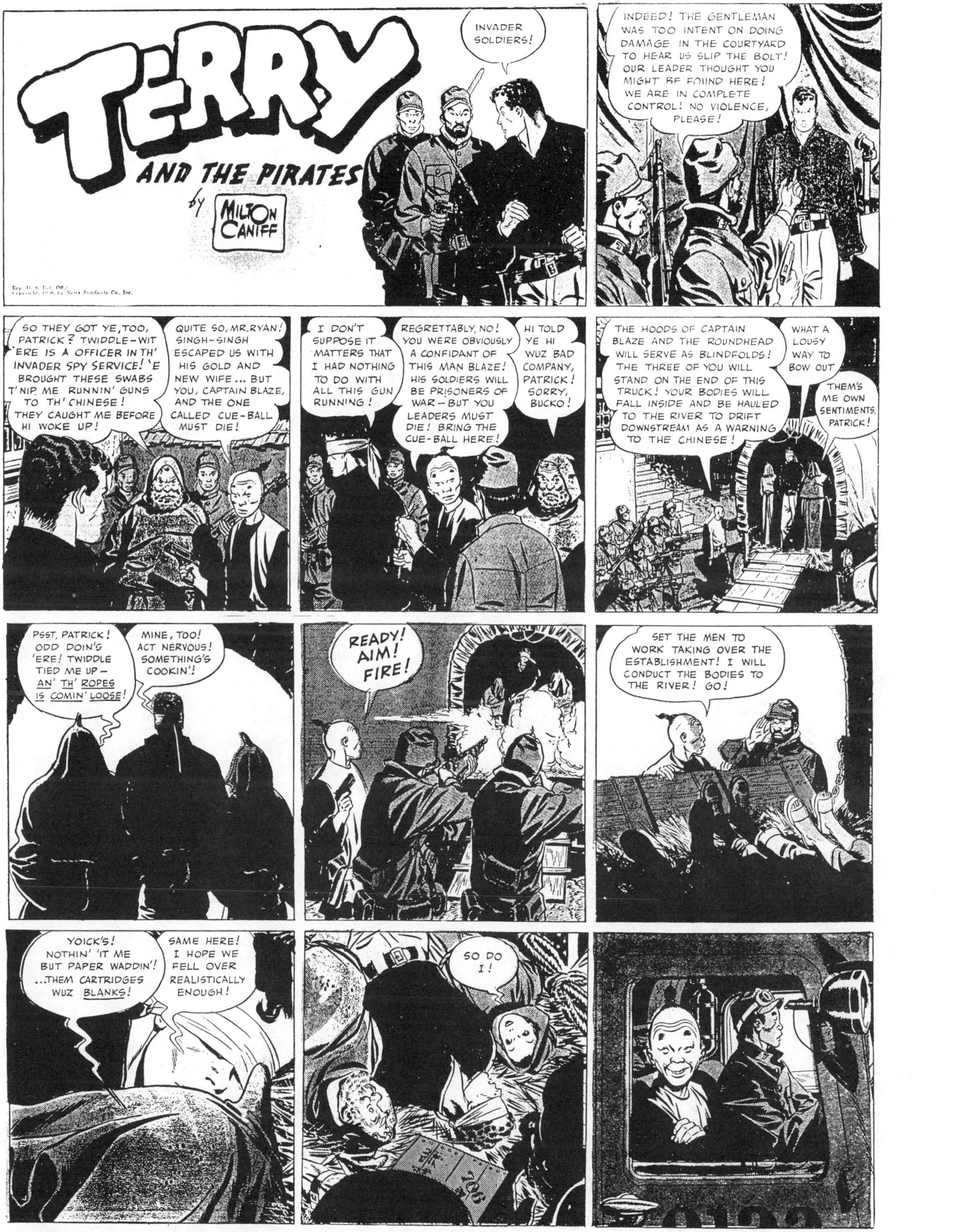
TERRY AND THE PIRATES
by MILTON CANIFF
Reg. U. S. Pat. Off.:
INVADER SOLDIERS!
INDEED! THE GENTLEMAN WAS TOO INTENT ON DOING DAMAGE IN THE COURTYARD TO HEAR US SLIP THE BOLT! OUR LEADER THOUGHT YOU MIGHT BE FOUND HERE! WE ARE IN COMPLETE CONTROL! NO VIOLENCE, PLEASE!
SO THEY GOT YE, TOO, PATRICK? TWIDDLE-WIT 'ERE IS A OFFICER IN TH' INVADER SPY SERVICE! 'E BROUGHT THESE SWABS T'NIP ME RUNNIN' GUNS TO TH' CHINESE! THEY CAUGHT ME BEFORE HI WOKE UP!
QUITE SO, MR. RYAN! SINGH-SINGH ESCAPED US WITH HIS GOLD AND NEW WIFE... BUT YOU, CAPTAIN BLAZE, AND THE ONE CALLED CUE-BALL MUST DIE!
I DON'T SUPPOSE IT MATTERS THAT I HAD NOTHING TO DO WITH ALL THIS GUN RUNNING!
REGRETTABLY, NO! YOU WERE OBVIOUSLY A CONFIDANT OF THIS MAN BLAZE! HIS SOLDIERS WILL BE PRISONERS OF WAR—BUT YOU LEADERS MUST DIE! BRING THE CUE-BALL HERE!
HI TOLD YE HI WUZ BAD COMPANY, PATRICK! SORRY, BUCKO!
THE HOODS OF CAPTAIN BLAZE AND THE ROUNDHEAD WILL SERVE AS BLINDFOLDS! THE THREE OF YOU WILL STAND ON THE END OF THIS TRUCK! YOUR BODIES WILL FALL INSIDE AND BE HAULED TO THE RIVER TO DRIFT DOWNSTREAM AS A WARNING TO THE CHINESE!
WHAT A LOUSY WAY TO BOW OUT
THEM'S ME OWN SENTIMENTS, PATRICK!
PSST, PATRICK! ODD DOIN'S 'ERE! TWIDDLE TIED ME UP— AN' TH' ROPES IS COMIN' LOOSE!
MINE, TOO! ACT NERVOUS! SOMETHING'S COOKIN'!
READY! AIM! FIRE!
SET THE MEN TO WORK TAKING OVER THE ESTABLISHMENT! I WILL CONDUCT THE BODIES TO THE RIVER! GO!
YOICK'S! NOTHIN' 'IT ME BUT PAPER WADDIN'! ..THEM CARTRIDGES WUZ BLANKS!
SAME HERE! I HOPE WE FELL OVER REALISTICALLY ENOUGH!
SO DO I!

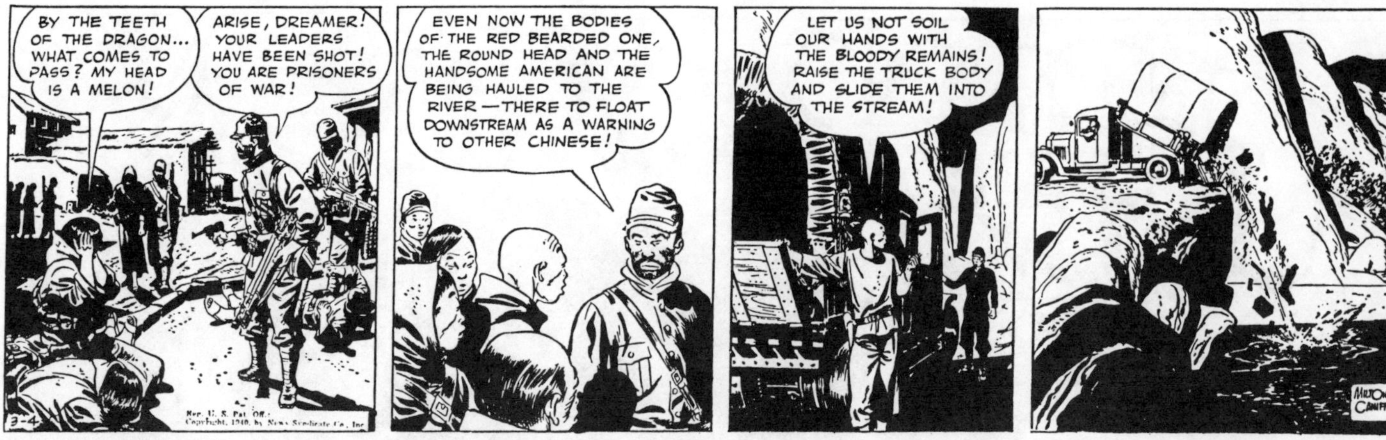
BY THE TEETH OF THE DRAGON... WHAT COMES TO PASS? MY HEAD IS A MELON!
ARISE, DREAMER! YOUR LEADERS HAVE BEEN SHOT! YOU ARE PRISONERS OF WAR!
3-4
Reg. U. S. Pat. Off.: Copyright, 1940, by News Syndicate Co., Inc.
EVEN NOW THE BODIES OF THE RED BEARDED ONE, THE ROUND HEAD AND THE HANDSOME AMERICAN ARE BEING HAULED TO THE RIVER—THERE TO FLOAT DOWNSTREAM AS A WARNING TO OTHER CHINESE!
LET US NOT SOIL OUR HANDS WITH THE BLOODY REMAINS! RAISE THE TRUCK BODY AND SLIDE THEM INTO THE STREAM!
MILTON CANIFF

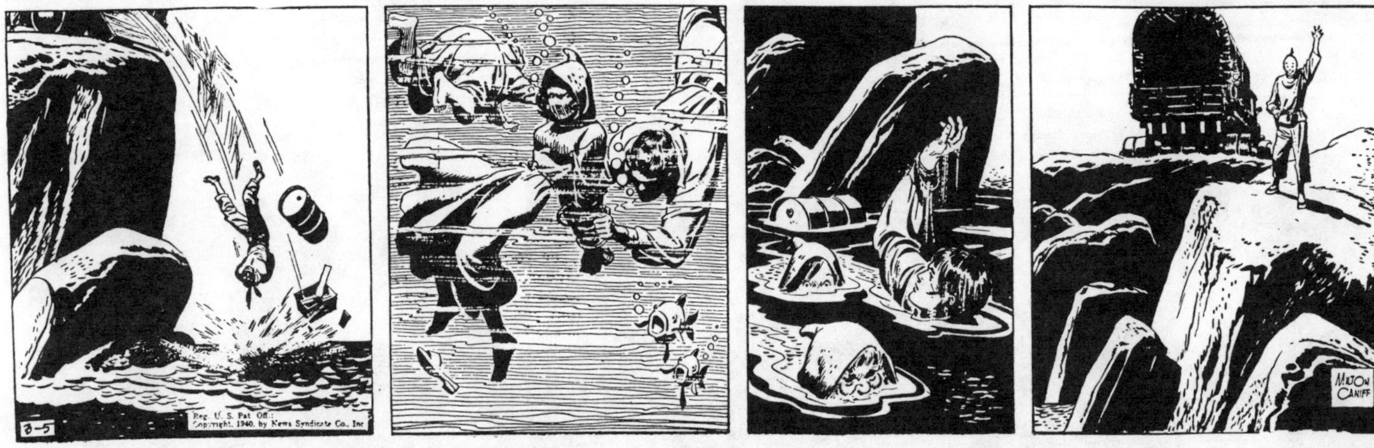
3-5
Reg. U. S. Pat. Off.: Copyright, 1940, by News Syndicate Co., Inc.
MILTON CANIFF

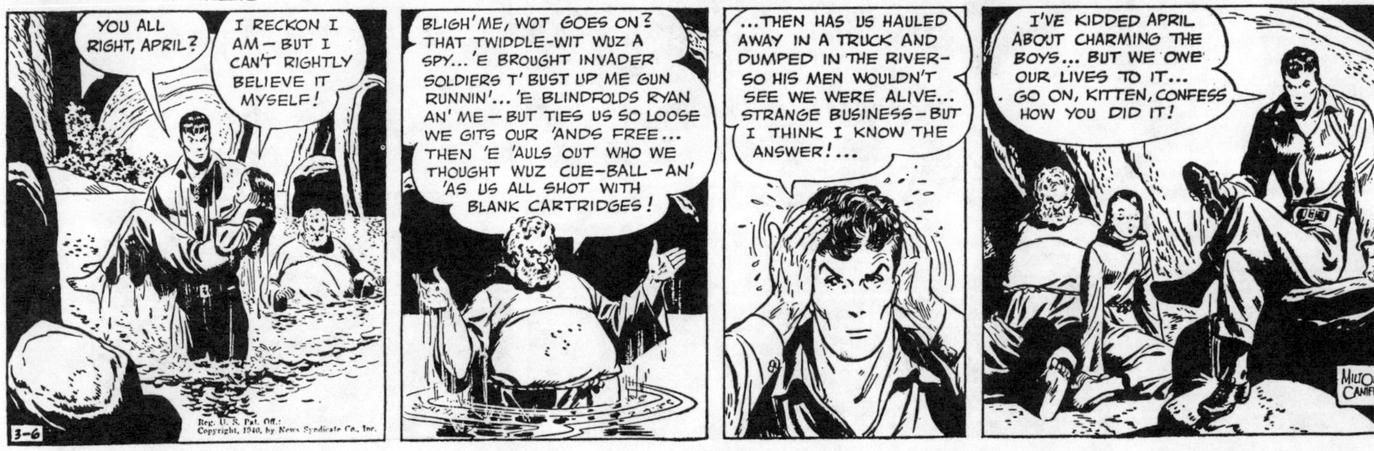
YOU ALL RIGHT, APRIL?
I RECKON I AM—BUT I CAN'T RIGHTLY BELIEVE IT MYSELF!
3-6
Reg. U. S. Pat. Off.: Copyright, 1940, by News Syndicate Co., Inc.
BLIGH'ME, WOT GOES ON? THAT TWIDDLE-WIT WUZ A SPY...'E BROUGHT INVADER SOLDIERS T' BUST UP ME GUN RUNNIN'...'E BLINDFOLDS RYAN AN' ME—BUT TIES US SO LOOSE WE GITS OUR 'ANDS FREE... THEN 'E 'AULS OUT WHO WE THOUGHT WUZ CUE-BALL—AN' 'AS US ALL SHOT WITH BLANK CARTRIDGES!
...THEN HAS US HAULED AWAY IN A TRUCK AND DUMPED IN THE RIVER-SO HIS MEN WOULDN'T SEE WE WERE ALIVE... STRANGE BUSINESS—BUT I THINK I KNOW THE ANSWER!...
I'VE KIDDED APRIL ABOUT CHARMING THE BOYS... BUT WE OWE OUR LIVES TO IT... GO ON, KITTEN, CONFESS HOW YOU DID IT!
MILTON CANIFF

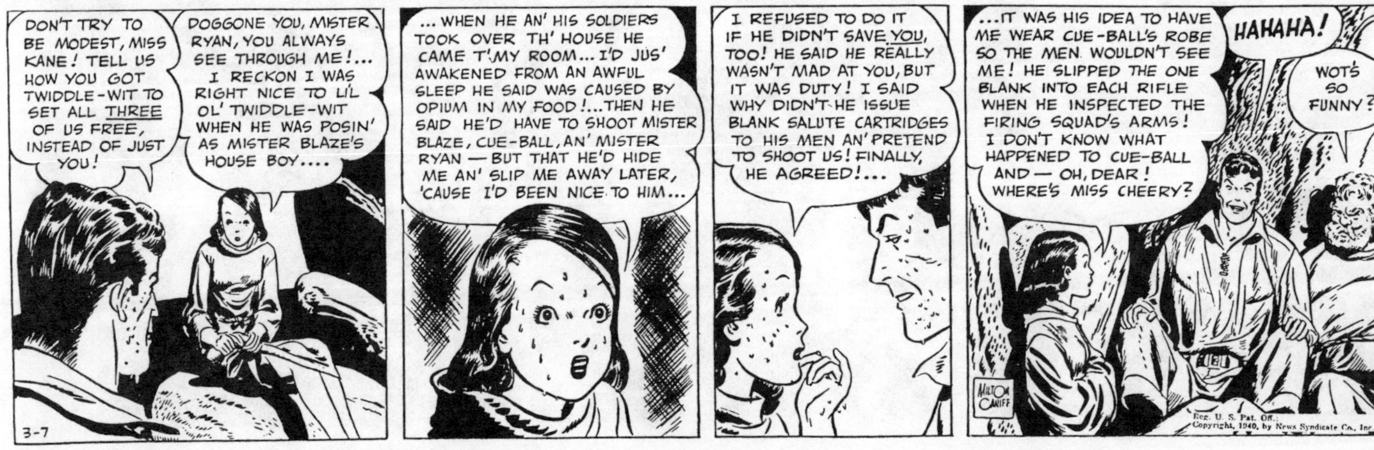
DON'T TRY TO BE MODEST, MISS KANE! TELL US HOW YOU GOT TWIDDLE-WIT TO SET ALL THREE OF US FREE, INSTEAD OF JUST YOU!
DOGGONE YOU, MISTER RYAN, YOU ALWAYS SEE THROUGH ME!... I RECKON I WAS RIGHT NICE TO LI'L OL' TWIDDLE-WIT WHEN HE WAS POSIN' AS MISTER BLAZE'S HOUSE BOY....
3-7
...WHEN HE AN' HIS SOLDIERS TOOK OVER TH' HOUSE HE CAME T' MY ROOM... I'D JUS' AWAKENED FROM AN AWFUL SLEEP HE SAID WAS CAUSED BY OPIUM IN MY FOOD!...THEN HE SAID HE'D HAVE TO SHOOT MISTER BLAZE, CUE-BALL, AN' MISTER RYAN—BUT THAT HE'D HIDE ME AN' SLIP ME AWAY LATER, 'CAUSE I'D BEEN NICE TO HIM...
I REFUSED TO DO IT IF HE DIDN'T SAVE YOU, TOO! HE SAID HE REALLY WASN'T MAD AT YOU, BUT IT WAS DUTY! I SAID WHY DIDN'T HE ISSUE BLANK SALUTE CARTRIDGES TO HIS MEN AN' PRETEND TO SHOOT US! FINALLY, HE AGREED!...
MILTON CANIFF
...IT WAS HIS IDEA TO HAVE ME WEAR CUE-BALL'S ROBE SO THE MEN WOULDN'T SEE ME! HE SLIPPED THE ONE BLANK INTO EACH RIFLE WHEN HE INSPECTED THE FIRING SQUAD'S ARMS! I DON'T KNOW WHAT HAPPENED TO CUE-BALL AND—OH, DEAR! WHERE'S MISS CHEERY?
HAHAHA!
WOT'S SO FUNNY?
Reg. U. S. Pat. Off.: Copyright, 1940, by News Syndicate Co., Inc.

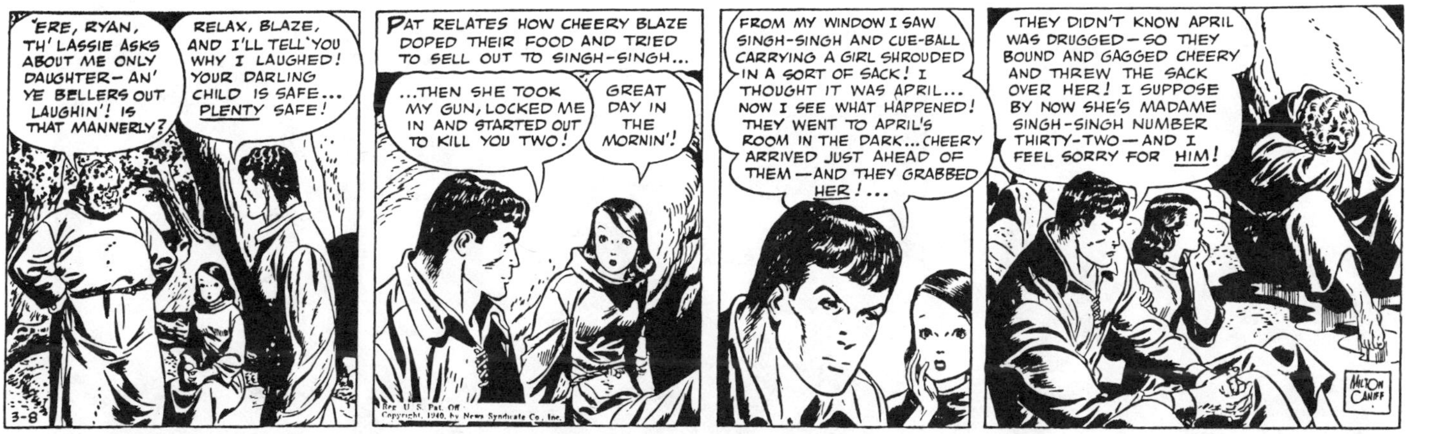
'ERE, RYAN, TH' LASSIE ASKS ABOUT ME ONLY DAUGHTER—AN' YE BELLERS OUT LAUGHIN'! IS THAT MANNERLY?
RELAX, BLAZE, AND I'LL TELL YOU WHY I LAUGHED! YOUR DARLING CHILD IS SAFE... PLENTY SAFE!
3-8
PAT RELATES HOW CHEERY BLAZE DOPED THEIR FOOD AND TRIED TO SELL OUT TO SINGH-SINGH...
...THEN SHE TOOK MY GUN, LOCKED ME IN AND STARTED OUT TO KILL YOU TWO!
GREAT DAY IN THE MORNIN'!
Reg. U. S. Pat. Off.
Copyright, 1940, by News Syndicate Co., Inc.
FROM MY WINDOW I SAW SINGH-SINGH AND CUE-BALL CARRYING A GIRL SHROUDED IN A SORT OF SACK! I THOUGHT IT WAS APRIL... NOW I SEE WHAT HAPPENED! THEY WENT TO APRIL'S ROOM IN THE DARK... CHEERY ARRIVED JUST AHEAD OF THEM—AND THEY GRABBED HER!...
THEY DIDN'T KNOW APRIL WAS DRUGGED—SO THEY BOUND AND GAGGED CHEERY AND THREW THE SACK OVER HER! I SUPPOSE BY NOW SHE'S MADAME SINGH-SINGH NUMBER THIRTY-TWO—AND I FEEL SORRY FOR HIM!
MILTON CANIFF

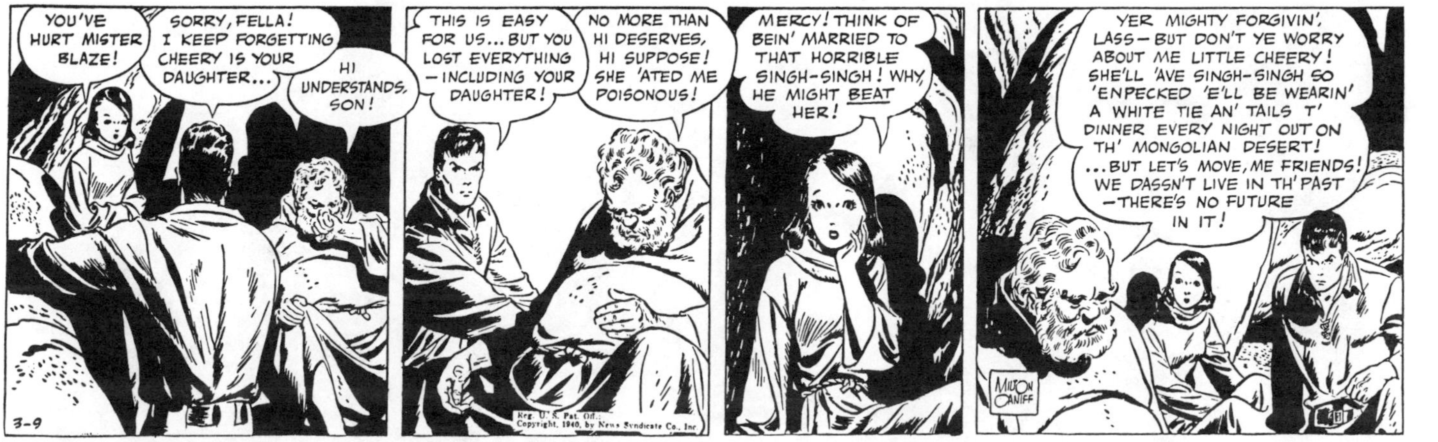
YOU'VE HURT MISTER BLAZE!
SORRY, FELLA! I KEEP FORGETTING CHEERY IS YOUR DAUGHTER...
HI UNDERSTANDS, SON!
3-9
THIS IS EASY FOR US... BUT YOU LOST EVERYTHING —INCLUDING YOUR DAUGHTER!
NO MORE THAN HI DESERVES, HI SUPPOSE! SHE 'ATED ME POISONOUS!
Reg. U. S. Pat. Off.
Copyright, 1940, by News Syndicate Co., Inc.
MERCY! THINK OF BEIN' MARRIED TO THAT HORRIBLE SINGH-SINGH! WHY, HE MIGHT BEAT HER!
YER MIGHTY FORGIVIN', LASS—BUT DON'T YE WORRY ABOUT ME LITTLE CHEERY! SHE'LL 'AVE SINGH-SINGH SO 'ENPECKED 'E'LL BE WEARIN' A WHITE TIE AN' TAILS T' DINNER EVERY NIGHT OUT ON TH' MONGOLIAN DESERT! ...BUT LET'S MOVE, ME FRIENDS! WE DASSN'T LIVE IN TH' PAST —THERE'S NO FUTURE IN IT!
MILTON CANIFF

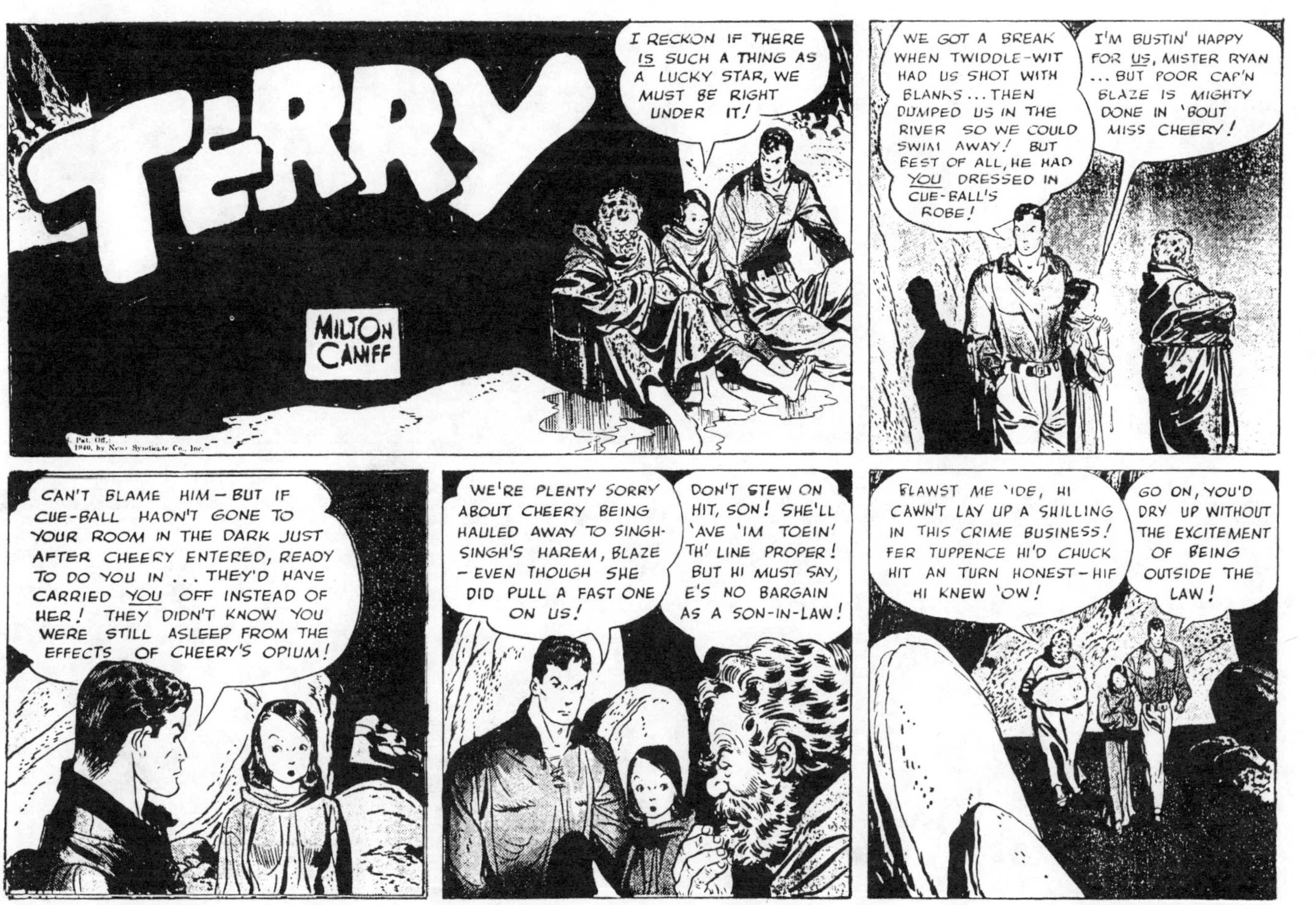
TERRY
MILTON CANIFF
I RECKON IF THERE IS SUCH A THING AS A LUCKY STAR, WE MUST BE RIGHT UNDER IT!
WE GOT A BREAK WHEN TWIDDLE-WIT HAD US SHOT WITH BLANKS... THEN DUMPED US IN THE RIVER SO WE COULD SWIM AWAY! BUT BEST OF ALL, HE HAD YOU DRESSED IN CUE-BALL'S ROBE!
I'M BUSTIN' HAPPY FOR US, MISTER RYAN ... BUT POOR CAP'N BLAZE IS MIGHTY DONE IN 'BOUT MISS CHEERY!
CAN'T BLAME HIM—BUT IF CUE-BALL HADN'T GONE TO YOUR ROOM IN THE DARK JUST AFTER CHEERY ENTERED, READY TO DO YOU IN... THEY'D HAVE CARRIED YOU OFF INSTEAD OF HER! THEY DIDN'T KNOW YOU WERE STILL ASLEEP FROM THE EFFECTS OF CHEERY'S OPIUM!
WE'RE PLENTY SORRY ABOUT CHEERY BEING HAULED AWAY TO SINGH-SINGH'S HAREM, BLAZE —EVEN THOUGH SHE DID PULL A FAST ONE ON US!
DON'T STEW ON HIT, SON! SHE'LL 'AVE 'IM TOEIN' TH' LINE PROPER! BUT HI MUST SAY, E'S NO BARGAIN AS A SON-IN-LAW!
BLAWST ME 'IDE, HI CAWN'T LAY UP A SHILLING IN THIS CRIME BUSINESS! FER TUPPENCE HI'D CHUCK HIT AN TURN HONEST—HIF HI KNEW 'OW!
GO ON, YOU'D DRY UP WITHOUT THE EXCITEMENT OF BEING OUTSIDE THE LAW!

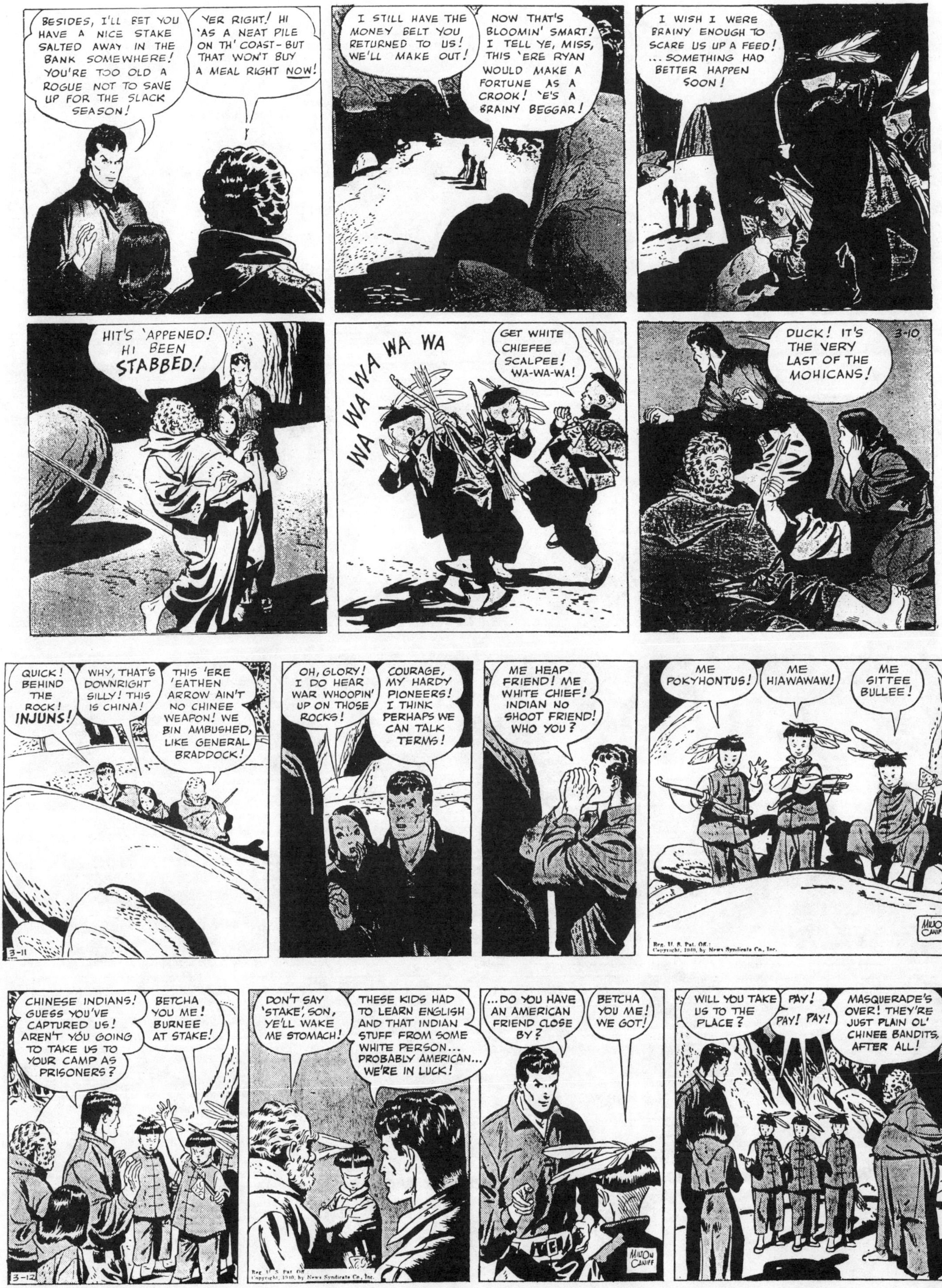

BESIDES, I'LL BET YOU HAVE A NICE STAKE SALTED AWAY IN THE BANK SOMEWHERE! YOU'RE TOO OLD A ROGUE NOT TO SAVE UP FOR THE SLACK SEASON!
YER RIGHT! HI 'AS A NEAT PILE ON TH' COAST – BUT THAT WON'T BUY A MEAL RIGHT NOW!
I STILL HAVE THE MONEY BELT YOU RETURNED TO US! WE'LL MAKE OUT!
NOW THAT'S BLOOMIN' SMART! I TELL YE, MISS, THIS 'ERE RYAN WOULD MAKE A FORTUNE AS A CROOK! 'E'S A BRAINY BEGGAR!
I WISH I WERE BRAINY ENOUGH TO SCARE US UP A FEED! ... SOMETHING HAD BETTER HAPPEN SOON!
HIT'S 'APPENED! HI BEEN STABBED!
WA WA WA WA WA WA
GET WHITE CHIEFEE SCALPEE! WA-WA-WA!
DUCK! IT'S THE VERY LAST OF THE MOHICANS!
3-10
QUICK! BEHIND THE ROCK! INJUNS!
WHY, THAT'S DOWNRIGHT SILLY! THIS IS CHINA!
THIS 'ERE 'EATHEN ARROW AIN'T NO CHINEE WEAPON! WE BIN AMBUSHED, LIKE GENERAL BRADDOCK!
3-11
OH, GLORY! I DO HEAR WAR WHOOPIN' UP ON THOSE ROCKS!
COURAGE, MY HARDY PIONEERS! I THINK PERHAPS WE CAN TALK TERMS!
ME HEAP FRIEND! ME WHITE CHIEF! INDIAN NO SHOOT FRIEND! WHO YOU?
ME POKYHONTUS!
ME HIAWAWAW!
ME SITTEE BULLEE!
MILTON CANIFF
Reg. U. S. Pat. Off.; Copyright, 1940, by News Syndicate Co., Inc.
CHINESE INDIANS! GUESS YOU'VE CAPTURED US! AREN'T YOU GOING TO TAKE US TO YOUR CAMP AS PRISONERS?
BETCHA YOU ME! BURNEE AT STAKE!
3-12
DON'T SAY 'STAKE', SON, YE'LL WAKE ME STOMACH!
THESE KIDS HAD TO LEARN ENGLISH AND THAT INDIAN STUFF FROM SOME WHITE PERSON... PROBABLY AMERICAN... WE'RE IN LUCK!
Reg. U. S. Pat. Off.
Copyright, 1940, by News Syndicate Co., Inc.
...DO YOU HAVE AN AMERICAN FRIEND CLOSE BY?
BETCHA YOU ME! WE GOT!
MILTON CANIFF
WILL YOU TAKE US TO THE PLACE?
PAY! PAY! PAY!
MASQUERADE'S OVER! THEY'RE JUST PLAIN OL' CHINEE BANDITS, AFTER ALL!

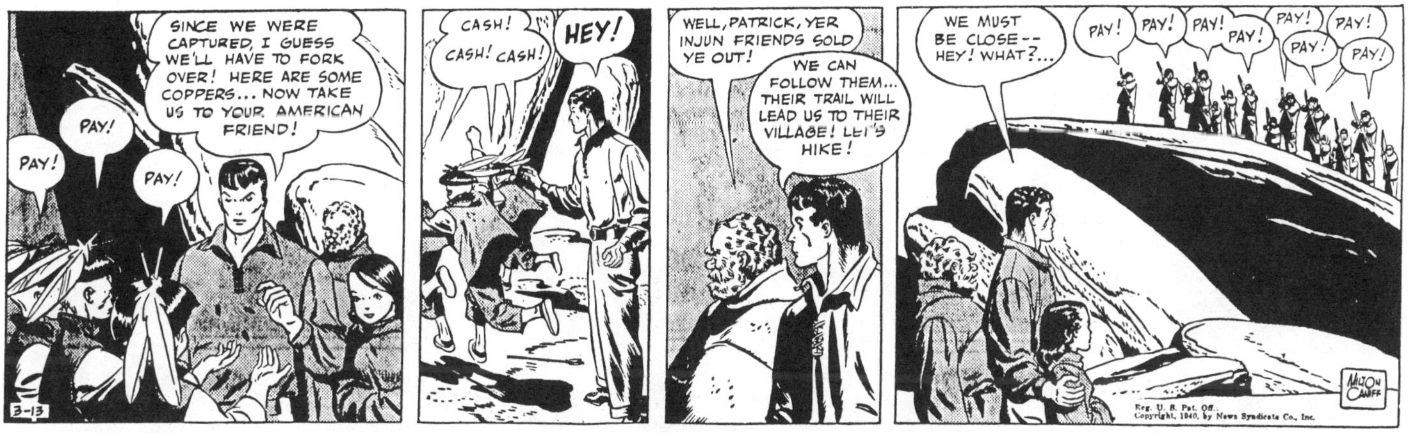
SINCE WE WERE CAPTURED, I GUESS WE'LL HAVE TO FORK OVER! HERE ARE SOME COPPERS... NOW TAKE US TO YOUR AMERICAN FRIEND!
PAY!
PAY!
PAY!
3-13
CASH!
CASH! CASH!
HEY!
WELL, PATRICK, YER INJUN FRIENDS SOLD YE OUT!
WE CAN FOLLOW THEM... THEIR TRAIL WILL LEAD US TO THEIR VILLAGE! LET'S HIKE!
WE MUST BE CLOSE-- HEY! WHAT?...
PAY!
PAY!
PAY!
PAY!
PAY!
PAY!
PAY!
PAY!
MILTON CANIFF
Reg. U. S. Pat. Off.
Copyright, 1940, by News Syndicate Co., Inc.

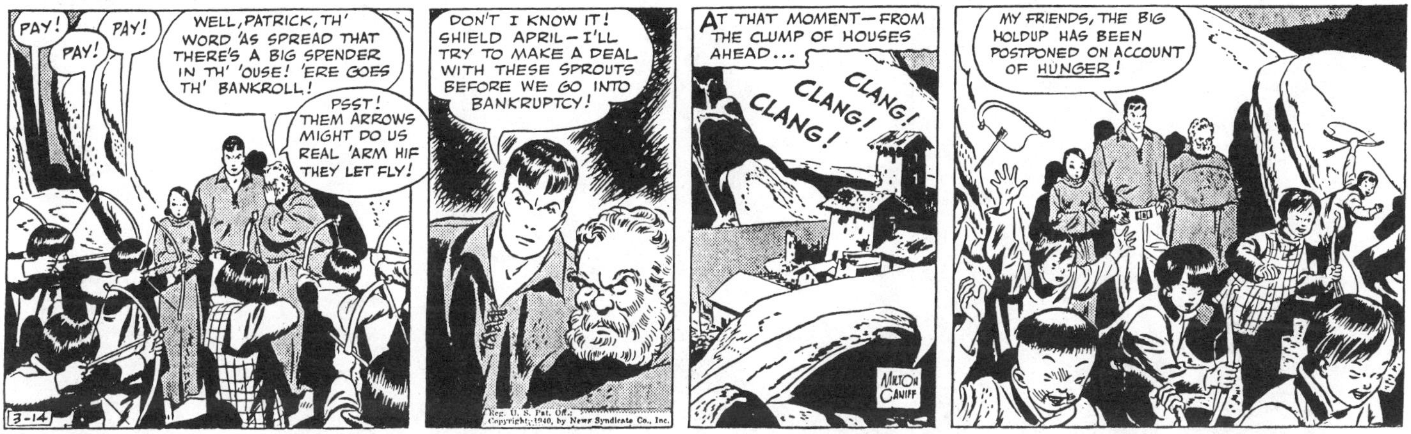
PAY!
PAY!
PAY!
WELL, PATRICK, TH' WORD 'AS SPREAD THAT THERE'S A BIG SPENDER IN TH' 'OUSE! 'ERE GOES TH' BANKROLL!
PSST! THEM ARROWS MIGHT DO US REAL 'ARM HIF THEY LET FLY!
3-14
DON'T I KNOW IT! SHIELD APRIL—I'LL TRY TO MAKE A DEAL WITH THESE SPROUTS BEFORE WE GO INTO BANKRUPTCY!
Reg. U. S. Pat. Off.
Copyright, 1940, by News Syndicate Co., Inc.
AT THAT MOMENT—FROM THE CLUMP OF HOUSES AHEAD...
CLANG!
CLANG!
CLANG!
MILTON CANIFF
MY FRIENDS, THE BIG HOLDUP HAS BEEN POSTPONED ON ACCOUNT OF HUNGER!

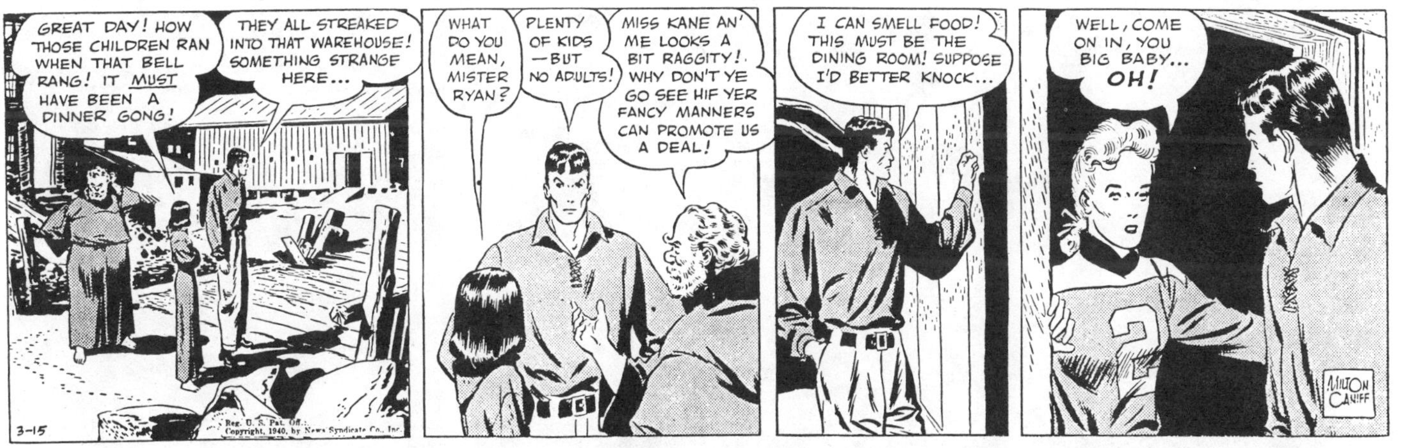
GREAT DAY! HOW THOSE CHILDREN RAN WHEN THAT BELL RANG! IT MUST HAVE BEEN A DINNER GONG!
THEY ALL STREAKED INTO THAT WAREHOUSE! SOMETHING STRANGE HERE...
3-15
Reg. U. S. Pat. Off.
Copyright, 1940, by News Syndicate Co., Inc.
WHAT DO YOU MEAN, MISTER RYAN?
PLENTY OF KIDS —BUT NO ADULTS!
MISS KANE AN' ME LOOKS A BIT RAGGITY! WHY DON'T YE GO SEE HIF YER FANCY MANNERS CAN PROMOTE US A DEAL!
I CAN SMELL FOOD! THIS MUST BE THE DINING ROOM! SUPPOSE I'D BETTER KNOCK...
WELL, COME ON IN, YOU BIG BABY... OH!
MILTON CANIFF

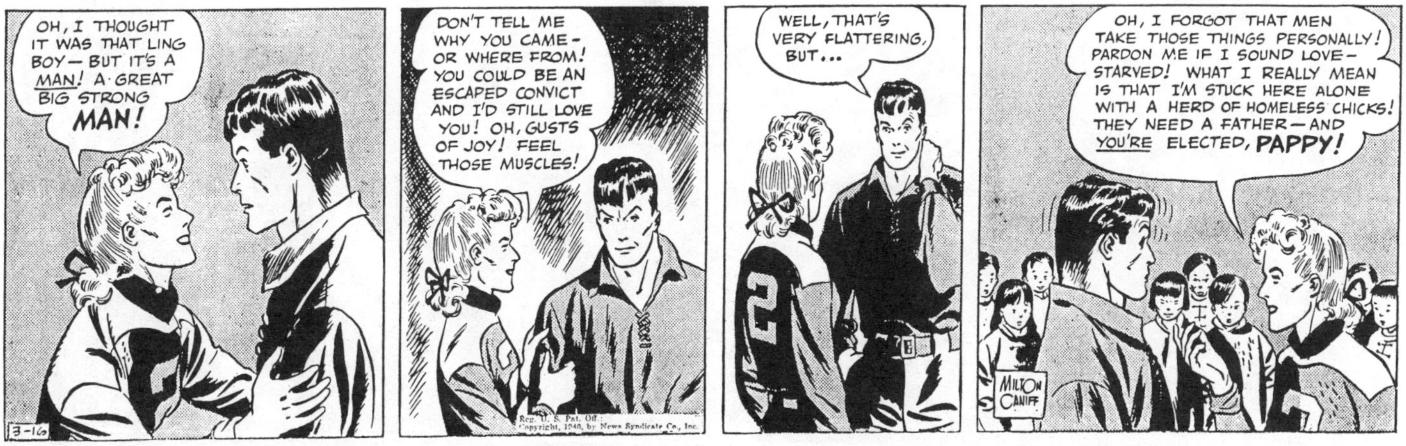
OH, I THOUGHT IT WAS THAT LING BOY— BUT IT'S A MAN! A GREAT BIG STRONG MAN!
3-16
DON'T TELL ME WHY YOU CAME- OR WHERE FROM! YOU COULD BE AN ESCAPED CONVICT AND I'D STILL LOVE YOU! OH, GUSTS OF JOY! FEEL THOSE MUSCLES!
Reg. U. S. Pat. Off.
Copyright, 1940, by News Syndicate Co., Inc.
WELL, THAT'S VERY FLATTERING, BUT...
OH, I FORGOT THAT MEN TAKE THOSE THINGS PERSONALLY! PARDON ME IF I SOUND LOVE-STARVED! WHAT I REALLY MEAN IS THAT I'M STUCK HERE ALONE WITH A HERD OF HOMELESS CHICKS! THEY NEED A FATHER—AND YOU'RE ELECTED, PAPPY!
MILTON CANIFF

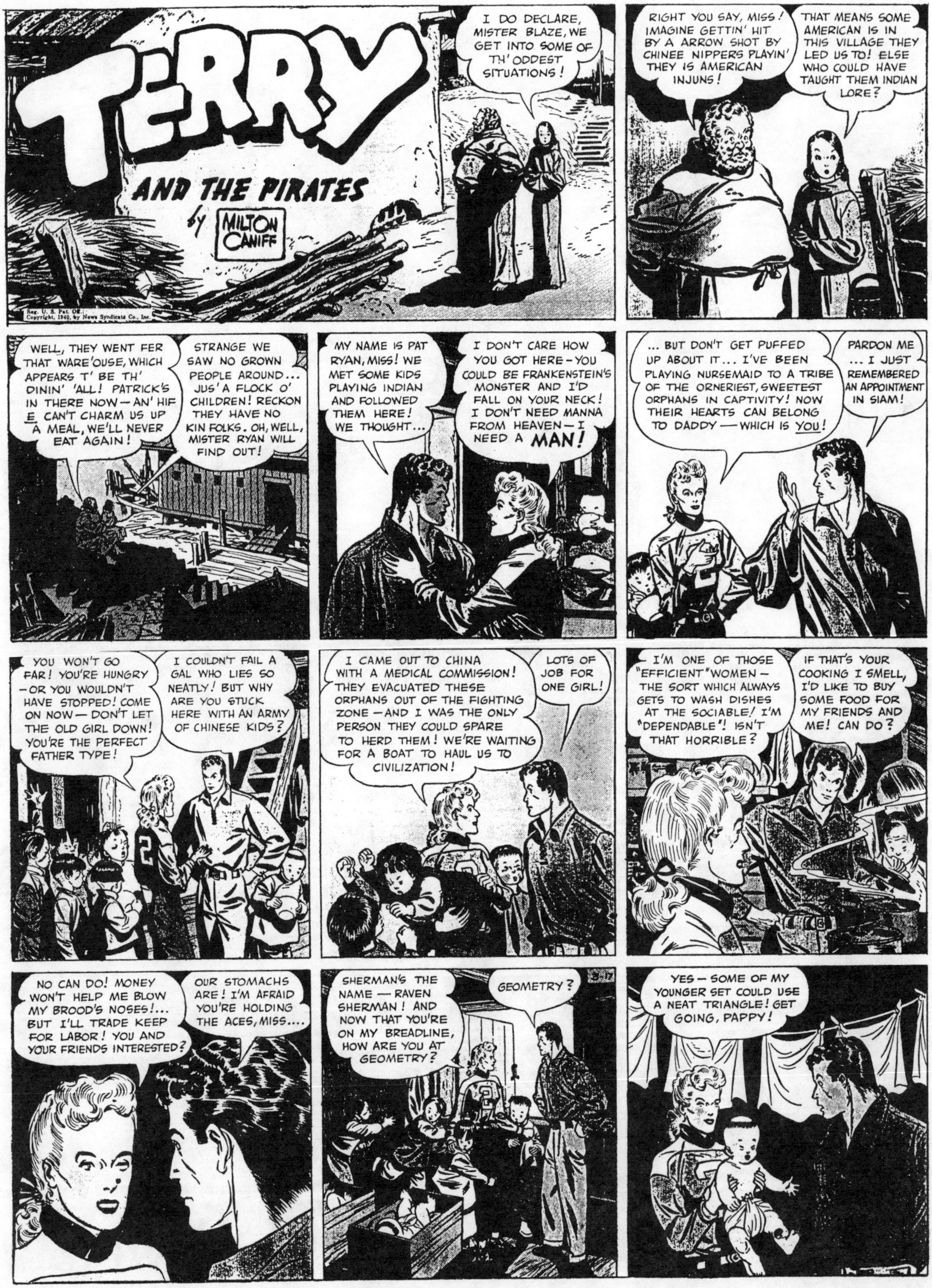
TERRY AND THE PIRATES
by MILTON CANIFF
Reg. U. S. Pat. Off.: Copyright, 1940, by News Syndicate Co., Inc.
I DO DECLARE, MISTER BLAZE, WE GET INTO SOME OF TH' ODDEST SITUATIONS!
RIGHT YOU SAY, MISS! IMAGINE GETTIN' HIT BY A ARROW SHOT BY CHINEE NIPPERS PLAYIN' THEY IS AMERICAN INJUNS!
THAT MEANS SOME AMERICAN IS IN THIS VILLAGE THEY LED US TO! ELSE WHO COULD HAVE TAUGHT THEM INDIAN LORE?
WELL, THEY WENT FER THAT WARE'OUSE, WHICH APPEARS T' BE TH' DININ' 'ALL! PATRICK'S IN THERE NOW—AN' HIF E CAN'T CHARM US UP A MEAL, WE'LL NEVER EAT AGAIN!
STRANGE WE SAW NO GROWN PEOPLE AROUND... JUS' A FLOCK O' CHILDREN! RECKON THEY HAVE NO KIN FOLKS. OH, WELL, MISTER RYAN WILL FIND OUT!
MY NAME IS PAT RYAN, MISS! WE MET SOME KIDS PLAYING INDIAN AND FOLLOWED THEM HERE! WE THOUGHT...
I DON'T CARE HOW YOU GOT HERE—YOU COULD BE FRANKENSTEIN'S MONSTER AND I'D FALL ON YOUR NECK! I DON'T NEED MANNA FROM HEAVEN—I NEED A MAN!
... BUT DON'T GET PUFFED UP ABOUT IT... I'VE BEEN PLAYING NURSEMAID TO A TRIBE OF THE ORNERIEST, SWEETEST ORPHANS IN CAPTIVITY! NOW THEIR HEARTS CAN BELONG TO DADDY — WHICH IS YOU!
PARDON ME ... I JUST REMEMBERED AN APPOINTMENT IN SIAM!
YOU WON'T GO FAR! YOU'RE HUNGRY —OR YOU WOULDN'T HAVE STOPPED! COME ON NOW— DON'T LET THE OLD GIRL DOWN! YOU'RE THE PERFECT FATHER TYPE!
I COULDN'T FAIL A GAL WHO LIES SO NEATLY! BUT WHY ARE YOU STUCK HERE WITH AN ARMY OF CHINESE KIDS?
I CAME OUT TO CHINA WITH A MEDICAL COMMISSION! THEY EVACUATED THESE ORPHANS OUT OF THE FIGHTING ZONE—AND I WAS THE ONLY PERSON THEY COULD SPARE TO HERD THEM! WE'RE WAITING FOR A BOAT TO HAUL US TO CIVILIZATION!
LOTS OF JOB FOR ONE GIRL!
I'M ONE OF THOSE "EFFICIENT" WOMEN— THE SORT WHICH ALWAYS GETS TO WASH DISHES AT THE SOCIABLE! I'M "DEPENDABLE"! ISN'T THAT HORRIBLE?
IF THAT'S YOUR COOKING I SMELL, I'D LIKE TO BUY SOME FOOD FOR MY FRIENDS AND ME! CAN DO?
NO CAN DO! MONEY WON'T HELP ME BLOW MY BROOD'S NOSES!... BUT I'LL TRADE KEEP FOR LABOR! YOU AND YOUR FRIENDS INTERESTED?
OUR STOMACHS ARE! I'M AFRAID YOU'RE HOLDING THE ACES, MISS....
SHERMAN'S THE NAME — RAVEN SHERMAN! AND NOW THAT YOU'RE ON MY BREADLINE, HOW ARE YOU AT GEOMETRY?
GEOMETRY?
YES — SOME OF MY YOUNGER SET COULD USE A NEAT TRIANGLE! GET GOING, PAPPY!

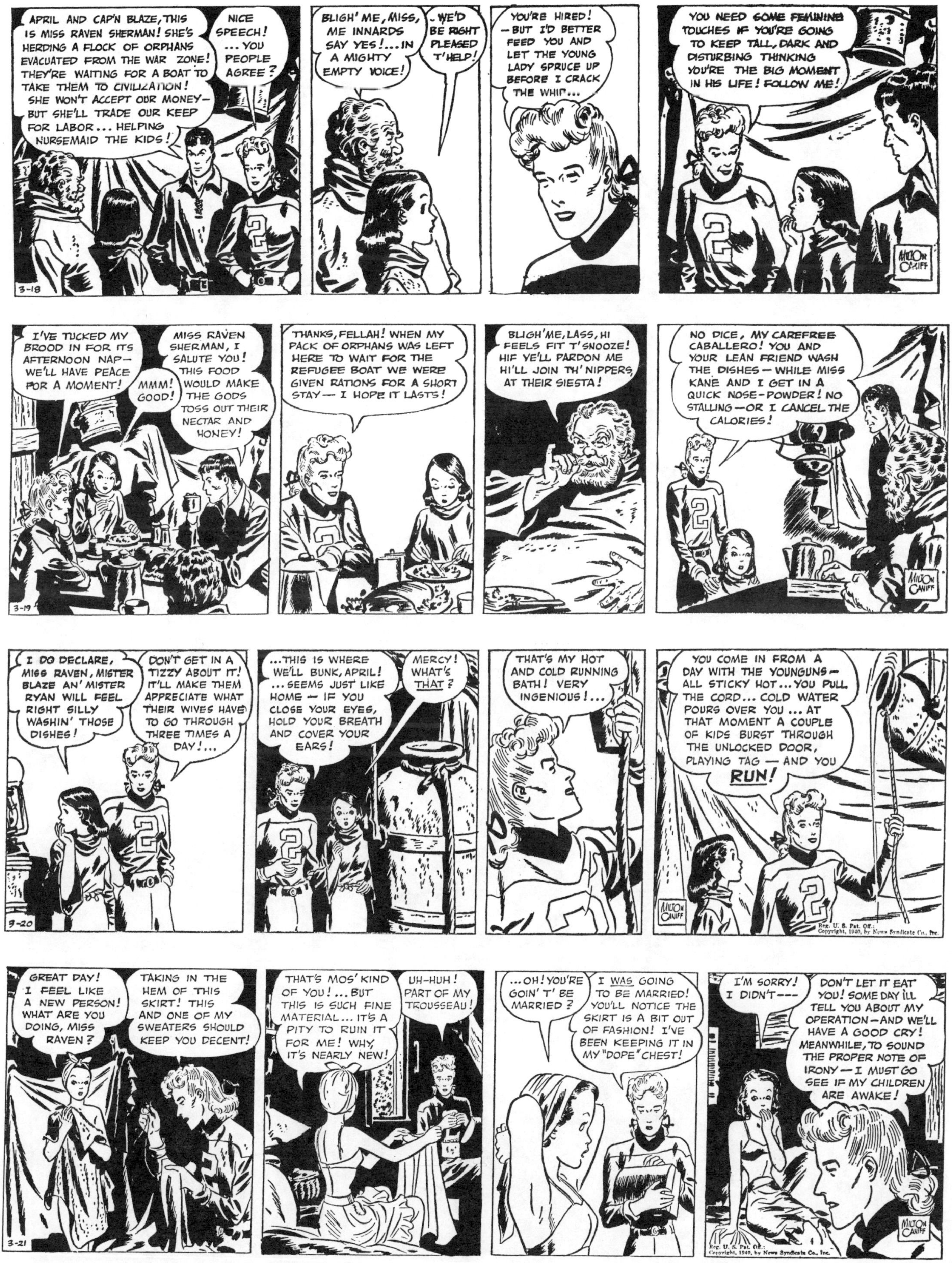

APRIL AND CAP'N BLAZE, THIS IS MISS RAVEN SHERMAN! SHE'S HERDING A FLOCK OF ORPHANS EVACUATED FROM THE WAR ZONE! THEY'RE WAITING FOR A BOAT TO TAKE THEM TO CIVILIZATION! SHE WON'T ACCEPT OUR MONEY— BUT SHE'LL TRADE OUR KEEP FOR LABOR... HELPING NURSEMAID THE KIDS!
NICE SPEECH! ...YOU PEOPLE AGREE?
BLIGH' ME, MISS, ME INNARDS SAY YES!... IN A MIGHTY EMPTY VOICE!
-WE'D BE RIGHT PLEASED T'HELP!
YOU'RE HIRED! —BUT I'D BETTER FEED YOU AND LET THE YOUNG LADY SPRUCE UP BEFORE I CRACK THE WHIP...
YOU NEED SOME FEMININE TOUCHES IF YOU'RE GOING TO KEEP TALL, DARK AND DISTURBING THINKING YOU'RE THE BIG MOMENT IN HIS LIFE! FOLLOW ME!
MILTON CANIFF
3-18
I'VE TUCKED MY BROOD IN FOR ITS AFTERNOON NAP— WE'LL HAVE PEACE FOR A MOMENT!
MISS RAVEN SHERMAN, I SALUTE YOU! THIS FOOD WOULD MAKE THE GODS TOSS OUT THEIR NECTAR AND HONEY!
MMM! GOOD!
THANKS, FELLAH! WHEN MY PACK OF ORPHANS WAS LEFT HERE TO WAIT FOR THE REFUGEE BOAT WE WERE GIVEN RATIONS FOR A SHORT STAY — I HOPE IT LASTS!
BLIGH'ME, LASS, HI FEELS FIT T'SNOOZE! HIF YE'LL PARDON ME HI'LL JOIN TH' NIPPERS AT THEIR SIESTA!
NO DICE, MY CAREFREE CABALLERO! YOU AND YOUR LEAN FRIEND WASH THE DISHES — WHILE MISS KANE AND I GET IN A QUICK NOSE-POWDER! NO STALLING — OR I CANCEL THE CALORIES!
MILTON CANIFF
3-19
I DO DECLARE, MISS RAVEN, MISTER BLAZE AN' MISTER RYAN WILL FEEL RIGHT SILLY WASHIN' THOSE DISHES!
DON'T GET IN A TIZZY ABOUT IT! IT'LL MAKE THEM APPRECIATE WHAT THEIR WIVES HAVE TO GO THROUGH THREE TIMES A DAY!...
...THIS IS WHERE WE'LL BUNK, APRIL! ...SEEMS JUST LIKE HOME — IF YOU CLOSE YOUR EYES, HOLD YOUR BREATH AND COVER YOUR EARS!
MERCY! WHAT'S THAT?
THAT'S MY HOT AND COLD RUNNING BATH! VERY INGENIOUS!...
YOU COME IN FROM A DAY WITH THE YOUNGUNS — ALL STICKY HOT... YOU PULL THE CORD... COLD WATER POURS OVER YOU... AT THAT MOMENT A COUPLE OF KIDS BURST THROUGH THE UNLOCKED DOOR, PLAYING TAG — AND YOU RUN!
MILTON CANIFF
3-20
GREAT DAY! I FEEL LIKE A NEW PERSON! WHAT ARE YOU DOING, MISS RAVEN?
TAKING IN THE HEM OF THIS SKIRT! THIS AND ONE OF MY SWEATERS SHOULD KEEP YOU DECENT!
THAT'S MOS' KIND OF YOU!... BUT THIS IS SUCH FINE MATERIAL... IT'S A PITY TO RUIN IT FOR ME! WHY, IT'S NEARLY NEW!
UH-HUH! PART OF MY TROUSSEAU!
...OH! YOU'RE GOIN' T' BE MARRIED?
I WAS GOING TO BE MARRIED! YOU'LL NOTICE THE SKIRT IS A BIT OUT OF FASHION! I'VE BEEN KEEPING IT IN MY "DOPE" CHEST!
I'M SORRY! I DIDN'T---
DON'T LET IT EAT YOU! SOME DAY I'LL TELL YOU ABOUT MY OPERATION — AND WE'LL HAVE A GOOD CRY! MEANWHILE, TO SOUND THE PROPER NOTE OF IRONY — I MUST GO SEE IF MY CHILDREN ARE AWAKE!
MILTON CANIFF
3-21

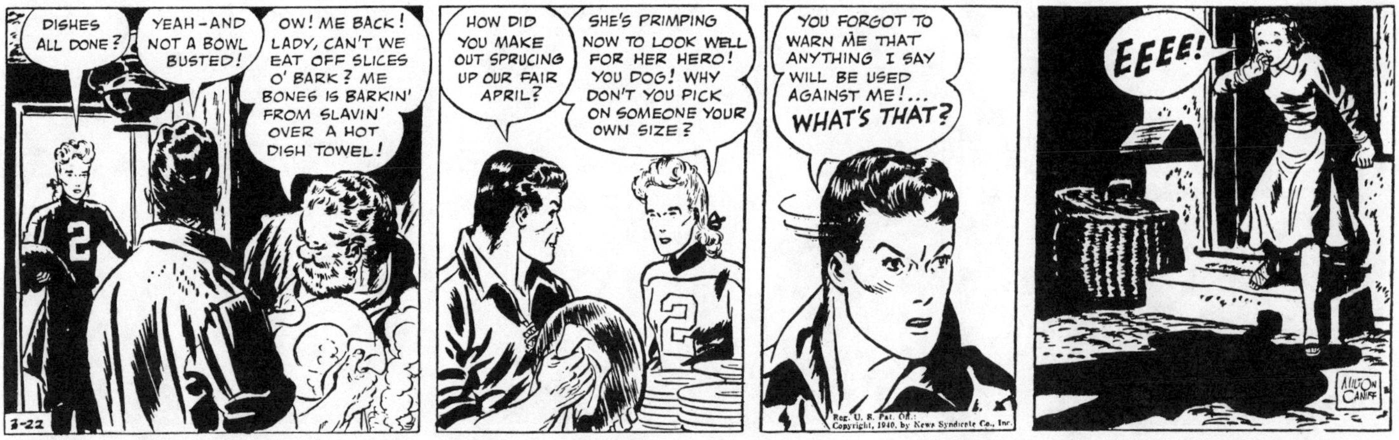
DISHES ALL DONE?
YEAH-AND NOT A BOWL BUSTED!
OW! ME BACK! LADY, CAN'T WE EAT OFF SLICES O' BARK? ME BONES IS BARKIN' FROM SLAVIN' OVER A HOT DISH TOWEL!
3-22
HOW DID YOU MAKE OUT SPRUCING UP OUR FAIR APRIL?
SHE'S PRIMPING NOW TO LOOK WELL FOR HER HERO! YOU DOG! WHY DON'T YOU PICK ON SOMEONE YOUR OWN SIZE?
YOU FORGOT TO WARN ME THAT ANYTHING I SAY WILL BE USED AGAINST ME!... WHAT'S THAT?
Reg. U. S. Pat. Off.; Copyright, 1940, by News Syndicate Co., Inc.
EEEE!
MILTON CANIFF

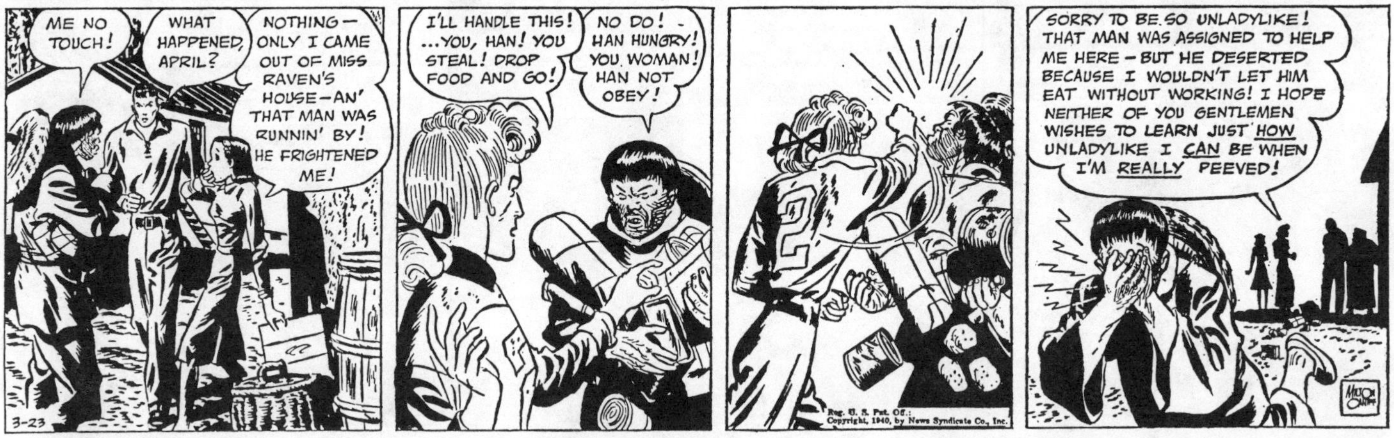
ME NO TOUCH!
WHAT HAPPENED, APRIL?
NOTHING— ONLY I CAME OUT OF MISS RAVEN'S HOUSE—AN' THAT MAN WAS RUNNIN' BY! HE FRIGHTENED ME!
3-23
I'LL HANDLE THIS! ...YOU, HAN! YOU STEAL! DROP FOOD AND GO!
NO DO! HAN HUNGRY! YOU WOMAN! HAN NOT OBEY!
Reg. U. S. Pat. Off.; Copyright, 1940, by News Syndicate Co., Inc.
SORRY TO BE SO UNLADYLIKE! THAT MAN WAS ASSIGNED TO HELP ME HERE—BUT HE DESERTED BECAUSE I WOULDN'T LET HIM EAT WITHOUT WORKING! I HOPE NEITHER OF YOU GENTLEMEN WISHES TO LEARN JUST HOW UNLADYLIKE I CAN BE WHEN I'M REALLY PEEVED!
MILTON CANIFF

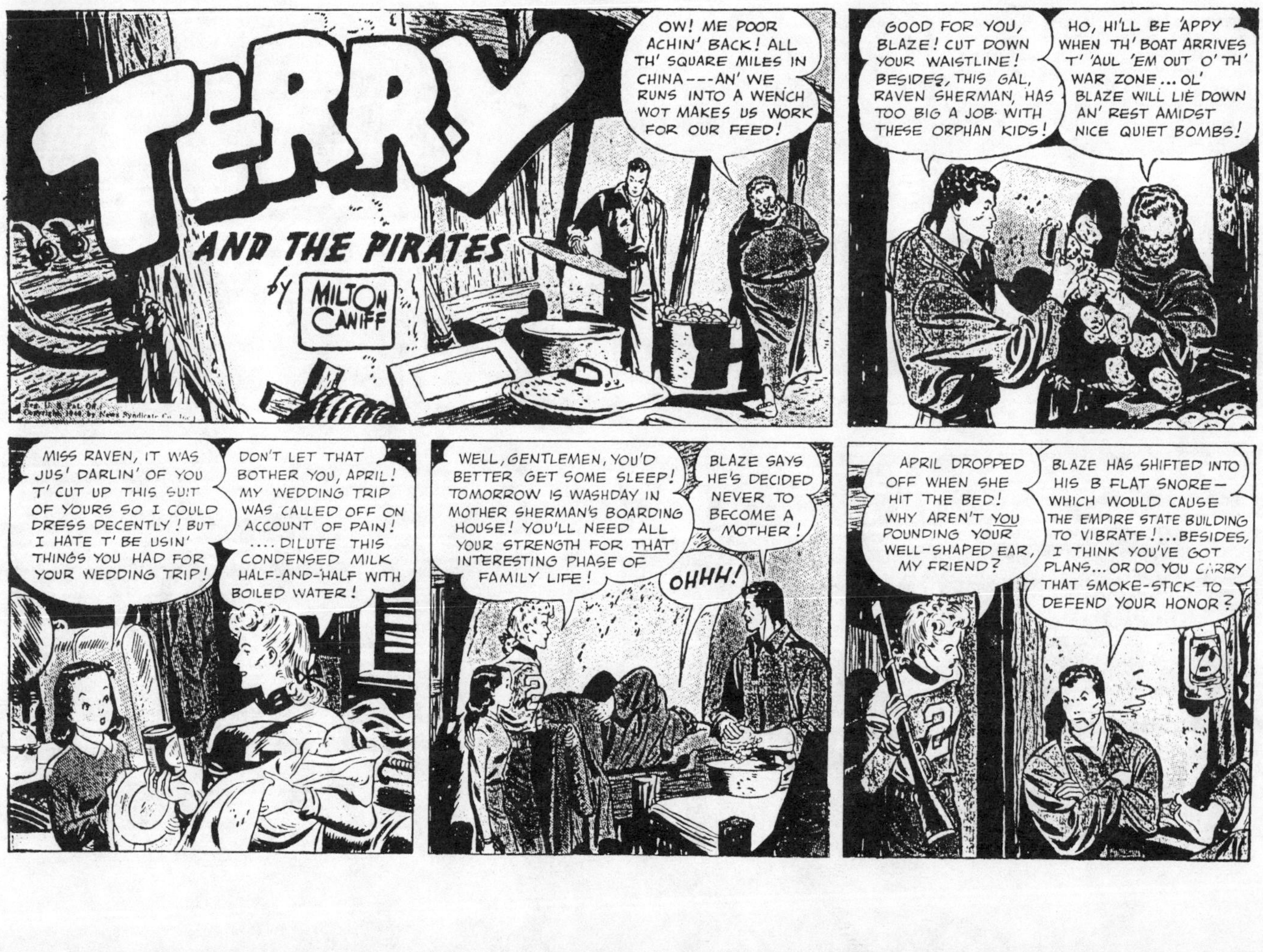
TERRY AND THE PIRATES
by MILTON CANIFF
OW! ME POOR ACHIN' BACK! ALL TH' SQUARE MILES IN CHINA---AN' WE RUNS INTO A WENCH WOT MAKES US WORK FOR OUR FEED!
GOOD FOR YOU, BLAZE! CUT DOWN YOUR WAISTLINE! BESIDES, THIS GAL, RAVEN SHERMAN, HAS TOO BIG A JOB WITH THESE ORPHAN KIDS!
HO, HI'LL BE 'APPY WHEN TH' BOAT ARRIVES T' 'AUL 'EM OUT O' TH' WAR ZONE... OL' BLAZE WILL LIE DOWN AN' REST AMIDST NICE QUIET BOMBS!
MISS RAVEN, IT WAS JUS' DARLIN' OF YOU T' CUT UP THIS SUIT OF YOURS SO I COULD DRESS DECENTLY! BUT I HATE T' BE USIN' THINGS YOU HAD FOR YOUR WEDDING TRIP!
DON'T LET THAT BOTHER YOU, APRIL! MY WEDDING TRIP WAS CALLED OFF ON ACCOUNT OF PAIN! .... DILUTE THIS CONDENSED MILK HALF-AND-HALF WITH BOILED WATER!
WELL, GENTLEMEN, YOU'D BETTER GET SOME SLEEP! TOMORROW IS WASHDAY IN MOTHER SHERMAN'S BOARDING HOUSE! YOU'LL NEED ALL YOUR STRENGTH FOR THAT INTERESTING PHASE OF FAMILY LIFE!
BLAZE SAYS HE'S DECIDED NEVER TO BECOME A MOTHER!
OHHH!
APRIL DROPPED OFF WHEN SHE HIT THE BED! WHY AREN'T YOU POUNDING YOUR WELL-SHAPED EAR, MY FRIEND?
BLAZE HAS SHIFTED INTO HIS B FLAT SNORE—WHICH WOULD CAUSE THE EMPIRE STATE BUILDING TO VIBRATE!... BESIDES, I THINK YOU'VE GOT PLANS... OR DO YOU CARRY THAT SMOKE-STICK TO DEFEND YOUR HONOR?

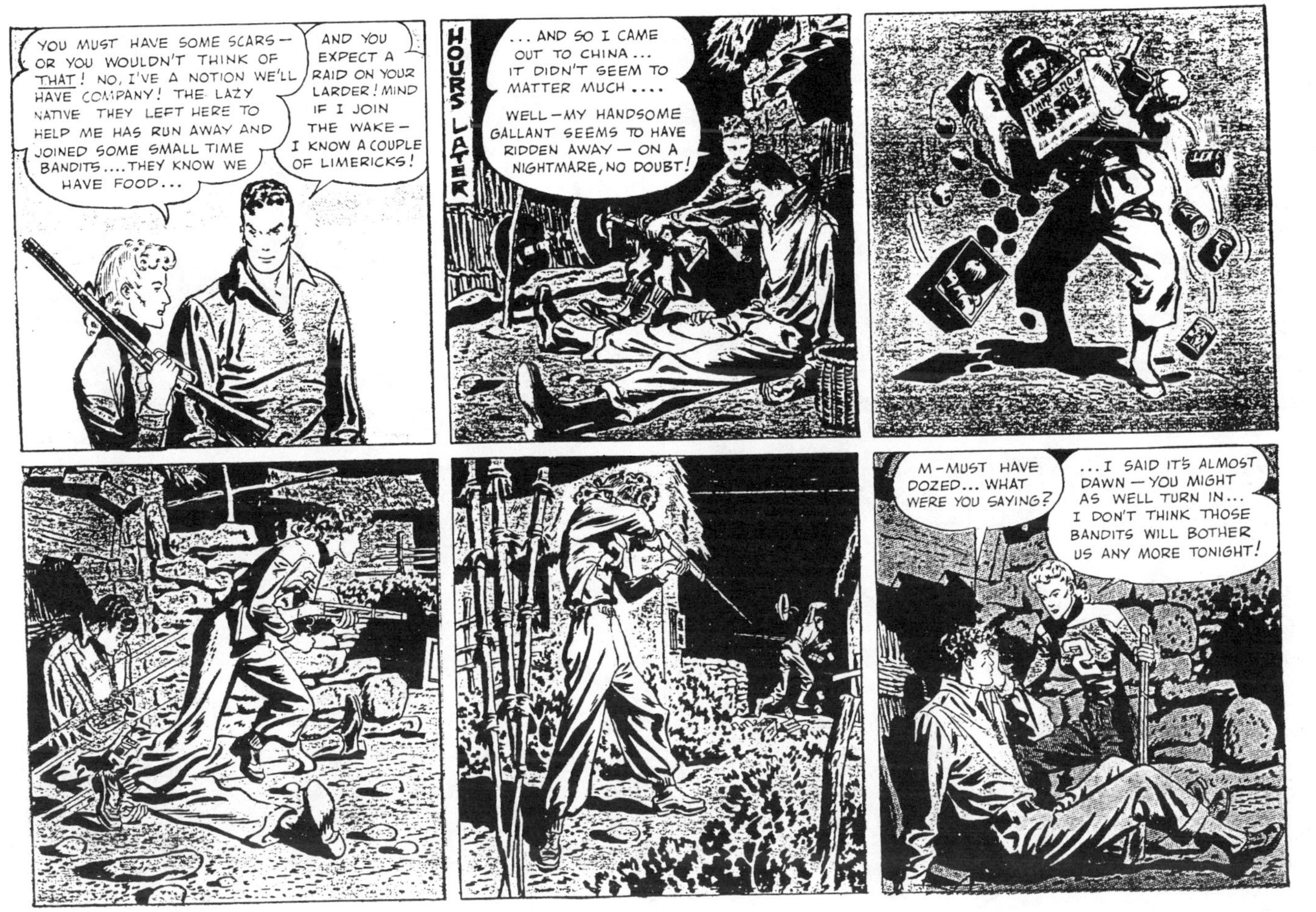
YOU MUST HAVE SOME SCARS— OR YOU WOULDN'T THINK OF THAT! NO, I'VE A NOTION WE'LL HAVE COMPANY! THE LAZY NATIVE THEY LEFT HERE TO HELP ME HAS RUN AWAY AND JOINED SOME SMALL TIME BANDITS.... THEY KNOW WE HAVE FOOD...
AND YOU EXPECT A RAID ON YOUR LARDER! MIND IF I JOIN THE WAKE— I KNOW A COUPLE OF LIMERICKS!
HOURS LATER
... AND SO I CAME OUT TO CHINA... IT DIDN'T SEEM TO MATTER MUCH ....
WELL—MY HANDSOME GALLANT SEEMS TO HAVE RIDDEN AWAY— ON A NIGHTMARE, NO DOUBT!
M-MUST HAVE DOZED... WHAT WERE YOU SAYING?
... I SAID IT'S ALMOST DAWN — YOU MIGHT AS WELL TURN IN... I DON'T THINK THOSE BANDITS WILL BOTHER US ANY MORE TONIGHT!

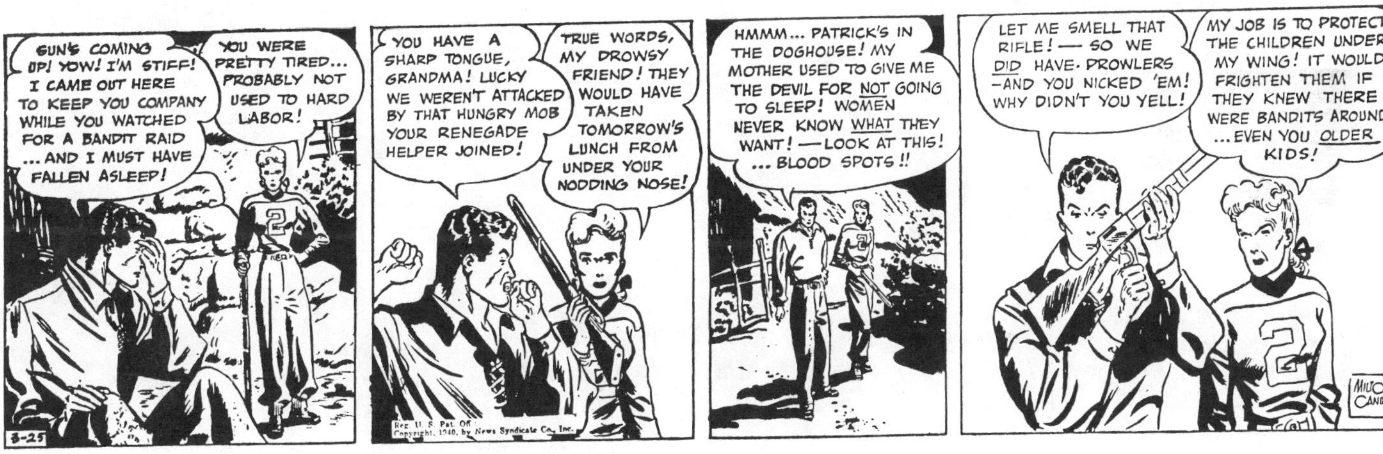
SUN'S COMING UP! YOW! I'M STIFF! I CAME OUT HERE TO KEEP YOU COMPANY WHILE YOU WATCHED FOR A BANDIT RAID ... AND I MUST HAVE FALLEN ASLEEP!
YOU WERE PRETTY TIRED... PROBABLY NOT USED TO HARD LABOR!
YOU HAVE A SHARP TONGUE, GRANDMA! LUCKY WE WEREN'T ATTACKED BY THAT HUNGRY MOB YOUR RENEGADE HELPER JOINED!
TRUE WORDS, MY DROWSY FRIEND! THEY WOULD HAVE TAKEN TOMORROW'S LUNCH FROM UNDER YOUR NODDING NOSE!
HMMM... PATRICK'S IN THE DOGHOUSE! MY MOTHER USED TO GIVE ME THE DEVIL FOR NOT GOING TO SLEEP! WOMEN NEVER KNOW WHAT THEY WANT! — LOOK AT THIS! ... BLOOD SPOTS!!
LET ME SMELL THAT RIFLE! — SO WE DID HAVE PROWLERS —AND YOU NICKED 'EM! WHY DIDN'T YOU YELL!
MY JOB IS TO PROTECT THE CHILDREN UNDER MY WING! IT WOULD FRIGHTEN THEM IF THEY KNEW THERE WERE BANDITS AROUND ... EVEN YOU OLDER KIDS!
3-25
Reg. U. S. Pat. Off. Copyright, 1940, by News Syndicate Co., Inc.
MILTON CANIFF

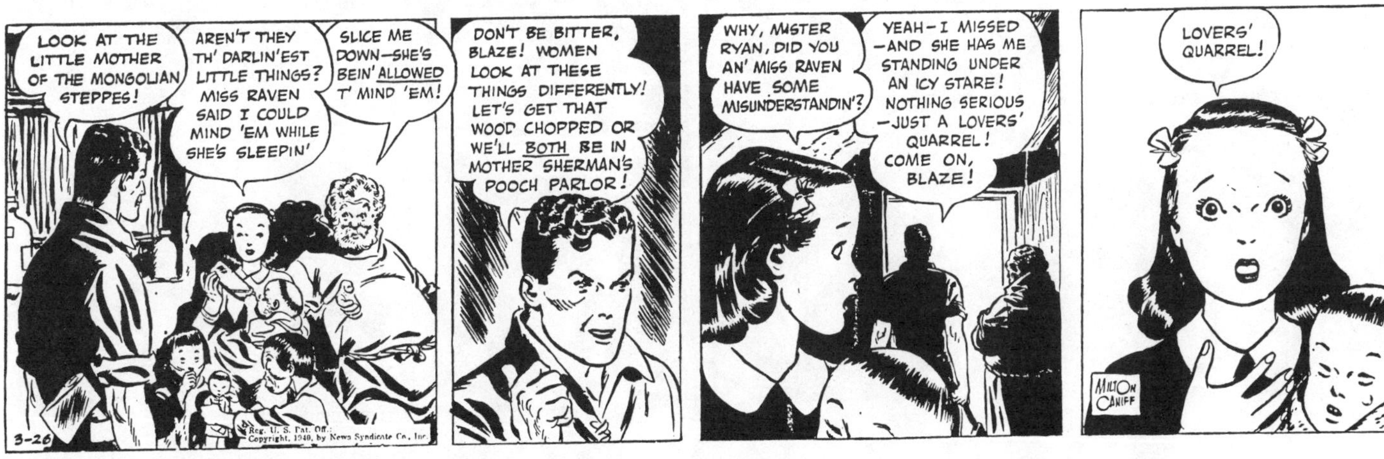
LOOK AT THE LITTLE MOTHER OF THE MONGOLIAN STEPPES!
AREN'T THEY TH' DARLIN'EST LITTLE THINGS? MISS RAVEN SAID I COULD MIND 'EM WHILE SHE'S SLEEPIN'
SLICE ME DOWN—SHE'S BEIN' ALLOWED T' MIND 'EM!
DON'T BE BITTER, BLAZE! WOMEN LOOK AT THESE THINGS DIFFERENTLY! LET'S GET THAT WOOD CHOPPED OR WE'LL BOTH BE IN MOTHER SHERMAN'S POOCH PARLOR!
WHY, MISTER RYAN, DID YOU AN' MISS RAVEN HAVE SOME MISUNDERSTANDIN'?
YEAH—I MISSED —AND SHE HAS ME STANDING UNDER AN ICY STARE! NOTHING SERIOUS —JUST A LOVERS' QUARREL! COME ON, BLAZE!
LOVERS' QUARREL!
3-26
Reg. U. S. Pat. Off. Copyright, 1940, by News Syndicate Co., Inc.
MILTON CANIFF

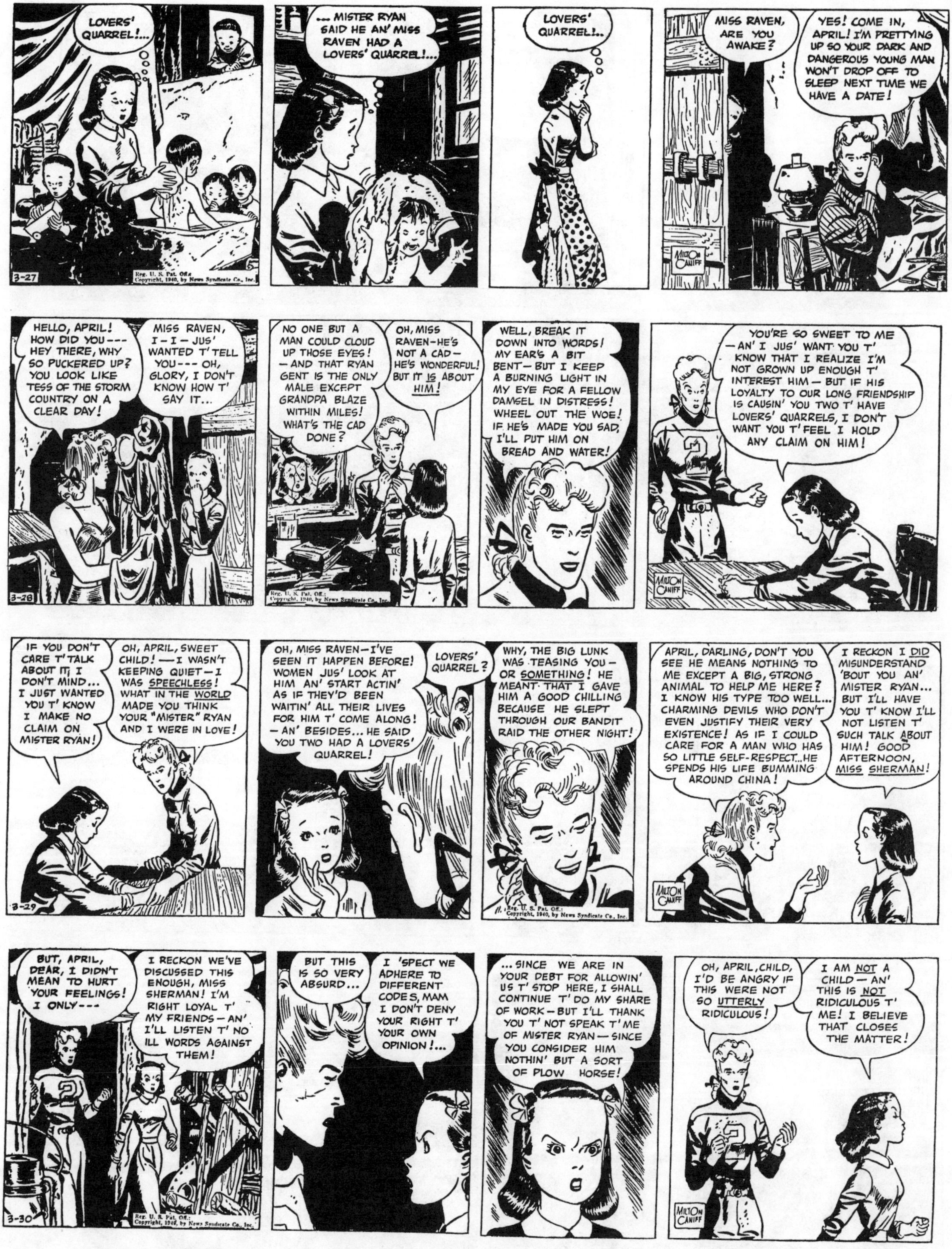

LOVERS' QUARREL!...
3-27
Reg. U. S. Pat. Off.; Copyright, 1940, by News Syndicate Co., Inc.
... MISTER RYAN SAID HE AN' MISS RAVEN HAD A LOVERS' QUARREL!...
LOVERS' QUARREL!..
MISS RAVEN, ARE YOU AWAKE?
YES! COME IN, APRIL! I'M PRETTYING UP SO YOUR DARK AND DANGEROUS YOUNG MAN WON'T DROP OFF TO SLEEP NEXT TIME WE HAVE A DATE!
MILTON CANIFF
HELLO, APRIL! HOW DID YOU--- HEY THERE, WHY SO PUCKERED UP? YOU LOOK LIKE TESS OF THE STORM COUNTRY ON A CLEAR DAY!
MISS RAVEN, I-I-JUS' WANTED T' TELL YOU--- OH, GLORY, I DON'T KNOW HOW T' SAY IT...
3-28
NO ONE BUT A MAN COULD CLOUD UP THOSE EYES! —AND THAT RYAN GENT IS THE ONLY MALE EXCEPT GRANDPA BLAZE WITHIN MILES! WHAT'S THE CAD DONE?
OH, MISS RAVEN—HE'S NOT A CAD—HE'S WONDERFUL! BUT IT IS ABOUT HIM!
Reg. U. S. Pat. Off.; Copyright, 1940, by News Syndicate Co., Inc.
WELL, BREAK IT DOWN INTO WORDS! MY EAR'S A BIT BENT—BUT I KEEP A BURNING LIGHT IN MY EYE FOR A FELLOW DAMSEL IN DISTRESS! WHEEL OUT THE WOE! IF HE'S MADE YOU SAD, I'LL PUT HIM ON BREAD AND WATER!
YOU'RE SO SWEET TO ME —AN' I JUS' WANT YOU T' KNOW THAT I REALIZE I'M NOT GROWN UP ENOUGH T' INTEREST HIM—BUT IF HIS LOYALTY TO OUR LONG FRIENDSHIP IS CAUSIN' YOU TWO T' HAVE LOVERS' QUARRELS, I DON'T WANT YOU T' FEEL I HOLD ANY CLAIM ON HIM!
MILTON CANIFF
IF YOU DON'T CARE T' TALK ABOUT IT, I DON'T MIND... I JUST WANTED YOU T' KNOW I MAKE NO CLAIM ON MISTER RYAN!
OH, APRIL, SWEET CHILD! —I WASN'T KEEPING QUIET—I WAS SPEECHLESS! WHAT IN THE WORLD MADE YOU THINK YOUR "MISTER" RYAN AND I WERE IN LOVE!
3-29
OH, MISS RAVEN—I'VE SEEN IT HAPPEN BEFORE! WOMEN JUS' LOOK AT HIM AN' START ACTIN' AS IF THEY'D BEEN WAITIN' ALL THEIR LIVES FOR HIM T' COME ALONG! —AN' BESIDES... HE SAID YOU TWO HAD A LOVERS' QUARREL!
LOVERS' QUARREL?
WHY, THE BIG LUNK WAS TEASING YOU—OR SOMETHING! HE MEANT THAT I GAVE HIM A GOOD CHILLING BECAUSE HE SLEPT THROUGH OUR BANDIT RAID THE OTHER NIGHT!
Reg. U. S. Pat. Off.; Copyright, 1940, by News Syndicate Co., Inc.
APRIL, DARLING, DON'T YOU SEE HE MEANS NOTHING TO ME EXCEPT A BIG, STRONG ANIMAL TO HELP ME HERE? I KNOW HIS TYPE TOO WELL... CHARMING DEVILS WHO DON'T EVEN JUSTIFY THEIR VERY EXISTENCE! AS IF I COULD CARE FOR A MAN WHO HAS SO LITTLE SELF-RESPECT...HE SPENDS HIS LIFE BUMMING AROUND CHINA!
I RECKON I DID MISUNDERSTAND 'BOUT YOU AN' MISTER RYAN... BUT I'LL HAVE YOU T' KNOW I'LL NOT LISTEN T' SUCH TALK ABOUT HIM! GOOD AFTERNOON, MISS SHERMAN!
MILTON CANIFF
BUT, APRIL, DEAR, I DIDN'T MEAN TO HURT YOUR FEELINGS! I ONLY---
I RECKON WE'VE DISCUSSED THIS ENOUGH, MISS SHERMAN! I'M RIGHT LOYAL T' MY FRIENDS—AN' I'LL LISTEN T' NO ILL WORDS AGAINST THEM!
3-30
Reg. U. S. Pat. Off.; Copyright, 1940, by News Syndicate Co., Inc.
BUT THIS IS SO VERY ABSURD...
I 'SPECT WE ADHERE TO DIFFERENT CODES, MAM I DON'T DENY YOUR RIGHT T' YOUR OWN OPINION!...
... SINCE WE ARE IN YOUR DEBT FOR ALLOWIN' US T' STOP HERE, I SHALL CONTINUE T' DO MY SHARE OF WORK—BUT I'LL THANK YOU T' NOT SPEAK T' ME OF MISTER RYAN—SINCE YOU CONSIDER HIM NOTHIN' BUT A SORT OF PLOW HORSE!
OH, APRIL, CHILD, I'D BE ANGRY IF THIS WERE NOT SO UTTERLY RIDICULOUS!
I AM NOT A CHILD—AN' THIS IS NOT RIDICULOUS T' ME! I BELIEVE THAT CLOSES THE MATTER!
MILTON CANIFF

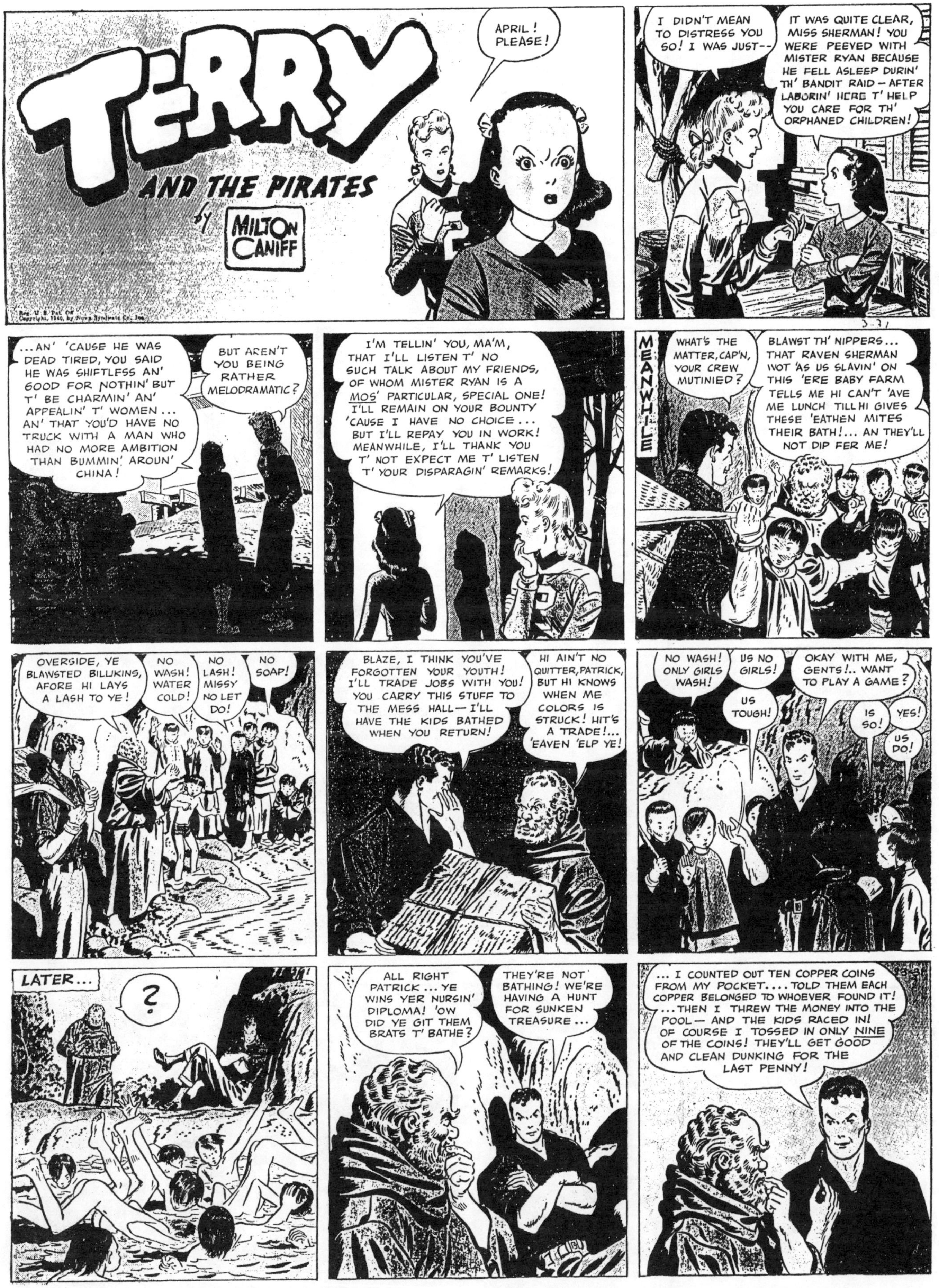
TERRY AND THE PIRATES
by MILTON CANIFF
Reg. U S Pat Off
Copyright, 1940, by News Syndicate Co. Inc.
APRIL! PLEASE!
I DIDN'T MEAN TO DISTRESS YOU SO! I WAS JUST--
IT WAS QUITE CLEAR, MISS SHERMAN! YOU WERE PEEVED WITH MISTER RYAN BECAUSE HE FELL ASLEEP DURIN' TH' BANDIT RAID—AFTER LABORIN' HERE T' HELP YOU CARE FOR TH' ORPHANED CHILDREN!
...AN' 'CAUSE HE WAS DEAD TIRED, YOU SAID HE WAS SHIFTLESS AN' GOOD FOR NOTHIN' BUT T' BE CHARMIN' AN' APPEALIN' T' WOMEN... AN' THAT YOU'D HAVE NO TRUCK WITH A MAN WHO HAD NO MORE AMBITION THAN BUMMIN' AROUN' CHINA!
BUT AREN'T YOU BEING RATHER MELODRAMATIC?
I'M TELLIN' YOU, MA'M, THAT I'LL LISTEN T' NO SUCH TALK ABOUT MY FRIENDS, OF WHOM MISTER RYAN IS A MOS' PARTICULAR, SPECIAL ONE! I'LL REMAIN ON YOUR BOUNTY 'CAUSE I HAVE NO CHOICE... BUT I'LL REPAY YOU IN WORK! MEANWHILE, I'LL THANK YOU T' NOT EXPECT ME T' LISTEN T' YOUR DISPARAGIN' REMARKS!
MEANWHILE
WHAT'S THE MATTER, CAP'N, YOUR CREW MUTINIED?
BLAWST TH' NIPPERS... THAT RAVEN SHERMAN WOT 'AS US SLAVIN' ON THIS 'ERE BABY FARM TELLS ME HI CAN'T 'AVE ME LUNCH TILL HI GIVES THESE 'EATHEN MITES THEIR BATH!... AN THEY'LL NOT DIP FER ME!
OVERSIDE, YE BLAWSTED BILLIKINS, AFORE HI LAYS A LASH TO YE!
NO WASH! WATER COLD!
NO LASH! MISSY NO LET DO!
NO SOAP!
BLAZE, I THINK YOU'VE FORGOTTEN YOUR YOUTH! I'LL TRADE JOBS WITH YOU! YOU CARRY THIS STUFF TO THE MESS HALL—I'LL HAVE THE KIDS BATHED WHEN YOU RETURN!
HI AIN'T NO QUITTER, PATRICK, BUT HI KNOWS WHEN ME COLORS IS STRUCK! HIT'S A TRADE!... 'EAVEN 'ELP YE!
NO WASH! ONLY GIRLS WASH!
US NO GIRLS!
US TOUGH!
OKAY WITH ME, GENTS!.. WANT TO PLAY A GAME?
IS SO!
YES!
US DO!
LATER...
?
ALL RIGHT PATRICK... YE WINS YER NURSIN' DIPLOMA! 'OW DID YE GIT THEM BRATS T' BATHE?
THEY'RE NOT BATHING! WE'RE HAVING A HUNT FOR SUNKEN TREASURE...
... I COUNTED OUT TEN COPPER COINS FROM MY POCKET.... TOLD THEM EACH COPPER BELONGED TO WHOEVER FOUND IT! ...THEN I THREW THE MONEY INTO THE POOL— AND THE KIDS RACED IN! OF COURSE I TOSSED IN ONLY NINE OF THE COINS! THEY'LL GET GOOD AND CLEAN DUNKING FOR THE LAST PENNY!

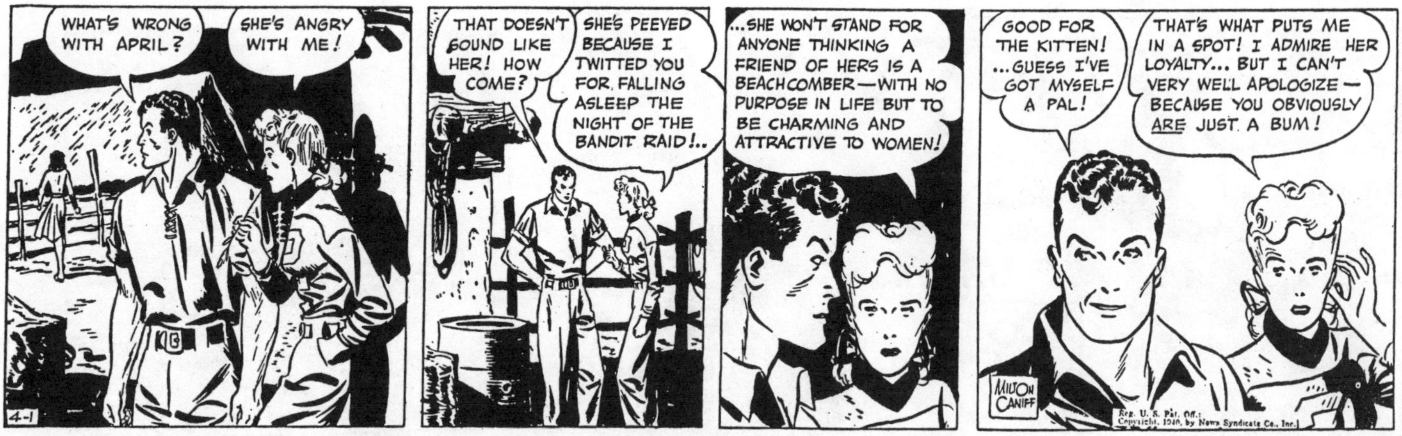
WHAT'S WRONG WITH APRIL?
SHE'S ANGRY WITH ME!
4-1
THAT DOESN'T SOUND LIKE HER! HOW COME?
SHE'S PEEVED BECAUSE I TWITTED YOU FOR FALLING ASLEEP THE NIGHT OF THE BANDIT RAID!..
...SHE WON'T STAND FOR ANYONE THINKING A FRIEND OF HERS IS A BEACHCOMBER—WITH NO PURPOSE IN LIFE BUT TO BE CHARMING AND ATTRACTIVE TO WOMEN!
GOOD FOR THE KITTEN! ...GUESS I'VE GOT MYSELF A PAL!
THAT'S WHAT PUTS ME IN A SPOT! I ADMIRE HER LOYALTY... BUT I CAN'T VERY WELL APOLOGIZE— BECAUSE YOU OBVIOUSLY ARE JUST A BUM!
MILTON CANIFF
Reg. U. S. Pat. Off.; Copyright, 1940, by News Syndicate Co., Inc.

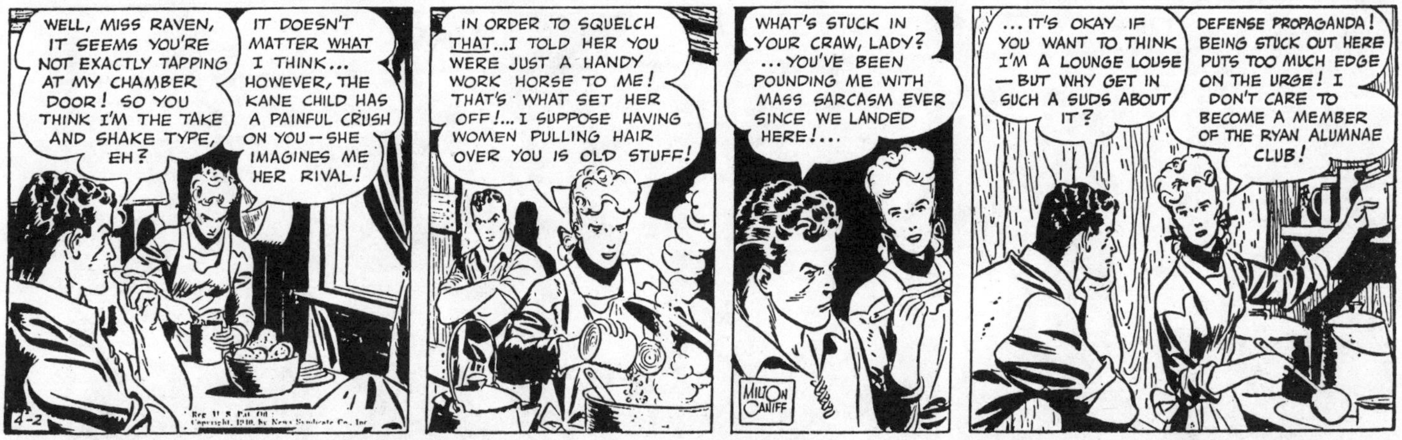
WELL, MISS RAVEN, IT SEEMS YOU'RE NOT EXACTLY TAPPING AT MY CHAMBER DOOR! SO YOU THINK I'M THE TAKE AND SHAKE TYPE, EH?
IT DOESN'T MATTER WHAT I THINK... HOWEVER, THE KANE CHILD HAS A PAINFUL CRUSH ON YOU—SHE IMAGINES ME HER RIVAL!
4-2
Reg. U. S. Pat. Off.; Copyright, 1940, by News Syndicate Co., Inc.
IN ORDER TO SQUELCH THAT...I TOLD HER YOU WERE JUST A HANDY WORK HORSE TO ME! THAT'S WHAT SET HER OFF!...I SUPPOSE HAVING WOMEN PULLING HAIR OVER YOU IS OLD STUFF!
WHAT'S STUCK IN YOUR CRAW, LADY? ...YOU'VE BEEN POUNDING ME WITH MASS SARCASM EVER SINCE WE LANDED HERE!...
MILTON CANIFF
...IT'S OKAY IF YOU WANT TO THINK I'M A LOUNGE LOUSE —BUT WHY GET IN SUCH A SUDS ABOUT IT?
DEFENSE PROPAGANDA! BEING STUCK OUT HERE PUTS TOO MUCH EDGE ON THE URGE! I DON'T CARE TO BECOME A MEMBER OF THE RYAN ALUMNAE CLUB!

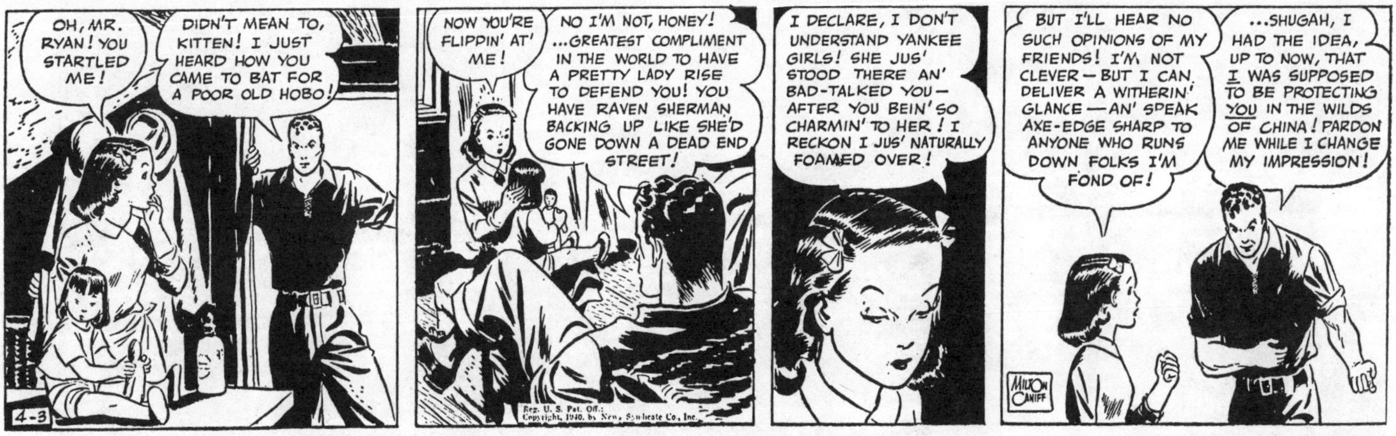
OH, MR. RYAN! YOU STARTLED ME!
DIDN'T MEAN TO, KITTEN! I JUST HEARD HOW YOU CAME TO BAT FOR A POOR OLD HOBO!
4-3
NOW YOU'RE FLIPPIN' AT ME!
NO I'M NOT, HONEY! ...GREATEST COMPLIMENT IN THE WORLD TO HAVE A PRETTY LADY RISE TO DEFEND YOU! YOU HAVE RAVEN SHERMAN BACKING UP LIKE SHE'D GONE DOWN A DEAD END STREET!
Reg. U. S. Pat. Off.; Copyright, 1940, by News Syndicate Co., Inc.
I DECLARE, I DON'T UNDERSTAND YANKEE GIRLS! SHE JUS' STOOD THERE AN' BAD-TALKED YOU— AFTER YOU BEIN' SO CHARMIN' TO HER! I RECKON I JUS' NATURALLY FOAMED OVER!
BUT I'LL HEAR NO SUCH OPINIONS OF MY FRIENDS! I'M NOT CLEVER—BUT I CAN DELIVER A WITHERIN' GLANCE—AN' SPEAK AXE-EDGE SHARP TO ANYONE WHO RUNS DOWN FOLKS I'M FOND OF!
...SHUGAH, I HAD THE IDEA, UP TO NOW, THAT I WAS SUPPOSED TO BE PROTECTING YOU IN THE WILDS OF CHINA! PARDON ME WHILE I CHANGE MY IMPRESSION!
MILTON CANIFF

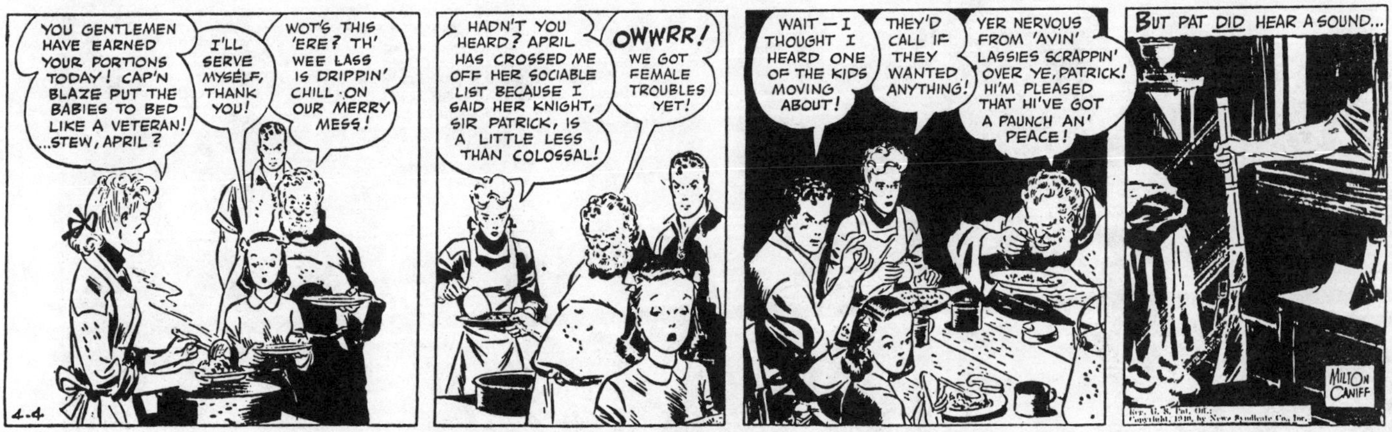
YOU GENTLEMEN HAVE EARNED YOUR PORTIONS TODAY! CAP'N BLAZE PUT THE BABIES TO BED LIKE A VETERAN! ...STEW, APRIL?
I'LL SERVE MYSELF, THANK YOU!
WOT'S THIS 'ERE? TH' WEE LASS IS DRIPPIN' CHILL ON OUR MERRY MESS!
4-4
HADN'T YOU HEARD? APRIL HAS CROSSED ME OFF HER SOCIABLE LIST BECAUSE I SAID HER KNIGHT, SIR PATRICK, IS A LITTLE LESS THAN COLOSSAL!
OWWRR! WE GOT FEMALE TROUBLES YET!
WAIT—I THOUGHT I HEARD ONE OF THE KIDS MOVING ABOUT!
THEY'D CALL IF THEY WANTED ANYTHING!
YER NERVOUS FROM 'AVIN' LASSIES SCRAPPIN' OVER YE, PATRICK! HI'M PLEASED THAT HI'VE GOT A PAUNCH AN' PEACE!
BUT PAT DID HEAR A SOUND...
MILTON CANIFF
Reg. U. S. Pat. Off.; Copyright, 1940, by News Syndicate Co., Inc.

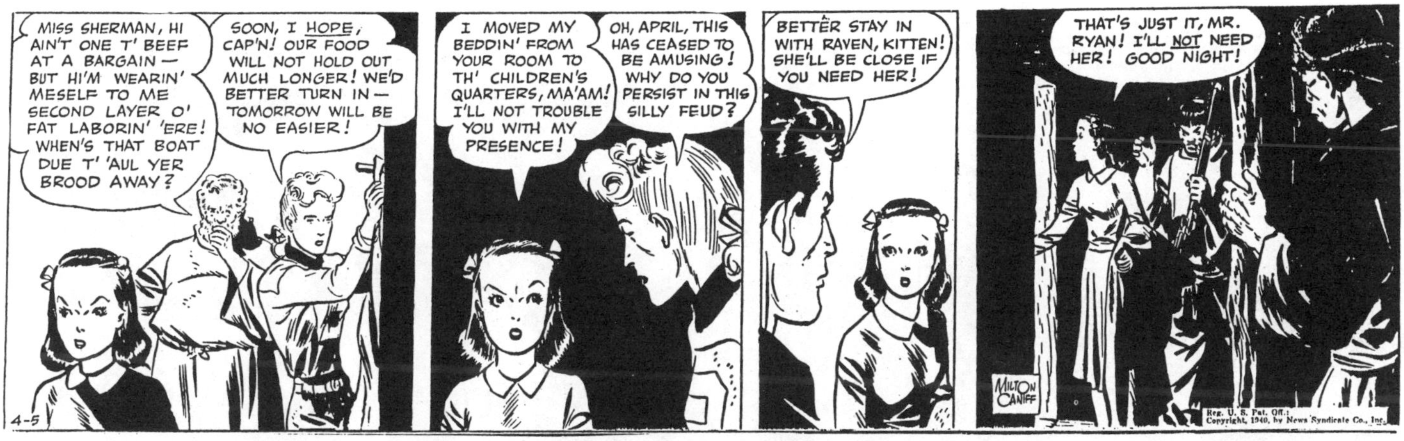
MISS SHERMAN, HI AIN'T ONE T' BEEF AT A BARGAIN — BUT HI'M WEARIN' MESELF TO ME SECOND LAYER O' FAT LABORIN' 'ERE! WHEN'S THAT BOAT DUE T' 'AUL YER BROOD AWAY?
SOON, I HOPE, CAP'N! OUR FOOD WILL NOT HOLD OUT MUCH LONGER! WE'D BETTER TURN IN — TOMORROW WILL BE NO EASIER!
I MOVED MY BEDDIN' FROM YOUR ROOM TO TH' CHILDREN'S QUARTERS, MA'AM! I'LL NOT TROUBLE YOU WITH MY PRESENCE!
OH, APRIL, THIS HAS CEASED TO BE AMUSING! WHY DO YOU PERSIST IN THIS SILLY FEUD?
BETTER STAY IN WITH RAVEN, KITTEN! SHE'LL BE CLOSE IF YOU NEED HER!
THAT'S JUST IT, MR. RYAN! I'LL NOT NEED HER! GOOD NIGHT!
MILTON CANIFF
4-5
Reg. U. S. Pat. Off.; Copyright, 1940, by News Syndicate Co., Inc.

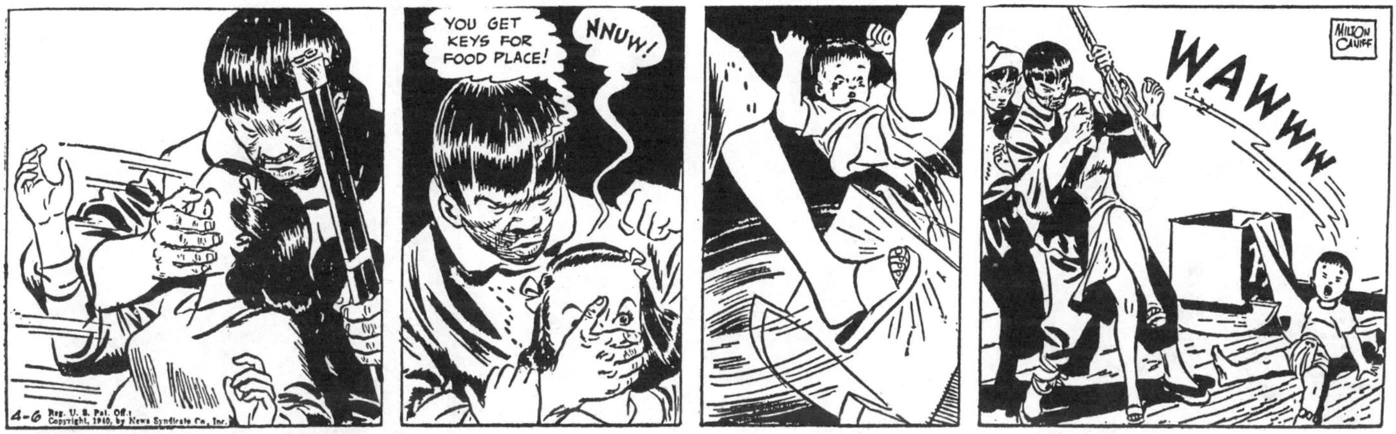
YOU GET KEYS FOR FOOD PLACE!
NNUW!
WAWWW
MILTON CANIFF
4-6
Reg. U. S. Pat. Off.; Copyright, 1940, by News Syndicate Co., Inc.

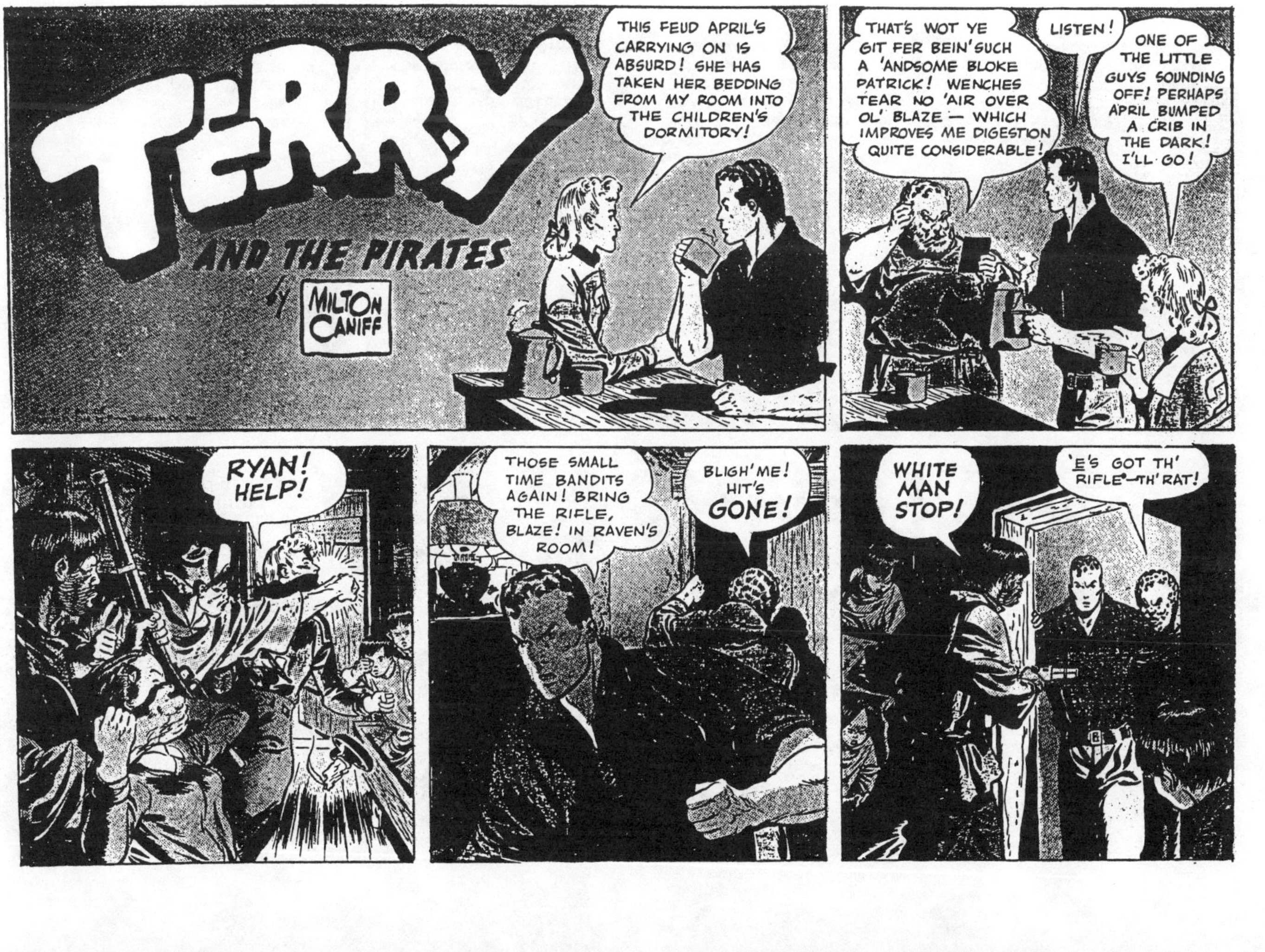
TERRY AND THE PIRATES
by MILTON CANIFF
THIS FEUD APRIL'S CARRYING ON IS ABSURD! SHE HAS TAKEN HER BEDDING FROM MY ROOM INTO THE CHILDREN'S DORMITORY!
THAT'S WOT YE GIT FER BEIN' SUCH A 'ANDSOME BLOKE PATRICK! WENCHES TEAR NO 'AIR OVER OL' BLAZE — WHICH IMPROVES ME DIGESTION QUITE CONSIDERABLE!
LISTEN!
ONE OF THE LITTLE GUYS SOUNDING OFF! PERHAPS APRIL BUMPED A CRIB IN THE DARK! I'LL GO!
RYAN! HELP!
THOSE SMALL TIME BANDITS AGAIN! BRING THE RIFLE, BLAZE! IN RAVEN'S ROOM!
BLIGH'ME! HIT'S GONE!
WHITE MAN STOP!
'E'S GOT TH' RIFLE — TH' RAT!

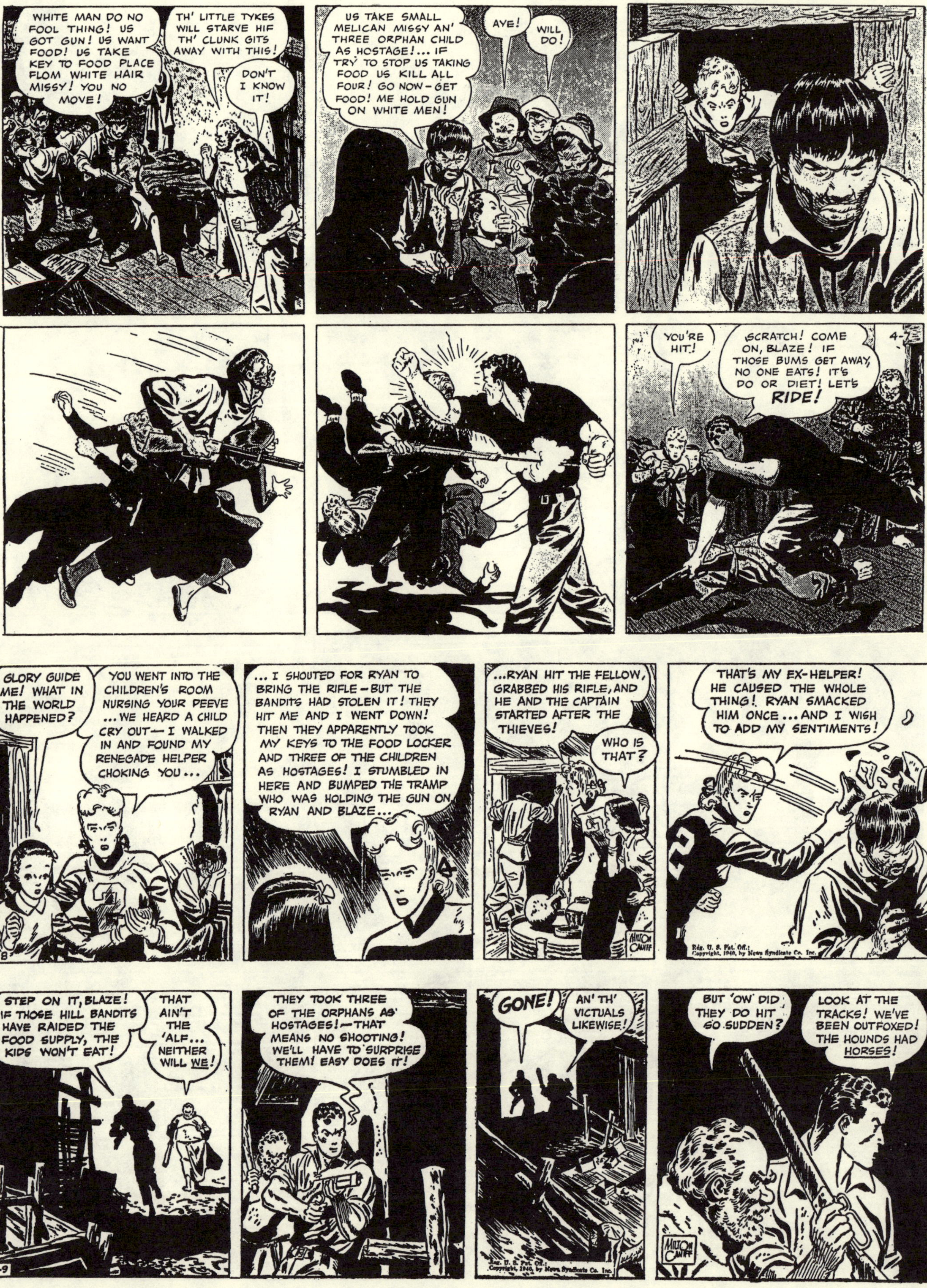

WHITE MAN DO NO FOOL THING! US GOT GUN! US WANT FOOD! US TAKE KEY TO FOOD PLACE FLOM WHITE HAIR MISSY! YOU NO MOVE!
TH' LITTLE TYKES WILL STARVE HIF TH' CLUNK GITS AWAY WITH THIS!
DON'T I KNOW IT!
US TAKE SMALL MELICAN MISSY AN' THREE ORPHAN CHILD AS HOSTAGE!... IF TRY TO STOP US TAKING FOOD US KILL ALL FOUR! GO NOW–GET FOOD! ME HOLD GUN ON WHITE MEN!
AYE!
WILL DO!
YOU'RE HIT!
SCRATCH! COME ON, BLAZE! IF THOSE BUMS GET AWAY, NO ONE EATS! IT'S DO OR DIET! LET'S RIDE!
4-7
GLORY GUIDE ME! WHAT IN THE WORLD HAPPENED?
YOU WENT INTO THE CHILDREN'S ROOM NURSING YOUR PEEVE ...WE HEARD A CHILD CRY OUT—I WALKED IN AND FOUND MY RENEGADE HELPER CHOKING YOU...
4-8
...I SHOUTED FOR RYAN TO BRING THE RIFLE–BUT THE BANDITS HAD STOLEN IT! THEY HIT ME AND I WENT DOWN! THEN THEY APPARENTLY TOOK MY KEYS TO THE FOOD LOCKER AND THREE OF THE CHILDREN AS HOSTAGES! I STUMBLED IN HERE AND BUMPED THE TRAMP WHO WAS HOLDING THE GUN ON RYAN AND BLAZE...
...RYAN HIT THE FELLOW, GRABBED HIS RIFLE, AND HE AND THE CAPTAIN STARTED AFTER THE THIEVES!
WHO IS THAT?
MILTON CANIFF
THAT'S MY EX-HELPER! HE CAUSED THE WHOLE THING! RYAN SMACKED HIM ONCE...AND I WISH TO ADD MY SENTIMENTS!
Reg. U. S. Pat. Off.: Copyright, 1940, by News Syndicate Co. Inc.
STEP ON IT, BLAZE! IF THOSE HILL BANDITS HAVE RAIDED THE FOOD SUPPLY, THE KIDS WON'T EAT!
THAT AIN'T THE 'ALF... NEITHER WILL WE!
4-9
THEY TOOK THREE OF THE ORPHANS AS HOSTAGES!—THAT MEANS NO SHOOTING! WE'LL HAVE TO SURPRISE THEM! EASY DOES IT!
GONE!
AN' TH' VICTUALS LIKEWISE!
Reg. U. S. Pat. Off.: Copyright, 1940, by News Syndicate Co. Inc.
BUT 'OW DID THEY DO HIT SO SUDDEN?
LOOK AT THE TRACKS! WE'VE BEEN OUTFOXED! THE HOUNDS HAD HORSES!
MILTON CANIFF

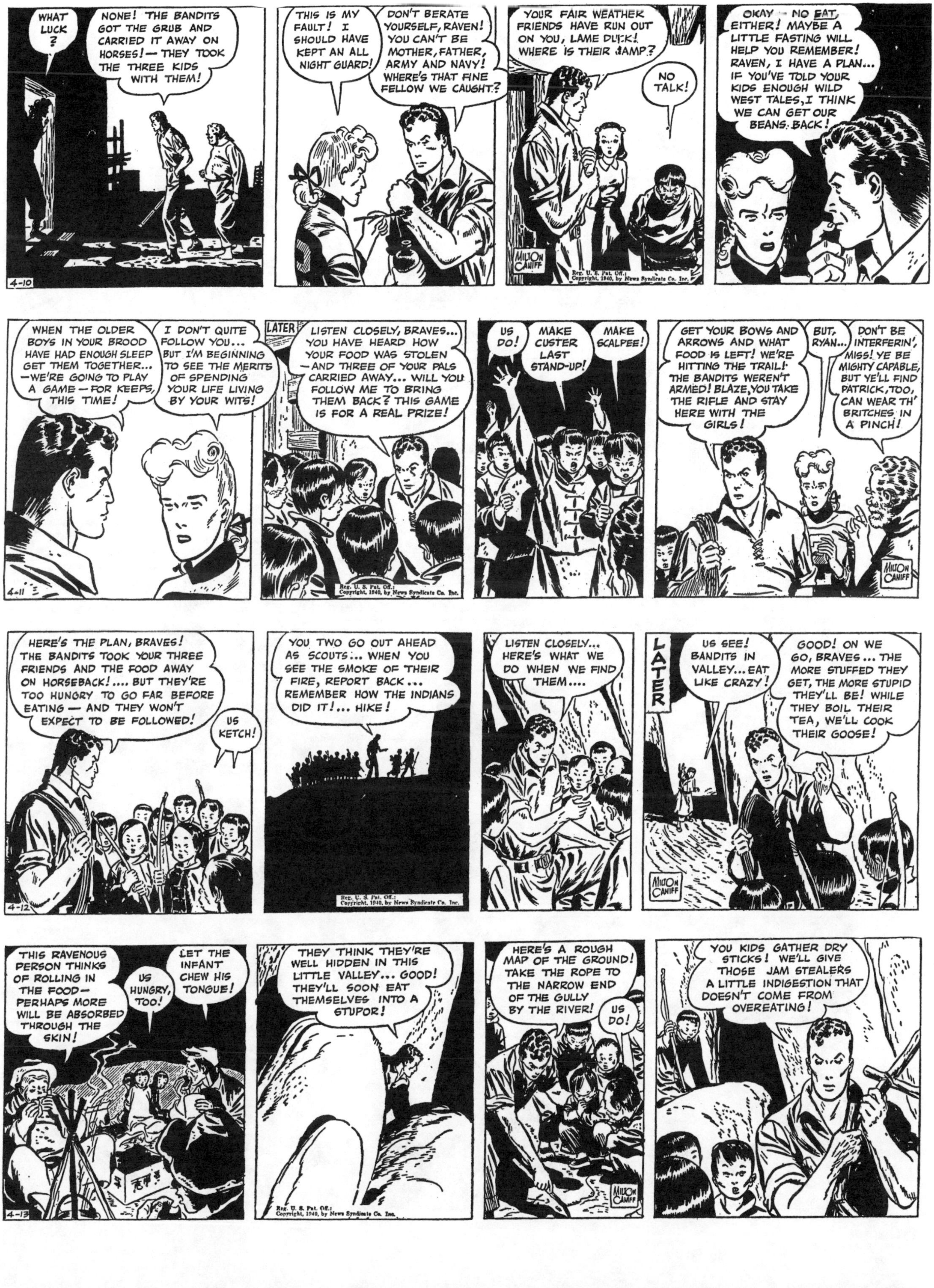
4-10
WHAT LUCK ?
NONE! THE BANDITS GOT THE GRUB AND CARRIED IT AWAY ON HORSES! — THEY TOOK THE THREE KIDS WITH THEM!
THIS IS MY FAULT! I SHOULD HAVE KEPT AN ALL NIGHT GUARD!
DON'T BERATE YOURSELF, RAVEN! YOU CAN'T BE MOTHER, FATHER, ARMY AND NAVY! WHERE'S THAT FINE FELLOW WE CAUGHT?
YOUR FAIR WEATHER FRIENDS HAVE RUN OUT ON YOU, LAME DUCK! WHERE IS THEIR CAMP?
NO TALK!
MILTON CANIFF
Reg. U. S. Pat. Off.: Copyright, 1940, by News Syndicate Co. Inc.
OKAY — NO EAT, EITHER! MAYBE A LITTLE FASTING WILL HELP YOU REMEMBER! RAVEN, I HAVE A PLAN... IF YOU'VE TOLD YOUR KIDS ENOUGH WILD WEST TALES, I THINK WE CAN GET OUR BEANS BACK!
4-11
WHEN THE OLDER BOYS IN YOUR BROOD HAVE HAD ENOUGH SLEEP GET THEM TOGETHER... —WE'RE GOING TO PLAY A GAME — FOR KEEPS, THIS TIME!
I DON'T QUITE FOLLOW YOU... BUT I'M BEGINNING TO SEE THE MERITS OF SPENDING YOUR LIFE LIVING BY YOUR WITS!
LATER
LISTEN CLOSELY, BRAVES... YOU HAVE HEARD HOW YOUR FOOD WAS STOLEN —AND THREE OF YOUR PALS CARRIED AWAY... WILL YOU FOLLOW ME TO BRING THEM BACK? THIS GAME IS FOR A REAL PRIZE!
Reg. U. S. Pat. Off.: Copyright, 1940, by News Syndicate Co. Inc.
US DO!
MAKE CUSTER LAST STAND-UP!
MAKE SCALPEE!
GET YOUR BOWS AND ARROWS AND WHAT FOOD IS LEFT! WE'RE HITTING THE TRAIL! THE BANDITS WEREN'T ARMED! BLAZE, YOU TAKE THE RIFLE AND STAY HERE WITH THE GIRLS!
BUT, RYAN...
DON'T BE INTERFERIN', MISS! YE BE MIGHTY CAPABLE, BUT YE'LL FIND PATRICK, TOO, CAN WEAR TH' BRITCHES IN A PINCH!
MILTON CANIFF
4-12
HERE'S THE PLAN, BRAVES! THE BANDITS TOOK YOUR THREE FRIENDS AND THE FOOD AWAY ON HORSEBACK! BUT THEY'RE TOO HUNGRY TO GO FAR BEFORE EATING — AND THEY WON'T EXPECT TO BE FOLLOWED!
US KETCH!
YOU TWO GO OUT AHEAD AS SCOUTS... WHEN YOU SEE THE SMOKE OF THEIR FIRE, REPORT BACK... REMEMBER HOW THE INDIANS DID IT!... HIKE!
Reg. U. S. Pat. Off.: Copyright, 1940, by News Syndicate Co. Inc.
LISTEN CLOSELY... HERE'S WHAT WE DO WHEN WE FIND THEM....
LATER
US SEE! BANDITS IN VALLEY... EAT LIKE CRAZY!
GOOD! ON WE GO, BRAVES... THE MORE STUFFED THEY GET, THE MORE STUPID THEY'LL BE! WHILE THEY BOIL THEIR TEA, WE'LL COOK THEIR GOOSE!
MILTON CANIFF
4-13
THIS RAVENOUS PERSON THINKS OF ROLLING IN THE FOOD— PERHAPS MORE WILL BE ABSORBED THROUGH THE SKIN!
US HUNGRY, TOO!
LET THE INFANT CHEW HIS TONGUE!
THEY THINK THEY'RE WELL HIDDEN IN THIS LITTLE VALLEY... GOOD! THEY'LL SOON EAT THEMSELVES INTO A STUPOR!
Reg. U. S. Pat. Off.: Copyright, 1940, by News Syndicate Co. Inc.
HERE'S A ROUGH MAP OF THE GROUND! TAKE THE ROPE TO THE NARROW END OF THE GULLY BY THE RIVER!
US DO!
MILTON CANIFF
YOU KIDS GATHER DRY STICKS! WE'LL GIVE THOSE JAM STEALERS A LITTLE INDIGESTION THAT DOESN'T COME FROM OVEREATING!

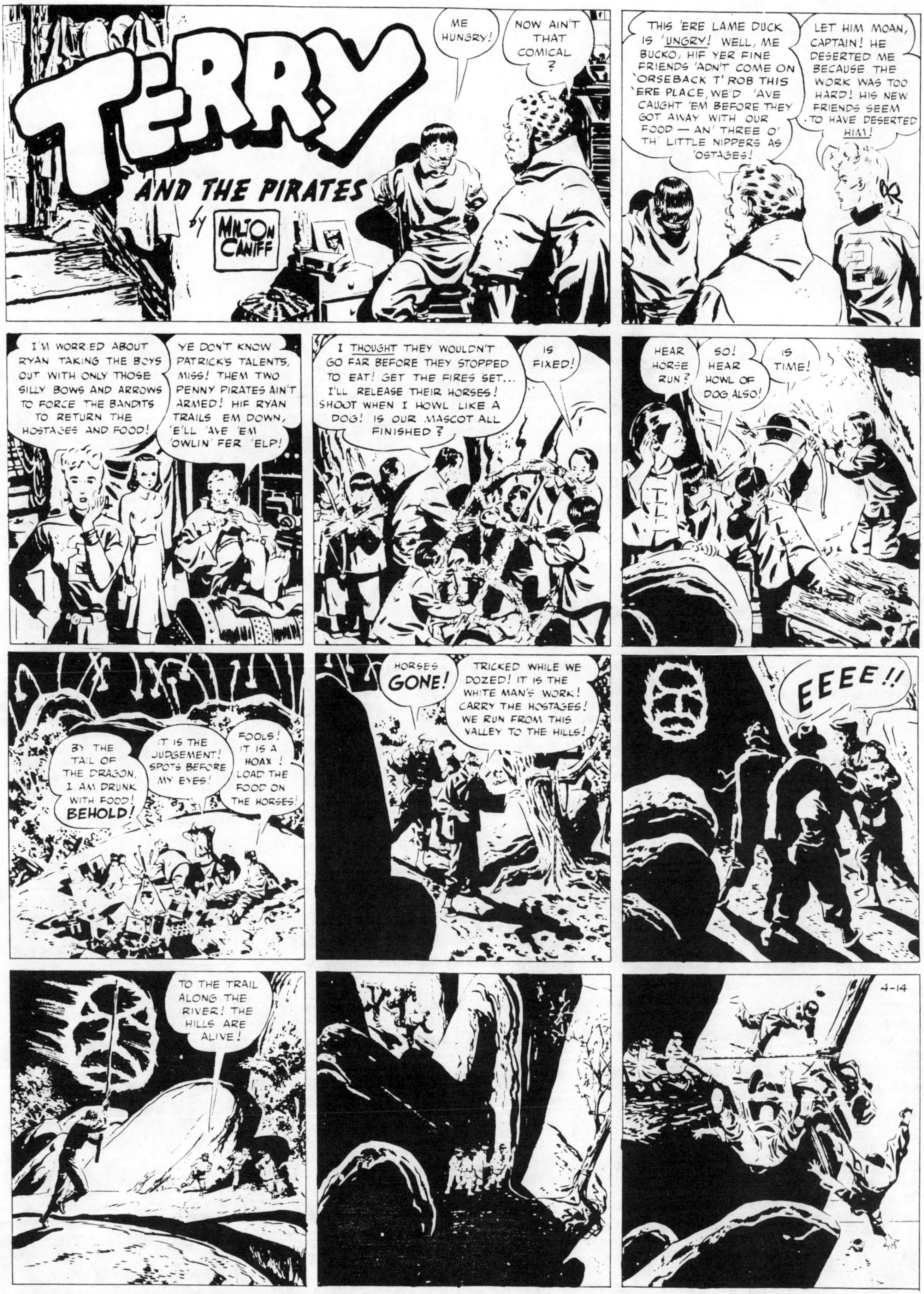

TERRY AND THE PIRATES
by MILTON CANIFF
ME HUNGRY!
NOW AIN'T THAT COMICAL ?
THIS 'ERE LAME DUCK IS 'UNGRY! WELL, ME BUCKO, HIF YER FINE FRIENDS 'ADN'T COME ON 'ORSEBACK T' ROB THIS 'ERE PLACE, WE'D 'AVE CAUGHT 'EM BEFORE THEY GOT AWAY WITH OUR FOOD — AN' THREE O' TH' LITTLE NIPPERS AS 'OSTAGES!
LET HIM MOAN, CAPTAIN! HE DESERTED ME BECAUSE THE WORK WAS TOO HARD! HIS NEW FRIENDS SEEM TO HAVE DESERTED HIM!
I'M WORRIED ABOUT RYAN TAKING THE BOYS OUT WITH ONLY THOSE SILLY BOWS AND ARROWS TO FORCE THE BANDITS TO RETURN THE HOSTAGES AND FOOD!
YE DON'T KNOW PATRICK'S TALENTS, MISS! THEM TWO PENNY PIRATES AIN'T ARMED! HIF RYAN TRAILS EM DOWN, 'E'LL 'AVE 'EM 'OWLIN' FER 'ELP!
I THOUGHT THEY WOULDN'T GO FAR BEFORE THEY STOPPED TO EAT! GET THE FIRES SET... I'LL RELEASE THEIR HORSES! SHOOT WHEN I HOWL LIKE A DOG! IS OUR MASCOT ALL FINISHED ?
IS FIXED!
HEAR HORSE RUN ?
SO! HEAR HOWL OF DOG ALSO!
IS TIME!
BY THE TAIL OF THE DRAGON, I AM DRUNK WITH FOOD! BEHOLD!
IT IS THE JUDGEMENT! SPOTS BEFORE MY EYES!
FOOLS! IT IS A HOAX ! LOAD THE FOOD ON THE HORSES!
HORSES GONE!
TRICKED WHILE WE DOZED! IT IS THE WHITE MAN'S WORK! CARRY THE HOSTAGES! WE RUN FROM THIS VALLEY TO THE HILLS!
EEEE!!
TO THE TRAIL ALONG THE RIVER! THE HILLS ARE ALIVE!
4-14

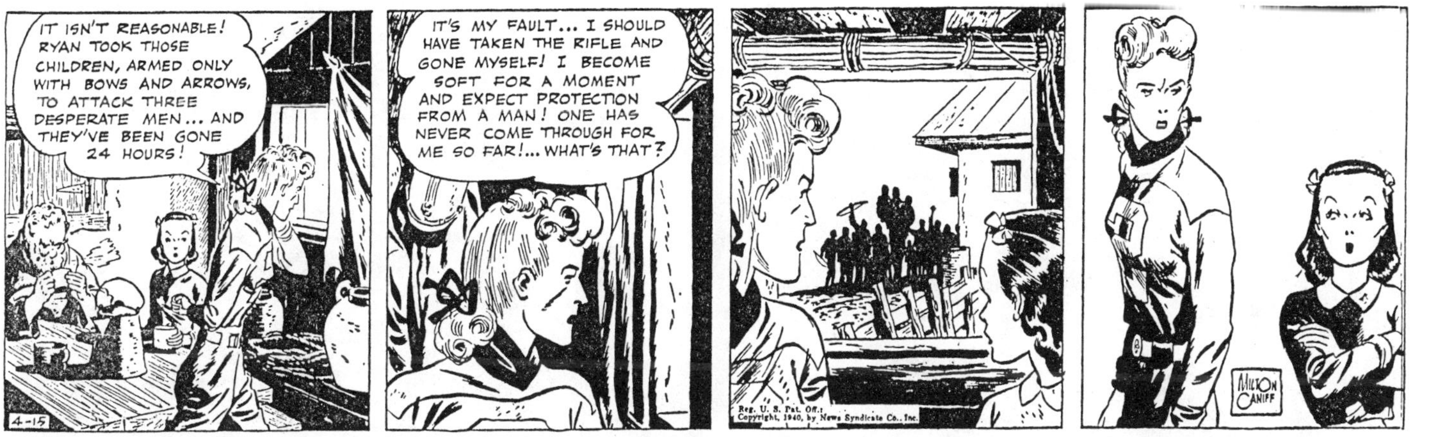
4-15
IT ISN'T REASONABLE! RYAN TOOK THOSE CHILDREN, ARMED ONLY WITH BOWS AND ARROWS, TO ATTACK THREE DESPERATE MEN... AND THEY'VE BEEN GONE 24 HOURS!
IT'S MY FAULT... I SHOULD HAVE TAKEN THE RIFLE AND GONE MYSELF! I BECOME SOFT FOR A MOMENT AND EXPECT PROTECTION FROM A MAN! ONE HAS NEVER COME THROUGH FOR ME SO FAR!... WHAT'S THAT?
Reg. U. S. Pat. Off.; Copyright, 1940, by News Syndicate Co., Inc.
MILTON CANIFF

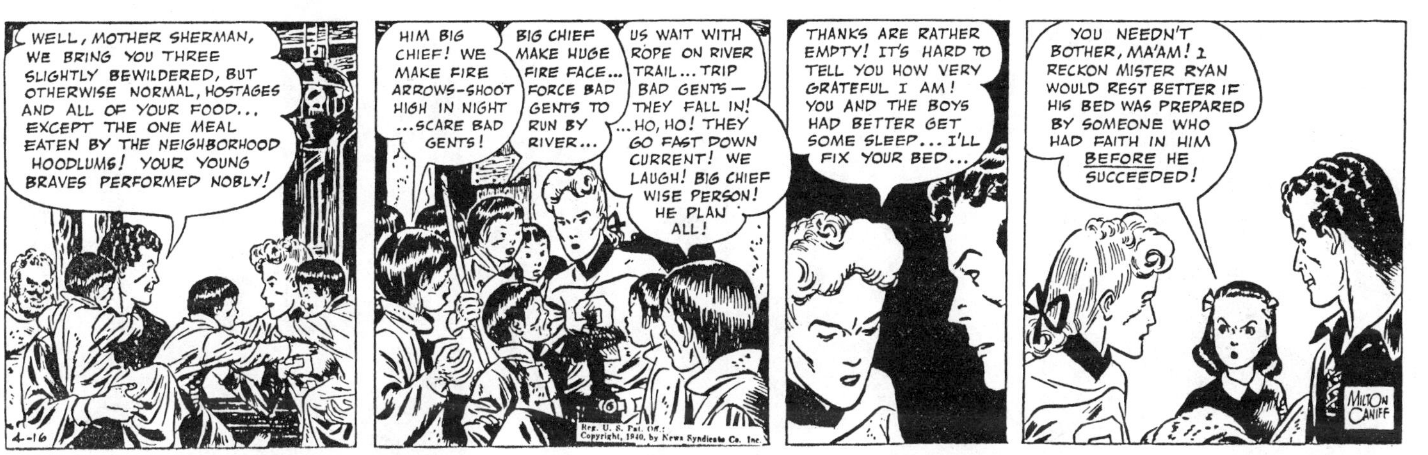
4-16
WELL, MOTHER SHERMAN, WE BRING YOU THREE SLIGHTLY BEWILDERED, BUT OTHERWISE NORMAL, HOSTAGES AND ALL OF YOUR FOOD... EXCEPT THE ONE MEAL EATEN BY THE NEIGHBORHOOD HOODLUMS! YOUR YOUNG BRAVES PERFORMED NOBLY!
HIM BIG CHIEF! WE MAKE FIRE ARROWS-SHOOT HIGH IN NIGHT ...SCARE BAD GENTS!
BIG CHIEF MAKE HUGE FIRE FACE... FORCE BAD GENTS TO RUN BY RIVER...
US WAIT WITH ROPE ON RIVER TRAIL... TRIP BAD GENTS — THEY FALL IN!
...HO, HO! THEY GO FAST DOWN CURRENT! WE LAUGH! BIG CHIEF WISE PERSON! HE PLAN ALL!
Reg. U. S. Pat. Off.; Copyright, 1940, by News Syndicate Co. Inc.
THANKS ARE RATHER EMPTY! IT'S HARD TO TELL YOU HOW VERY GRATEFUL I AM! YOU AND THE BOYS HAD BETTER GET SOME SLEEP... I'LL FIX YOUR BED...
YOU NEEDN'T BOTHER, MA'AM! I RECKON MISTER RYAN WOULD REST BETTER IF HIS BED WAS PREPARED BY SOMEONE WHO HAD FAITH IN HIM BEFORE HE SUCCEEDED!
MILTON CANIFF

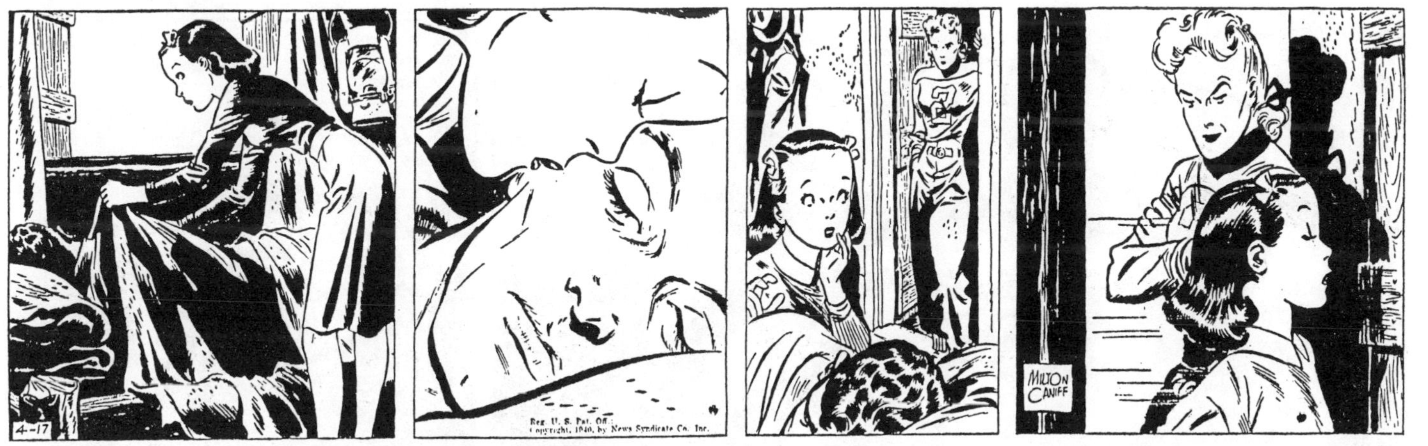
4-17
Reg. U. S. Pat. Off.; Copyright, 1940, by News Syndicate Co. Inc.
MILTON CANIFF

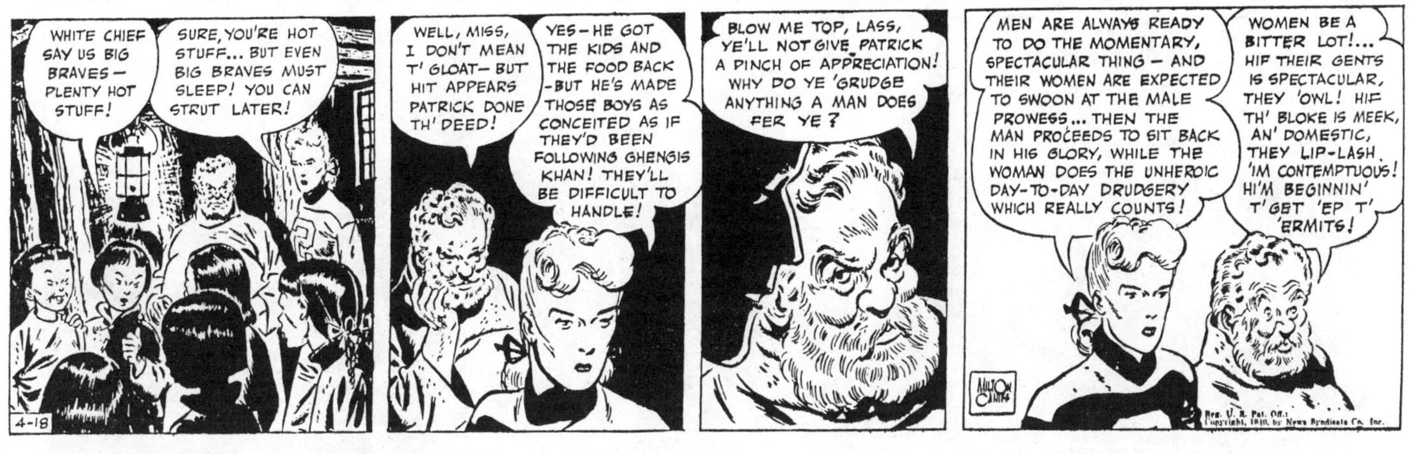
4-18
WHITE CHIEF SAY US BIG BRAVES — PLENTY HOT STUFF!
SURE, YOU'RE HOT STUFF... BUT EVEN BIG BRAVES MUST SLEEP! YOU CAN STRUT LATER!
WELL, MISS, I DON'T MEAN T' GLOAT — BUT HIT APPEARS PATRICK DONE TH' DEED!
YES — HE GOT THE KIDS AND THE FOOD BACK — BUT HE'S MADE THOSE BOYS AS CONCEITED AS IF THEY'D BEEN FOLLOWING GHENGIS KHAN! THEY'LL BE DIFFICULT TO HANDLE!
BLOW ME TOP, LASS, YE'LL NOT GIVE PATRICK A PINCH OF APPRECIATION! WHY DO YE 'GRUDGE ANYTHING A MAN DOES FER YE?
MILTON CANIFF
MEN ARE ALWAYS READY TO DO THE MOMENTARY, SPECTACULAR THING — AND THEIR WOMEN ARE EXPECTED TO SWOON AT THE MALE PROWESS... THEN THE MAN PROCEEDS TO SIT BACK IN HIS GLORY, WHILE THE WOMAN DOES THE UNHEROIC DAY-TO-DAY DRUDGERY WHICH REALLY COUNTS!
WOMEN BE A BITTER LOT!... HIF THEIR GENTS IS SPECTACULAR, THEY 'OWL! HIF TH' BLOKE IS MEEK, AN' DOMESTIC, THEY LIP-LASH 'IM CONTEMPTUOUS! HI'M BEGINNIN' T'GET 'EP T' 'ERMITS!
Reg. U. S. Pat. Off.; Copyright, 1940, by News Syndicate Co. Inc.

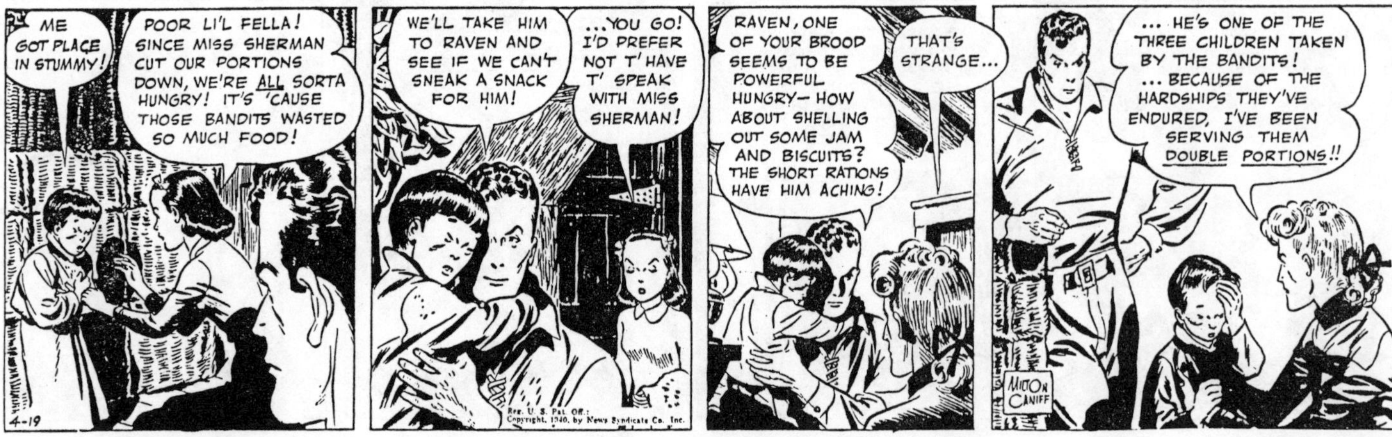
ME GOT PLACE IN STUMMY!
POOR LI'L FELLA! SINCE MISS SHERMAN CUT OUR PORTIONS DOWN, WE'RE ALL SORTA HUNGRY! IT'S 'CAUSE THOSE BANDITS WASTED SO MUCH FOOD!
4-19
WE'LL TAKE HIM TO RAVEN AND SEE IF WE CAN'T SNEAK A SNACK FOR HIM!
...YOU GO! I'D PREFER NOT T' HAVE T' SPEAK WITH MISS SHERMAN!
Reg. U. S. Pat. Off.; Copyright, 1940, by News Syndicate Co. Inc.
RAVEN, ONE OF YOUR BROOD SEEMS TO BE POWERFUL HUNGRY— HOW ABOUT SHELLING OUT SOME JAM AND BISCUITS? THE SHORT RATIONS HAVE HIM ACHING!
THAT'S STRANGE...
MILTON CANIFF
... HE'S ONE OF THE THREE CHILDREN TAKEN BY THE BANDITS! ... BECAUSE OF THE HARDSHIPS THEY'VE ENDURED, I'VE BEEN SERVING THEM DOUBLE PORTIONS!!

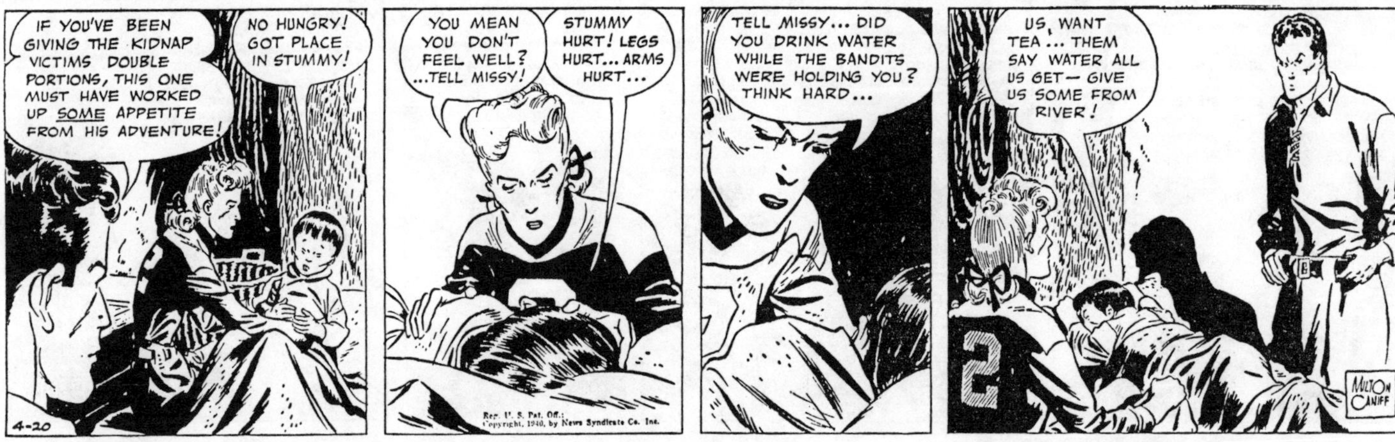
IF YOU'VE BEEN GIVING THE KIDNAP VICTIMS DOUBLE PORTIONS, THIS ONE MUST HAVE WORKED UP SOME APPETITE FROM HIS ADVENTURE!
NO HUNGRY! GOT PLACE IN STUMMY!
4-20
YOU MEAN YOU DON'T FEEL WELL? ...TELL MISSY!
STUMMY HURT! LEGS HURT... ARMS HURT...
Reg. U. S. Pat. Off.; Copyright, 1940, by News Syndicate Co. Inc.
TELL MISSY... DID YOU DRINK WATER WHILE THE BANDITS WERE HOLDING YOU? THINK HARD...
US, WANT TEA... THEM SAY WATER ALL US GET— GIVE US SOME FROM RIVER!
MILTON CANIFF

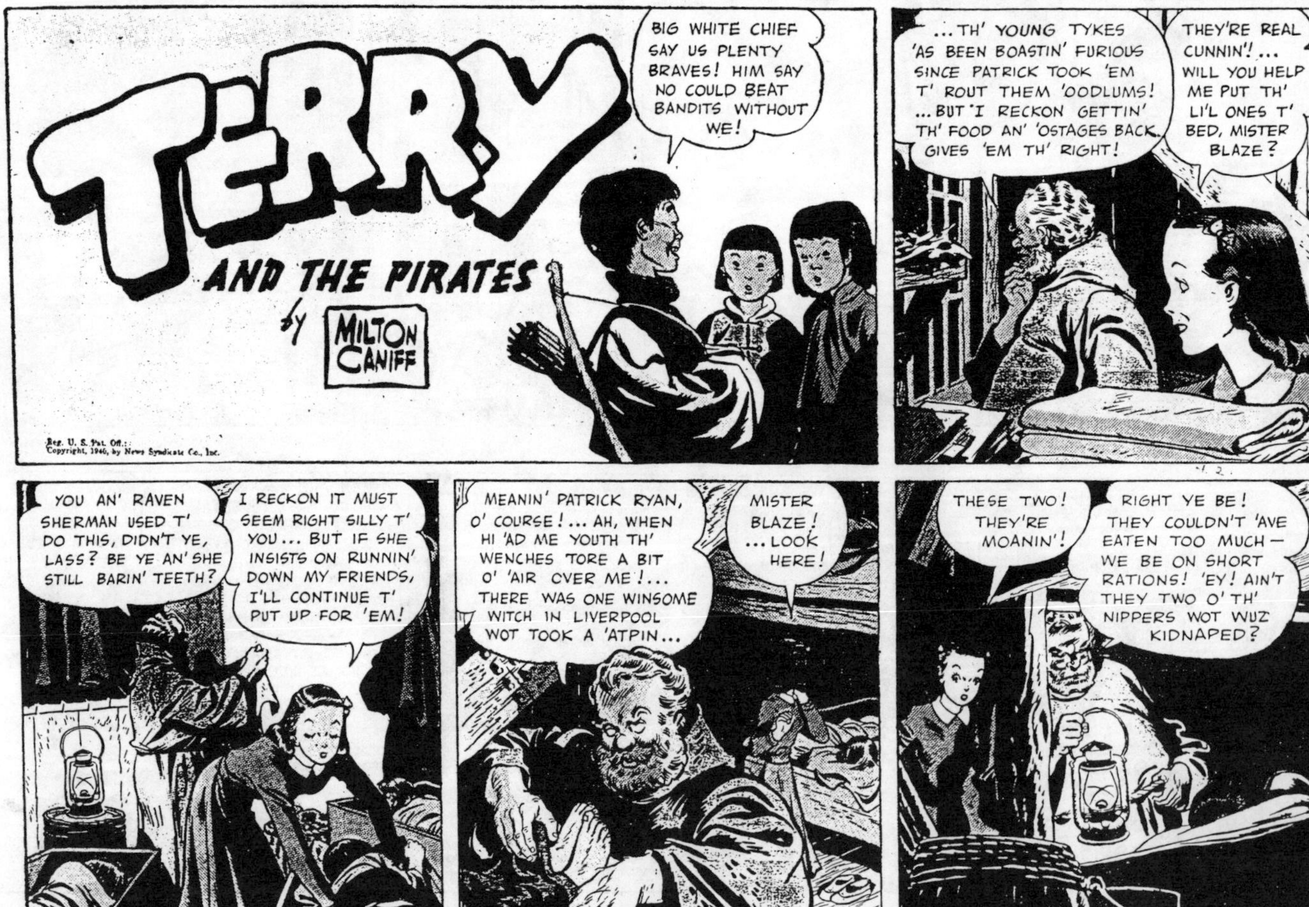
TERRY AND THE PIRATES
by MILTON CANIFF
Reg. U. S. Pat. Off.; Copyright, 1940, by News Syndicate Co., Inc.
BIG WHITE CHIEF SAY US PLENTY BRAVES! HIM SAY NO COULD BEAT BANDITS WITHOUT WE!
...TH' YOUNG TYKES 'AS BEEN BOASTIN' FURIOUS SINCE PATRICK TOOK 'EM T' ROUT THEM 'OODLUMS! ...BUT 'I RECKON GETTIN' TH' FOOD AN' 'OSTAGES BACK GIVES 'EM TH' RIGHT!
THEY'RE REAL CUNNIN'!... WILL YOU HELP ME PUT TH' LI'L ONES T' BED, MISTER BLAZE?
YOU AN' RAVEN SHERMAN USED T' DO THIS, DIDN'T YE, LASS? BE YE AN' SHE STILL BARIN' TEETH?
I RECKON IT MUST SEEM RIGHT SILLY T' YOU... BUT IF SHE INSISTS ON RUNNIN' DOWN MY FRIENDS, I'LL CONTINUE T' PUT UP FOR 'EM!
MEANIN' PATRICK RYAN, O' COURSE!... AH, WHEN HI 'AD ME YOUTH TH' WENCHES TORE A BIT O' 'AIR OVER ME!... THERE WAS ONE WINSOME WITCH IN LIVERPOOL WOT TOOK A 'ATPIN...
MISTER BLAZE! ...LOOK HERE!
THESE TWO! THEY'RE MOANIN'!
RIGHT YE BE! THEY COULDN'T 'AVE EATEN TOO MUCH— WE BE ON SHORT RATIONS! 'EY! AIN'T THEY TWO O' TH' NIPPERS WOT WUZ KIDNAPED?

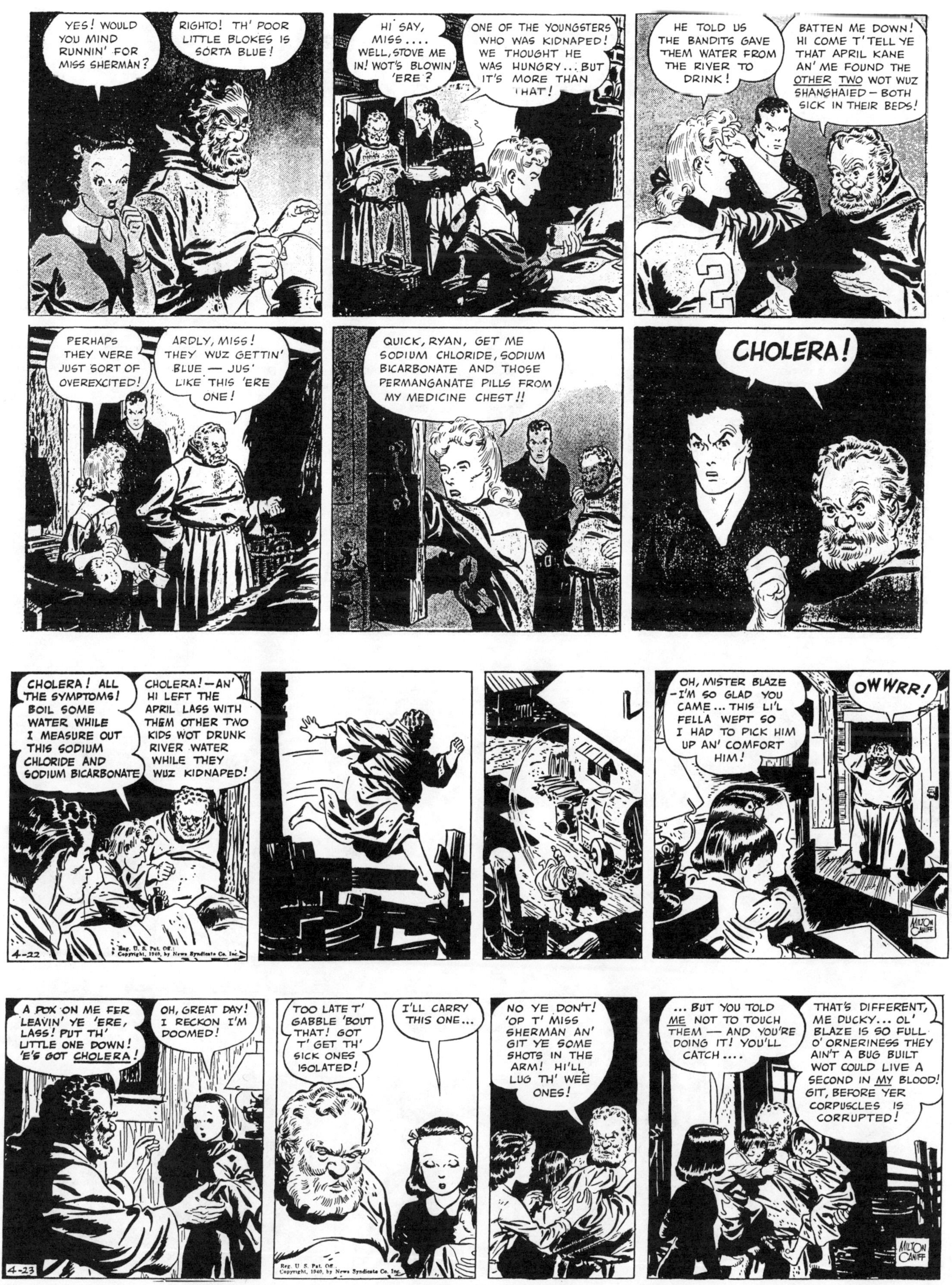
YES! WOULD YOU MIND RUNNIN' FOR MISS SHERMAN?
RIGHTO! TH' POOR LITTLE BLOKES IS SORTA BLUE!
HI SAY, MISS.... WELL, STOVE ME IN! WOT'S BLOWIN' 'ERE?
ONE OF THE YOUNGSTERS WHO WAS KIDNAPED! WE THOUGHT HE WAS HUNGRY... BUT IT'S MORE THAN THAT!
HE TOLD US THE BANDITS GAVE THEM WATER FROM THE RIVER TO DRINK!
BATTEN ME DOWN! HI COME T'TELL YE THAT APRIL KANE AN' ME FOUND THE OTHER TWO WOT WUZ SHANGHAIED — BOTH SICK IN THEIR BEDS!
PERHAPS THEY WERE JUST SORT OF OVEREXCITED!
ARDLY, MISS! THEY WUZ GETTIN' BLUE — JUS' LIKE THIS 'ERE ONE!
QUICK, RYAN, GET ME SODIUM CHLORIDE, SODIUM BICARBONATE AND THOSE PERMANGANATE PILLS FROM MY MEDICINE CHEST!!
CHOLERA!
CHOLERA! ALL THE SYMPTOMS! BOIL SOME WATER WHILE I MEASURE OUT THIS SODIUM CHLORIDE AND SODIUM BICARBONATE
CHOLERA! — AN' HI LEFT THE APRIL LASS WITH THEM OTHER TWO KIDS WOT DRUNK RIVER WATER WHILE THEY WUZ KIDNAPED!
4-22
Reg. U. S. Pat. Off.: Copyright, 1940, by News Syndicate Co. Inc.
OH, MISTER BLAZE — I'M SO GLAD YOU CAME... THIS LI'L FELLA WEPT SO I HAD TO PICK HIM UP AN' COMFORT HIM!
OWWRR!
MILTON CANIFF
A POX ON ME FER LEAVIN' YE 'ERE, LASS! PUT TH' LITTLE ONE DOWN! 'E'S GOT CHOLERA!
OH, GREAT DAY! I RECKON I'M DOOMED!
4-23
TOO LATE T' GABBLE 'BOUT THAT! GOT T' GET TH' SICK ONES ISOLATED!
I'LL CARRY THIS ONE...
Reg. U. S. Pat. Off.: Copyright, 1940, by News Syndicate Co. Inc.
NO YE DON'T! 'OP T' MISS SHERMAN AN' GIT YE SOME SHOTS IN THE ARM! HI'LL LUG TH' WEE ONES!
... BUT YOU TOLD ME NOT TO TOUCH THEM — AND YOU'RE DOING IT! YOU'LL CATCH....
THAT'S DIFFERENT, ME DUCKY... OL' BLAZE IS SO FULL O' ORNERINESS THEY AIN'T A BUG BUILT WOT COULD LIVE A SECOND IN MY BLOOD! GIT, BEFORE YER CORPUSCLES IS CORRUPTED!
MILTON CANIFF

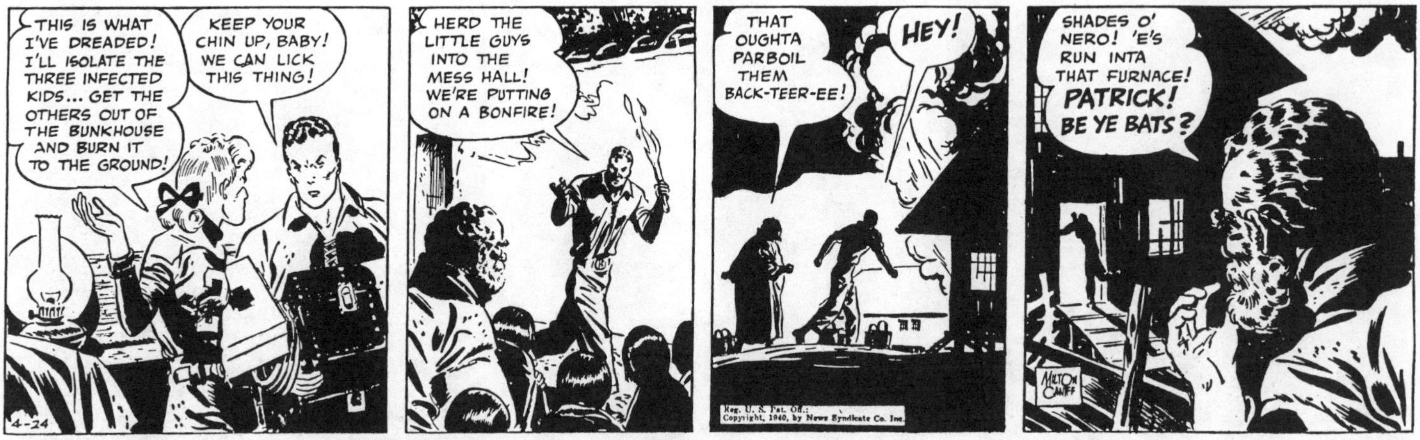
THIS IS WHAT I'VE DREADED! I'LL ISOLATE THE THREE INFECTED KIDS... GET THE OTHERS OUT OF THE BUNKHOUSE AND BURN IT TO THE GROUND!
KEEP YOUR CHIN UP, BABY! WE CAN LICK THIS THING!
4-24
HERD THE LITTLE GUYS INTO THE MESS HALL! WE'RE PUTTING ON A BONFIRE!
THAT OUGHTA PARBOIL THEM BACK-TEER-EE!
HEY!
Reg. U. S. Pat. Off.: Copyright, 1940, by News Syndicate Co. Inc.
SHADES O' NERO! 'E'S RUN INTA THAT FURNACE! PATRICK! BE YE BATS?
MILTON CANIFF

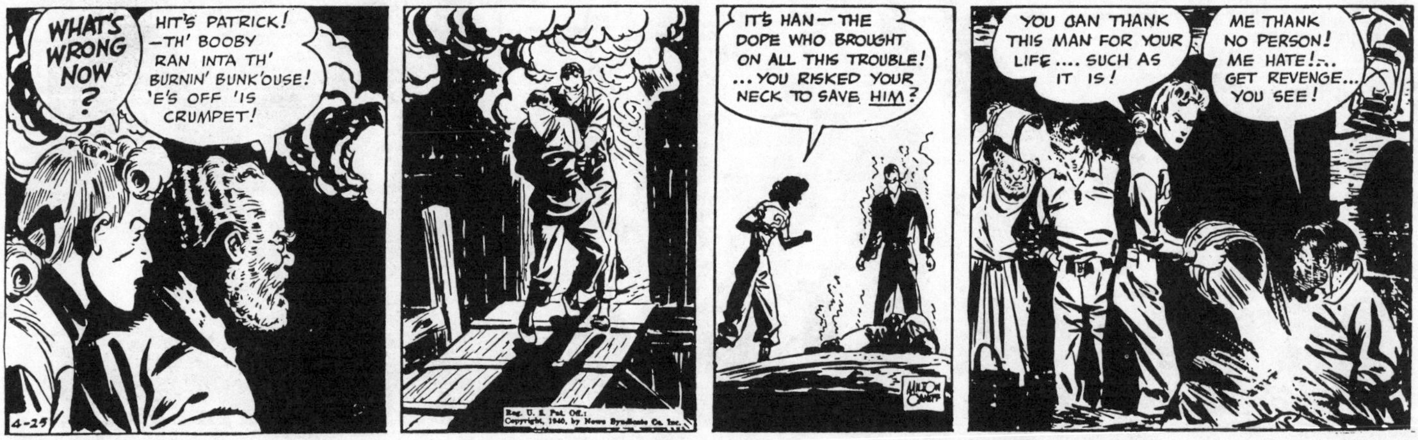
WHAT'S WRONG NOW?
HIT'S PATRICK! —TH' BOOBY RAN INTA TH' BURNIN' BUNK'OUSE! 'E'S OFF 'IS CRUMPET!
4-25
Reg. U. S. Pat. Off.: Copyright, 1940, by News Syndicate Co. Inc.
IT'S HAN—THE DOPE WHO BROUGHT ON ALL THIS TROUBLE! ...YOU RISKED YOUR NECK TO SAVE HIM?
MILTON CANIFF
YOU CAN THANK THIS MAN FOR YOUR LIFE.... SUCH AS IT IS!
ME THANK NO PERSON! ME HATE!... GET REVENGE... YOU SEE!

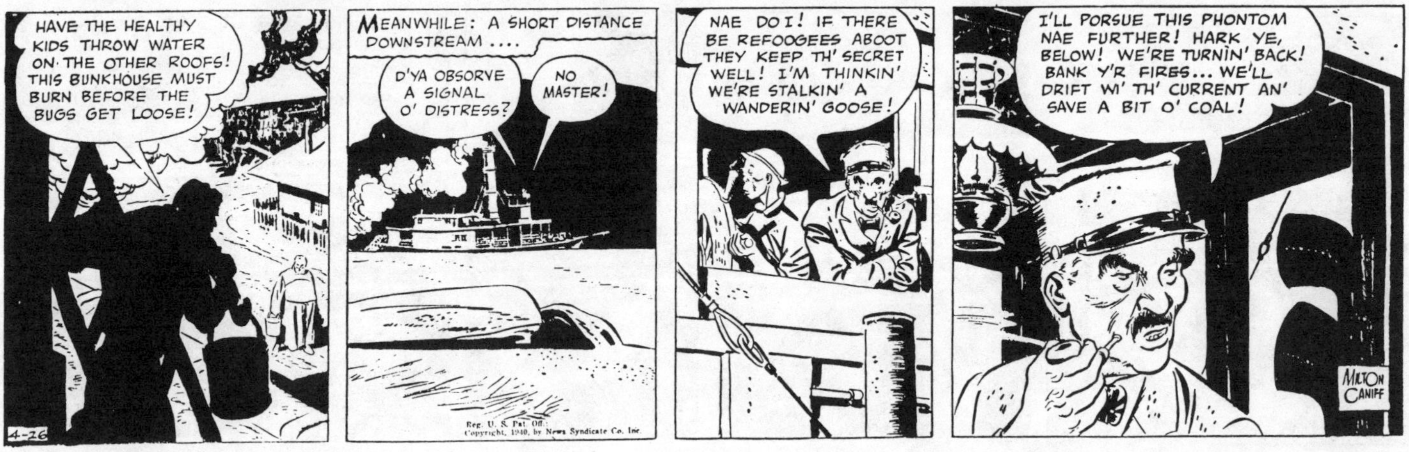
HAVE THE HEALTHY KIDS THROW WATER ON THE OTHER ROOFS! THIS BUNKHOUSE MUST BURN BEFORE THE BUGS GET LOOSE!
4-26
MEANWHILE: A SHORT DISTANCE DOWNSTREAM ....
D'YA OBSERVE A SIGNAL O' DISTRESS?
NO MASTER!
Reg. U. S. Pat. Off.: Copyright, 1940, by News Syndicate Co. Inc.
NAE DO I! IF THERE BE REFOOGEES ABOOT THEY KEEP TH' SECRET WELL! I'M THINKIN' WE'RE STALKIN' A WANDERIN' GOOSE!
I'LL PORSUE THIS PHONTOM NAE FURTHER! HARK YE, BELOW! WE'RE TURNIN' BACK! BANK Y'R FIRES... WE'LL DRIFT WI' TH' CURRENT AN' SAVE A BIT O' COAL!
MILTON CANIFF

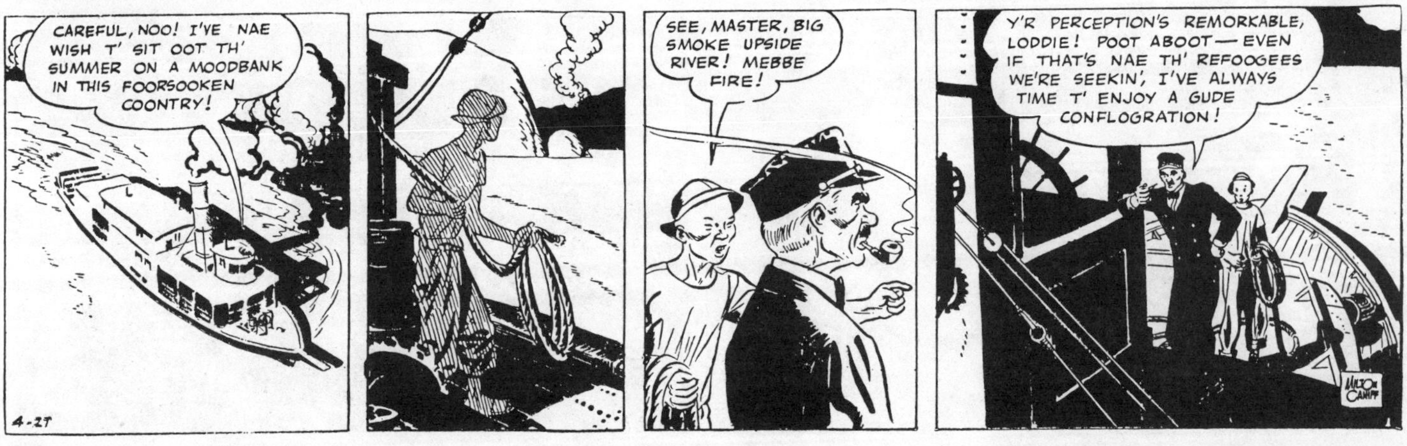
CAREFUL, NOO! I'VE NAE WISH T' SIT OOT TH' SUMMER ON A MOODBANK IN THIS FOORSOOKEN COONTRY!
4-27
SEE, MASTER, BIG SMOKE UPSIDE RIVER! MEBBE FIRE!
Y'R PERCEPTION'S REMORKABLE, LODDIE! POOT ABOOT—EVEN IF THAT'S NAE TH' REFOOGEES WE'RE SEEKIN', I'VE ALWAYS TIME T' ENJOY A GUDE CONFLOGRATION!
MILTON CANIFF

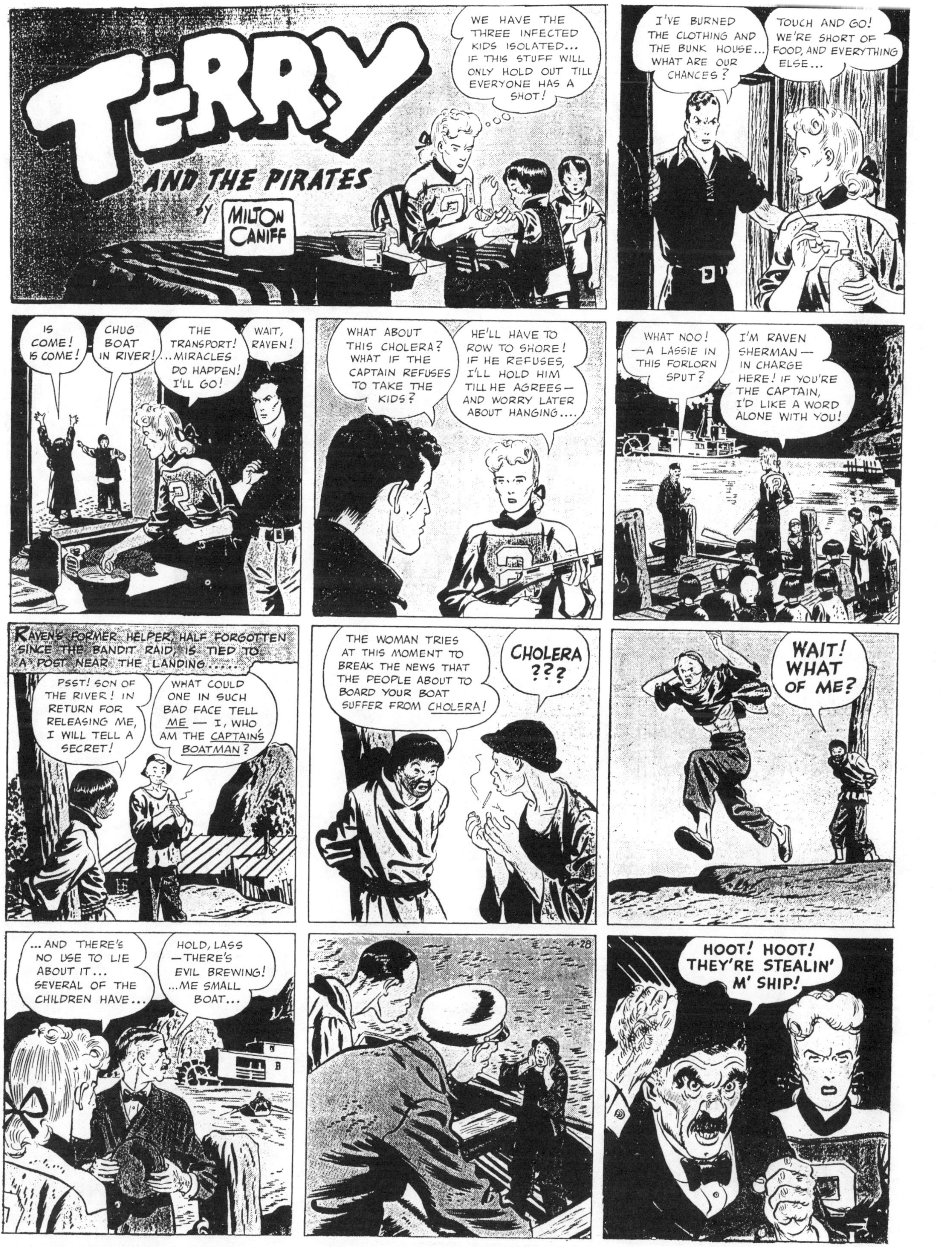
TERRY AND THE PIRATES
by MILTON CANIFF
WE HAVE THE THREE INFECTED KIDS ISOLATED... IF THIS STUFF WILL ONLY HOLD OUT TILL EVERYONE HAS A SHOT!
I'VE BURNED THE CLOTHING AND THE BUNK HOUSE... WHAT ARE OUR CHANCES?
TOUCH AND GO! WE'RE SHORT OF FOOD, AND EVERYTHING ELSE...
IS COME! IS COME!
CHUG BOAT IN RIVER!
THE TRANSPORT! ...MIRACLES DO HAPPEN! I'LL GO!
WAIT, RAVEN!
WHAT ABOUT THIS CHOLERA? WHAT IF THE CAPTAIN REFUSES TO TAKE THE KIDS?
HE'LL HAVE TO ROW TO SHORE! IF HE REFUSES, I'LL HOLD HIM TILL HE AGREES— AND WORRY LATER ABOUT HANGING....
WHAT NOO! —A LASSIE IN THIS FORLORN SPUT?
I'M RAVEN SHERMAN — IN CHARGE HERE! IF YOU'RE THE CAPTAIN, I'D LIKE A WORD ALONE WITH YOU!
RAVEN'S FORMER HELPER, HALF FORGOTTEN SINCE THE BANDIT RAID, IS TIED TO A POST NEAR THE LANDING.....
PSST! SON OF THE RIVER! IN RETURN FOR RELEASING ME, I WILL TELL A SECRET!
WHAT COULD ONE IN SUCH BAD FACE TELL ME — I, WHO AM THE CAPTAIN'S BOATMAN?
THE WOMAN TRIES AT THIS MOMENT TO BREAK THE NEWS THAT THE PEOPLE ABOUT TO BOARD YOUR BOAT SUFFER FROM CHOLERA!
CHOLERA ???
WAIT! WHAT OF ME?
...AND THERE'S NO USE TO LIE ABOUT IT... SEVERAL OF THE CHILDREN HAVE...
HOLD, LASS —THERE'S EVIL BREWING! ...ME SMALL BOAT...
4-28
HOOT! HOOT! THEY'RE STEALIN' M' SHIP!

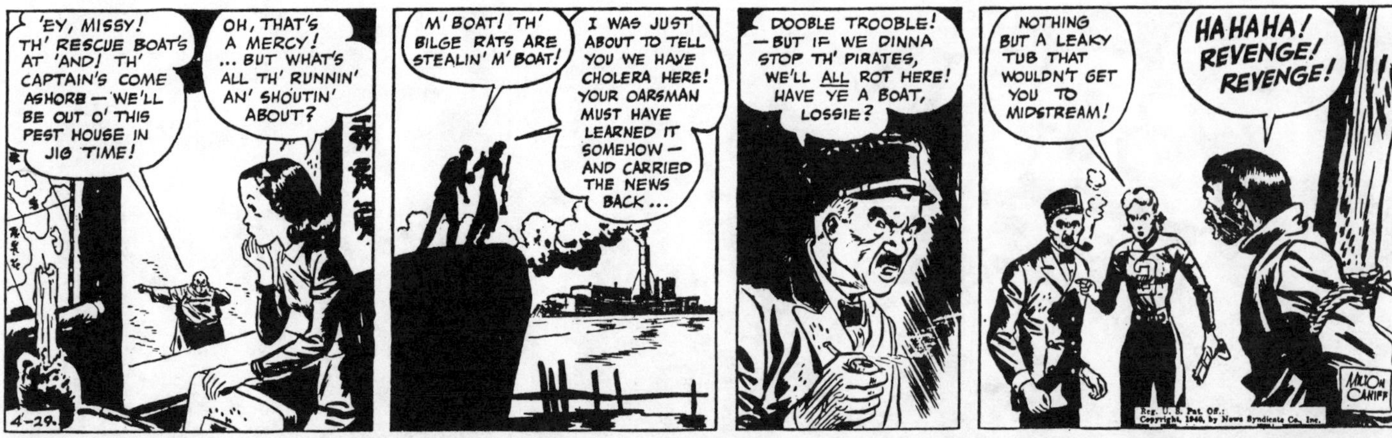
'EY, MISSY! TH' RESCUE BOAT'S AT 'AND! TH' CAPTAIN'S COME ASHORE — WE'LL BE OUT O' THIS PEST HOUSE IN JIG TIME!
OH, THAT'S A MERCY! ... BUT WHAT'S ALL TH' RUNNIN' AN' SHOUTIN' ABOUT?
4-29.
M' BOAT! TH' BILGE RATS ARE STEALIN' M' BOAT!
I WAS JUST ABOUT TO TELL YOU WE HAVE CHOLERA HERE! YOUR OARSMAN MUST HAVE LEARNED IT SOMEHOW — AND CARRIED THE NEWS BACK...
DOOBLE TROOBLE! — BUT IF WE DINNA STOP TH' PIRATES, WE'LL ALL ROT HERE! HAVE YE A BOAT, LOSSIE?
NOTHING BUT A LEAKY TUB THAT WOULDN'T GET YOU TO MIDSTREAM!
HAHAHA! REVENGE! REVENGE!
MILTON CANIFF
Reg. U. S. Pat. Off.; Copyright, 1940, by News Syndicate Co. Inc.

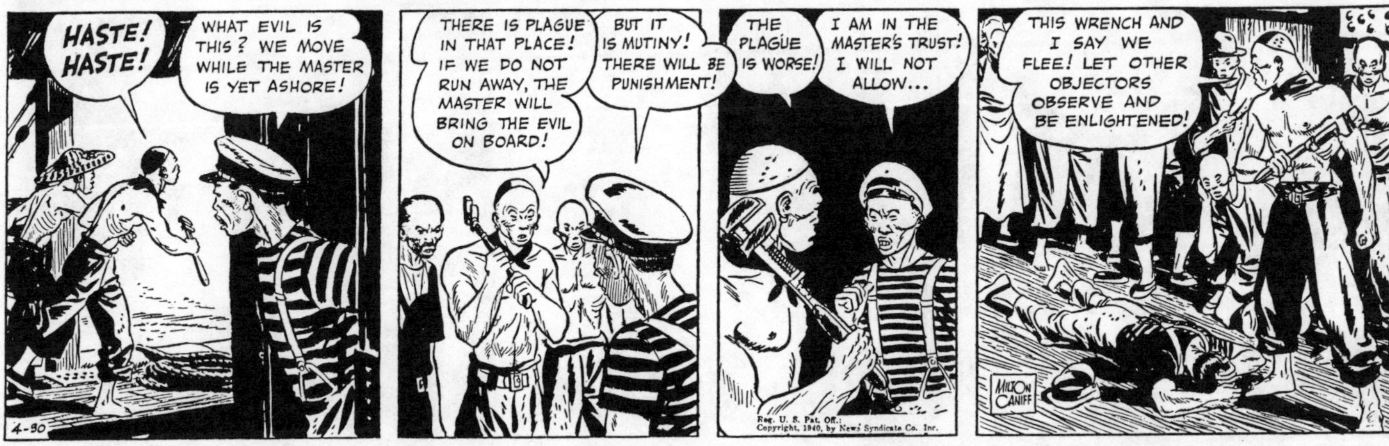
HASTE! HASTE!
WHAT EVIL IS THIS? WE MOVE WHILE THE MASTER IS YET ASHORE!
4-30
THERE IS PLAGUE IN THAT PLACE! IF WE DO NOT RUN AWAY, THE MASTER WILL BRING THE EVIL ON BOARD!
BUT IT IS MUTINY! THERE WILL BE PUNISHMENT!
THE PLAGUE IS WORSE!
I AM IN THE MASTER'S TRUST! I WILL NOT ALLOW...
Reg. U. S. Pat. Off.; Copyright, 1940, by News Syndicate Co. Inc.
THIS WRENCH AND I SAY WE FLEE! LET OTHER OBJECTORS OBSERVE AND BE ENLIGHTENED!
MILTON CANIFF

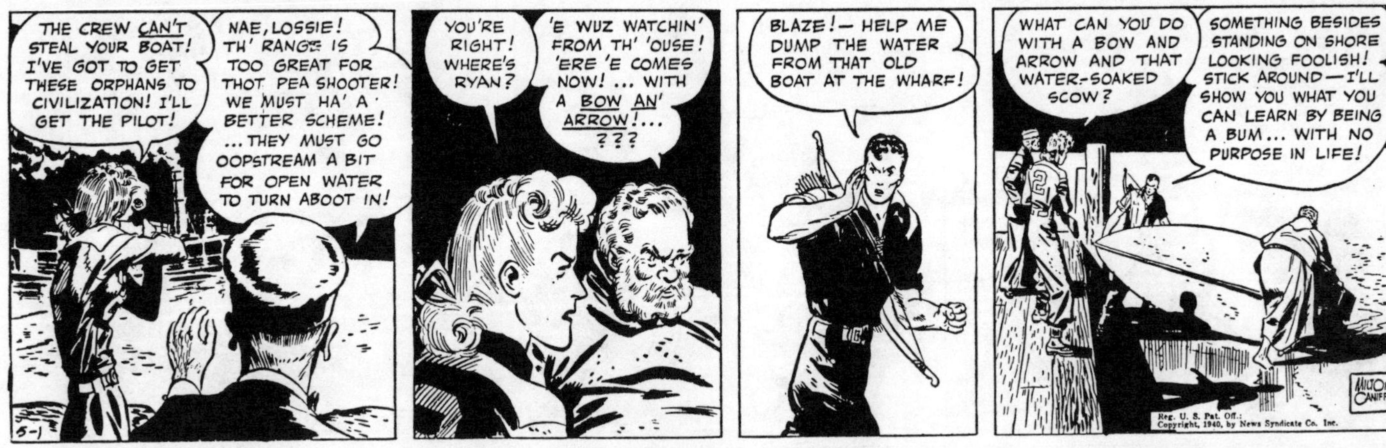
THE CREW CAN'T STEAL YOUR BOAT! I'VE GOT TO GET THESE ORPHANS TO CIVILIZATION! I'LL GET THE PILOT!
NAE, LOSSIE! TH' RANGE IS TOO GREAT FOR THOT PEA SHOOTER! WE MUST HA' A BETTER SCHEME! ... THEY MUST GO OOPSTREAM A BIT FOR OPEN WATER TO TURN ABOOT IN!
5-1
YOU'RE RIGHT! WHERE'S RYAN?
'E WUZ WATCHIN' FROM TH' 'OUSE! 'ERE 'E COMES NOW! ... WITH A BOW AN' ARROW!... ???
BLAZE! — HELP ME DUMP THE WATER FROM THAT OLD BOAT AT THE WHARF!
WHAT CAN YOU DO WITH A BOW AND ARROW AND THAT WATER-SOAKED SCOW?
SOMETHING BESIDES STANDING ON SHORE LOOKING FOOLISH! STICK AROUND — I'LL SHOW YOU WHAT YOU CAN LEARN BY BEING A BUM ... WITH NO PURPOSE IN LIFE!
MILTON CANIFF
Reg. U. S. Pat. Off.; Copyright, 1940, by News Syndicate Co. Inc.

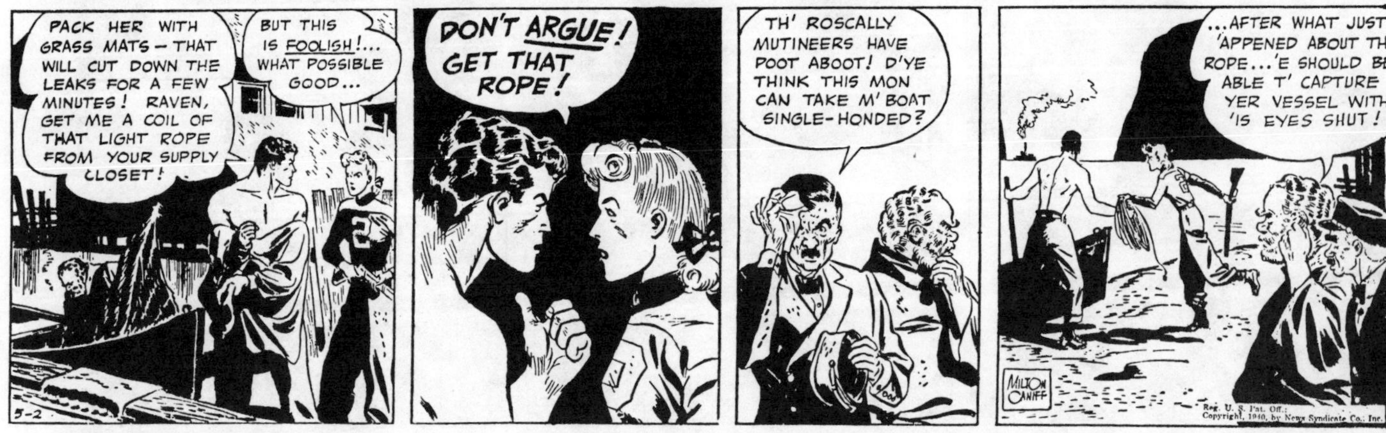
PACK HER WITH GRASS MATS — THAT WILL CUT DOWN THE LEAKS FOR A FEW MINUTES! RAVEN, GET ME A COIL OF THAT LIGHT ROPE FROM YOUR SUPPLY CLOSET!
BUT THIS IS FOOLISH!... WHAT POSSIBLE GOOD...
5-2
DON'T ARGUE! GET THAT ROPE!
TH' ROSCALLY MUTINEERS HAVE POOT ABOOT! D'YE THINK THIS MON CAN TAKE M' BOAT SINGLE-HONDED?
MILTON CANIFF
...AFTER WHAT JUST 'APPENED ABOUT TH' ROPE ... 'E SHOULD BE ABLE T' CAPTURE YER VESSEL WITH 'IS EYES SHUT!
Reg. U. S. Pat. Off.; Copyright, 1940, by News Syndicate Co. Inc.

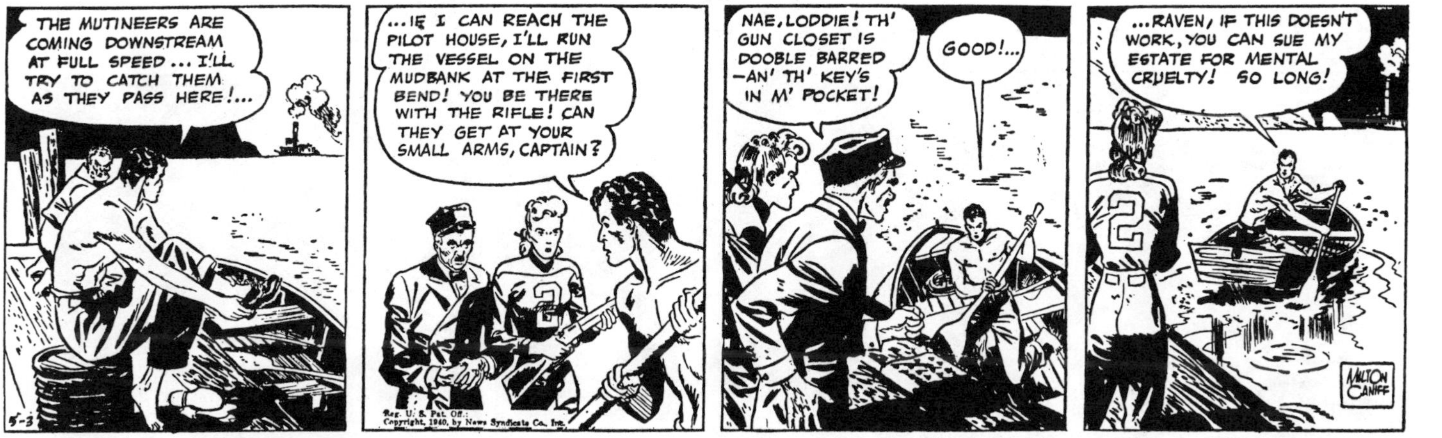
THE MUTINEERS ARE COMING DOWNSTREAM AT FULL SPEED... I'LL TRY TO CATCH THEM AS THEY PASS HERE!...
5-3
...IF I CAN REACH THE PILOT HOUSE, I'LL RUN THE VESSEL ON THE MUDBANK AT THE FIRST BEND! YOU BE THERE WITH THE RIFLE! CAN THEY GET AT YOUR SMALL ARMS, CAPTAIN?
Reg. U. S. Pat. Off.; Copyright, 1940, by News Syndicate Co. Inc.
NAE, LODDIE! TH' GUN CLOSET IS DOOBLE BARRED —AN' TH' KEY'S IN M' POCKET!
GOOD!...
...RAVEN, IF THIS DOESN'T WORK, YOU CAN SUE MY ESTATE FOR MENTAL CRUELTY! SO LONG!
MILTON CANIFF

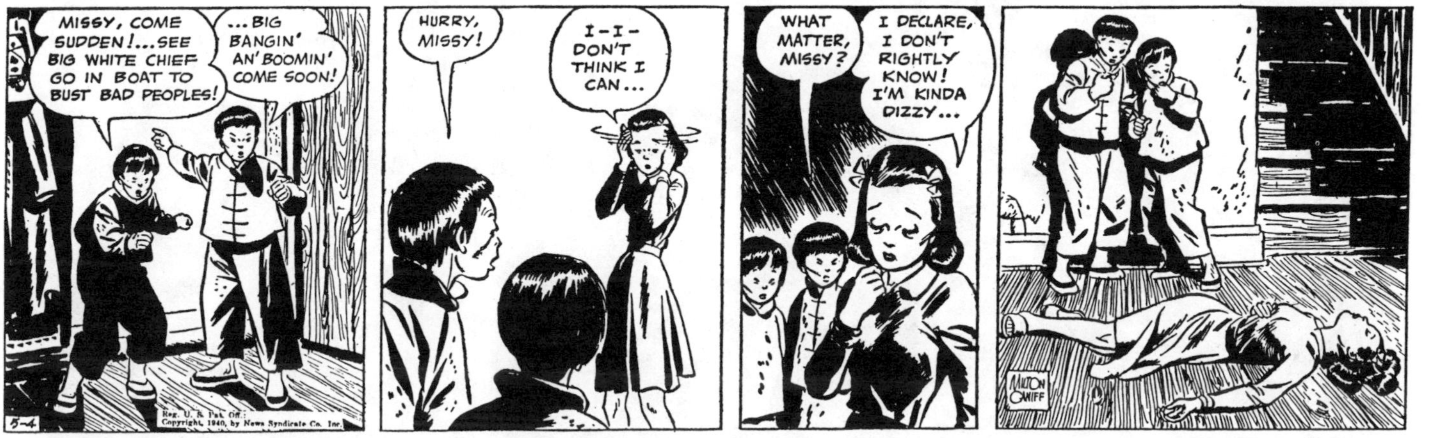
MISSY, COME SUDDEN!...SEE BIG WHITE CHIEF GO IN BOAT TO BUST BAD PEOPLES!
...BIG BANGIN' AN' BOOMIN' COME SOON!
5-4
Reg. U. S. Pat. Off.; Copyright, 1940, by News Syndicate Co. Inc.
HURRY, MISSY!
I-I-DON'T THINK I CAN...
WHAT MATTER, MISSY?
I DECLARE, I DON'T RIGHTLY KNOW! I'M KINDA DIZZY...
MILTON CANIFF

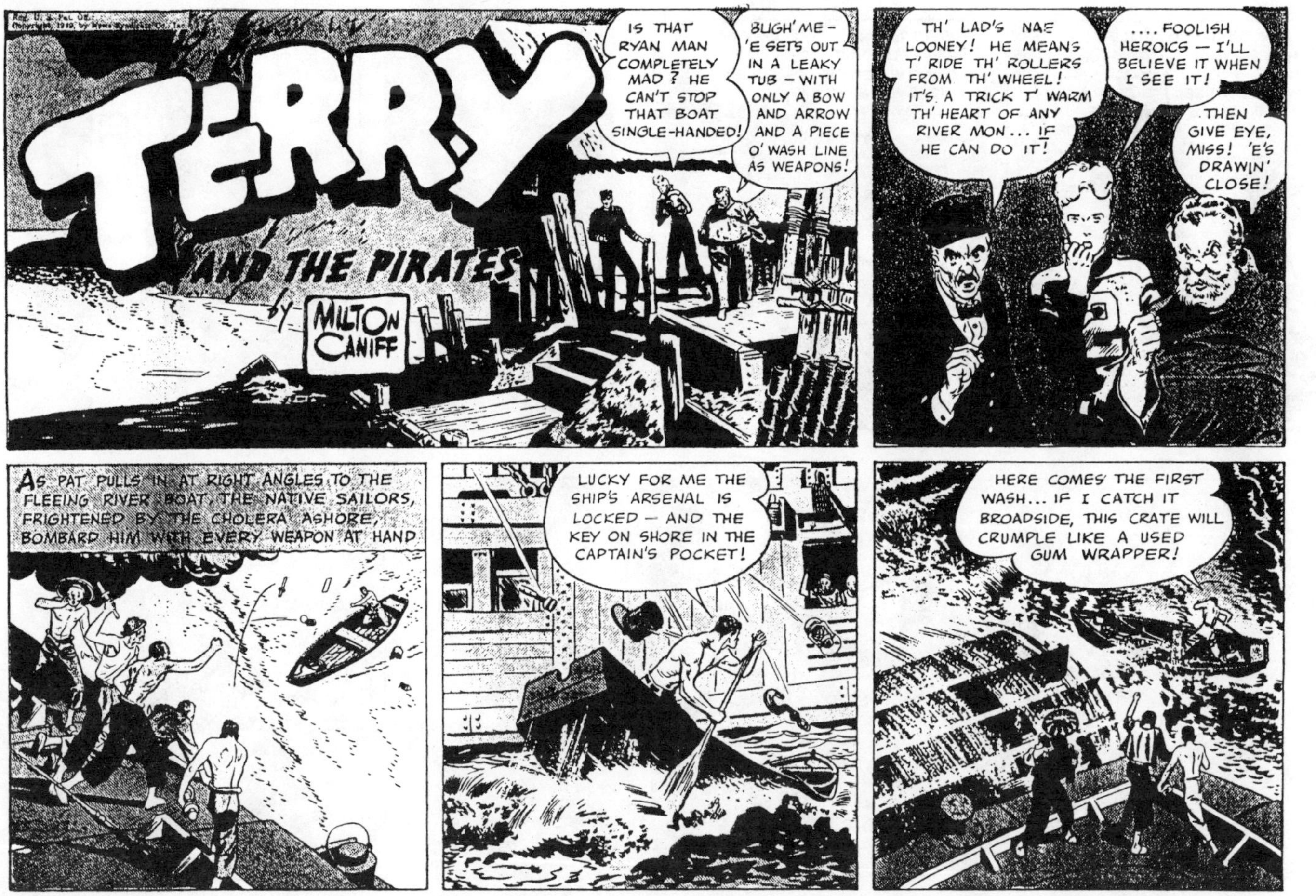
TERRY AND THE PIRATES by MILTON CANIFF
IS THAT RYAN MAN COMPLETELY MAD? HE CAN'T STOP THAT BOAT SINGLE-HANDED!
BUGH' ME—'E SETS OUT IN A LEAKY TUB—WITH ONLY A BOW AND ARROW AND A PIECE O' WASH LINE AS WEAPONS!
TH' LAD'S NAE LOONEY! HE MEANS T' RIDE TH' ROLLERS FROM TH' WHEEL! IT'S A TRICK T' WARM TH' HEART OF ANY RIVER MON... IF HE CAN DO IT!
....FOOLISH HEROICS—I'LL BELIEVE IT WHEN I SEE IT!
THEN GIVE EYE, MISS! 'E'S DRAWIN' CLOSE!
AS PAT PULLS IN AT RIGHT ANGLES TO THE FLEEING RIVER BOAT, THE NATIVE SAILORS, FRIGHTENED BY THE CHOLERA ASHORE, BOMBARD HIM WITH EVERY WEAPON AT HAND
LUCKY FOR ME THE SHIP'S ARSENAL IS LOCKED—AND THE KEY ON SHORE IN THE CAPTAIN'S POCKET!
HERE COMES THE FIRST WASH... IF I CATCH IT BROADSIDE, THIS CRATE WILL CRUMPLE LIKE A USED GUM WRAPPER!

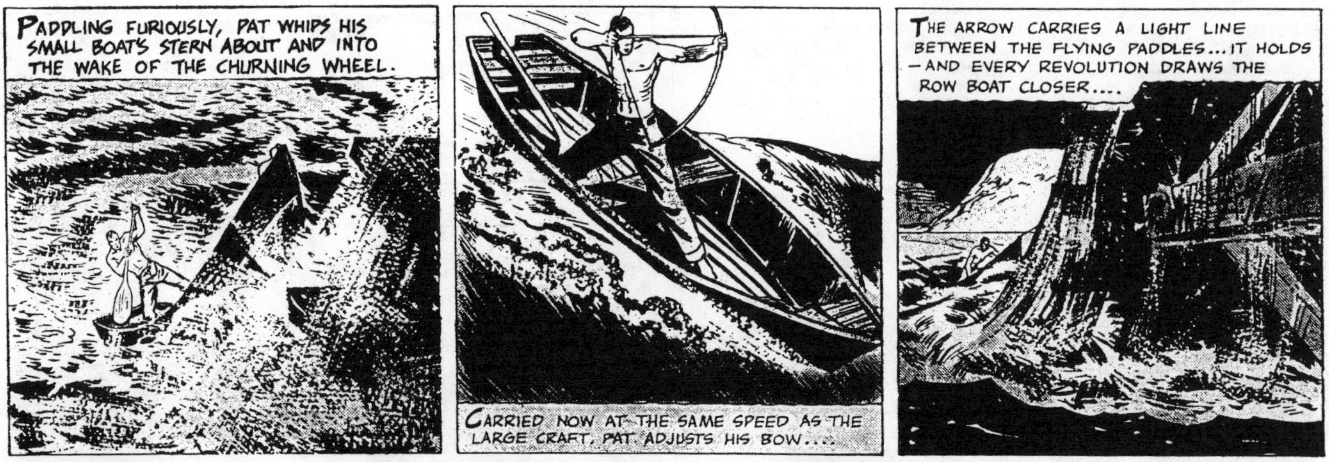
PADDLING FURIOUSLY, PAT WHIPS HIS SMALL BOAT'S STERN ABOUT AND INTO THE WAKE OF THE CHURNING WHEEL.
CARRIED NOW AT THE SAME SPEED AS THE LARGE CRAFT, PAT ADJUSTS HIS BOW....
THE ARROW CARRIES A LIGHT LINE BETWEEN THE FLYING PADDLES... IT HOLDS —AND EVERY REVOLUTION DRAWS THE ROW BOAT CLOSER....

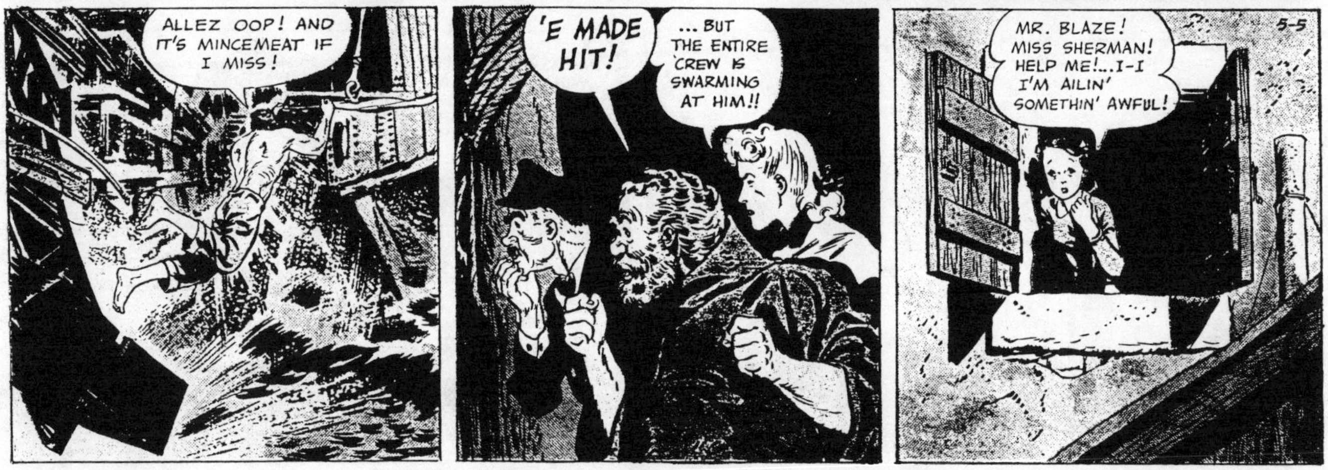
ALLEZ OOP! AND IT'S MINCEMEAT IF I MISS!
'E MADE HIT!
... BUT THE ENTIRE CREW IS SWARMING AT HIM!!
5-5
MR. BLAZE! MISS SHERMAN! HELP ME!...I-I I'M AILIN' SOMETHIN' AWFUL!

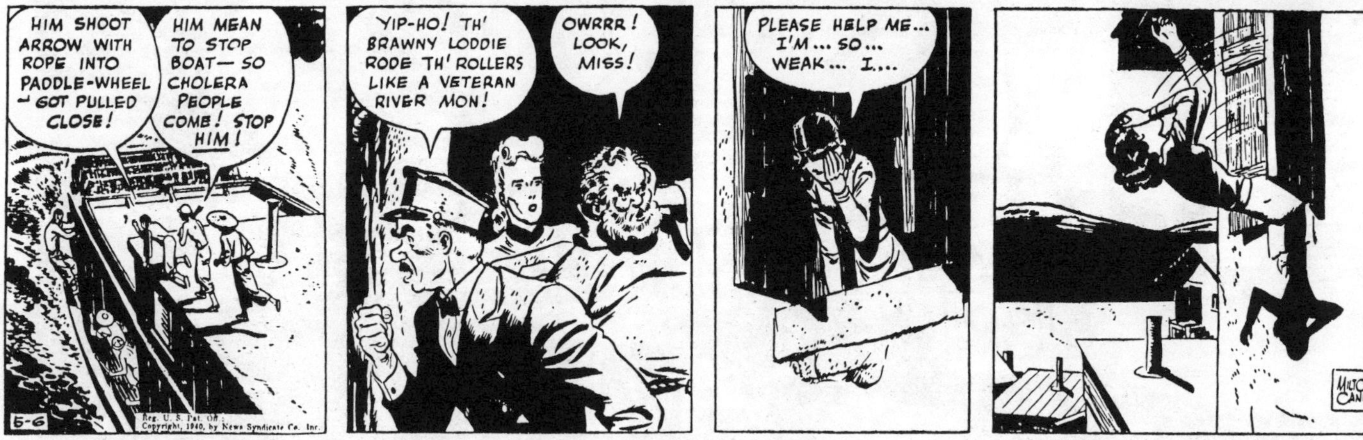
HIM SHOOT ARROW WITH ROPE INTO PADDLE-WHEEL — GOT PULLED CLOSE!
HIM MEAN TO STOP BOAT— SO CHOLERA PEOPLE COME! STOP HIM!
5-6
Reg. U. S. Pat. Off.; Copyright, 1940, by News Syndicate Co. Inc.
YIP-HO! TH' BRAWNY LODDIE RODE TH' ROLLERS LIKE A VETERAN RIVER MON!
OWRRR! LOOK, MISS!
PLEASE HELP ME... I'M... SO... WEAK... I...
MILTON CANIFF

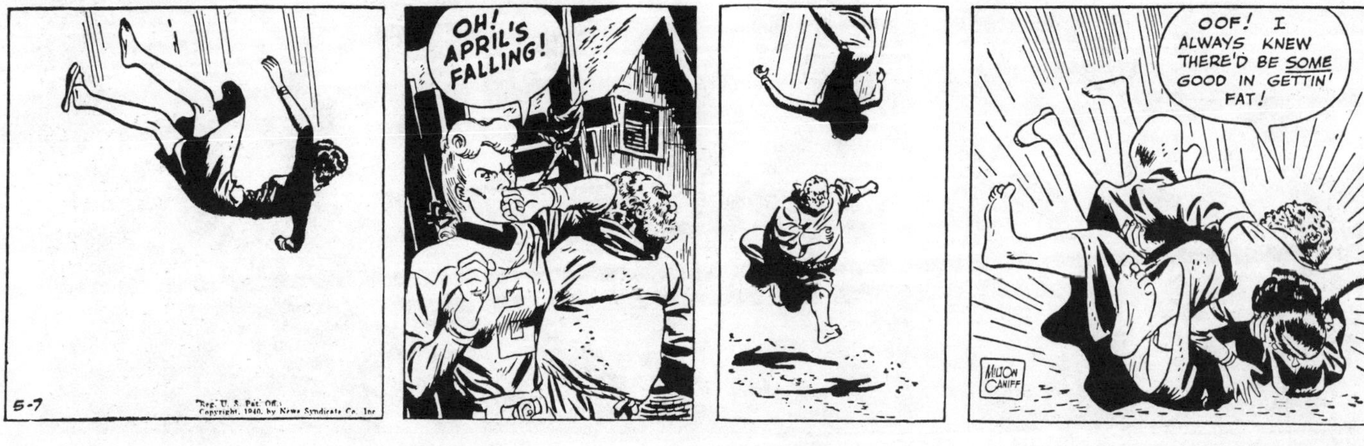
5-7
Reg. U. S. Pat. Off.; Copyright, 1940, by News Syndicate Co. Inc.
OH! APRIL'S FALLING!
OOF! I ALWAYS KNEW THERE'D BE SOME GOOD IN GETTIN' FAT!
MILTON CANIFF

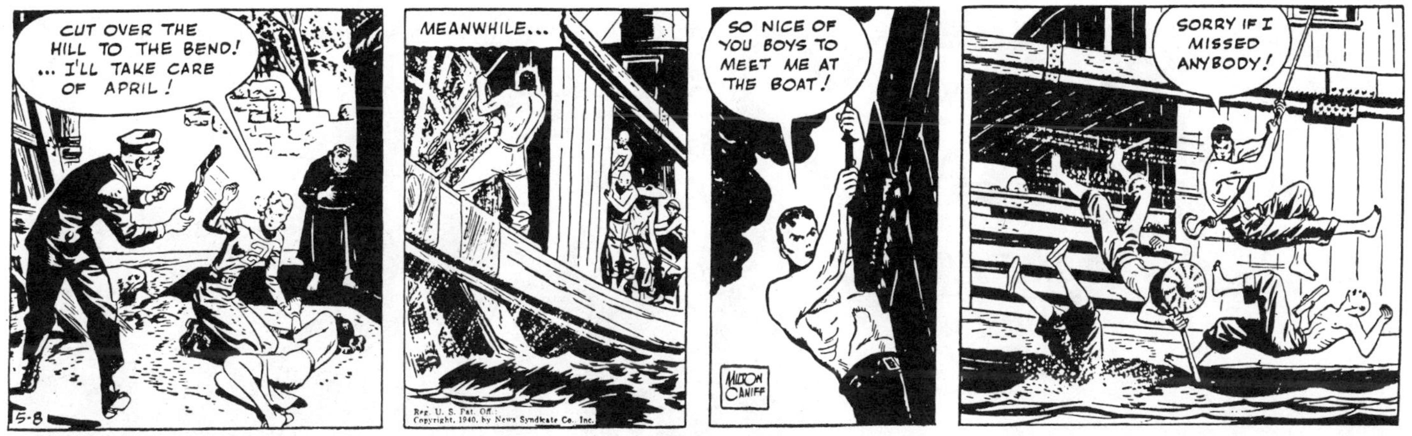
5-8
CUT OVER THE HILL TO THE BEND! ... I'LL TAKE CARE OF APRIL!
MEANWHILE...
Reg. U. S. Pat. Off.: Copyright, 1940, by News Syndicate Co. Inc.
SO NICE OF YOU BOYS TO MEET ME AT THE BOAT!
MILTON CANIFF
SORRY IF I MISSED ANYBODY!

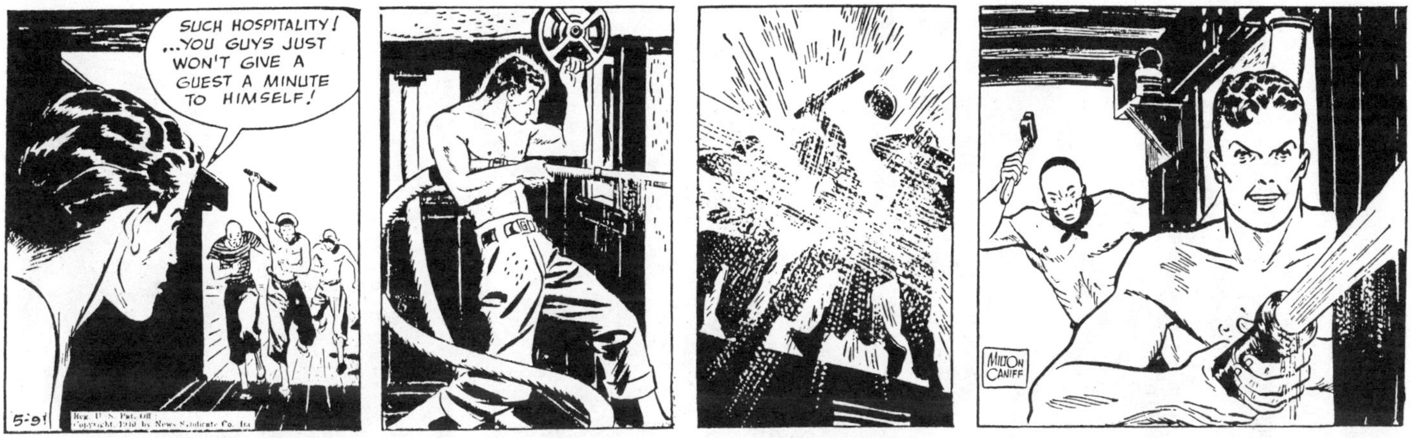
5-9
SUCH HOSPITALITY! ...YOU GUYS JUST WON'T GIVE A GUEST A MINUTE TO HIMSELF!
Reg. U. S. Pat. Off.: Copyright, 1940, by News Syndicate Co. Inc.
MILTON CANIFF

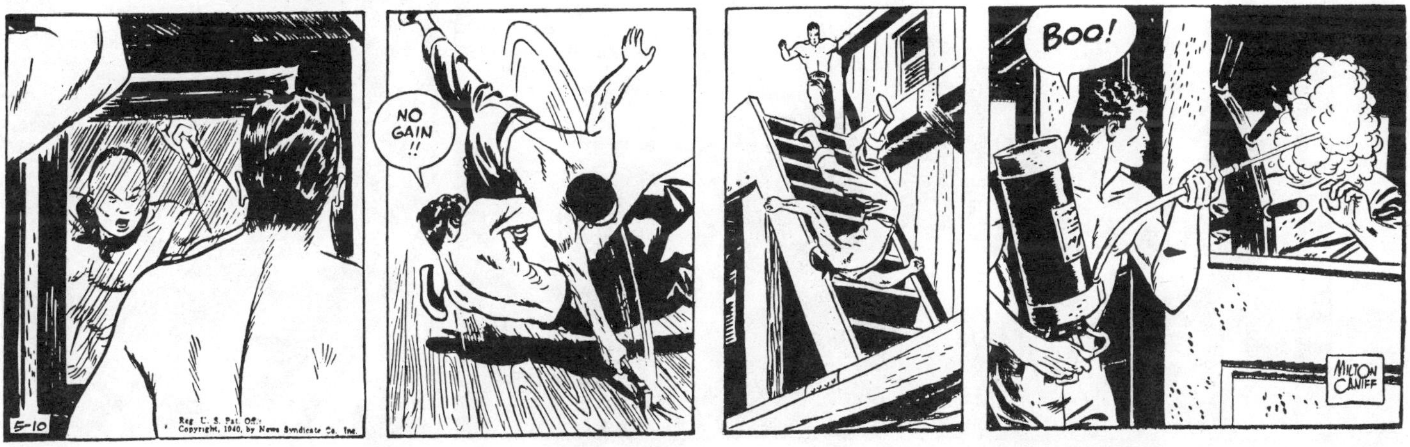
5-10
Reg. U. S. Pat. Off.: Copyright, 1940, by News Syndicate Co. Inc.
NO GAIN !!
BOO!
MILTON CANIFF

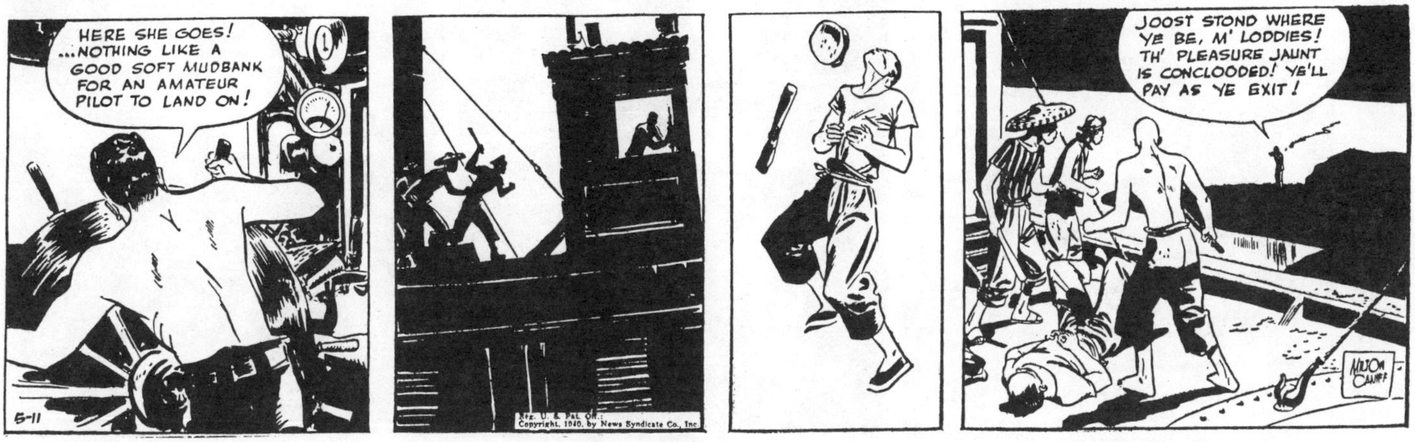
5-11
HERE SHE GOES! ...NOTHING LIKE A GOOD SOFT MUDBANK FOR AN AMATEUR PILOT TO LAND ON!
Reg. U. S. Pat. Off.: Copyright, 1940, by News Syndicate Co. Inc.
JOOST STOND WHERE YE BE, M' LODDIES! TH' PLEASURE JAUNT IS CONCLOODED! YE'LL PAY AS YE EXIT!
MILTON CANIFF

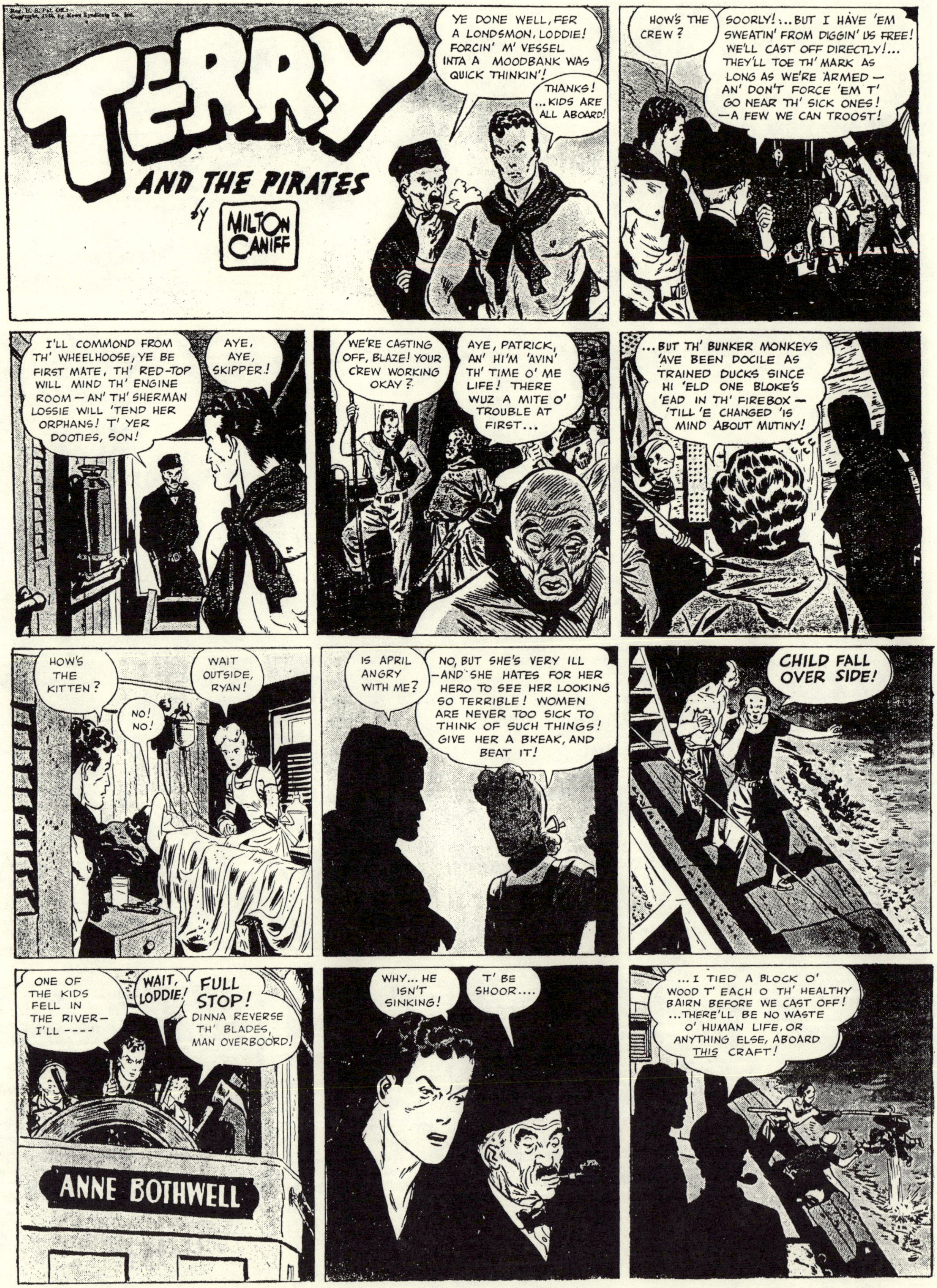
TERRY AND THE PIRATES
by MILTON CANIFF
YE DONE WELL, FER A LONDSMON, LODDIE! FORCIN' M' VESSEL INTA A MOODBANK WAS QUICK THINKIN'!
THANKS! ...KIDS ARE ALL ABOARD!
HOW'S THE CREW?
SOORLY! ...BUT I HAVE 'EM SWEATIN' FROM DIGGIN' US FREE! WE'LL CAST OFF DIRECTLY! ... THEY'LL TOE TH' MARK AS LONG AS WE'RE ARMED — AN' DON'T FORCE 'EM T' GO NEAR TH' SICK ONES! —A FEW WE CAN TROOST!
I'LL COMMOND FROM TH' WHEELHOOSE, YE BE FIRST MATE. TH' RED-TOP WILL MIND TH' ENGINE ROOM — AN' TH' SHERMAN LOSSIE WILL 'TEND HER ORPHANS! T' YER DOOTIES, SON!
AYE, AYE, SKIPPER!
WE'RE CASTING OFF, BLAZE! YOUR CREW WORKING OKAY?
AYE, PATRICK, AN' HI'M 'AVIN' TH' TIME O' ME LIFE! THERE WUZ A MITE O' TROUBLE AT FIRST...
...BUT TH' BUNKER MONKEYS 'AVE BEEN DOCILE AS TRAINED DUCKS SINCE HI 'ELD ONE BLOKE'S 'EAD IN TH' FIREBOX — 'TILL 'E CHANGED 'IS MIND ABOUT MUTINY!
HOW'S THE KITTEN?
NO! NO!
WAIT OUTSIDE, RYAN!
IS APRIL ANGRY WITH ME?
NO, BUT SHE'S VERY ILL —AND SHE HATES FOR HER HERO TO SEE HER LOOKING SO TERRIBLE! WOMEN ARE NEVER TOO SICK TO THINK OF SUCH THINGS! GIVE HER A BREAK, AND BEAT IT!
CHILD FALL OVER SIDE!
ONE OF THE KIDS FELL IN THE RIVER— I'LL ----
WAIT, LODDIE!
FULL STOP!
DINNA REVERSE TH' BLADES, MAN OVERBOORD!
ANNE BOTHWELL
WHY... HE ISN'T SINKING!
T' BE SHOOR....
...I TIED A BLOCK O' WOOD T' EACH O TH' HEALTHY BAIRN BEFORE WE CAST OFF! ...THERE'LL BE NO WASTE O' HUMAN LIFE, OR ANYTHING ELSE, ABOARD THIS CRAFT!

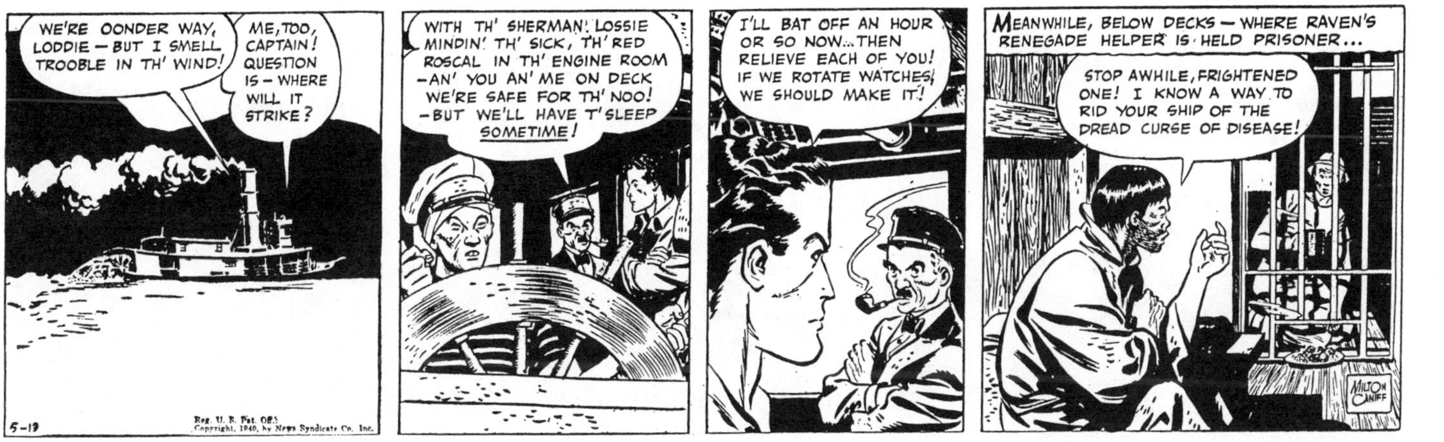
WE'RE OONDER WAY, LODDIE — BUT I SMELL TROOBLE IN TH' WIND!
ME, TOO, CAPTAIN! QUESTION IS — WHERE WILL IT STRIKE?
5-13
Reg. U. S. Pat. Off.: Copyright, 1940, by News Syndicate Co. Inc.
WITH TH' SHERMAN LOSSIE MINDIN' TH' SICK, TH' RED ROSCAL IN TH' ENGINE ROOM —AN' YOU AN' ME ON DECK WE'RE SAFE FOR TH' NOO! —BUT WE'LL HAVE T' SLEEP SOMETIME!
I'LL BAT OFF AN HOUR OR SO NOW... THEN RELIEVE EACH OF YOU! IF WE ROTATE WATCHES, WE SHOULD MAKE IT!
MEANWHILE, BELOW DECKS — WHERE RAVEN'S RENEGADE HELPER IS HELD PRISONER...
STOP AWHILE, FRIGHTENED ONE! I KNOW A WAY TO RID YOUR SHIP OF THE DREAD CURSE OF DISEASE!
MILTON CANIFF

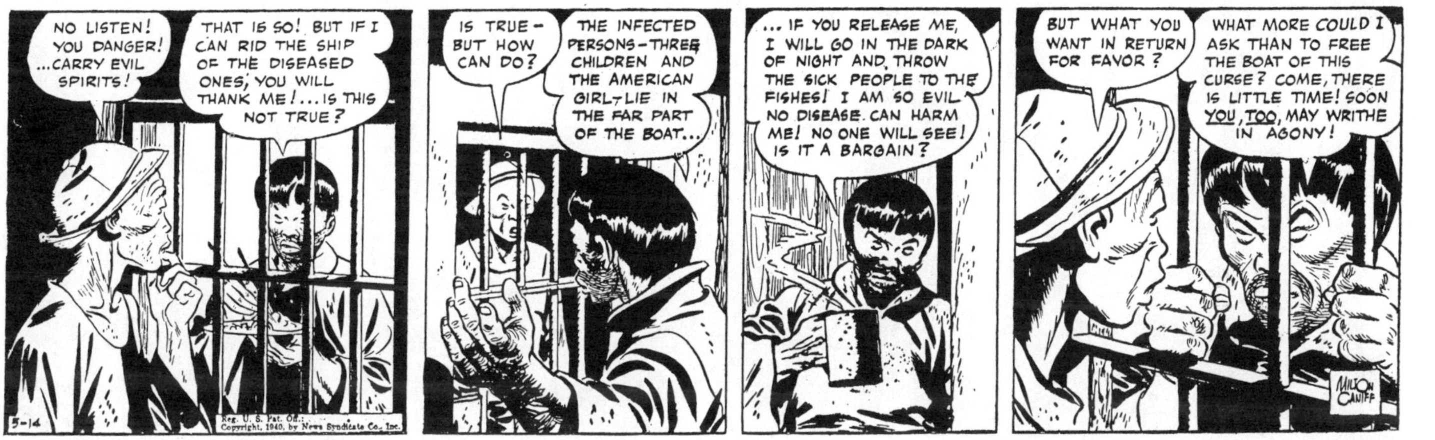
NO LISTEN! YOU DANGER! ...CARRY EVIL SPIRITS!
THAT IS SO! BUT IF I CAN RID THE SHIP OF THE DISEASED ONES, YOU WILL THANK ME!... IS THIS NOT TRUE?
5-14
Reg. U. S. Pat. Off.: Copyright, 1940, by News Syndicate Co., Inc.
IS TRUE — BUT HOW CAN DO?
THE INFECTED PERSONS — THREE CHILDREN AND THE AMERICAN GIRL — LIE IN THE FAR PART OF THE BOAT...
... IF YOU RELEASE ME, I WILL GO IN THE DARK OF NIGHT AND THROW THE SICK PEOPLE TO THE FISHES! I AM SO EVIL NO DISEASE CAN HARM ME! NO ONE WILL SEE! IS IT A BARGAIN?
BUT WHAT YOU WANT IN RETURN FOR FAVOR?
WHAT MORE COULD I ASK THAN TO FREE THE BOAT OF THIS CURSE? COME, THERE IS LITTLE TIME! SOON YOU, TOO, MAY WRITHE IN AGONY!
MILTON CANIFF

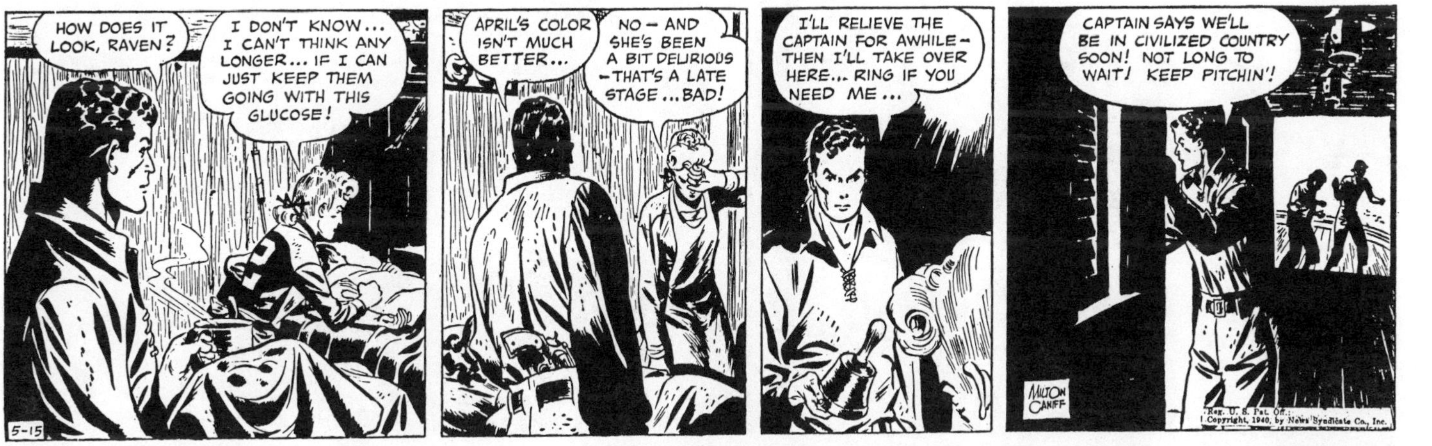
HOW DOES IT LOOK, RAVEN?
I DON'T KNOW... I CAN'T THINK ANY LONGER... IF I CAN JUST KEEP THEM GOING WITH THIS GLUCOSE!
5-15
APRIL'S COLOR ISN'T MUCH BETTER...
NO — AND SHE'S BEEN A BIT DELIRIOUS — THAT'S A LATE STAGE ...BAD!
I'LL RELIEVE THE CAPTAIN FOR AWHILE — THEN I'LL TAKE OVER HERE... RING IF YOU NEED ME...
MILTON CANIFF
CAPTAIN SAYS WE'LL BE IN CIVILIZED COUNTRY SOON! NOT LONG TO WAIT! KEEP PITCHIN'!
Reg. U. S. Pat. Off.: Copyright, 1940, by News Syndicate Co., Inc.

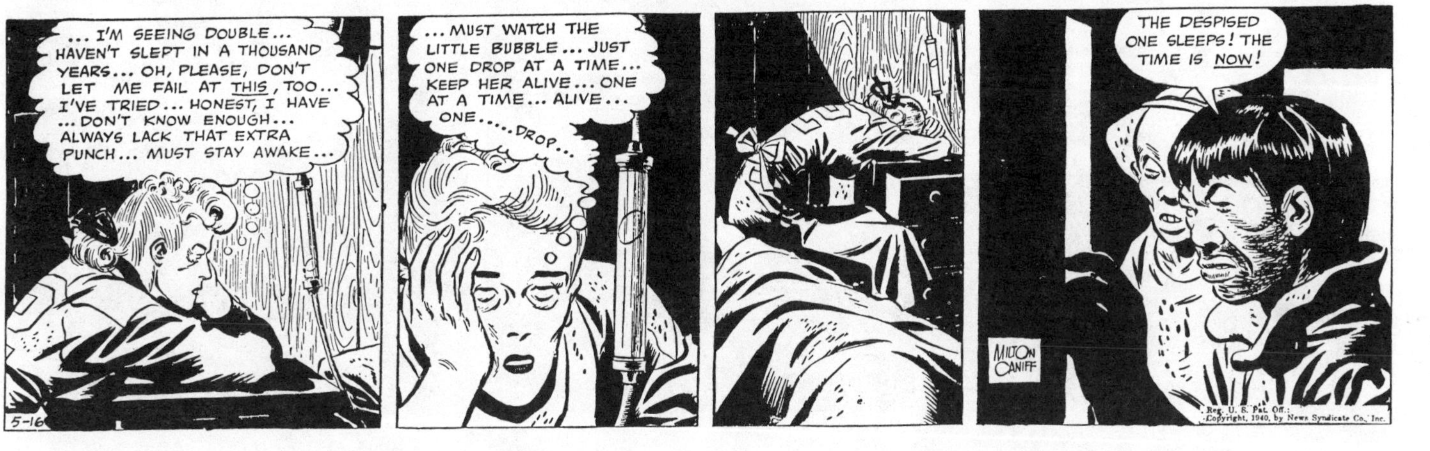
... I'M SEEING DOUBLE... HAVEN'T SLEPT IN A THOUSAND YEARS... OH, PLEASE, DON'T LET ME FAIL AT THIS, TOO... I'VE TRIED... HONEST, I HAVE ...DON'T KNOW ENOUGH... ALWAYS LACK THAT EXTRA PUNCH... MUST STAY AWAKE...
5-16
... MUST WATCH THE LITTLE BUBBLE ... JUST ONE DROP AT A TIME... KEEP HER ALIVE ... ONE AT A TIME... ALIVE... ONE..... DROP....
MILTON CANIFF
THE DESPISED ONE SLEEPS! THE TIME IS NOW!
Reg. U. S. Pat. Off.: Copyright, 1940, by News Syndicate Co., Inc.

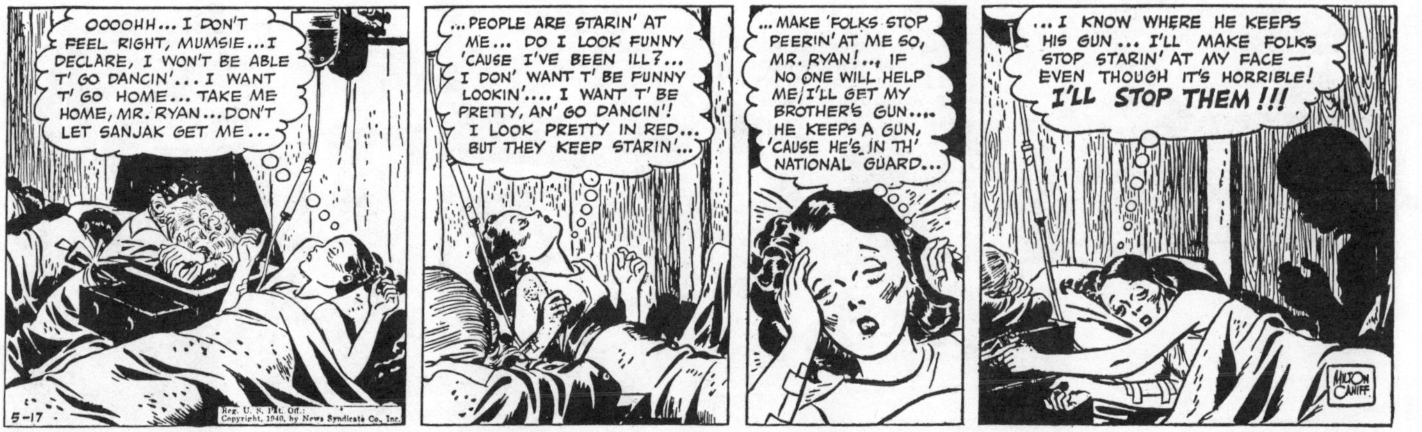
OOOOHH... I DON'T FEEL RIGHT, MUMSIE... I DECLARE, I WON'T BE ABLE T' GO DANCIN'... I WANT T' GO HOME... TAKE ME HOME, MR. RYAN... DON'T LET SANJAK GET ME...
5-17
Reg. U. S. Pat. Off.: Copyright, 1940, by News Syndicate Co. Inc.
...PEOPLE ARE STARIN' AT ME... DO I LOOK FUNNY 'CAUSE I'VE BEEN ILL?... I DON' WANT T' BE FUNNY LOOKIN'.... I WANT T' BE PRETTY, AN' GO DANCIN'! I LOOK PRETTY IN RED... BUT THEY KEEP STARIN'...
...MAKE 'FOLKS STOP PEERIN' AT ME SO, MR. RYAN!.., IF NO ONE WILL HELP ME, I'LL GET MY BROTHER'S GUN.... HE KEEPS A GUN, 'CAUSE HE'S IN TH' NATIONAL GUARD...
...I KNOW WHERE HE KEEPS HIS GUN... I'LL MAKE FOLKS STOP STARIN' AT MY FACE — EVEN THOUGH IT'S HORRIBLE! I'LL STOP THEM!!!
MILTON CANIFF

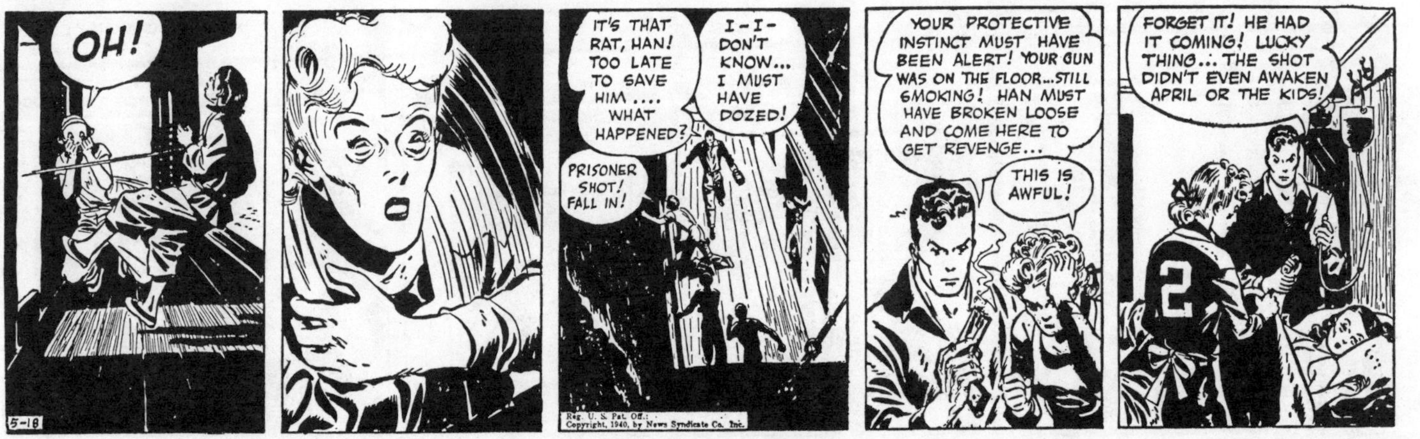
OH!
5-18
IT'S THAT RAT, HAN! TOO LATE TO SAVE HIM.... WHAT HAPPENED?
I-I- DON'T KNOW... I MUST HAVE DOZED!
PRISONER SHOT! FALL IN!
Reg. U. S. Pat. Off.: Copyright, 1940, by News Syndicate Co. Inc.
YOUR PROTECTIVE INSTINCT MUST HAVE BEEN ALERT! YOUR GUN WAS ON THE FLOOR...STILL SMOKING! HAN MUST HAVE BROKEN LOOSE AND COME HERE TO GET REVENGE...
THIS IS AWFUL!
FORGET IT! HE HAD IT COMING! LUCKY THING... THE SHOT DIDN'T EVEN AWAKEN APRIL OR THE KIDS!

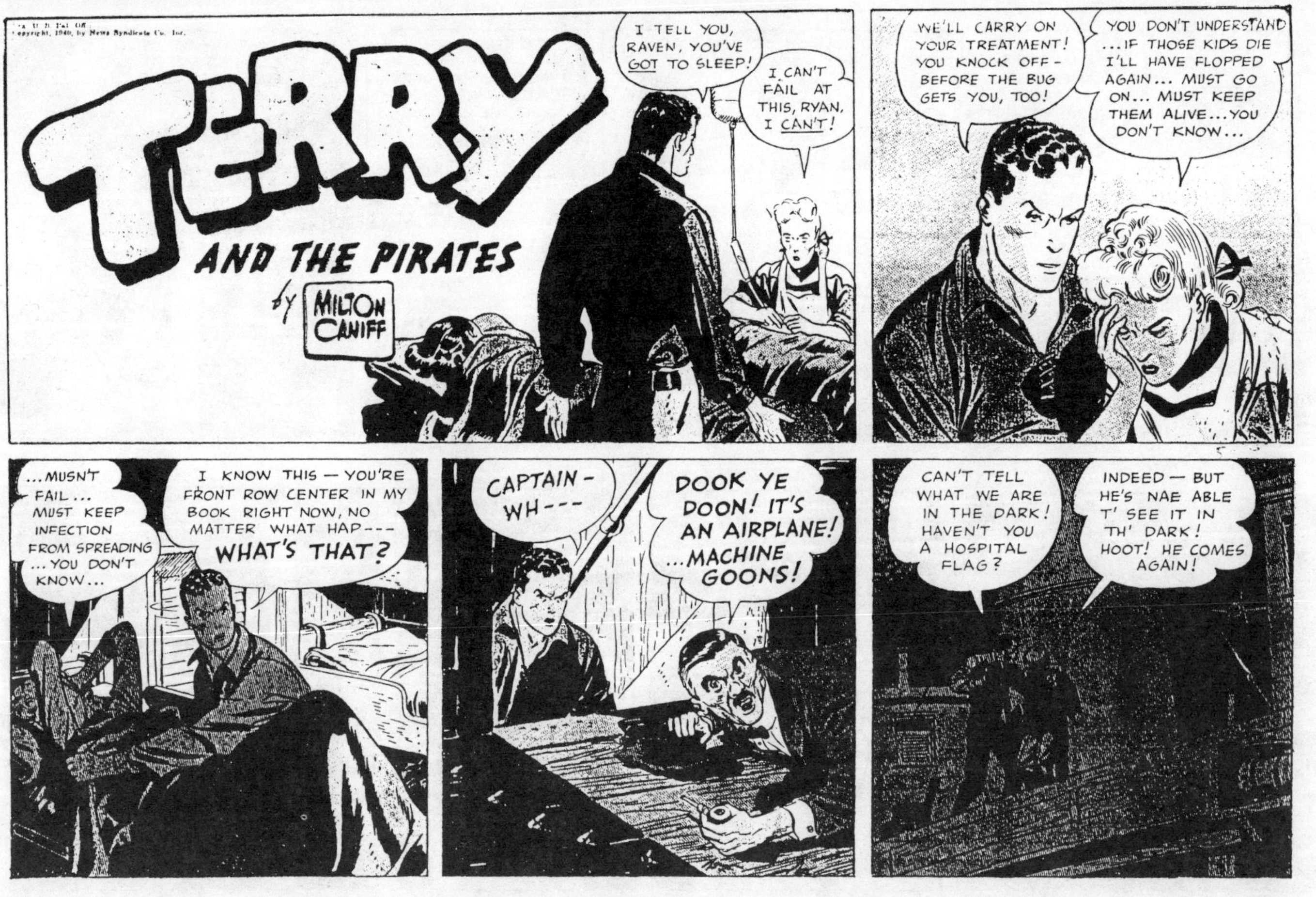
TERRY AND THE PIRATES by MILTON CANIFF
I TELL YOU, RAVEN, YOU'VE GOT TO SLEEP!
I CAN'T FAIL AT THIS, RYAN, I CAN'T!
WE'LL CARRY ON YOUR TREATMENT! YOU KNOCK OFF - BEFORE THE BUG GETS YOU, TOO!
YOU DON'T UNDERSTAND ...IF THOSE KIDS DIE I'LL HAVE FLOPPED AGAIN... MUST GO ON... MUST KEEP THEM ALIVE... YOU DON'T KNOW...
...MUSN'T FAIL... MUST KEEP INFECTION FROM SPREADING ...YOU DON'T KNOW...
I KNOW THIS — YOU'RE FRONT ROW CENTER IN MY BOOK RIGHT NOW, NO MATTER WHAT HAP---
WHAT'S THAT?
CAPTAIN - WH---
DOOK YE DOON! IT'S AN AIRPLANE! ...MACHINE GOONS!
CAN'T TELL WHAT WE ARE IN THE DARK! HAVEN'T YOU A HOSPITAL FLAG?
INDEED — BUT HE'S NAE ABLE T' SEE IT IN TH' DARK! HOOT! HE COMES AGAIN!

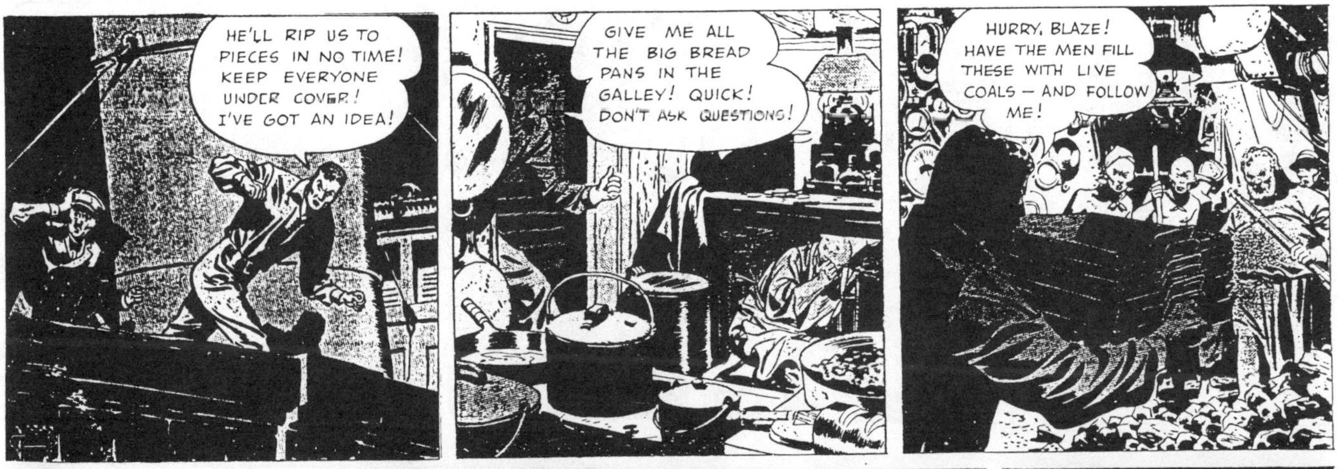
HE'LL RIP US TO PIECES IN NO TIME! KEEP EVERYONE UNDER COVER! I'VE GOT AN IDEA!
GIVE ME ALL THE BIG BREAD PANS IN THE GALLEY! QUICK! DON'T ASK QUESTIONS!
HURRY, BLAZE! HAVE THE MEN FILL THESE WITH LIVE COALS — AND FOLLOW ME!

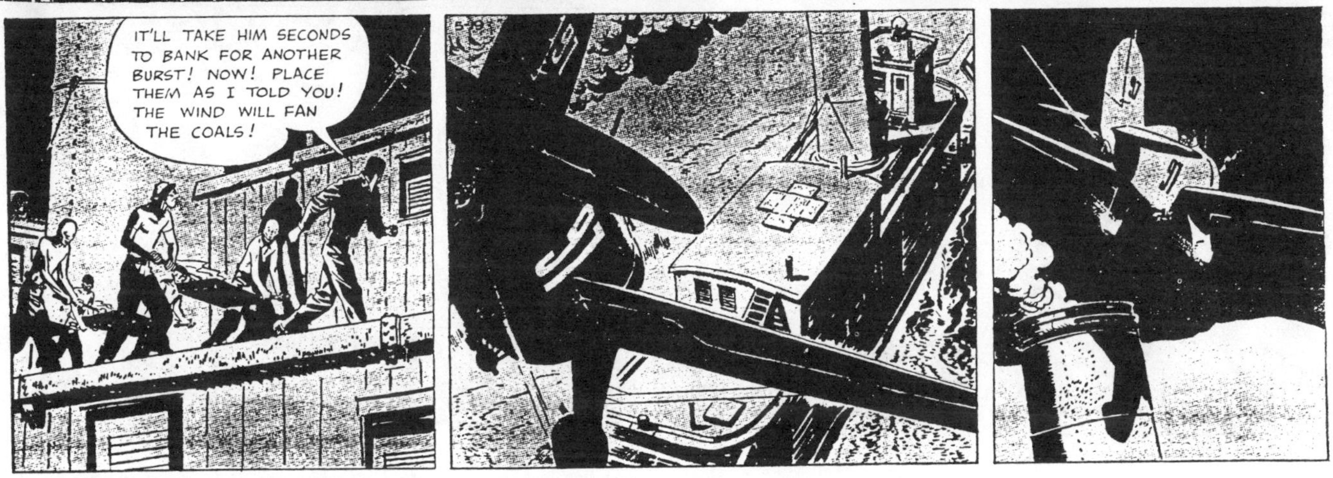
IT'LL TAKE HIM SECONDS TO BANK FOR ANOTHER BURST! NOW! PLACE THEM AS I TOLD YOU! THE WIND WILL FAN THE COALS!

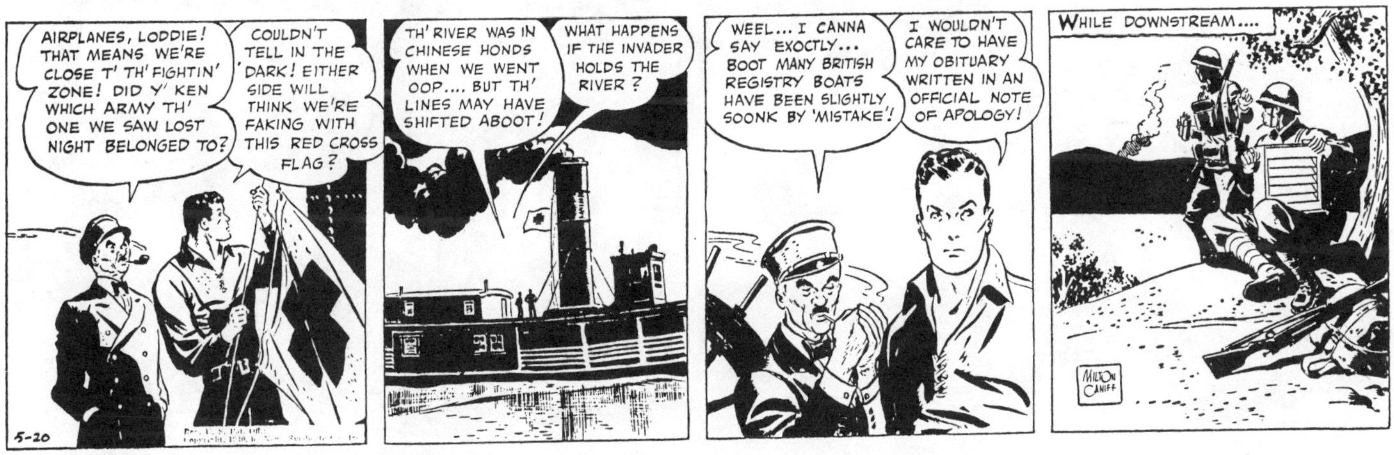
AIRPLANES, LODDIE! THAT MEANS WE'RE CLOSE T' TH' FIGHTIN' ZONE! DID Y' KEN WHICH ARMY TH' ONE WE SAW LOST NIGHT BELONGED TO?
COULDN'T TELL IN THE DARK! EITHER SIDE WILL THINK WE'RE FAKING WITH THIS RED CROSS FLAG?
5-20
TH' RIVER WAS IN CHINESE HONDS WHEN WE WENT OOP.... BUT TH' LINES MAY HAVE SHIFTED ABOOT!
WHAT HAPPENS IF THE INVADER HOLDS THE RIVER?
WEEL... I CANNA SAY EXOCTLY... BOOT MANY BRITISH REGISTRY BOATS HAVE BEEN SLIGHTLY SOONK BY 'MISTAKE'!
I WOULDN'T CARE TO HAVE MY OBITUARY WRITTEN IN AN OFFICIAL NOTE OF APOLOGY!
WHILE DOWNSTREAM....
MILTON CANIFF

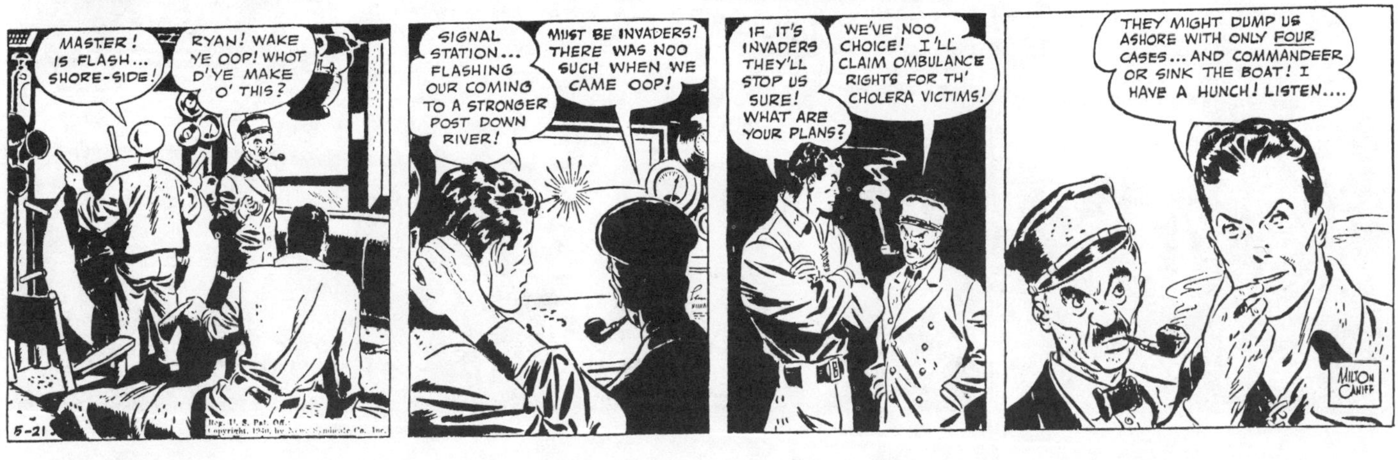
MASTER! IS FLASH... SHORE-SIDE!
RYAN! WAKE YE OOP! WHOT D'YE MAKE O' THIS?
5-21
SIGNAL STATION... FLASHING OUR COMING TO A STRONGER POST DOWN RIVER!
MUST BE INVADERS! THERE WAS NOO SUCH WHEN WE CAME OOP!
Reg. U. S. Pat. Off. Copyright, 1940, by News Syndicate Co. Inc.
IF IT'S INVADERS THEY'LL STOP US SURE! WHAT ARE YOUR PLANS?
WE'VE NOO CHOICE! I'LL CLAIM OMBULANCE RIGHTS FOR TH' CHOLERA VICTIMS!
THEY MIGHT DUMP US ASHORE WITH ONLY FOUR CASES... AND COMMANDEER OR SINK THE BOAT! I HAVE A HUNCH! LISTEN....
MILTON CANIFF

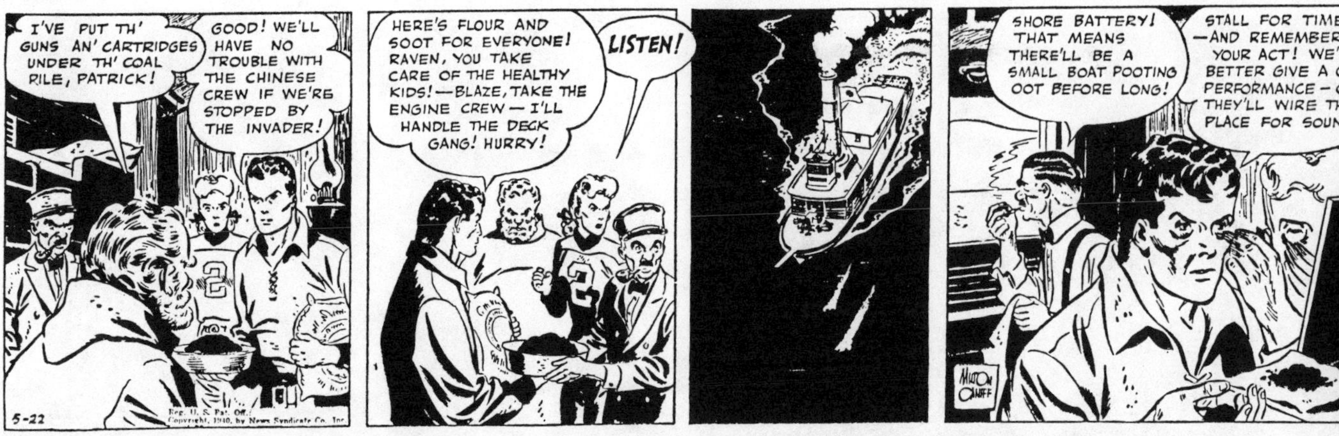
I'VE PUT TH' GUNS AN' CARTRIDGES UNDER TH' COAL PILE, PATRICK!
GOOD! WE'LL HAVE NO TROUBLE WITH THE CHINESE CREW IF WE'RE STOPPED BY THE INVADER!
HERE'S FLOUR AND SOOT FOR EVERYONE! RAVEN, YOU TAKE CARE OF THE HEALTHY KIDS! —BLAZE, TAKE THE ENGINE CREW — I'LL HANDLE THE DECK GANG! HURRY!
LISTEN!
SHORE BATTERY! THAT MEANS THERE'LL BE A SMALL BOAT POOTING OOT BEFORE LONG!
STALL FOR TIME —AND REMEMBER YOUR ACT! WE'D BETTER GIVE A GOOD PERFORMANCE — OR THEY'LL WIRE THE PLACE FOR SOUND!
MILTON CANIFF
5-22
Reg. U. S. Pat. Off.
Copyright, 1940, by News Syndicate Co. Inc.

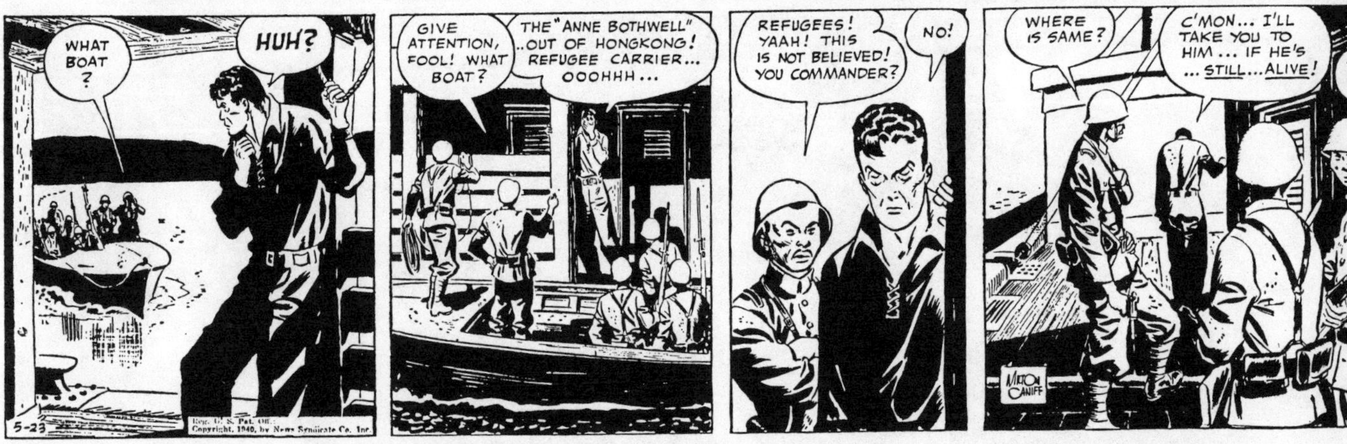
WHAT BOAT ?
HUH?
GIVE ATTENTION, FOOL! WHAT BOAT?
THE "ANNE BOTHWELL" ..OUT OF HONGKONG! REFUGEE CARRIER... OOOHHH...
REFUGEES! YAAH! THIS IS NOT BELIEVED! YOU COMMANDER?
NO!
WHERE IS SAME?
C'MON... I'LL TAKE YOU TO HIM... IF HE'S ...STILL...ALIVE!
MILTON CANIFF
5-23
Reg. U. S. Pat. Off.
Copyright, 1940, by News Syndicate Co. Inc.

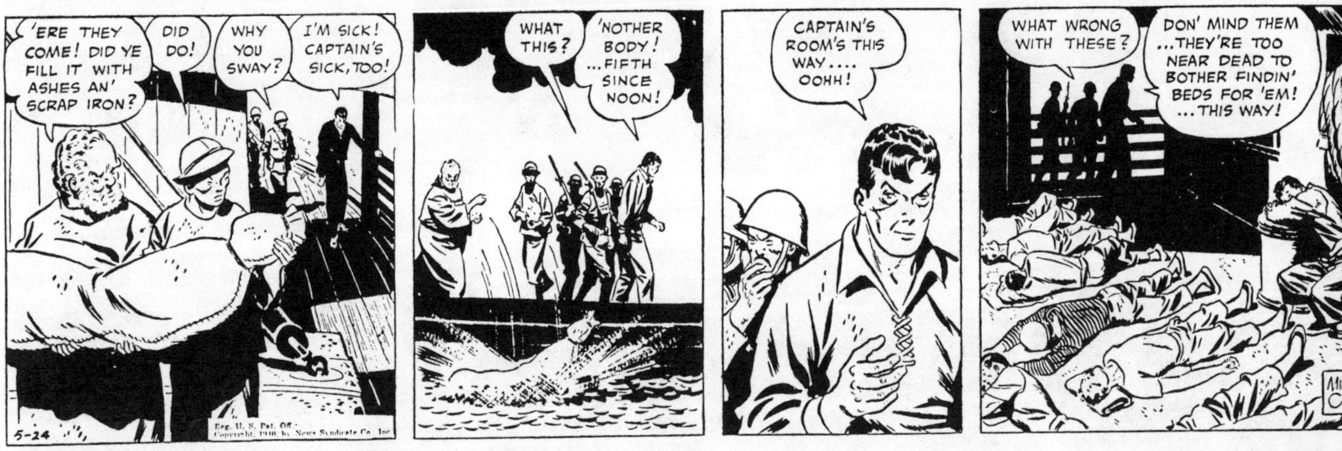
'ERE THEY COME! DID YE FILL IT WITH ASHES AN' SCRAP IRON?
DID DO!
WHY YOU SWAY?
I'M SICK! CAPTAIN'S SICK, TOO!
WHAT THIS?
'NOTHER BODY! ...FIFTH SINCE NOON!
CAPTAIN'S ROOM'S THIS WAY.... OOHH!
WHAT WRONG WITH THESE?
DON' MIND THEM ...THEY'RE TOO NEAR DEAD TO BOTHER FINDIN' BEDS FOR 'EM! ...THIS WAY!
MILTON CANIFF
5-24
Reg. U. S. Pat. Off.
Copyright, 1940, by News Syndicate Co. Inc.

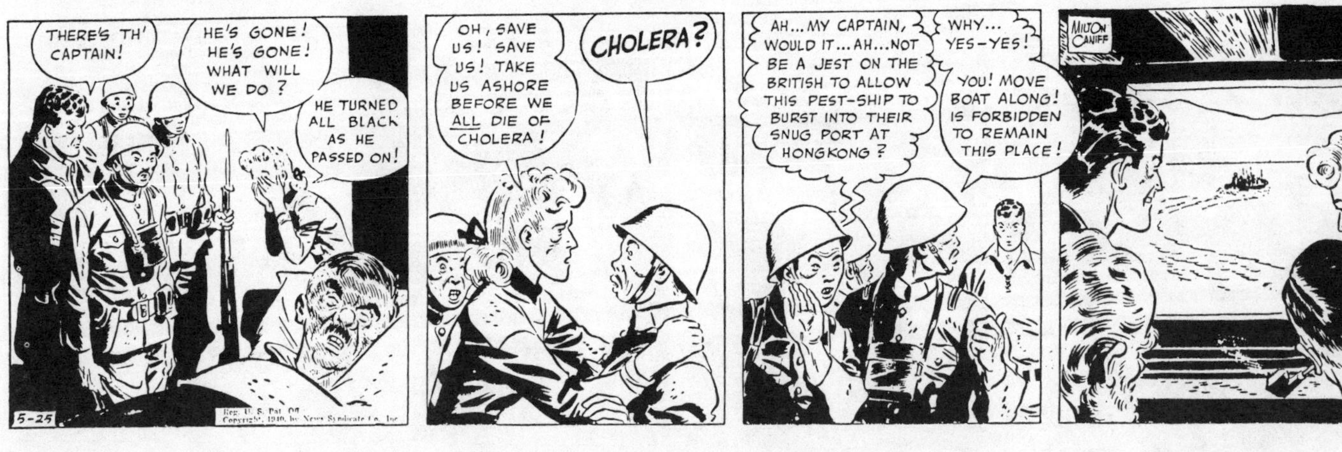
THERE'S TH' CAPTAIN!
HE'S GONE! HE'S GONE! WHAT WILL WE DO ?
HE TURNED ALL BLACK AS HE PASSED ON!
OH, SAVE US! SAVE US! TAKE US ASHORE BEFORE WE ALL DIE OF CHOLERA!
CHOLERA?
AH... MY CAPTAIN, WOULD IT... AH... NOT BE A JEST ON THE BRITISH TO ALLOW THIS PEST-SHIP TO BURST INTO THEIR SNUG PORT AT HONGKONG ?
WHY... YES-YES!
YOU! MOVE BOAT ALONG! IS FORBIDDEN TO REMAIN THIS PLACE!
MILTON CANIFF
5-25
Reg. U. S. Pat. Off.
Copyright, 1940, by News Syndicate Co. Inc.

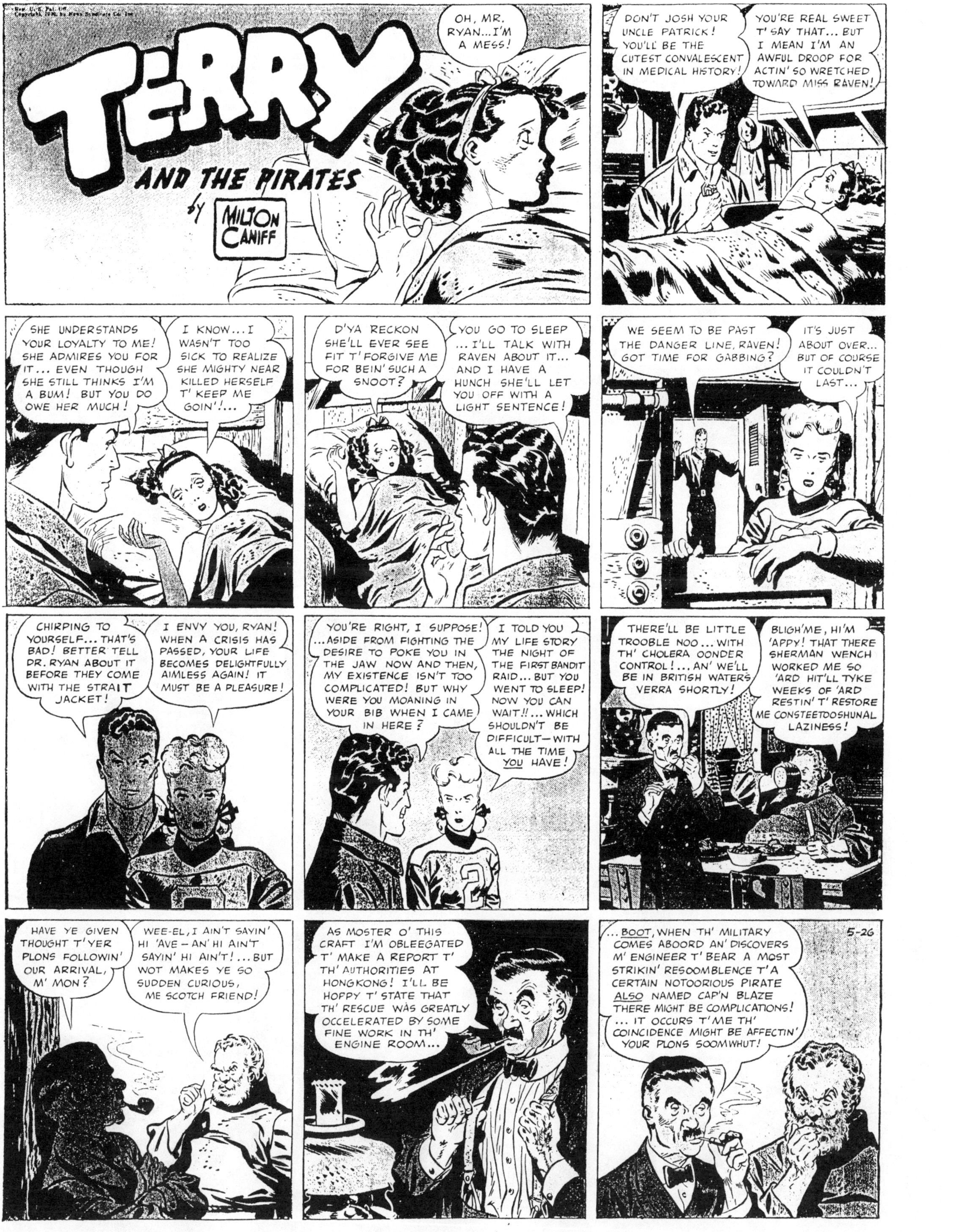
TERRY AND THE PIRATES
by MILTON CANIFF
OH, MR. RYAN...I'M A MESS!
DON'T JOSH YOUR UNCLE PATRICK! YOU'LL BE THE CUTEST CONVALESCENT IN MEDICAL HISTORY!
YOU'RE REAL SWEET T' SAY THAT... BUT I MEAN I'M AN AWFUL DROOP FOR ACTIN' SO WRETCHED TOWARD MISS RAVEN!
SHE UNDERSTANDS YOUR LOYALTY TO ME! SHE ADMIRES YOU FOR IT... EVEN THOUGH SHE STILL THINKS I'M A BUM! BUT YOU DO OWE HER MUCH!
I KNOW...I WASN'T TOO SICK TO REALIZE SHE MIGHTY NEAR KILLED HERSELF T' KEEP ME GOIN'!...
D'YA RECKON SHE'LL EVER SEE FIT T' FORGIVE ME FOR BEIN' SUCH A SNOOT?
YOU GO TO SLEEP ... I'LL TALK WITH RAVEN ABOUT IT... AND I HAVE A HUNCH SHE'LL LET YOU OFF WITH A LIGHT SENTENCE!
WE SEEM TO BE PAST THE DANGER LINE, RAVEN! GOT TIME FOR GABBING?
IT'S JUST ABOUT OVER... BUT OF COURSE IT COULDN'T LAST...
CHIRPING TO YOURSELF... THAT'S BAD! BETTER TELL DR. RYAN ABOUT IT BEFORE THEY COME WITH THE STRAIT JACKET!
I ENVY YOU, RYAN! WHEN A CRISIS HAS PASSED, YOUR LIFE BECOMES DELIGHTFULLY AIMLESS AGAIN! IT MUST BE A PLEASURE!
YOU'RE RIGHT, I SUPPOSE! ...ASIDE FROM FIGHTING THE DESIRE TO POKE YOU IN THE JAW NOW AND THEN, MY EXISTENCE ISN'T TOO COMPLICATED! BUT WHY WERE YOU MOANING IN YOUR BIB WHEN I CAME IN HERE?
I TOLD YOU MY LIFE STORY THE NIGHT OF THE FIRST BANDIT RAID... BUT YOU WENT TO SLEEP! NOW YOU CAN WAIT!!... WHICH SHOULDN'T BE DIFFICULT—WITH ALL THE TIME YOU HAVE!
THERE'LL BE LITTLE TROOBLE NOO... WITH TH' CHOLERA OONDER CONTROL!... AN' WE'LL BE IN BRITISH WATERS VERRA SHORTLY!
BLIGH'ME, HI'M 'APPY! THAT THERE SHERMAN WENCH WORKED ME SO 'ARD HIT'LL TYKE WEEKS OF 'ARD RESTIN' T' RESTORE ME CONSTEETOOSHUNAL LAZINESS!
HAVE YE GIVEN THOUGHT T'YER PLONS FOLLOWIN' OUR ARRIVAL, M' MON?
WEE-EL, I AIN'T SAYIN' HI 'AVE—AN' HI AIN'T SAYIN' HI AIN'T!... BUT WOT MAKES YE SO SUDDEN CURIOUS, ME SCOTCH FRIEND!
AS MOSTER O' THIS CRAFT I'M OBLEEGATED T' MAKE A REPORT T' TH' AUTHORITIES AT HONGKONG! I'LL BE HOPPY T' STATE THAT TH' RESCUE WAS GREATLY OCCELERATED BY SOME FINE WORK IN TH' ENGINE ROOM...
...BOOT, WHEN TH' MILITARY COMES ABOORD AN' DISCOVERS M' ENGINEER T' BEAR A MOST STRIKIN' RESOOMBLENCE T'A CERTAIN NOTOORIOUS PIRATE ALSO NAMED CAP'N BLAZE THERE MIGHT BE COMPLICATIONS! ... IT OCCURS T'ME TH' COINCIDENCE MIGHT BE AFFECTIN' YOUR PLONS SOOMWHUT!
5-26

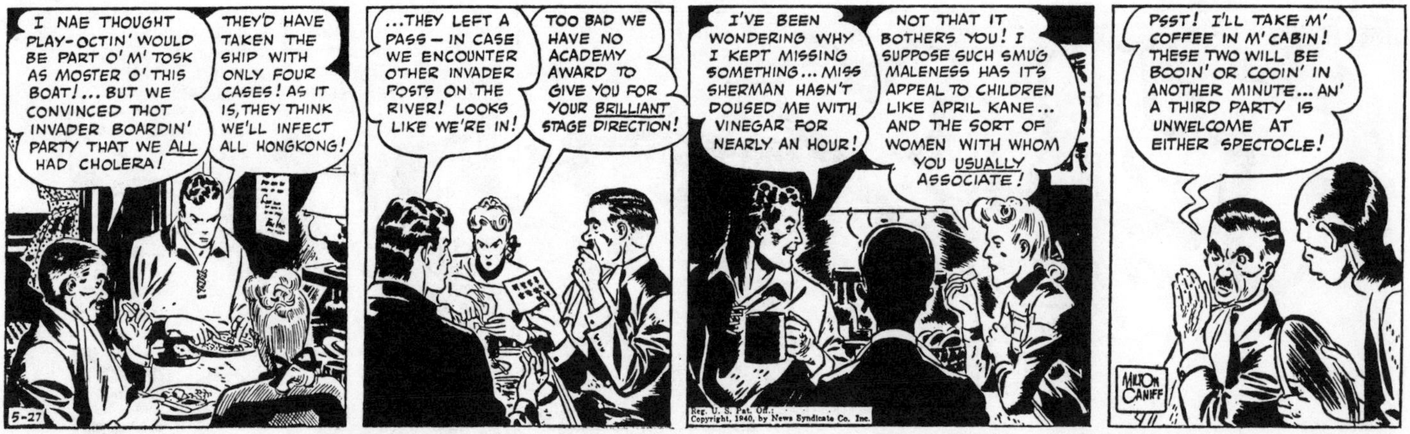
I NAE THOUGHT PLAY-OCTIN' WOULD BE PART O' M' TOSK AS MOSTER O' THIS BOAT! ... BUT WE CONVINCED THOT INVADER BOARDIN' PARTY THAT WE ALL HAD CHOLERA!
THEY'D HAVE TAKEN THE SHIP WITH ONLY FOUR CASES! AS IT IS, THEY THINK WE'LL INFECT ALL HONGKONG!
5-27
...THEY LEFT A PASS — IN CASE WE ENCOUNTER OTHER INVADER POSTS ON THE RIVER! LOOKS LIKE WE'RE IN!
TOO BAD WE HAVE NO ACADEMY AWARD TO GIVE YOU FOR YOUR BRILLIANT STAGE DIRECTION!
I'VE BEEN WONDERING WHY I KEPT MISSING SOMETHING... MISS SHERMAN HASN'T DOUSED ME WITH VINEGAR FOR NEARLY AN HOUR!
NOT THAT IT BOTHERS YOU! I SUPPOSE SUCH SMUG MALENESS HAS IT'S APPEAL TO CHILDREN LIKE APRIL KANE... AND THE SORT OF WOMEN WITH WHOM YOU USUALLY ASSOCIATE!
Reg. U. S. Pat. Off.: Copyright, 1940, by News Syndicate Co. Inc.
PSST! I'LL TAKE M' COFFEE IN M' CABIN! THESE TWO WILL BE BOOIN' OR COOIN' IN ANOTHER MINUTE... AN' A THIRD PARTY IS UNWELCOME AT EITHER SPECTOCLE!
MILTON CANIFF

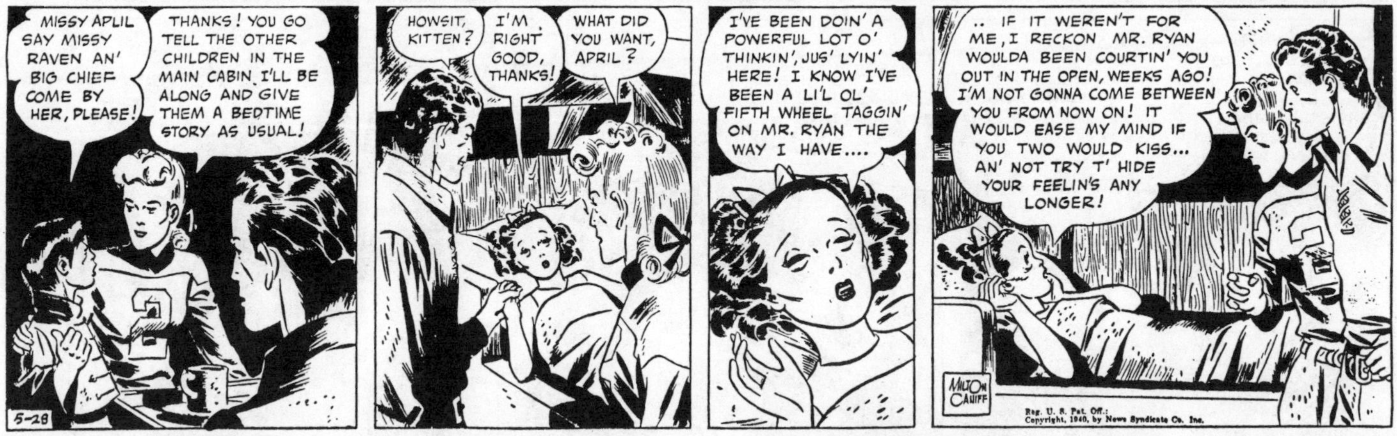
MISSY APLIL SAY MISSY RAVEN AN' BIG CHIEF COME BY HER, PLEASE!
THANKS! YOU GO TELL THE OTHER CHILDREN IN THE MAIN CABIN. I'LL BE ALONG AND GIVE THEM A BEDTIME STORY AS USUAL!
5-28
HOWSIT, KITTEN?
I'M RIGHT GOOD, THANKS!
WHAT DID YOU WANT, APRIL?
I'VE BEEN DOIN' A POWERFUL LOT O' THINKIN', JUS' LYIN' HERE! I KNOW I'VE BEEN A LI'L OL' FIFTH WHEEL TAGGIN' ON MR. RYAN THE WAY I HAVE....
.. IF IT WEREN'T FOR ME, I RECKON MR. RYAN WOULDA BEEN COURTIN' YOU OUT IN THE OPEN, WEEKS AGO! I'M NOT GONNA COME BETWEEN YOU FROM NOW ON! IT WOULD EASE MY MIND IF YOU TWO WOULD KISS... AN' NOT TRY T' HIDE YOUR FEELIN'S ANY LONGER!
MILTON CANIFF
Reg. U. S. Pat. Off.: Copyright, 1940, by News Syndicate Co. Inc.

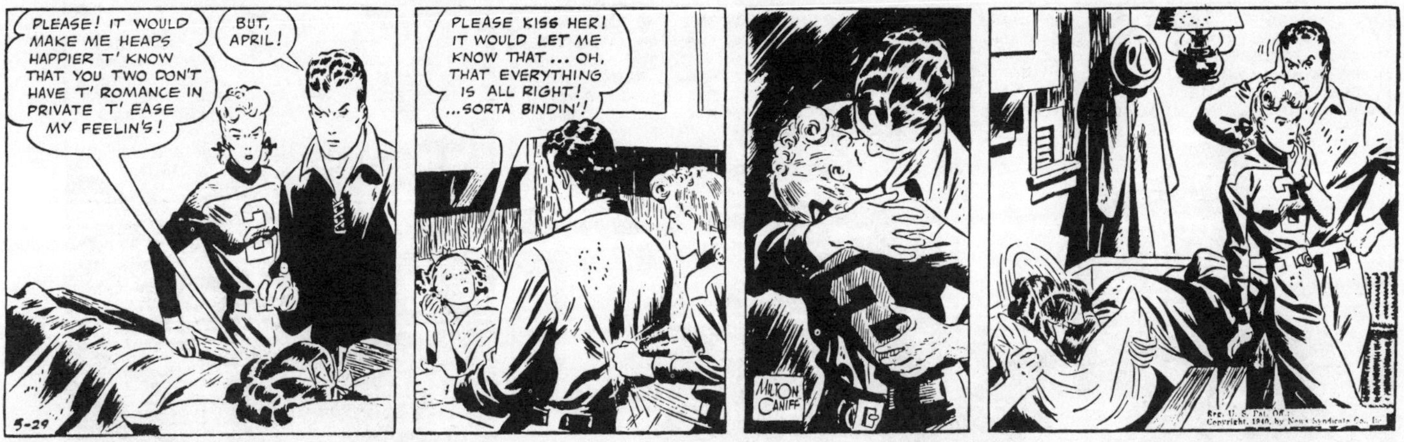
PLEASE! IT WOULD MAKE ME HEAPS HAPPIER T' KNOW THAT YOU TWO DON'T HAVE T' ROMANCE IN PRIVATE T' EASE MY FEELIN'S!
BUT, APRIL!
5-29
PLEASE KISS HER! IT WOULD LET ME KNOW THAT ... OH, THAT EVERYTHING IS ALL RIGHT! ...SORTA BINDIN'!
MILTON CANIFF
Reg. U. S. Pat. Off.: Copyright, 1940, by News Syndicate Co. Inc.

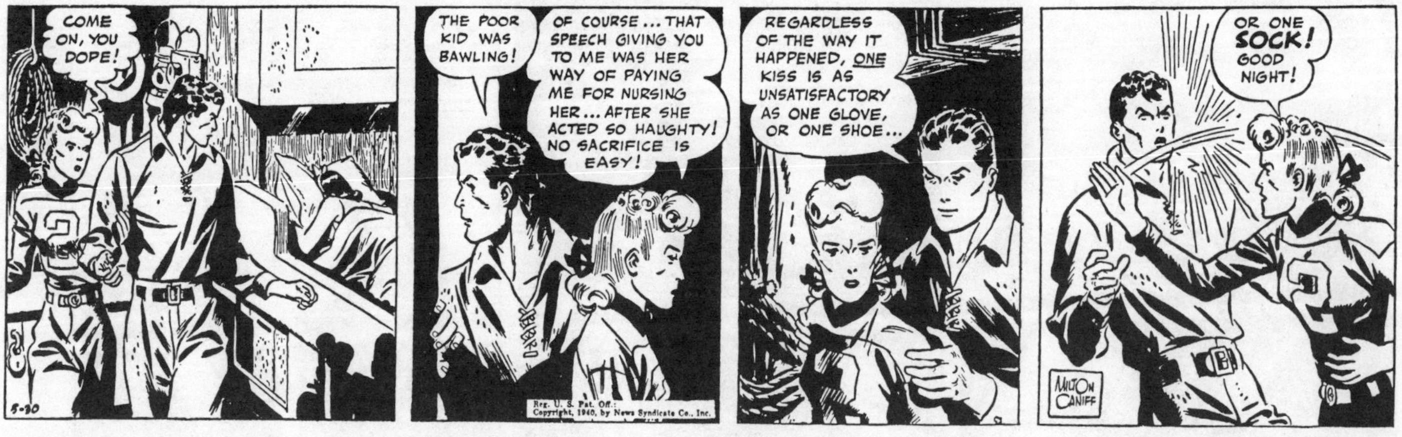
COME ON, YOU DOPE!
5-30
THE POOR KID WAS BAWLING!
OF COURSE ... THAT SPEECH GIVING YOU TO ME WAS HER WAY OF PAYING ME FOR NURSING HER ... AFTER SHE ACTED SO HAUGHTY! NO SACRIFICE IS EASY!
Reg. U. S. Pat. Off.: Copyright, 1940, by News Syndicate Co. Inc.
REGARDLESS OF THE WAY IT HAPPENED, ONE KISS IS AS UNSATISFACTORY AS ONE GLOVE, OR ONE SHOE...
OR ONE SOCK! GOOD NIGHT!
MILTON CANIFF

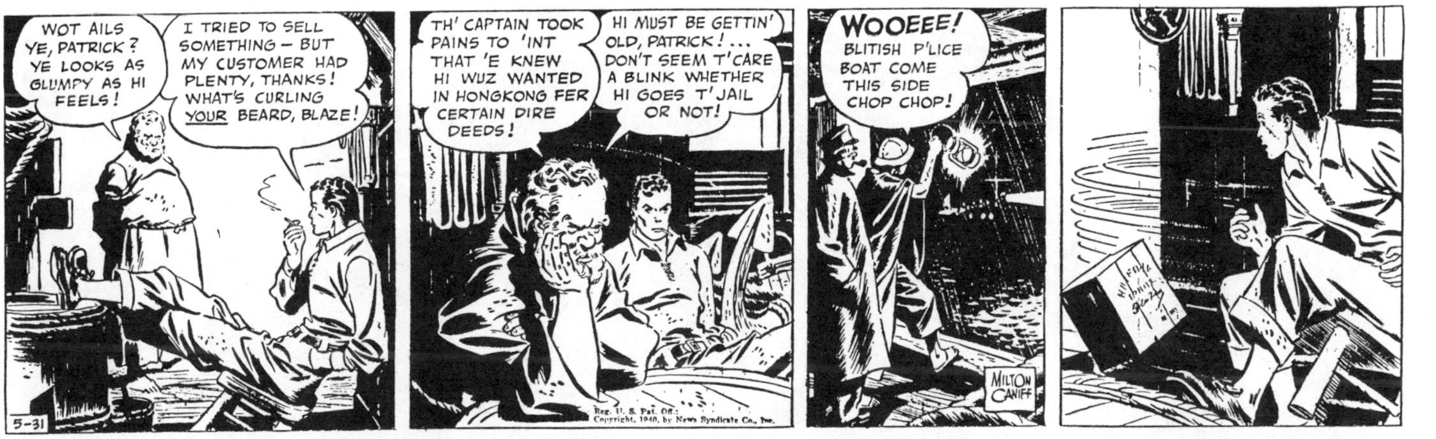
WOT AILS YE, PATRICK? YE LOOKS AS GLUMPY AS HI FEELS!
I TRIED TO SELL SOMETHING – BUT MY CUSTOMER HAD PLENTY, THANKS! WHAT'S CURLING YOUR BEARD, BLAZE!
5-31
TH' CAPTAIN TOOK PAINS TO 'INT THAT 'E KNEW HI WUZ WANTED IN HONGKONG FER CERTAIN DIRE DEEDS!
HI MUST BE GETTIN' OLD, PATRICK!... DON'T SEEM T'CARE A BLINK WHETHER HI GOES T' JAIL OR NOT!
Reg. U. S. Pat. Off.: Copyright, 1940, by News Syndicate Co., Inc.
WOOEEE! BLITISH P'LICE BOAT COME THIS SIDE CHOP CHOP!
MILTON CANIFF

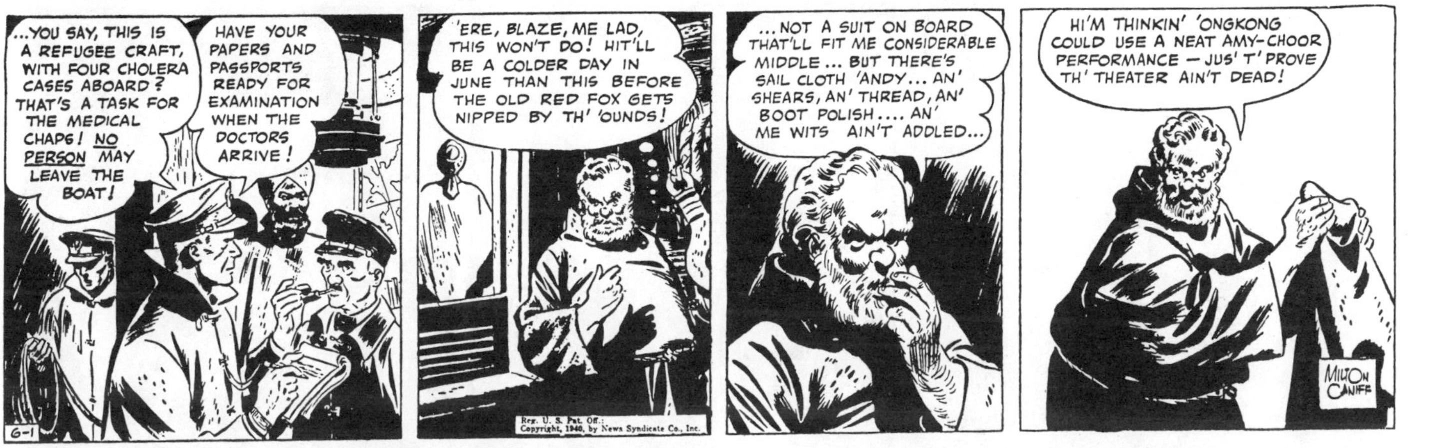
...YOU SAY, THIS IS A REFUGEE CRAFT, WITH FOUR CHOLERA CASES ABOARD? THAT'S A TASK FOR THE MEDICAL CHAPS! NO PERSON MAY LEAVE THE BOAT!
HAVE YOUR PAPERS AND PASSPORTS READY FOR EXAMINATION WHEN THE DOCTORS ARRIVE!
6-1
'ERE, BLAZE, ME LAD, THIS WON'T DO! HIT'LL BE A COLDER DAY IN JUNE THAN THIS BEFORE THE OLD RED FOX GETS NIPPED BY TH' 'OUNDS!
Reg. U. S. Pat. Off.: Copyright, 1940, by News Syndicate Co., Inc.
...NOT A SUIT ON BOARD THAT'LL FIT ME CONSIDERABLE MIDDLE ... BUT THERE'S SAIL CLOTH 'ANDY... AN' SHEARS, AN' THREAD, AN' BOOT POLISH.... AN' ME WITS AIN'T ADDLED...
HI'M THINKIN' 'ONGKONG COULD USE A NEAT AMY-CHOOR PERFORMANCE – JUS' T' PROVE TH' THEATER AIN'T DEAD!
MILTON CANIFF

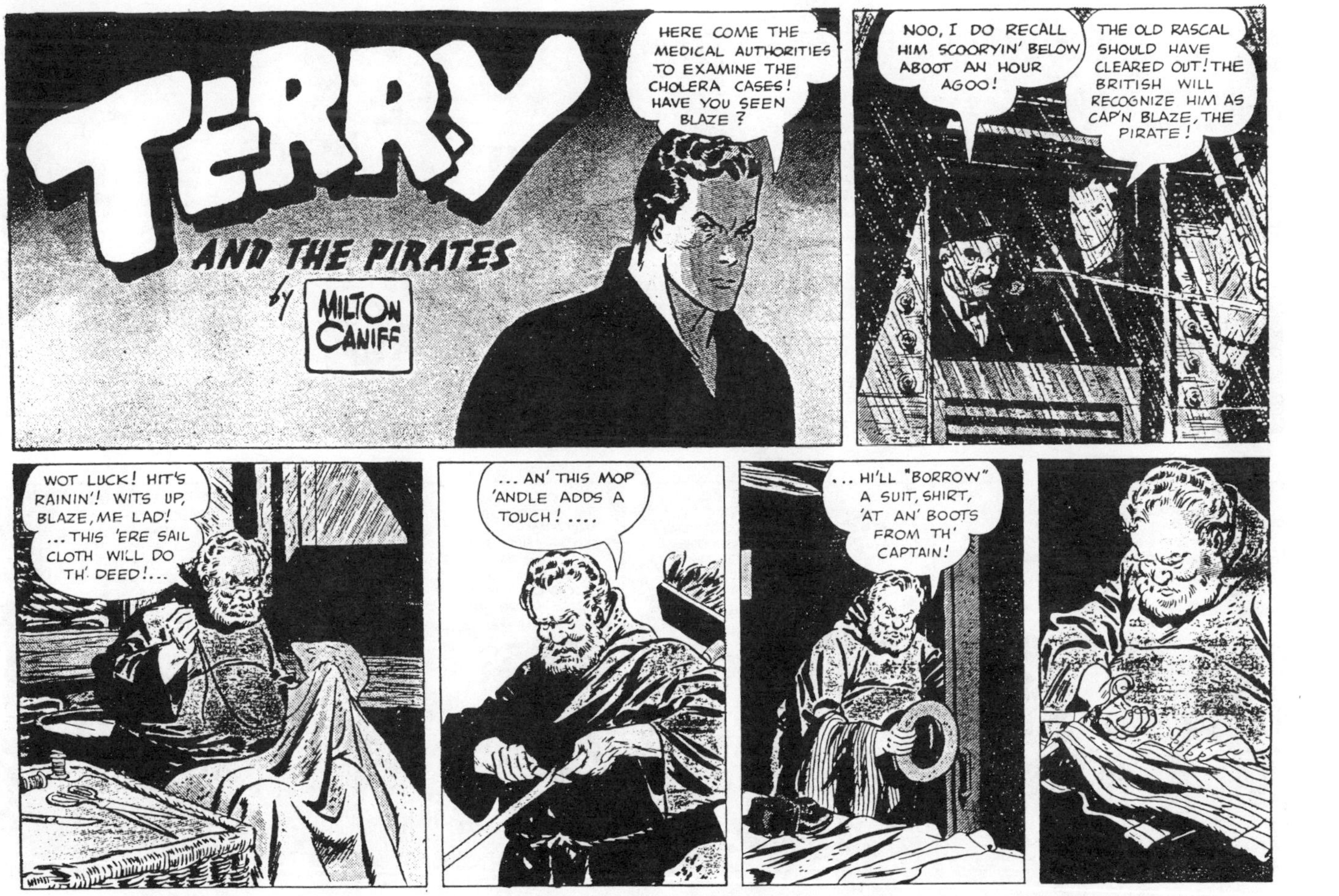
TERRY AND THE PIRATES
by MILTON CANIFF
HERE COME THE MEDICAL AUTHORITIES TO EXAMINE THE CHOLERA CASES! HAVE YOU SEEN BLAZE?
NOO, I DO RECALL HIM SCOORYIN' BELOW ABOOT AN HOUR AGOO!
THE OLD RASCAL SHOULD HAVE CLEARED OUT! THE BRITISH WILL RECOGNIZE HIM AS CAP'N BLAZE, THE PIRATE!
WOT LUCK! HIT'S RAININ'! WITS UP, BLAZE, ME LAD! ...THIS 'ERE SAIL CLOTH WILL DO TH' DEED!...
... AN' THIS MOP 'ANDLE ADDS A TOUCH! ....
... HI'LL "BORROW" A SUIT, SHIRT, 'AT AN' BOOTS FROM TH' CAPTAIN!

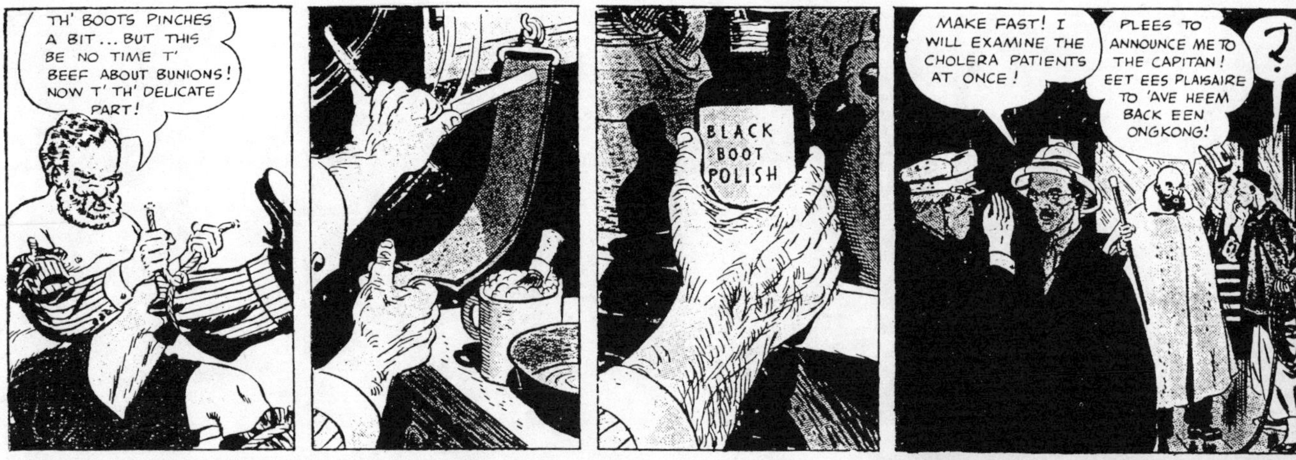
TH' BOOTS PINCHES A BIT... BUT THIS BE NO TIME T' BEEF ABOUT BUNIONS! NOW T' TH' DELICATE PART!
BLACK BOOT POLISH
MAKE FAST! I WILL EXAMINE THE CHOLERA PATIENTS AT ONCE!
PLEES TO ANNOUNCE ME TO THE CAPITAN! EET EES PLAISAIRE TO 'AVE HEEM BACK EEN ONGKONG!
?

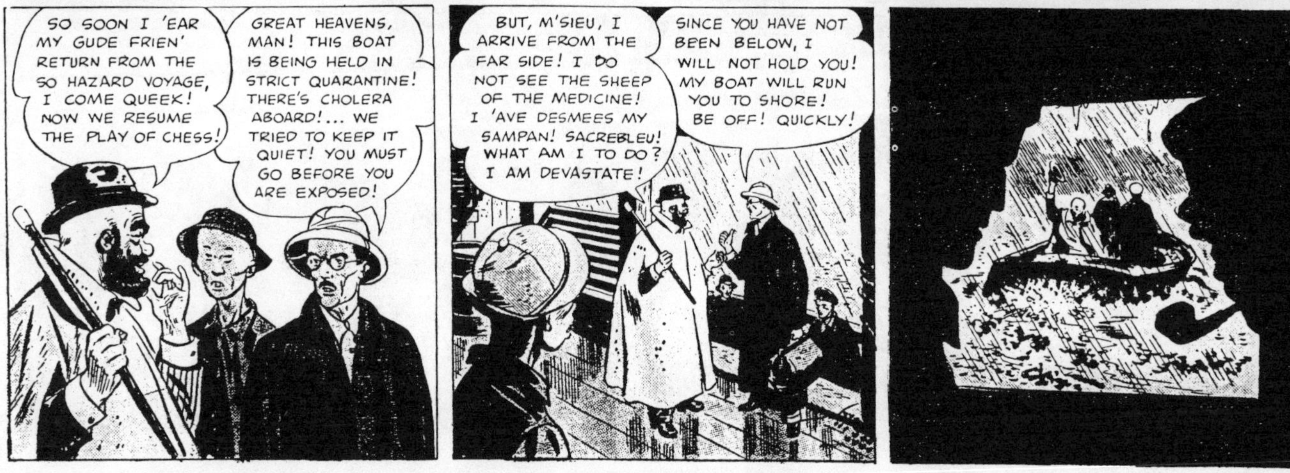
SO SOON I 'EAR MY GUDE FRIEN' RETURN FROM THE SO HAZARD VOYAGE, I COME QUEEK! NOW WE RESUME THE PLAY OF CHESS!
GREAT HEAVENS, MAN! THIS BOAT IS BEING HELD IN STRICT QUARANTINE! THERE'S CHOLERA ABOARD!... WE TRIED TO KEEP IT QUIET! YOU MUST GO BEFORE YOU ARE EXPOSED!
BUT, M'SIEU, I ARRIVE FROM THE FAR SIDE! I DO NOT SEE THE SHEEP OF THE MEDICINE! I 'AVE DESMEES MY SAMPAN! SACREBLEU! WHAT AM I TO DO? I AM DEVASTATE!
SINCE YOU HAVE NOT BEEN BELOW, I WILL NOT HOLD YOU! MY BOAT WILL RUN YOU TO SHORE! BE OFF! QUICKLY!

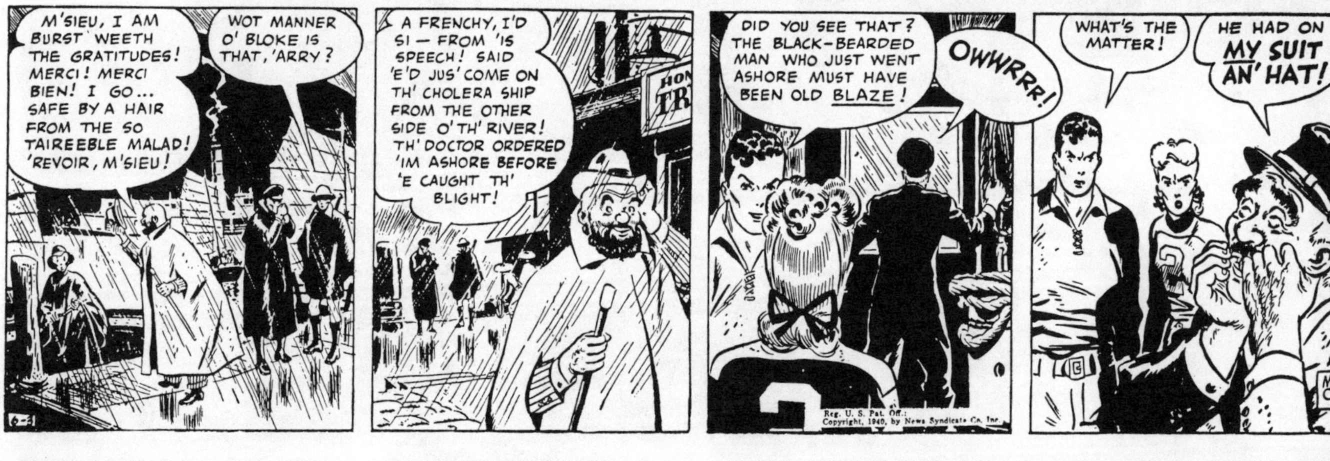
M'SIEU, I AM BURST WEETH THE GRATITUDES! MERCI! MERCI BIEN! I GO... SAFE BY A HAIR FROM THE SO TAIREEBLE MALAD! 'REVOIR, M'SIEU!
WOT MANNER O' BLOKE IS THAT, 'ARRY?
6-1
A FRENCHY, I'D SI — FROM 'IS SPEECH! SAID 'E'D JUS' COME ON TH' CHOLERA SHIP FROM THE OTHER SIDE O' TH' RIVER! TH' DOCTOR ORDERED 'IM ASHORE BEFORE 'E CAUGHT TH' BLIGHT!
DID YOU SEE THAT? THE BLACK-BEARDED MAN WHO JUST WENT ASHORE MUST HAVE BEEN OLD BLAZE!
OWWRRR!
Reg. U. S. Pat. Off.: Copyright, 1940, by News Syndicate Co. Inc.
WHAT'S THE MATTER!
HE HAD ON MY SUIT AN' HAT!
MILTON CANIFF

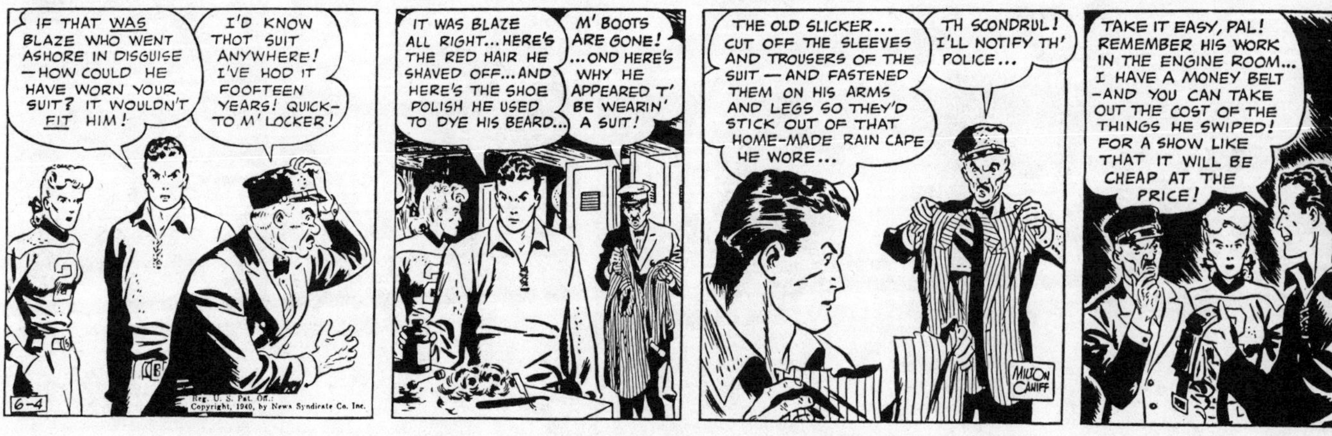
IF THAT WAS BLAZE WHO WENT ASHORE IN DISGUISE — HOW COULD HE HAVE WORN YOUR SUIT? IT WOULDN'T FIT HIM!
I'D KNOW THOT SUIT ANYWHERE! I'VE HOD IT FOOFTEEN YEARS! QUICK — TO M' LOCKER!
6-4
Reg. U. S. Pat. Off.: Copyright, 1940, by News Syndicate Co. Inc.
IT WAS BLAZE ALL RIGHT... HERE'S THE RED HAIR HE SHAVED OFF... AND HERE'S THE SHOE POLISH HE USED TO DYE HIS BEARD...
M' BOOTS ARE GONE! ...OND HERE'S WHY HE APPEARED T' BE WEARIN' A SUIT!
THE OLD SLICKER... CUT OFF THE SLEEVES AND TROUSERS OF THE SUIT — AND FASTENED THEM ON HIS ARMS AND LEGS SO THEY'D STICK OUT OF THAT HOME-MADE RAIN CAPE HE WORE...
TH SCONDRUL! I'LL NOTIFY TH' POLICE...
MILTON CANIFF
TAKE IT EASY, PAL! REMEMBER HIS WORK IN THE ENGINE ROOM... I HAVE A MONEY BELT — AND YOU CAN TAKE OUT THE COST OF THE THINGS HE SWIPED! FOR A SHOW LIKE THAT IT WILL BE CHEAP AT THE PRICE!

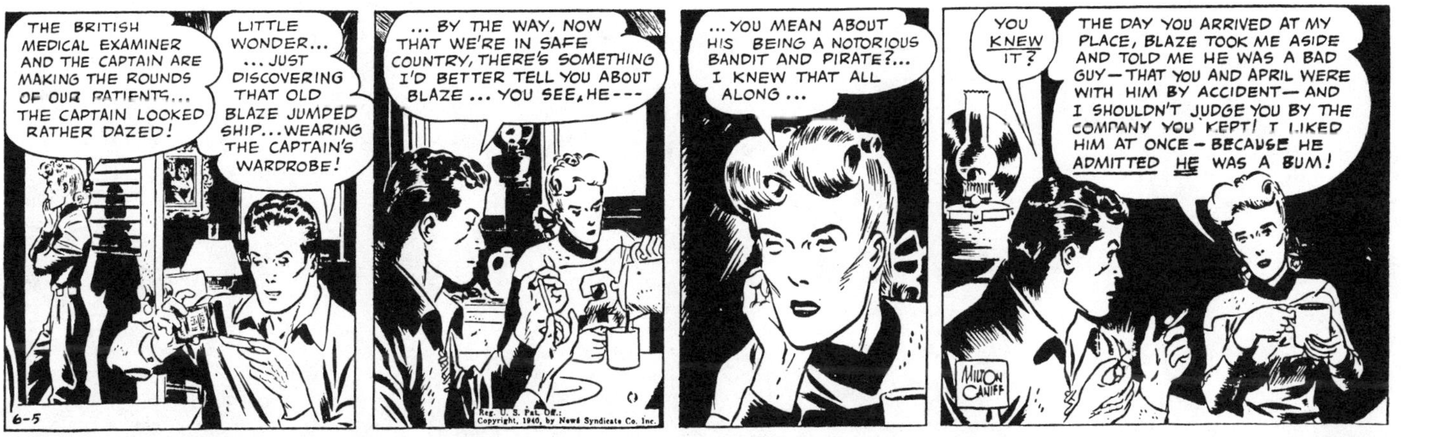
THE BRITISH MEDICAL EXAMINER AND THE CAPTAIN ARE MAKING THE ROUNDS OF OUR PATIENTS... THE CAPTAIN LOOKED RATHER DAZED!
LITTLE WONDER... ...JUST DISCOVERING THAT OLD BLAZE JUMPED SHIP...WEARING THE CAPTAIN'S WARDROBE!
...BY THE WAY, NOW THAT WE'RE IN SAFE COUNTRY, THERE'S SOMETHING I'D BETTER TELL YOU ABOUT BLAZE ... YOU SEE, HE---
...YOU MEAN ABOUT HIS BEING A NOTORIOUS BANDIT AND PIRATE?... I KNEW THAT ALL ALONG...
YOU KNEW IT?
THE DAY YOU ARRIVED AT MY PLACE, BLAZE TOOK ME ASIDE AND TOLD ME HE WAS A BAD GUY—THAT YOU AND APRIL WERE WITH HIM BY ACCIDENT—AND I SHOULDN'T JUDGE YOU BY THE COMPANY YOU KEPT! I LIKED HIM AT ONCE—BECAUSE HE ADMITTED HE WAS A BUM!
MILTON CANIFF
6-5
Reg. U. S. Pat. Off.: Copyright, 1940, by News Syndicate Co. Inc.

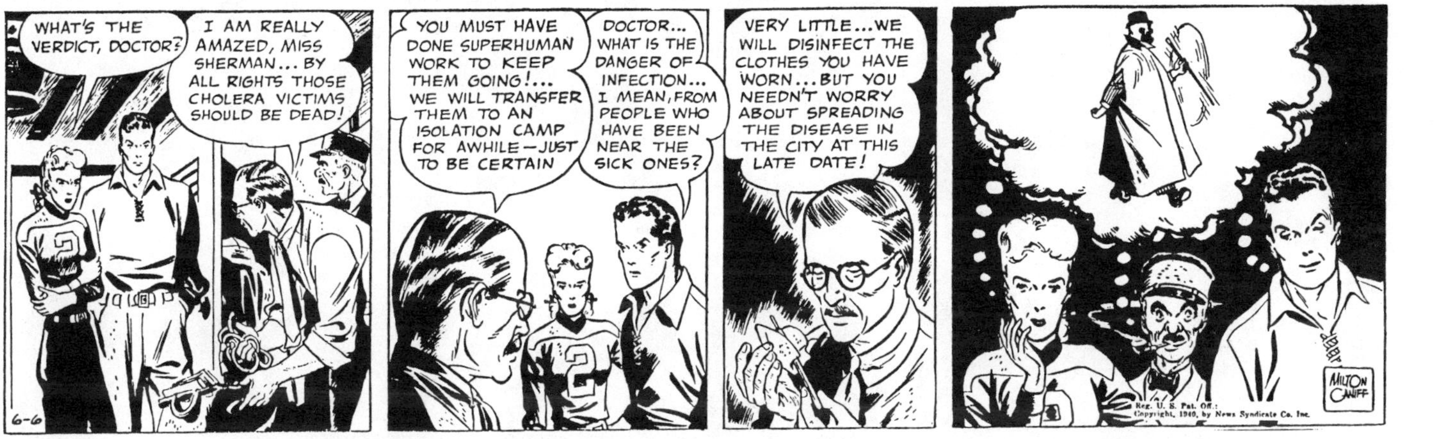
WHAT'S THE VERDICT, DOCTOR?
I AM REALLY AMAZED, MISS SHERMAN... BY ALL RIGHTS THOSE CHOLERA VICTIMS SHOULD BE DEAD!
YOU MUST HAVE DONE SUPERHUMAN WORK TO KEEP THEM GOING!... WE WILL TRANSFER THEM TO AN ISOLATION CAMP FOR AWHILE—JUST TO BE CERTAIN
DOCTOR... WHAT IS THE DANGER OF INFECTION... I MEAN, FROM PEOPLE WHO HAVE BEEN NEAR THE SICK ONES?
VERY LITTLE...WE WILL DISINFECT THE CLOTHES YOU HAVE WORN...BUT YOU NEEDN'T WORRY ABOUT SPREADING THE DISEASE IN THE CITY AT THIS LATE DATE!
MILTON CANIFF
6-6
Reg. U. S. Pat. Off.: Copyright, 1940, by News Syndicate Co. Inc.

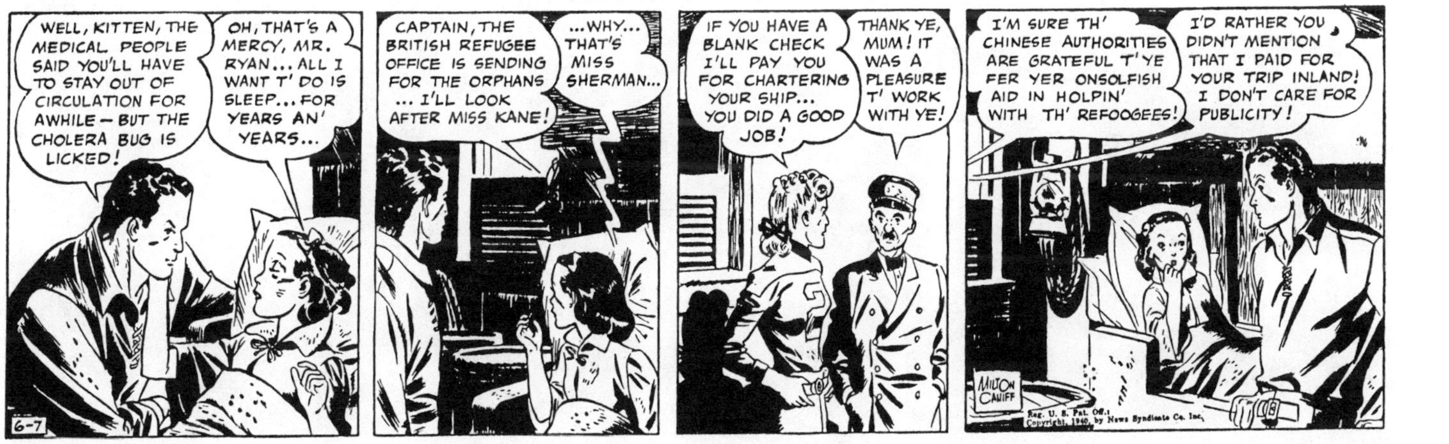
WELL, KITTEN, THE MEDICAL PEOPLE SAID YOU'LL HAVE TO STAY OUT OF CIRCULATION FOR AWHILE—BUT THE CHOLERA BUG IS LICKED!
OH, THAT'S A MERCY, MR. RYAN... ALL I WANT T' DO IS SLEEP... FOR YEARS AN' YEARS...
CAPTAIN, THE BRITISH REFUGEE OFFICE IS SENDING FOR THE ORPHANS ...I'LL LOOK AFTER MISS KANE!
...WHY... THAT'S MISS SHERMAN...
IF YOU HAVE A BLANK CHECK I'LL PAY YOU FOR CHARTERING YOUR SHIP... YOU DID A GOOD JOB!
THANK YE, MUM! IT WAS A PLEASURE T' WORK WITH YE!
I'M SURE TH' CHINESE AUTHORITIES ARE GRATEFUL T'YE FER YER ONSOLFISH AID IN HOLPIN' WITH TH' REFOOGEES!
I'D RATHER YOU DIDN'T MENTION THAT I PAID FOR YOUR TRIP INLAND! I DON'T CARE FOR PUBLICITY!
MILTON CANIFF
6-7
Reg. U. S. Pat. Off.: Copyright, 1940, by News Syndicate Co. Inc.

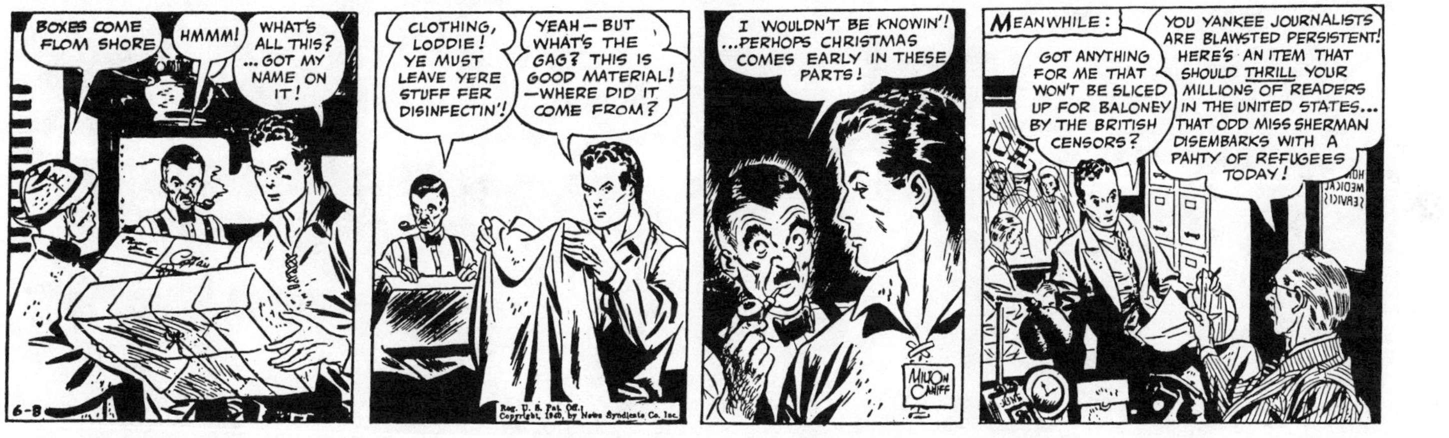
BOXES COME FLOM SHORE
HMMM!
WHAT'S ALL THIS? ...GOT MY NAME ON IT!
CLOTHING, LODDIE! YE MUST LEAVE YERE STUFF FER DISINFECTIN'!
YEAH—BUT WHAT'S THE GAG? THIS IS GOOD MATERIAL! —WHERE DID IT COME FROM?
I WOULDN'T BE KNOWIN'! ...PERHOPS CHRISTMAS COMES EARLY IN THESE PARTS!
MEANWHILE:
GOT ANYTHING FOR ME THAT WON'T BE SLICED UP FOR BALONEY BY THE BRITISH CENSORS?
YOU YANKEE JOURNALISTS ARE BLAWSTED PERSISTENT! HERE'S AN ITEM THAT SHOULD THRILL YOUR MILLIONS OF READERS IN THE UNITED STATES... THAT ODD MISS SHERMAN DISEMBARKS WITH A PAHTY OF REFUGEES TODAY!
MEDICAL SERVICES
MILTON CANIFF
6-8
Reg. U. S. Pat. Off.: Copyright, 1940, by News Syndicate Co. Inc.

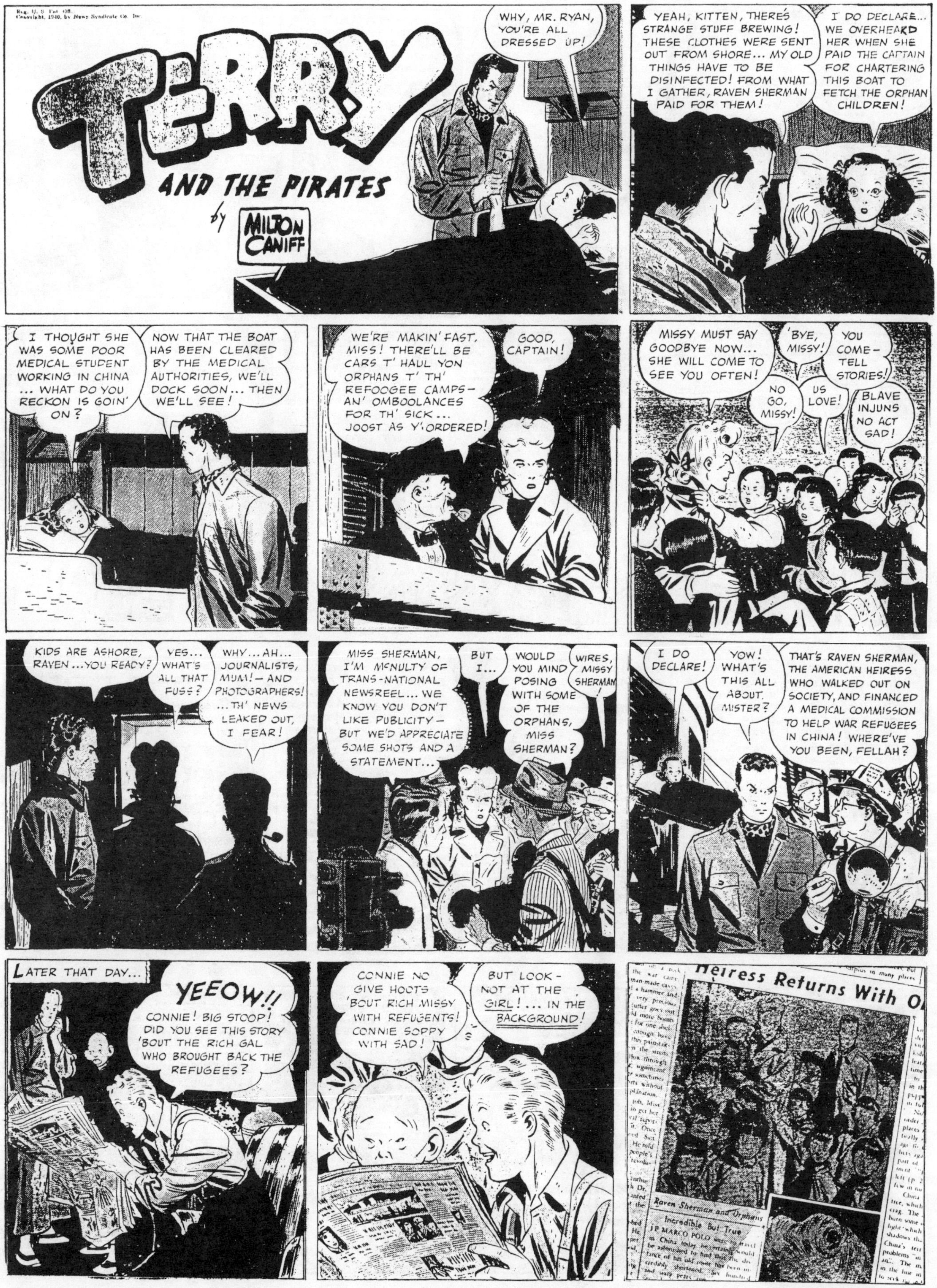

Reg. U. S. Pat. Off.
Copyright, 1940, by News Syndicate Co. Inc.
TERRY AND THE PIRATES
by MILTON CANIFF
WHY, MR. RYAN, YOU'RE ALL DRESSED UP!
YEAH, KITTEN, THERE'S STRANGE STUFF BREWING! THESE CLOTHES WERE SENT OUT FROM SHORE... MY OLD THINGS HAVE TO BE DISINFECTED! FROM WHAT I GATHER, RAVEN SHERMAN PAID FOR THEM!
I DO DECLARE... WE OVERHEARD HER WHEN SHE PAID THE CAPTAIN FOR CHARTERING THIS BOAT TO FETCH THE ORPHAN CHILDREN!
I THOUGHT SHE WAS SOME POOR MEDICAL STUDENT WORKING IN CHINA ... WHAT DO YOU RECKON IS GOIN' ON?
NOW THAT THE BOAT HAS BEEN CLEARED BY THE MEDICAL AUTHORITIES, WE'LL DOCK SOON... THEN WE'LL SEE!
WE'RE MAKIN' FAST, MISS! THERE'LL BE CARS T' HAUL YON ORPHANS T' TH' REFOOGEE CAMPS-AN' OMBOOLANCES FOR TH' SICK... JOOST AS Y' ORDERED!
GOOD, CAPTAIN!
MISSY MUST SAY GOODBYE NOW... SHE WILL COME TO SEE YOU OFTEN!
'BYE, MISSY!
YOU COME-TELL STORIES!
NO GO, MISSY!
US LOVE!
BLAVE INJUNS NO ACT SAD!
KIDS ARE ASHORE, RAVEN ... YOU READY?
YES... WHAT'S ALL THAT FUSS?
WHY... AH... JOURNALISTS, MUM!- AND PHOTOGRAPHERS! ...TH' NEWS LEAKED OUT, I FEAR!
MISS SHERMAN, I'M McNULTY OF TRANS-NATIONAL NEWSREEL... WE KNOW YOU DON'T LIKE PUBLICITY- BUT WE'D APPRECIATE SOME SHOTS AND A STATEMENT...
BUT I...
WOULD YOU MIND POSING WITH SOME OF THE ORPHANS, MISS SHERMAN?
WIRES, MISSY SHERMAN!
I DO DECLARE!
YOW! WHAT'S THIS ALL ABOUT, MISTER?
THAT'S RAVEN SHERMAN, THE AMERICAN HEIRESS WHO WALKED OUT ON SOCIETY, AND FINANCED A MEDICAL COMMISSION TO HELP WAR REFUGEES IN CHINA! WHERE'VE YOU BEEN, FELLAH?
LATER THAT DAY...
YEEOW!!
CONNIE! BIG STOOP! DID YOU SEE THIS STORY 'BOUT THE RICH GAL WHO BROUGHT BACK THE REFUGEES?
CONNIE NO GIVE HOOTS 'BOUT RICH MISSY WITH REFUGENTS! CONNIE SOPPY WITH SAD!
BUT LOOK- NOT AT THE GIRL! ... IN THE BACKGROUND!
Heiress Returns With O
Raven Sherman and Orphans
Incredible But True

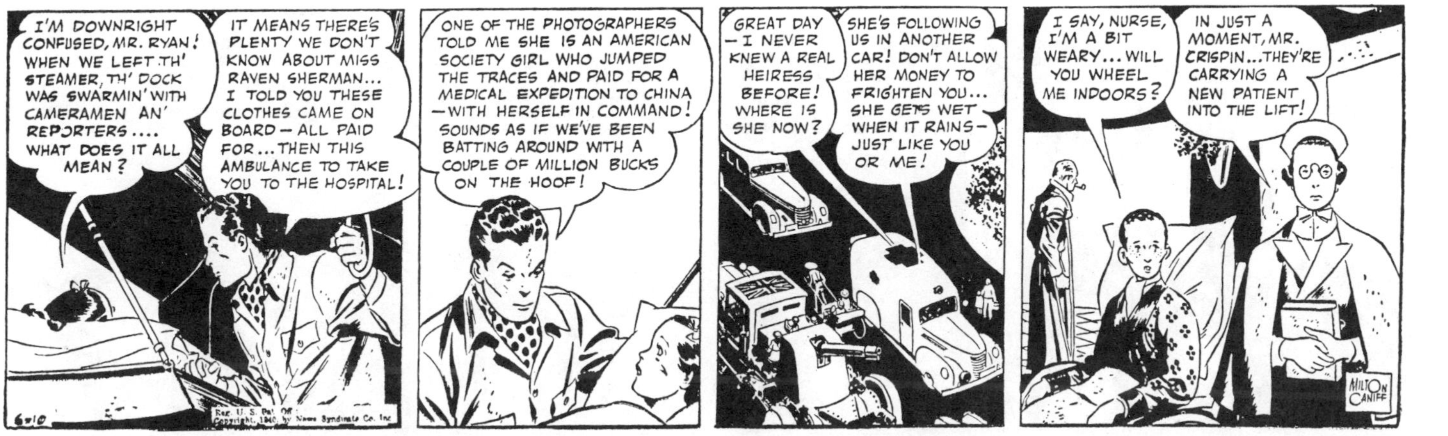
I'M DOWNRIGHT CONFUSED, MR. RYAN! WHEN WE LEFT TH' STEAMER, TH' DOCK WAS SWARMIN' WITH CAMERAMEN AN' REPORTERS.... WHAT DOES IT ALL MEAN?
IT MEANS THERE'S PLENTY WE DON'T KNOW ABOUT MISS RAVEN SHERMAN... I TOLD YOU THESE CLOTHES CAME ON BOARD — ALL PAID FOR... THEN THIS AMBULANCE TO TAKE YOU TO THE HOSPITAL!
ONE OF THE PHOTOGRAPHERS TOLD ME SHE IS AN AMERICAN SOCIETY GIRL WHO JUMPED THE TRACES AND PAID FOR A MEDICAL EXPEDITION TO CHINA — WITH HERSELF IN COMMAND! SOUNDS AS IF WE'VE BEEN BATTING AROUND WITH A COUPLE OF MILLION BUCKS ON THE HOOF!
GREAT DAY — I NEVER KNEW A REAL HEIRESS BEFORE! WHERE IS SHE NOW?
SHE'S FOLLOWING US IN ANOTHER CAR! DON'T ALLOW HER MONEY TO FRIGHTEN YOU... SHE GETS WET WHEN IT RAINS — JUST LIKE YOU OR ME!
I SAY, NURSE, I'M A BIT WEARY... WILL YOU WHEEL ME INDOORS?
IN JUST A MOMENT, MR. CRISPIN... THEY'RE CARRYING A NEW PATIENT INTO THE LIFT!
6-10
Reg. U. S. Pat. Off.: Copyright, 1940, by News Syndicate Co. Inc.
MILTON CANIFF

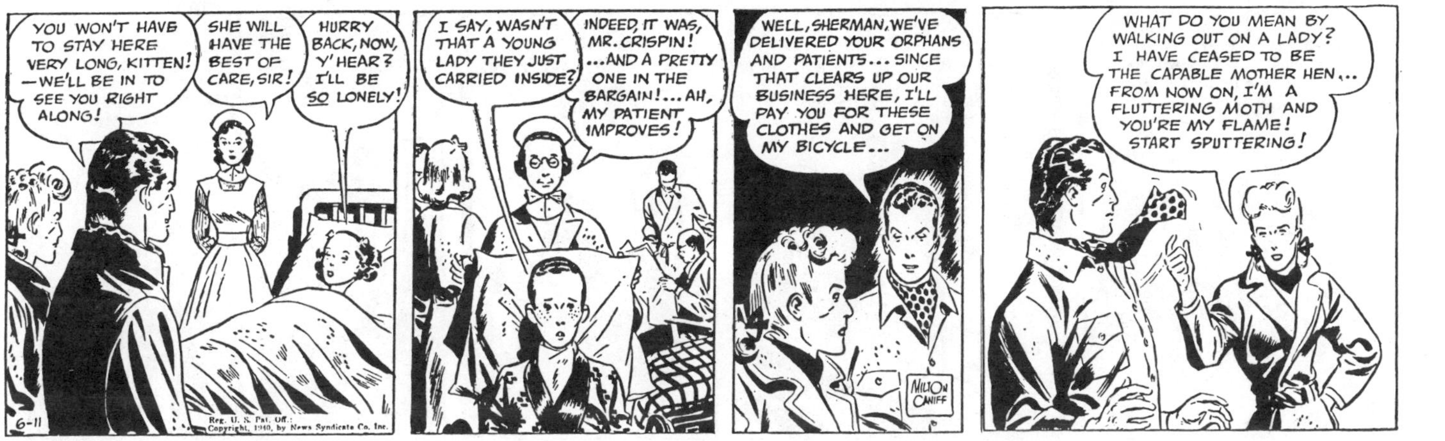
YOU WON'T HAVE TO STAY HERE VERY LONG, KITTEN! — WE'LL BE IN TO SEE YOU RIGHT ALONG!
SHE WILL HAVE THE BEST OF CARE, SIR!
HURRY BACK, NOW, Y' HEAR? I'LL BE SO LONELY!
I SAY, WASN'T THAT A YOUNG LADY THEY JUST CARRIED INSIDE?
INDEED, IT WAS, MR. CRISPIN! ...AND A PRETTY ONE IN THE BARGAIN!... AH, MY PATIENT IMPROVES!
WELL, SHERMAN, WE'VE DELIVERED YOUR ORPHANS AND PATIENTS... SINCE THAT CLEARS UP OUR BUSINESS HERE, I'LL PAY YOU FOR THESE CLOTHES AND GET ON MY BICYCLE...
WHAT DO YOU MEAN BY WALKING OUT ON A LADY? I HAVE CEASED TO BE THE CAPABLE MOTHER HEN... FROM NOW ON, I'M A FLUTTERING MOTH AND YOU'RE MY FLAME! START SPUTTERING!
6-11
Reg. U. S. Pat. Off.: Copyright, 1940, by News Syndicate Co. Inc.
MILTON CANIFF

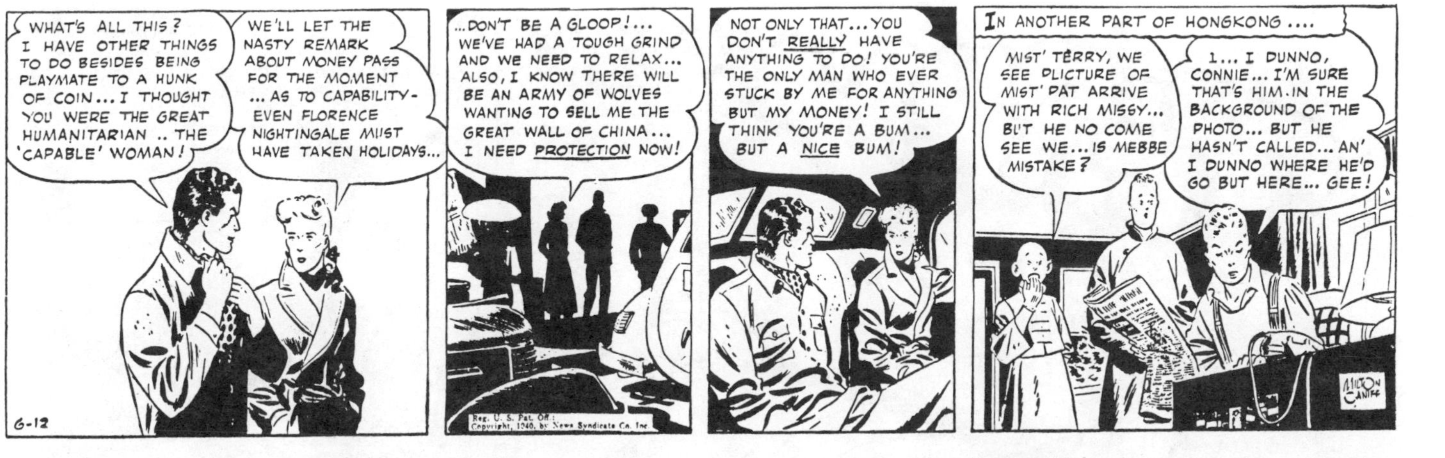
WHAT'S ALL THIS? I HAVE OTHER THINGS TO DO BESIDES BEING PLAYMATE TO A HUNK OF COIN... I THOUGHT YOU WERE THE GREAT HUMANITARIAN .. THE 'CAPABLE' WOMAN!
WE'LL LET THE NASTY REMARK ABOUT MONEY PASS FOR THE MOMENT ... AS TO CAPABILITY - EVEN FLORENCE NIGHTINGALE MUST HAVE TAKEN HOLIDAYS...
...DON'T BE A GLOOP!... WE'VE HAD A TOUGH GRIND AND WE NEED TO RELAX... ALSO, I KNOW THERE WILL BE AN ARMY OF WOLVES WANTING TO SELL ME THE GREAT WALL OF CHINA... I NEED PROTECTION NOW!
NOT ONLY THAT... YOU DON'T REALLY HAVE ANYTHING TO DO! YOU'RE THE ONLY MAN WHO EVER STUCK BY ME FOR ANYTHING BUT MY MONEY! I STILL THINK YOU'RE A BUM... BUT A NICE BUM!
IN ANOTHER PART OF HONGKONG ....
MIST' TERRY, WE SEE PLICTURE OF MIST' PAT ARRIVE WITH RICH MISSY... BUT HE NO COME SEE WE... IS MEBBE MISTAKE?
I... I DUNNO, CONNIE... I'M SURE THAT'S HIM IN THE BACKGROUND OF THE PHOTO... BUT HE HASN'T CALLED... AN' I DUNNO WHERE HE'D GO BUT HERE... GEE!
6-12
Reg. U. S. Pat. Off.: Copyright, 1940, by News Syndicate Co. Inc.
MILTON CANIFF

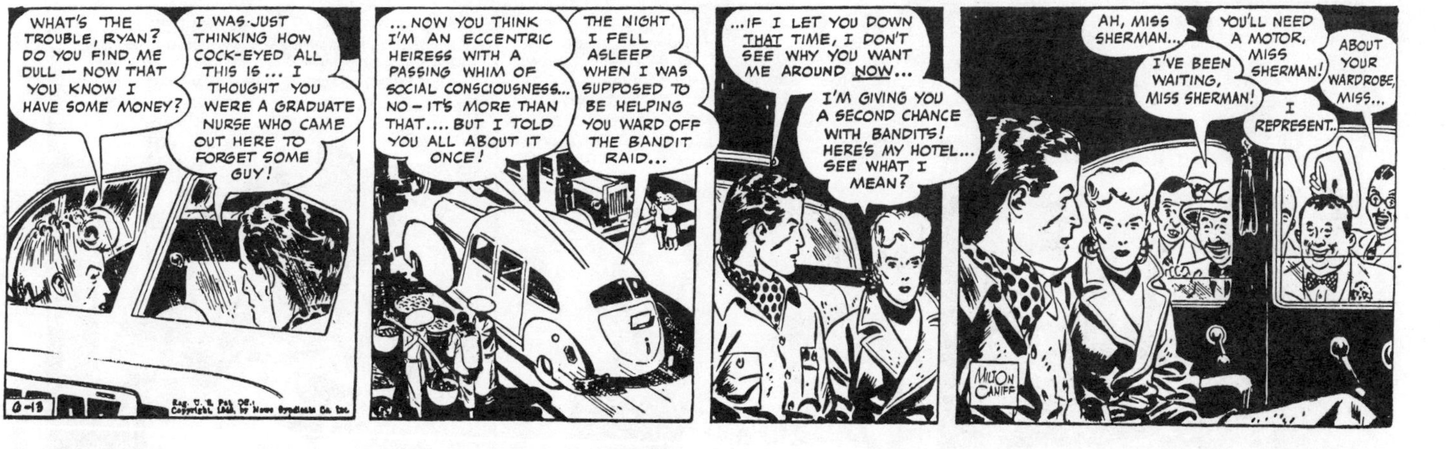
WHAT'S THE TROUBLE, RYAN? DO YOU FIND ME DULL — NOW THAT YOU KNOW I HAVE SOME MONEY?
I WAS JUST THINKING HOW COCK-EYED ALL THIS IS... I THOUGHT YOU WERE A GRADUATE NURSE WHO CAME OUT HERE TO FORGET SOME GUY!
... NOW YOU THINK I'M AN ECCENTRIC HEIRESS WITH A PASSING WHIM OF SOCIAL CONSCIOUSNESS... NO — IT'S MORE THAN THAT.... BUT I TOLD YOU ALL ABOUT IT ONCE!
THE NIGHT I FELL ASLEEP WHEN I WAS SUPPOSED TO BE HELPING YOU WARD OFF THE BANDIT RAID...
...IF I LET YOU DOWN THAT TIME, I DON'T SEE WHY YOU WANT ME AROUND NOW...
I'M GIVING YOU A SECOND CHANCE WITH BANDITS! HERE'S MY HOTEL... SEE WHAT I MEAN?
AH, MISS SHERMAN...
I'VE BEEN WAITING, MISS SHERMAN!
YOU'LL NEED A MOTOR, MISS SHERMAN!
I REPRESENT...
ABOUT YOUR WARDROBE, MISS...
6-13
Reg. U. S. Pat. Off.: Copyright, 1940, by News Syndicate Co. Inc.
MILTON CANIFF

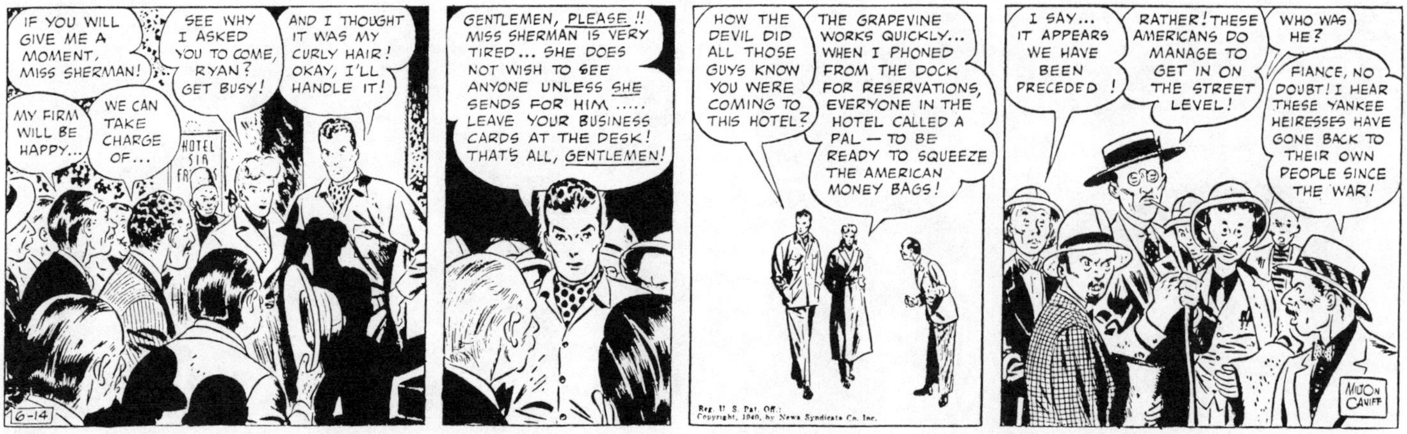
IF YOU WILL GIVE ME A MOMENT, MISS SHERMAN!
MY FIRM WILL BE HAPPY...
WE CAN TAKE CHARGE OF...
SEE WHY I ASKED YOU TO COME, RYAN? GET BUSY!
AND I THOUGHT IT WAS MY CURLY HAIR! OKAY, I'LL HANDLE IT!
HOTEL SIR FRA
6-14
GENTLEMEN, PLEASE!! MISS SHERMAN IS VERY TIRED... SHE DOES NOT WISH TO SEE ANYONE UNLESS SHE SENDS FOR HIM..... LEAVE YOUR BUSINESS CARDS AT THE DESK! THAT'S ALL, GENTLEMEN!
HOW THE DEVIL DID ALL THOSE GUYS KNOW YOU WERE COMING TO THIS HOTEL?
THE GRAPEVINE WORKS QUICKLY... WHEN I PHONED FROM THE DOCK FOR RESERVATIONS, EVERYONE IN THE HOTEL CALLED A PAL — TO BE READY TO SQUEEZE THE AMERICAN MONEY BAGS!
Reg. U. S. Pat. Off.: Copyright, 1940, by News Syndicate Co. Inc.
I SAY... IT APPEARS WE HAVE BEEN PRECEDED!
RATHER! THESE AMERICANS DO MANAGE TO GET IN ON THE STREET LEVEL!
WHO WAS HE?
FIANCE, NO DOUBT! I HEAR THESE YANKEE HEIRESSES HAVE GONE BACK TO THEIR OWN PEOPLE SINCE THE WAR!
MILTON CANIFF

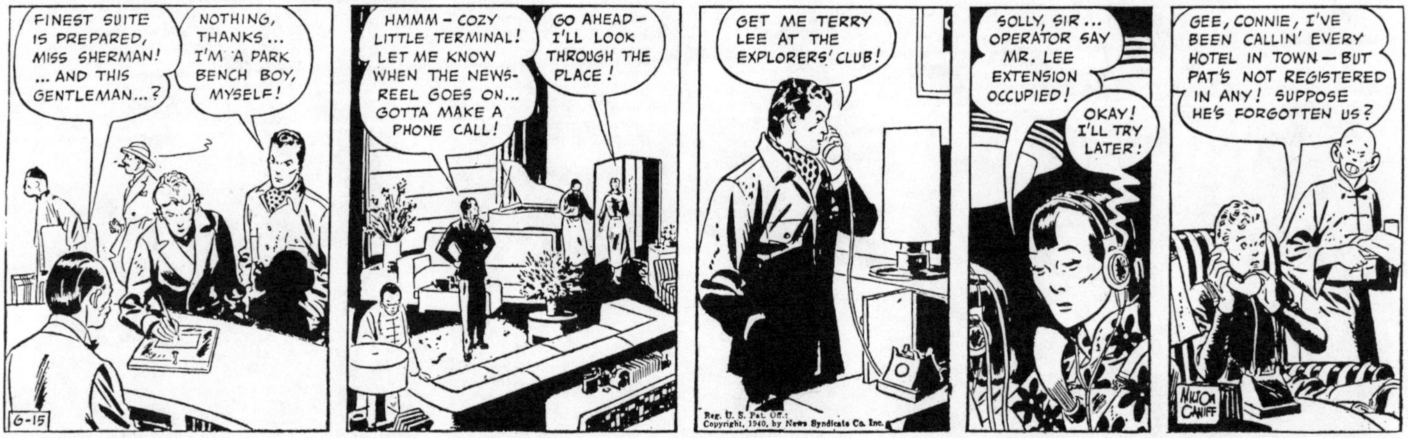
FINEST SUITE IS PREPARED, MISS SHERMAN! ... AND THIS GENTLEMAN...?
NOTHING, THANKS... I'M A PARK BENCH BOY, MYSELF!
6-15
HMMM - COZY LITTLE TERMINAL! LET ME KNOW WHEN THE NEWS-REEL GOES ON... GOTTA MAKE A PHONE CALL!
GO AHEAD - I'LL LOOK THROUGH THE PLACE!
GET ME TERRY LEE AT THE EXPLORERS' CLUB!
Reg. U. S. Pat. Off.: Copyright, 1940, by News Syndicate Co. Inc.
SOLLY, SIR... OPERATOR SAY MR. LEE EXTENSION OCCUPIED!
OKAY! I'LL TRY LATER!
GEE, CONNIE, I'VE BEEN CALLIN' EVERY HOTEL IN TOWN — BUT PAT'S NOT REGISTERED IN ANY! SUPPOSE HE'S FORGOTTEN US?
MILTON CANIFF

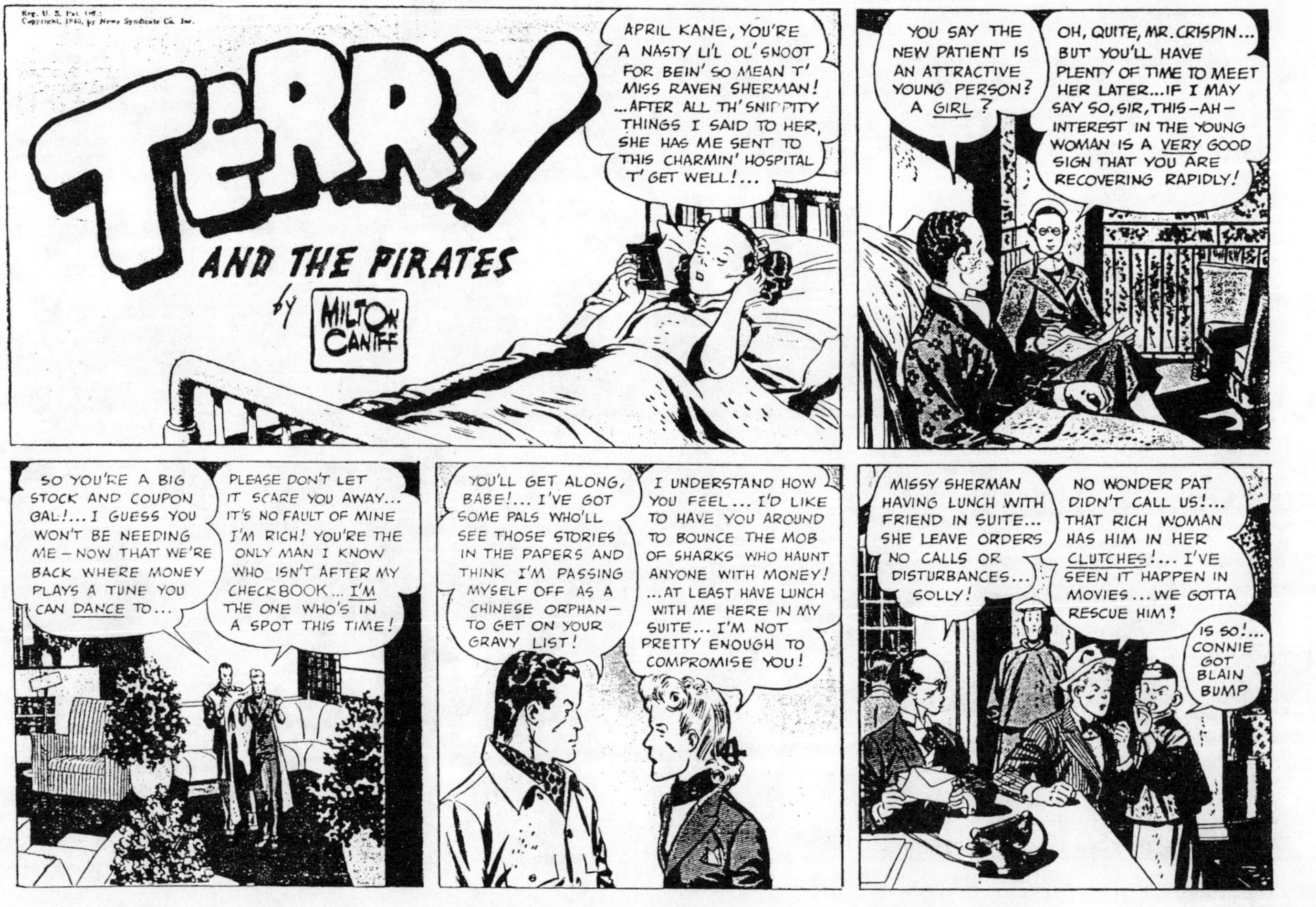
Reg. U. S. Pat. Off.: Copyright, 1940, by News Syndicate Co. Inc.
TERRY AND THE PIRATES
by MILTON CANIFF
APRIL KANE, YOU'RE A NASTY LI'L OL' SNOOT FOR BEIN' SO MEAN T' MISS RAVEN SHERMAN! ...AFTER ALL TH' SNIPPITY THINGS I SAID TO HER, SHE HAS ME SENT TO THIS CHARMIN' HOSPITAL T' GET WELL!...
YOU SAY THE NEW PATIENT IS AN ATTRACTIVE YOUNG PERSON? A GIRL?
OH, QUITE, MR. CRISPIN... BUT YOU'LL HAVE PLENTY OF TIME TO MEET HER LATER... IF I MAY SAY SO, SIR, THIS - AH - INTEREST IN THE YOUNG WOMAN IS A VERY GOOD SIGN THAT YOU ARE RECOVERING RAPIDLY!
SO YOU'RE A BIG STOCK AND COUPON GAL!... I GUESS YOU WON'T BE NEEDING ME — NOW THAT WE'RE BACK WHERE MONEY PLAYS A TUNE YOU CAN DANCE TO...
PLEASE DON'T LET IT SCARE YOU AWAY... IT'S NO FAULT OF MINE I'M RICH! YOU'RE THE ONLY MAN I KNOW WHO ISN'T AFTER MY CHECKBOOK... I'M THE ONE WHO'S IN A SPOT THIS TIME!
YOU'LL GET ALONG, BABE!... I'VE GOT SOME PALS WHO'LL SEE THOSE STORIES IN THE PAPERS AND THINK I'M PASSING MYSELF OFF AS A CHINESE ORPHAN — TO GET ON YOUR GRAVY LIST!
I UNDERSTAND HOW YOU FEEL... I'D LIKE TO HAVE YOU AROUND TO BOUNCE THE MOB OF SHARKS WHO HAUNT ANYONE WITH MONEY! ...AT LEAST HAVE LUNCH WITH ME HERE IN MY SUITE... I'M NOT PRETTY ENOUGH TO COMPROMISE YOU!
MISSY SHERMAN HAVING LUNCH WITH FRIEND IN SUITE... SHE LEAVE ORDERS NO CALLS OR DISTURBANCES... SOLLY!
NO WONDER PAT DIDN'T CALL US!... THAT RICH WOMAN HAS HIM IN HER CLUTCHES!... I'VE SEEN IT HAPPEN IN MOVIES... WE GOTTA RESCUE HIM!
IS SO!... CONNIE GOT BLAIN BUMP

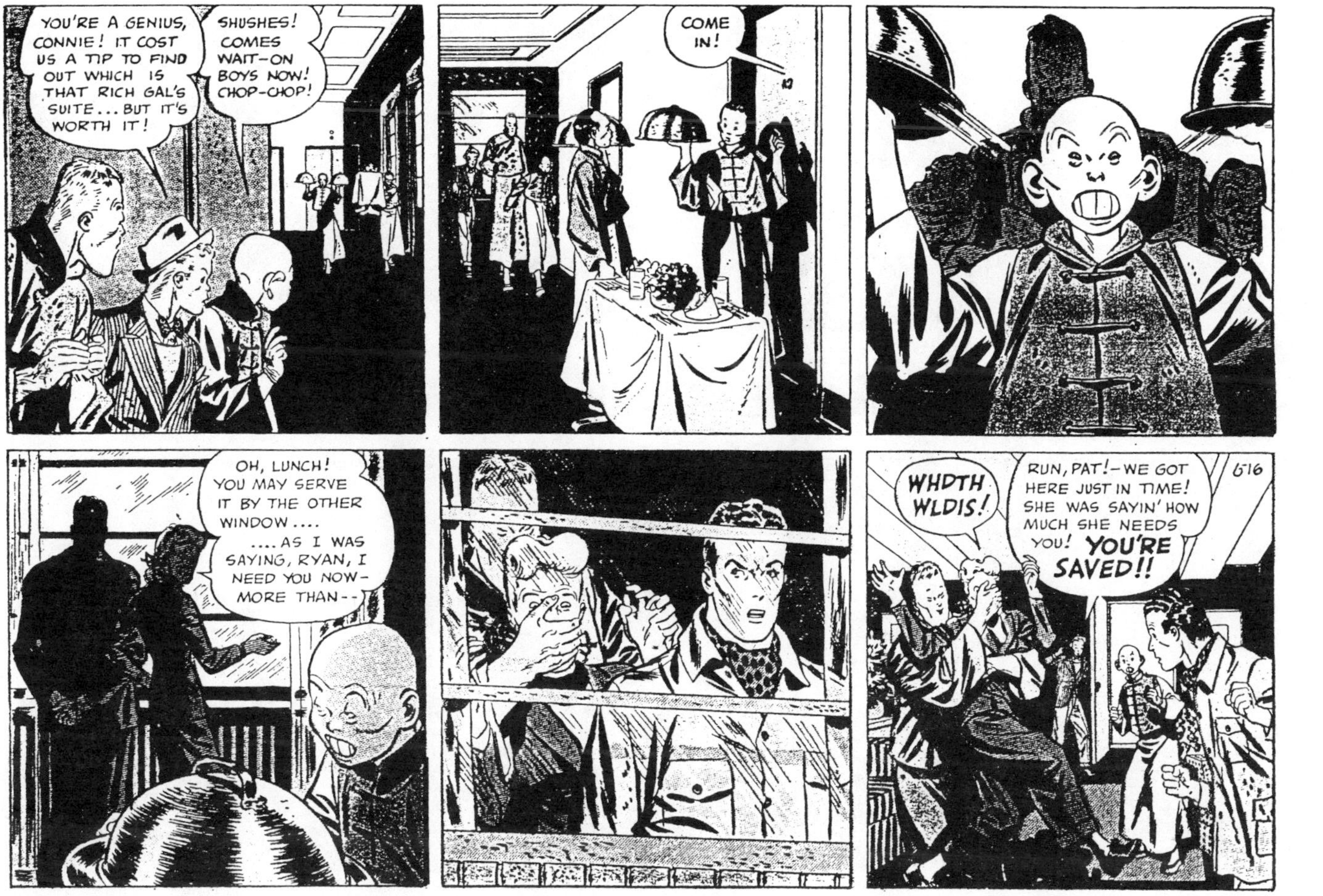
YOU'RE A GENIUS, CONNIE! IT COST US A TIP TO FIND OUT WHICH IS THAT RICH GAL'S SUITE... BUT IT'S WORTH IT!
SHUSHES! COMES WAIT-ON BOYS NOW! CHOP-CHOP!
COME IN!
OH, LUNCH! YOU MAY SERVE IT BY THE OTHER WINDOW....
....AS I WAS SAYING, RYAN, I NEED YOU NOW-MORE THAN--
6-16
WHDTH WLDIS!
RUN, PAT!—WE GOT HERE JUST IN TIME! SHE WAS SAYIN' HOW MUCH SHE NEEDS YOU! YOU'RE SAVED!!

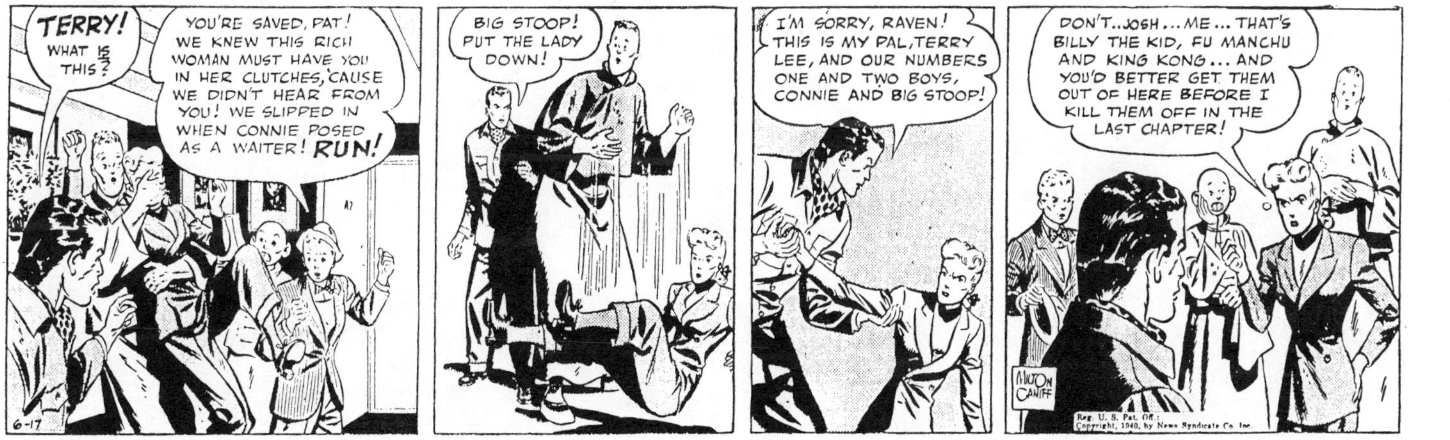
TERRY! WHAT IS THIS?
YOU'RE SAVED, PAT! WE KNEW THIS RICH WOMAN MUST HAVE YOU IN HER CLUTCHES, 'CAUSE WE DIDN'T HEAR FROM YOU! WE SLIPPED IN WHEN CONNIE POSED AS A WAITER! RUN!
6-17
BIG STOOP! PUT THE LADY DOWN!
I'M SORRY, RAVEN! THIS IS MY PAL, TERRY LEE, AND OUR NUMBERS ONE AND TWO BOYS, CONNIE AND BIG STOOP!
DON'T...JOSH...ME...THAT'S BILLY THE KID, FU MANCHU AND KING KONG... AND YOU'D BETTER GET THEM OUT OF HERE BEFORE I KILL THEM OFF IN THE LAST CHAPTER!
MILTON CANIFF
Reg. U. S. Pat. Off.:
Copyright, 1940, by News Syndicate Co. Inc.

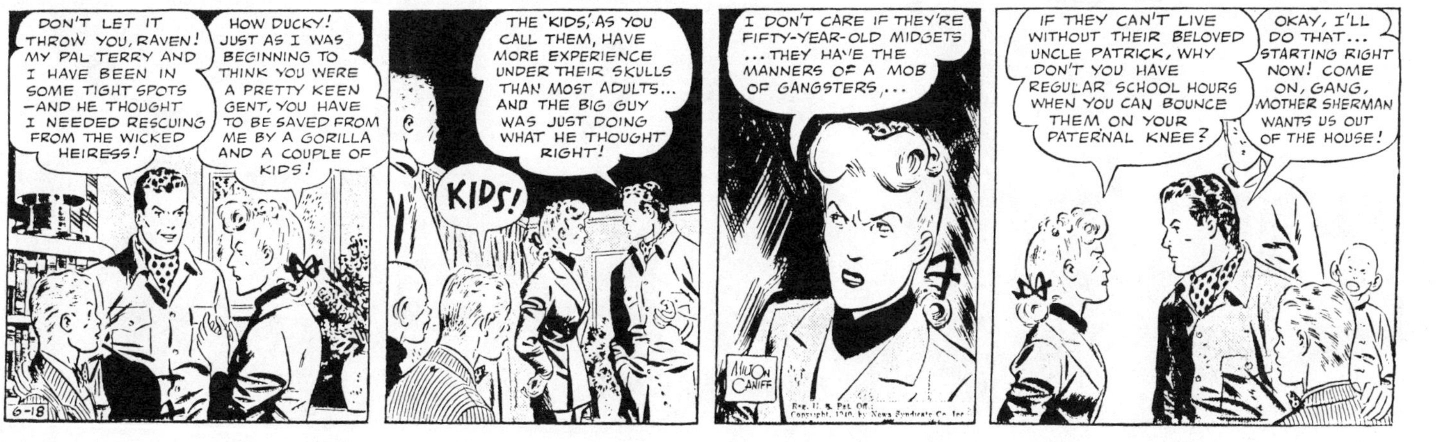
DON'T LET IT THROW YOU, RAVEN! MY PAL TERRY AND I HAVE BEEN IN SOME TIGHT SPOTS —AND HE THOUGHT I NEEDED RESCUING FROM THE WICKED HEIRESS!
HOW DUCKY! JUST AS I WAS BEGINNING TO THINK YOU WERE A PRETTY KEEN GENT, YOU HAVE TO BE SAVED FROM ME BY A GORILLA AND A COUPLE OF KIDS!
6-18
THE 'KIDS,' AS YOU CALL THEM, HAVE MORE EXPERIENCE UNDER THEIR SKULLS THAN MOST ADULTS... AND THE BIG GUY WAS JUST DOING WHAT HE THOUGHT RIGHT!
KIDS!
I DON'T CARE IF THEY'RE FIFTY-YEAR-OLD MIDGETS ...THEY HAVE THE MANNERS OF A MOB OF GANGSTERS,...
MILTON CANIFF
IF THEY CAN'T LIVE WITHOUT THEIR BELOVED UNCLE PATRICK, WHY DON'T YOU HAVE REGULAR SCHOOL HOURS WHEN YOU CAN BOUNCE THEM ON YOUR PATERNAL KNEE?
OKAY, I'LL DO THAT... STARTING RIGHT NOW! COME ON, GANG, MOTHER SHERMAN WANTS US OUT OF THE HOUSE!

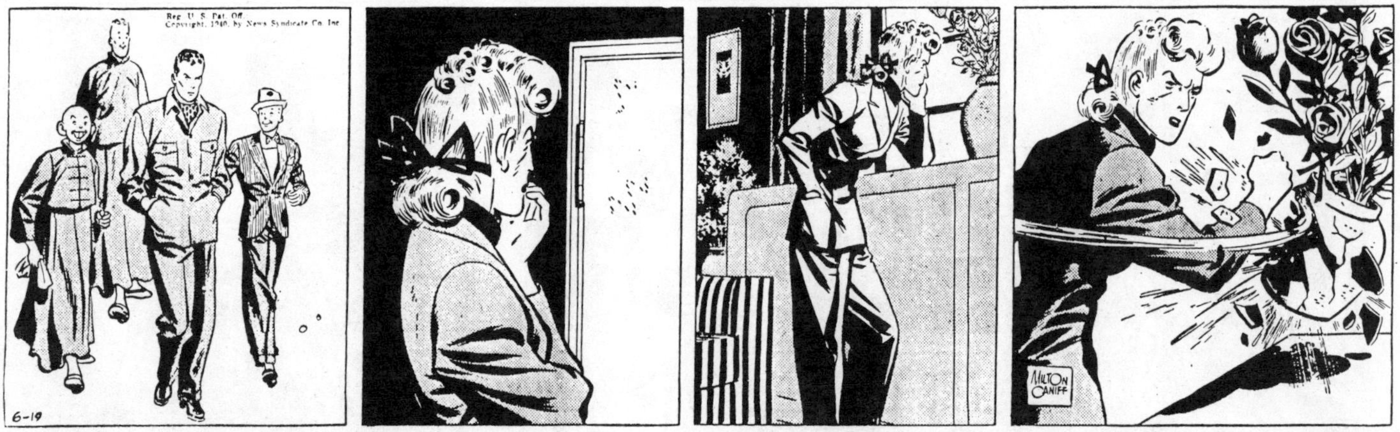
Reg. U. S. Pat. Off.
Copyright, 1940, by News Syndicate Co. Inc.
6-19
MILTON CANIFF

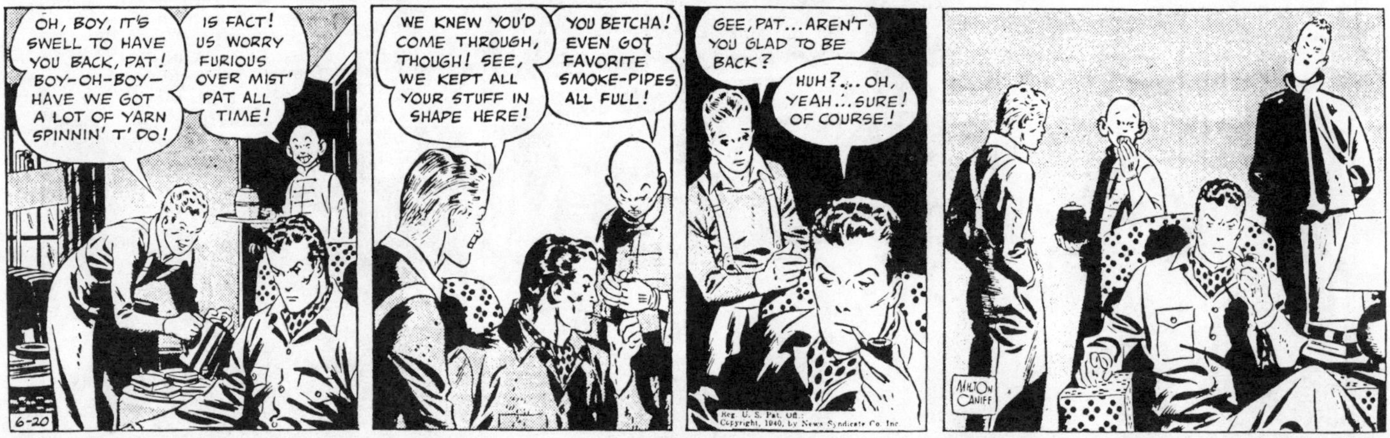
OH, BOY, IT'S SWELL TO HAVE YOU BACK, PAT! BOY-OH-BOY—HAVE WE GOT A LOT OF YARN SPINNIN' T' DO!
IS FACT! US WORRY FURIOUS OVER MIST' PAT ALL TIME!
WE KNEW YOU'D COME THROUGH, THOUGH! SEE, WE KEPT ALL YOUR STUFF IN SHAPE HERE!
YOU BETCHA! EVEN GOT FAVORITE SMOKE-PIPES ALL FULL!
GEE, PAT... AREN'T YOU GLAD TO BE BACK?
HUH?... OH, YEAH... SURE! OF COURSE!
6-20
Reg. U. S. Pat. Off.
Copyright, 1940, by News Syndicate Co. Inc.
MILTON CANIFF

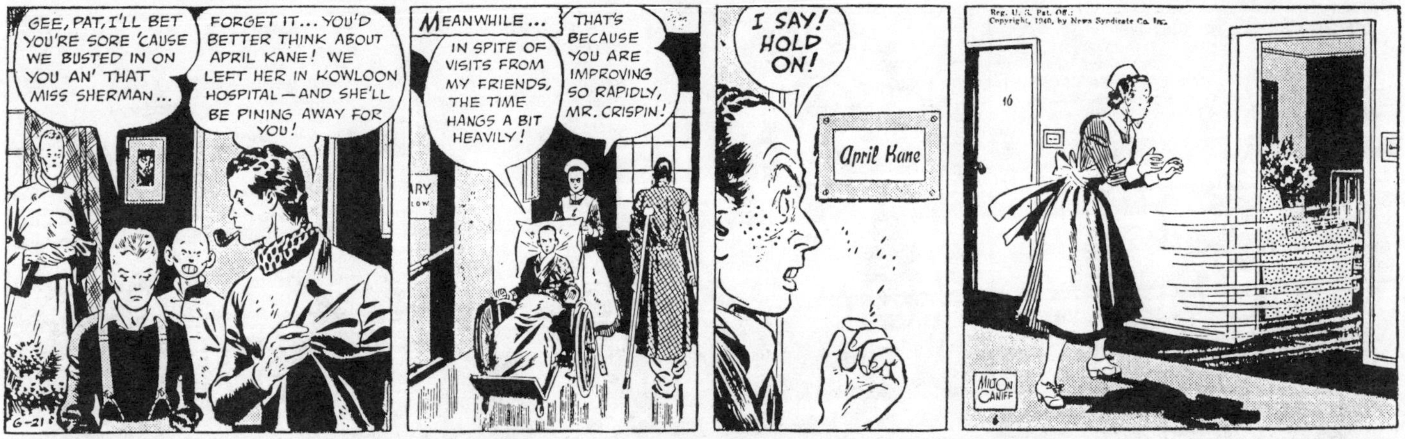
GEE, PAT, I'LL BET YOU'RE SORE 'CAUSE WE BUSTED IN ON YOU AN' THAT MISS SHERMAN...
FORGET IT... YOU'D BETTER THINK ABOUT APRIL KANE! WE LEFT HER IN KOWLOON HOSPITAL—AND SHE'LL BE PINING AWAY FOR YOU!
6-21
MEANWHILE...
IN SPITE OF VISITS FROM MY FRIENDS, THE TIME HANGS A BIT HEAVILY!
THAT'S BECAUSE YOU ARE IMPROVING SO RAPIDLY, MR. CRISPIN!
I SAY! HOLD ON!
April Kane
Reg. U. S. Pat. Off.
Copyright, 1940, by News Syndicate Co. Inc.
16
MILTON CANIFF

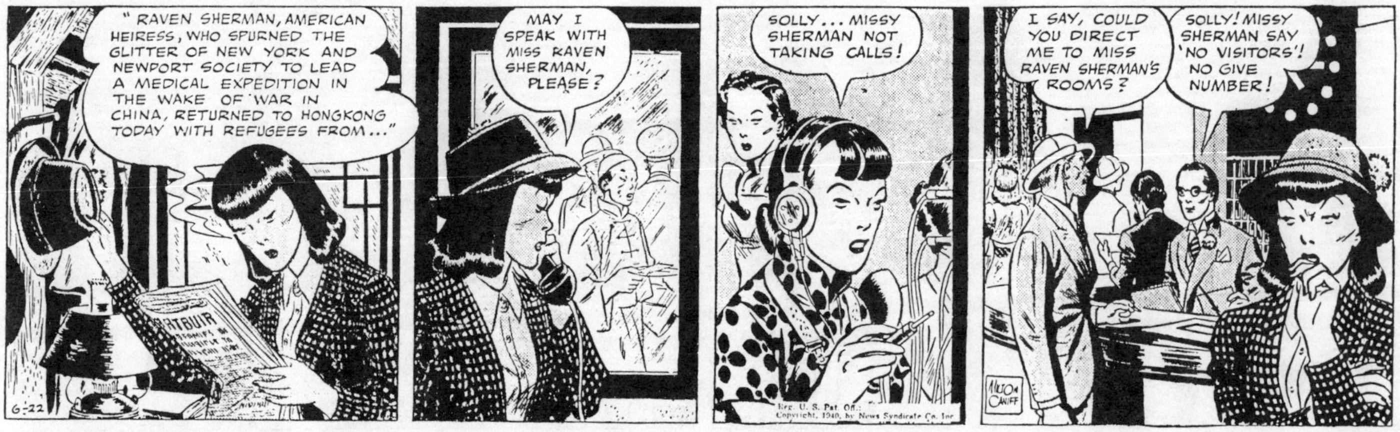
" RAVEN SHERMAN, AMERICAN HEIRESS, WHO SPURNED THE GLITTER OF NEW YORK AND NEWPORT SOCIETY TO LEAD A MEDICAL EXPEDITION IN THE WAKE OF WAR IN CHINA, RETURNED TO HONGKONG TODAY WITH REFUGEES FROM..."
6-22
MAY I SPEAK WITH MISS RAVEN SHERMAN, PLEASE?
SOLLY... MISSY SHERMAN NOT TAKING CALLS!
Reg. U. S. Pat. Off.
Copyright, 1940, by News Syndicate Co. Inc.
I SAY, COULD YOU DIRECT ME TO MISS RAVEN SHERMAN'S ROOMS?
SOLLY! MISSY SHERMAN SAY 'NO VISITORS'! NO GIVE NUMBER!
MILTON CANIFF

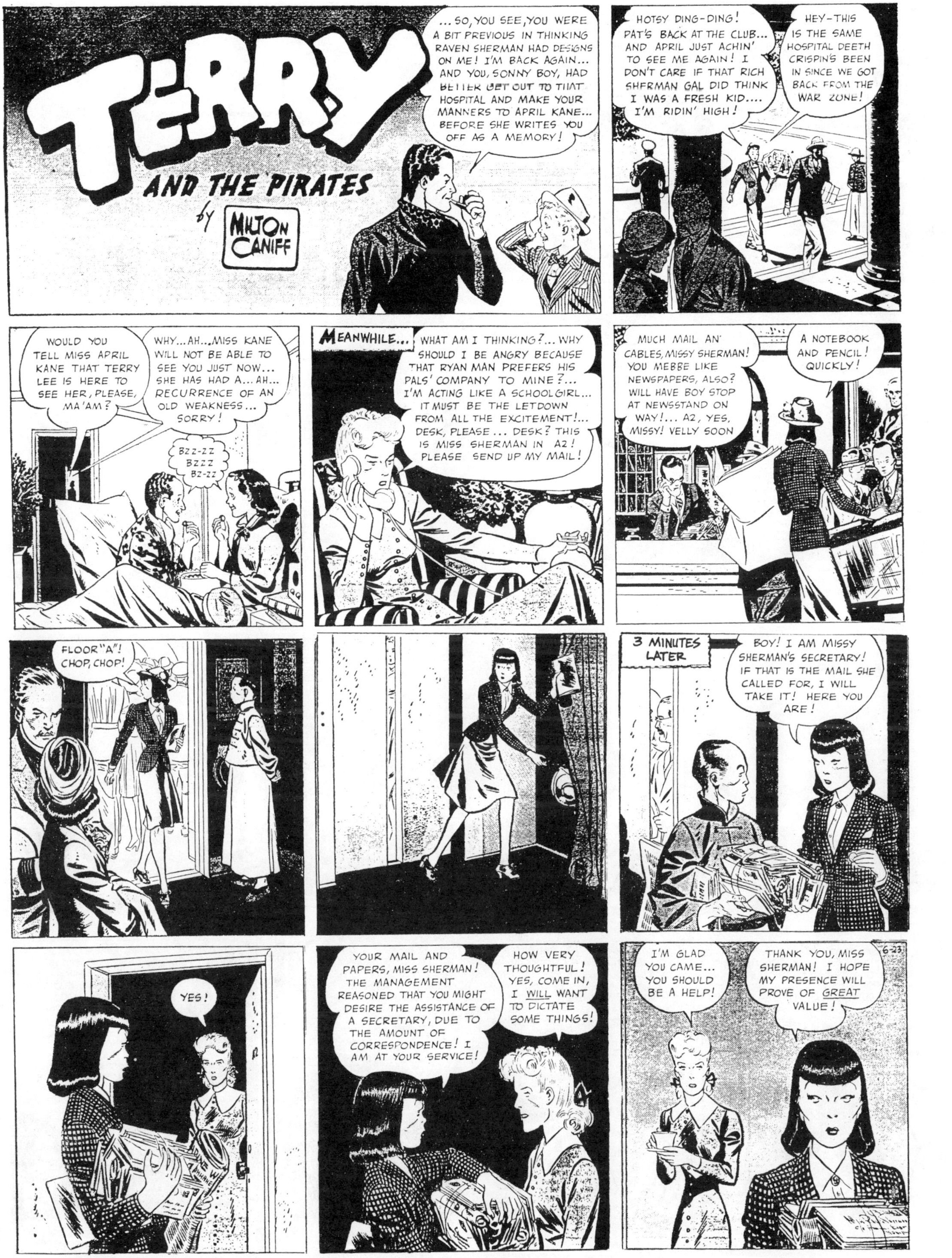
TERRY AND THE PIRATES
by MILTON CANIFF
...SO, YOU SEE, YOU WERE A BIT PREVIOUS IN THINKING RAVEN SHERMAN HAD DESIGNS ON ME! I'M BACK AGAIN... AND YOU, SONNY BOY, HAD BETTER GET OUT TO THAT HOSPITAL AND MAKE YOUR MANNERS TO APRIL KANE... BEFORE SHE WRITES YOU OFF AS A MEMORY!
HOTSY DING-DING! PAT'S BACK AT THE CLUB... AND APRIL JUST ACHIN' TO SEE ME AGAIN! I DON'T CARE IF THAT RICH SHERMAN GAL DID THINK I WAS A FRESH KID.... I'M RIDIN' HIGH!
HEY-THIS IS THE SAME HOSPITAL DEETH CRISPIN'S BEEN IN SINCE WE GOT BACK FROM THE WAR ZONE!
WOULD YOU TELL MISS APRIL KANE THAT TERRY LEE IS HERE TO SEE HER, PLEASE, MA'AM?
WHY...AH...MISS KANE WILL NOT BE ABLE TO SEE YOU JUST NOW... SHE HAS HAD A...AH... RECURRENCE OF AN OLD WEAKNESS... SORRY!
BZZ-ZZ BZZZ BZ-ZZ
MEANWHILE...
WHAT AM I THINKING?... WHY SHOULD I BE ANGRY BECAUSE THAT RYAN MAN PREFERS HIS PALS' COMPANY TO MINE?... I'M ACTING LIKE A SCHOOLGIRL... IT MUST BE THE LETDOWN FROM ALL THE EXCITEMENT!... DESK, PLEASE... DESK? THIS IS MISS SHERMAN IN A2! PLEASE SEND UP MY MAIL!
MUCH MAIL AN' CABLES, MISSY SHERMAN! YOU MEBBE LIKE NEWSPAPERS, ALSO? WILL HAVE BOY STOP AT NEWSSTAND ON WAY!... A2, YES, MISSY! VELLY SOON
A NOTEBOOK AND PENCIL! QUICKLY!
FLOOR "A"! CHOP, CHOP!
3 MINUTES LATER
BOY! I AM MISSY SHERMAN'S SECRETARY! IF THAT IS THE MAIL SHE CALLED FOR, I WILL TAKE IT! HERE YOU ARE!
YES!
YOUR MAIL AND PAPERS, MISS SHERMAN! THE MANAGEMENT REASONED THAT YOU MIGHT DESIRE THE ASSISTANCE OF A SECRETARY, DUE TO THE AMOUNT OF CORRESPONDENCE! I AM AT YOUR SERVICE!
HOW VERY THOUGHTFUL! YES, COME IN, I WILL WANT TO DICTATE SOME THINGS!
I'M GLAD YOU CAME... YOU SHOULD BE A HELP!
THANK YOU, MISS SHERMAN! I HOPE MY PRESENCE WILL PROVE OF GREAT VALUE!
6-23

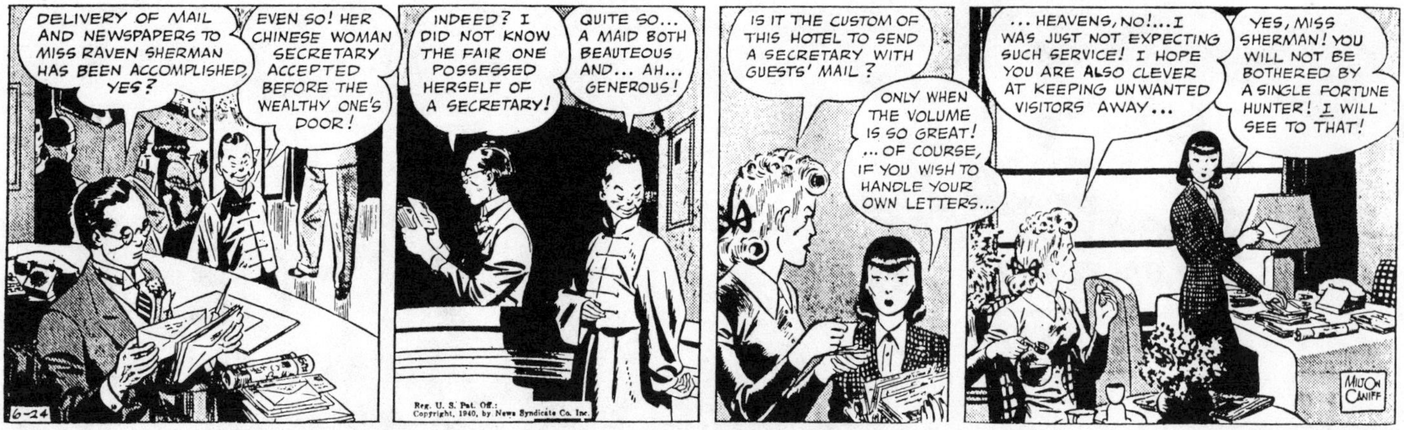
DELIVERY OF MAIL AND NEWSPAPERS TO MISS RAVEN SHERMAN HAS BEEN ACCOMPLISHED, YES?
EVEN SO! HER CHINESE WOMAN SECRETARY ACCEPTED BEFORE THE WEALTHY ONE'S DOOR!
6-24
INDEED? I DID NOT KNOW THE FAIR ONE POSSESSED HERSELF OF A SECRETARY!
QUITE SO... A MAID BOTH BEAUTEOUS AND... AH... GENEROUS!
Reg. U. S. Pat. Off.; Copyright, 1940, by News Syndicate Co. Inc.
IS IT THE CUSTOM OF THIS HOTEL TO SEND A SECRETARY WITH GUESTS' MAIL?
ONLY WHEN THE VOLUME IS SO GREAT! ... OF COURSE, IF YOU WISH TO HANDLE YOUR OWN LETTERS...
... HEAVENS, NO!... I WAS JUST NOT EXPECTING SUCH SERVICE! I HOPE YOU ARE ALSO CLEVER AT KEEPING UNWANTED VISITORS AWAY...
YES, MISS SHERMAN! YOU WILL NOT BE BOTHERED BY A SINGLE FORTUNE HUNTER! I WILL SEE TO THAT!
MILTON CANIFF

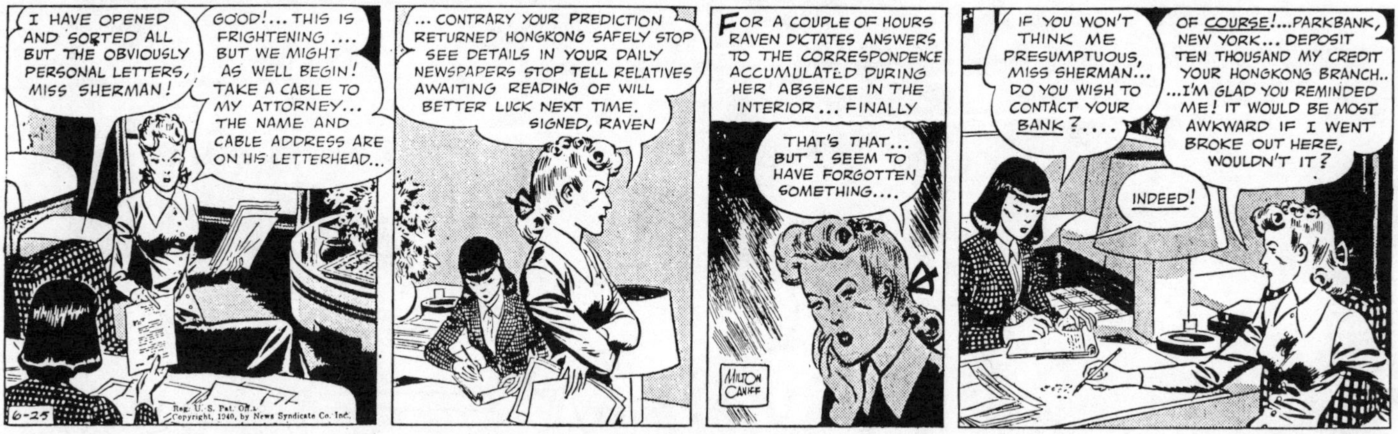
I HAVE OPENED AND SORTED ALL BUT THE OBVIOUSLY PERSONAL LETTERS, MISS SHERMAN!
GOOD!... THIS IS FRIGHTENING.... BUT WE MIGHT AS WELL BEGIN! TAKE A CABLE TO MY ATTORNEY... THE NAME AND CABLE ADDRESS ARE ON HIS LETTERHEAD...
6-25
Reg. U. S. Pat. Off.; Copyright, 1940, by News Syndicate Co. Inc.
... CONTRARY YOUR PREDICTION RETURNED HONGKONG SAFELY STOP SEE DETAILS IN YOUR DAILY NEWSPAPERS STOP TELL RELATIVES AWAITING READING OF WILL BETTER LUCK NEXT TIME. SIGNED, RAVEN
FOR A COUPLE OF HOURS RAVEN DICTATES ANSWERS TO THE CORRESPONDENCE ACCUMULATED DURING HER ABSENCE IN THE INTERIOR... FINALLY
THAT'S THAT... BUT I SEEM TO HAVE FORGOTTEN SOMETHING....
MILTON CANIFF
IF YOU WON'T THINK ME PRESUMPTUOUS, MISS SHERMAN... DO YOU WISH TO CONTACT YOUR BANK?....
OF COURSE!...PARKBANK, NEW YORK... DEPOSIT TEN THOUSAND MY CREDIT YOUR HONGKONG BRANCH.. ...I'M GLAD YOU REMINDED ME! IT WOULD BE MOST AWKWARD IF I WENT BROKE OUT HERE, WOULDN'T IT?
INDEED!

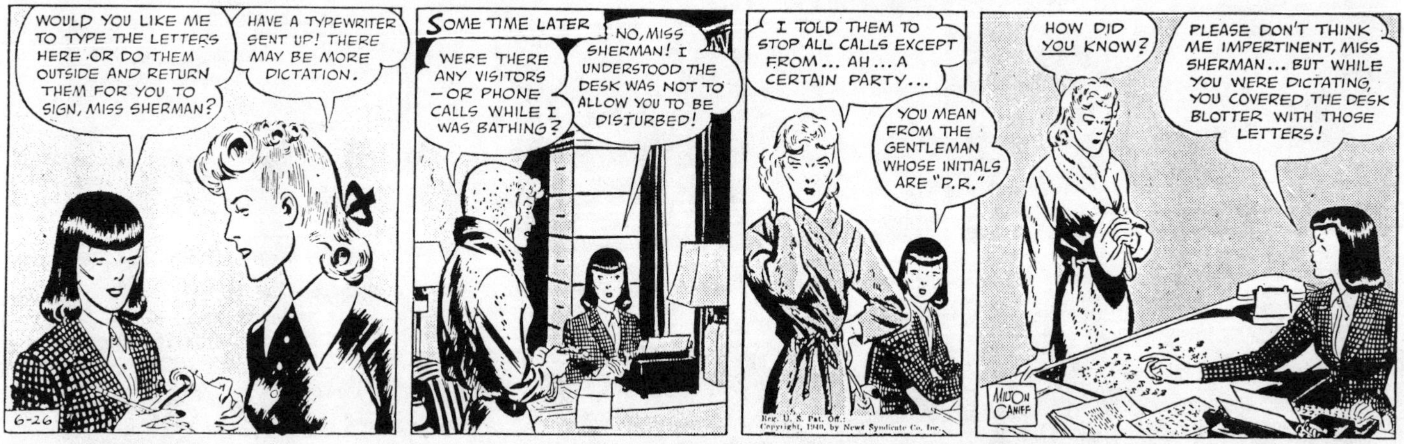
WOULD YOU LIKE ME TO TYPE THE LETTERS HERE OR DO THEM OUTSIDE AND RETURN THEM FOR YOU TO SIGN, MISS SHERMAN?
HAVE A TYPEWRITER SENT UP! THERE MAY BE MORE DICTATION.
6-26
SOME TIME LATER
WERE THERE ANY VISITORS -OR PHONE CALLS WHILE I WAS BATHING?
NO, MISS SHERMAN! I UNDERSTOOD THE DESK WAS NOT TO ALLOW YOU TO BE DISTURBED!
I TOLD THEM TO STOP ALL CALLS EXCEPT FROM... AH... A CERTAIN PARTY...
YOU MEAN FROM THE GENTLEMAN WHOSE INITIALS ARE "P.R."
Reg. U. S. Pat. Off.; Copyright, 1940, by News Syndicate Co. Inc.
HOW DID YOU KNOW?
PLEASE DON'T THINK ME IMPERTINENT, MISS SHERMAN... BUT WHILE YOU WERE DICTATING, YOU COVERED THE DESK BLOTTER WITH THOSE LETTERS!
MILTON CANIFF

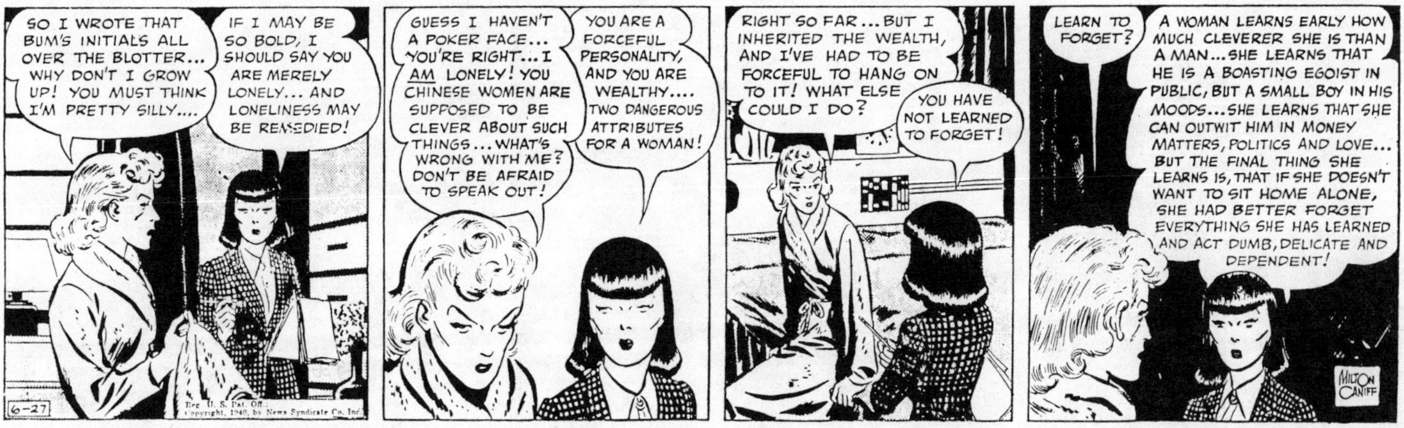
SO I WROTE THAT BUM'S INITIALS ALL OVER THE BLOTTER... WHY DON'T I GROW UP! YOU MUST THINK I'M PRETTY SILLY....
IF I MAY BE SO BOLD, I SHOULD SAY YOU ARE MERELY LONELY... AND LONELINESS MAY BE REMEDIED!
6-27
Reg. U. S. Pat. Off.; Copyright, 1940, by News Syndicate Co. Inc.
GUESS I HAVEN'T A POKER FACE... YOU'RE RIGHT... I AM LONELY! YOU CHINESE WOMEN ARE SUPPOSED TO BE CLEVER ABOUT SUCH THINGS... WHAT'S WRONG WITH ME? DON'T BE AFRAID TO SPEAK OUT!
YOU ARE A FORCEFUL PERSONALITY, AND YOU ARE WEALTHY.... TWO DANGEROUS ATTRIBUTES FOR A WOMAN!
RIGHT SO FAR... BUT I INHERITED THE WEALTH, AND I'VE HAD TO BE FORCEFUL TO HANG ON TO IT! WHAT ELSE COULD I DO?
YOU HAVE NOT LEARNED TO FORGET!
LEARN TO FORGET?
A WOMAN LEARNS EARLY HOW MUCH CLEVERER SHE IS THAN A MAN... SHE LEARNS THAT HE IS A BOASTING EGOIST IN PUBLIC, BUT A SMALL BOY IN HIS MOODS... SHE LEARNS THAT SHE CAN OUTWIT HIM IN MONEY MATTERS, POLITICS AND LOVE... BUT THE FINAL THING SHE LEARNS IS, THAT IF SHE DOESN'T WANT TO SIT HOME ALONE, SHE HAD BETTER FORGET EVERYTHING SHE HAS LEARNED AND ACT DUMB, DELICATE AND DEPENDENT!
MILTON CANIFF

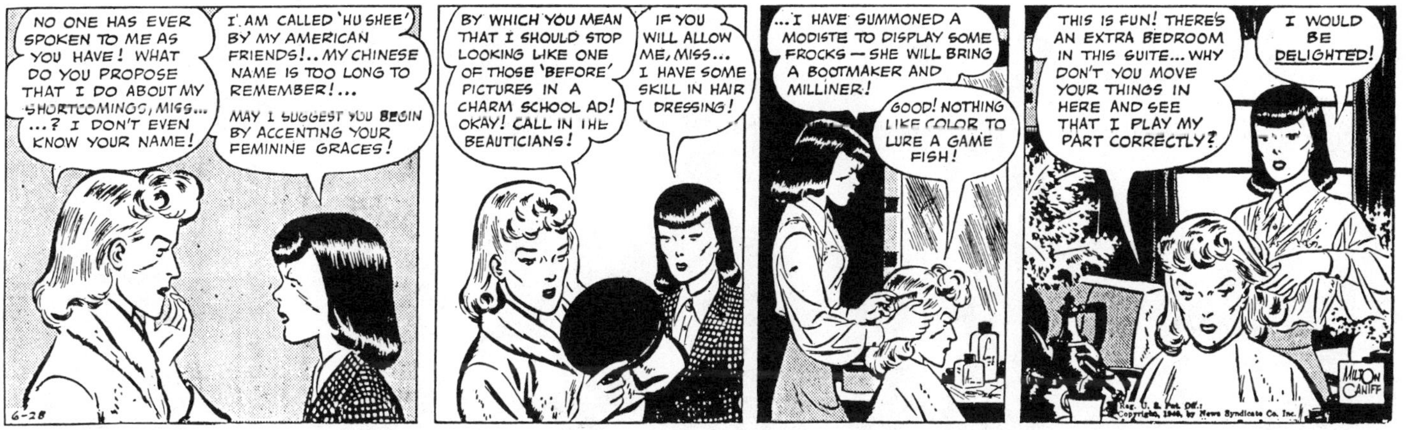
NO ONE HAS EVER SPOKEN TO ME AS YOU HAVE! WHAT DO YOU PROPOSE THAT I DO ABOUT MY SHORTCOMINGS, MISS... ...? I DON'T EVEN KNOW YOUR NAME!
I AM CALLED 'HU SHEE' BY MY AMERICAN FRIENDS!.. MY CHINESE NAME IS TOO LONG TO REMEMBER!...
MAY I SUGGEST YOU BEGIN BY ACCENTING YOUR FEMININE GRACES!
BY WHICH YOU MEAN THAT I SHOULD STOP LOOKING LIKE ONE OF THOSE 'BEFORE' PICTURES IN A CHARM SCHOOL AD! OKAY! CALL IN THE BEAUTICIANS!
IF YOU WILL ALLOW ME, MISS... I HAVE SOME SKILL IN HAIR DRESSING!
...I HAVE SUMMONED A MODISTE TO DISPLAY SOME FROCKS — SHE WILL BRING A BOOTMAKER AND MILLINER!
GOOD! NOTHING LIKE COLOR TO LURE A GAME FISH!
THIS IS FUN! THERE'S AN EXTRA BEDROOM IN THIS SUITE... WHY DON'T YOU MOVE YOUR THINGS IN HERE AND SEE THAT I PLAY MY PART CORRECTLY?
I WOULD BE DELIGHTED!
6-28
MILTON CANIFF
Reg. U. S. Pat. Off.: Copyright, 1940, by News Syndicate Co. Inc.

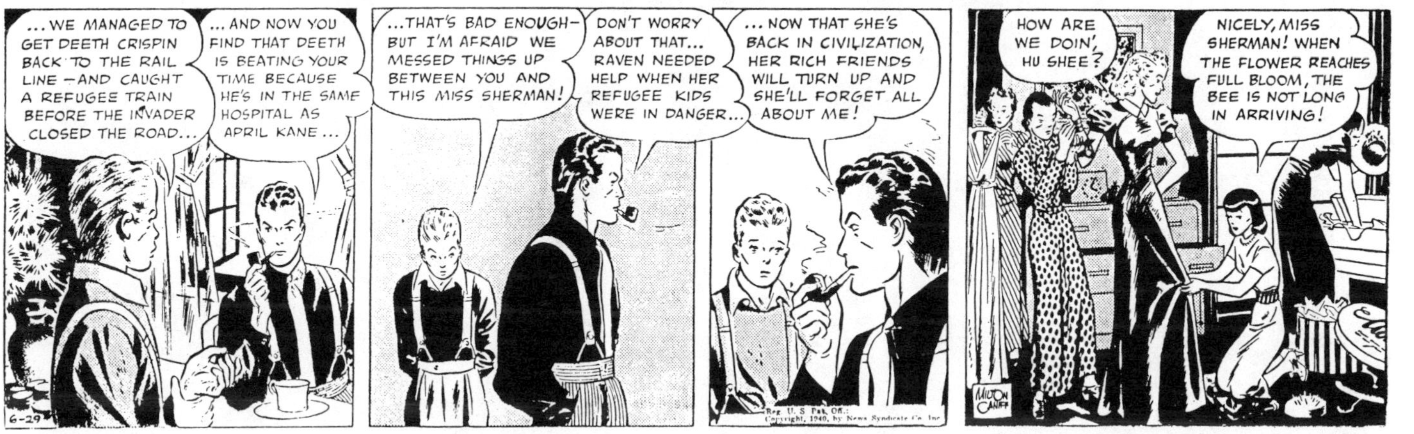
...WE MANAGED TO GET DEETH CRISPIN BACK TO THE RAIL LINE — AND CAUGHT A REFUGEE TRAIN BEFORE THE INVADER CLOSED THE ROAD...
...AND NOW YOU FIND THAT DEETH IS BEATING YOUR TIME BECAUSE HE'S IN THE SAME HOSPITAL AS APRIL KANE...
...THAT'S BAD ENOUGH— BUT I'M AFRAID WE MESSED THINGS UP BETWEEN YOU AND THIS MISS SHERMAN!
DON'T WORRY ABOUT THAT... RAVEN NEEDED HELP WHEN HER REFUGEE KIDS WERE IN DANGER...
...NOW THAT SHE'S BACK IN CIVILIZATION, HER RICH FRIENDS WILL TURN UP AND SHE'LL FORGET ALL ABOUT ME!
HOW ARE WE DOIN', HU SHEE?
NICELY, MISS SHERMAN! WHEN THE FLOWER REACHES FULL BLOOM, THE BEE IS NOT LONG IN ARRIVING!
6-29
Reg. U. S. Pat. Off.: Copyright, 1940, by News Syndicate Co. Inc.
MILTON CANIFF

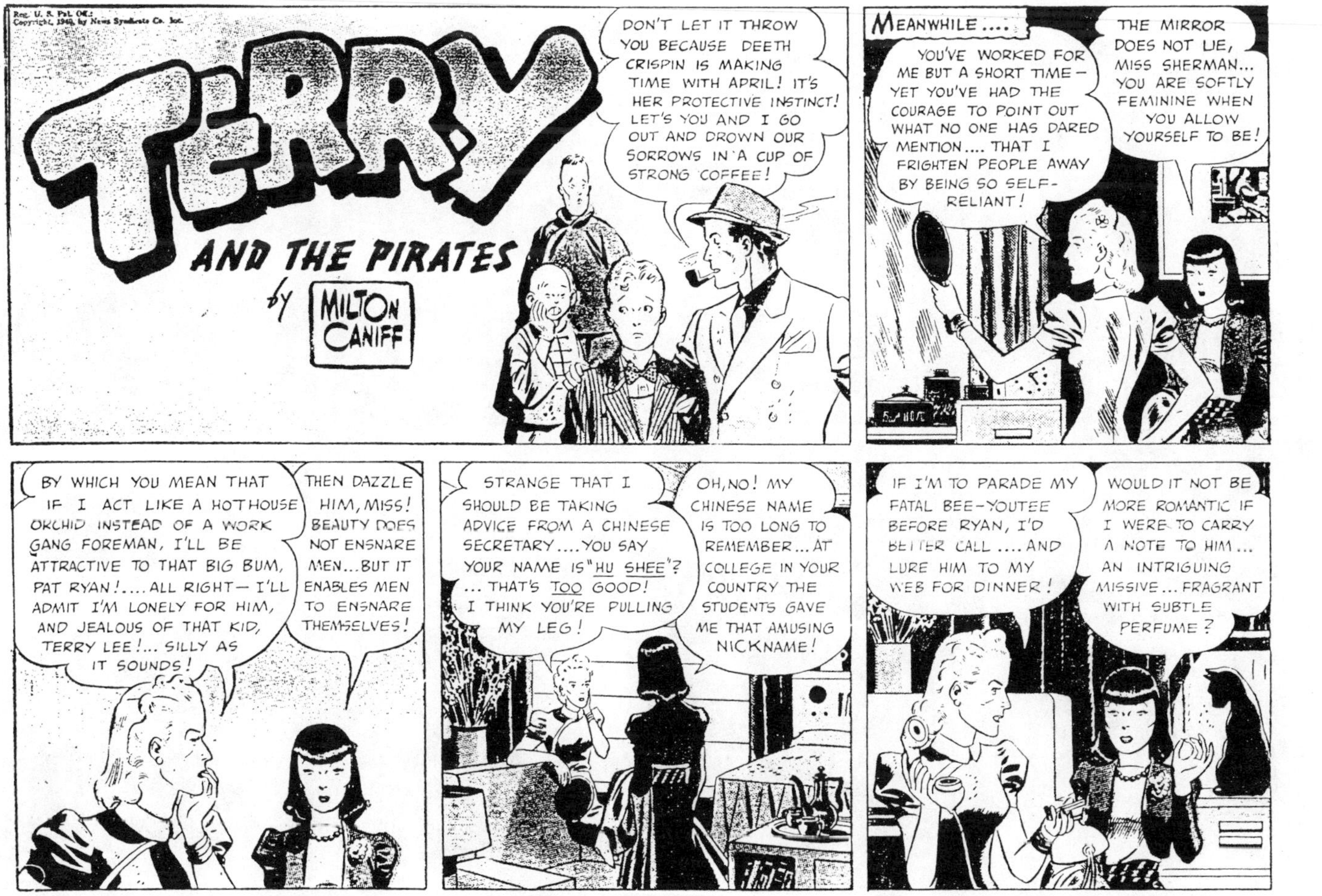
Reg. U. S. Pat. Off.: Copyright, 1940, by News Syndicate Co. Inc.
TERRY AND THE PIRATES by MILTON CANIFF
DON'T LET IT THROW YOU BECAUSE DEETH CRISPIN IS MAKING TIME WITH APRIL! IT'S HER PROTECTIVE INSTINCT! LET'S YOU AND I GO OUT AND DROWN OUR SORROWS IN A CUP OF STRONG COFFEE!
MEANWHILE....
YOU'VE WORKED FOR ME BUT A SHORT TIME — YET YOU'VE HAD THE COURAGE TO POINT OUT WHAT NO ONE HAS DARED MENTION.... THAT I FRIGHTEN PEOPLE AWAY BY BEING SO SELF-RELIANT!
THE MIRROR DOES NOT LIE, MISS SHERMAN... YOU ARE SOFTLY FEMININE WHEN YOU ALLOW YOURSELF TO BE!
BY WHICH YOU MEAN THAT IF I ACT LIKE A HOTHOUSE ORCHID INSTEAD OF A WORK GANG FOREMAN, I'LL BE ATTRACTIVE TO THAT BIG BUM, PAT RYAN!.... ALL RIGHT— I'LL ADMIT I'M LONELY FOR HIM, AND JEALOUS OF THAT KID, TERRY LEE!... SILLY AS IT SOUNDS!
THEN DAZZLE HIM, MISS! BEAUTY DOES NOT ENSNARE MEN... BUT IT ENABLES MEN TO ENSNARE THEMSELVES!
STRANGE THAT I SHOULD BE TAKING ADVICE FROM A CHINESE SECRETARY.... YOU SAY YOUR NAME IS "HU SHEE"? ... THAT'S TOO GOOD! I THINK YOU'RE PULLING MY LEG!
OH, NO! MY CHINESE NAME IS TOO LONG TO REMEMBER... AT COLLEGE IN YOUR COUNTRY THE STUDENTS GAVE ME THAT AMUSING NICKNAME!
IF I'M TO PARADE MY FATAL BEE-YOUTEE BEFORE RYAN, I'D BETTER CALL.... AND LURE HIM TO MY WEB FOR DINNER!
WOULD IT NOT BE MORE ROMANTIC IF I WERE TO CARRY A NOTE TO HIM... AN INTRIGUING MISSIVE... FRAGRANT WITH SUBTLE PERFUME?

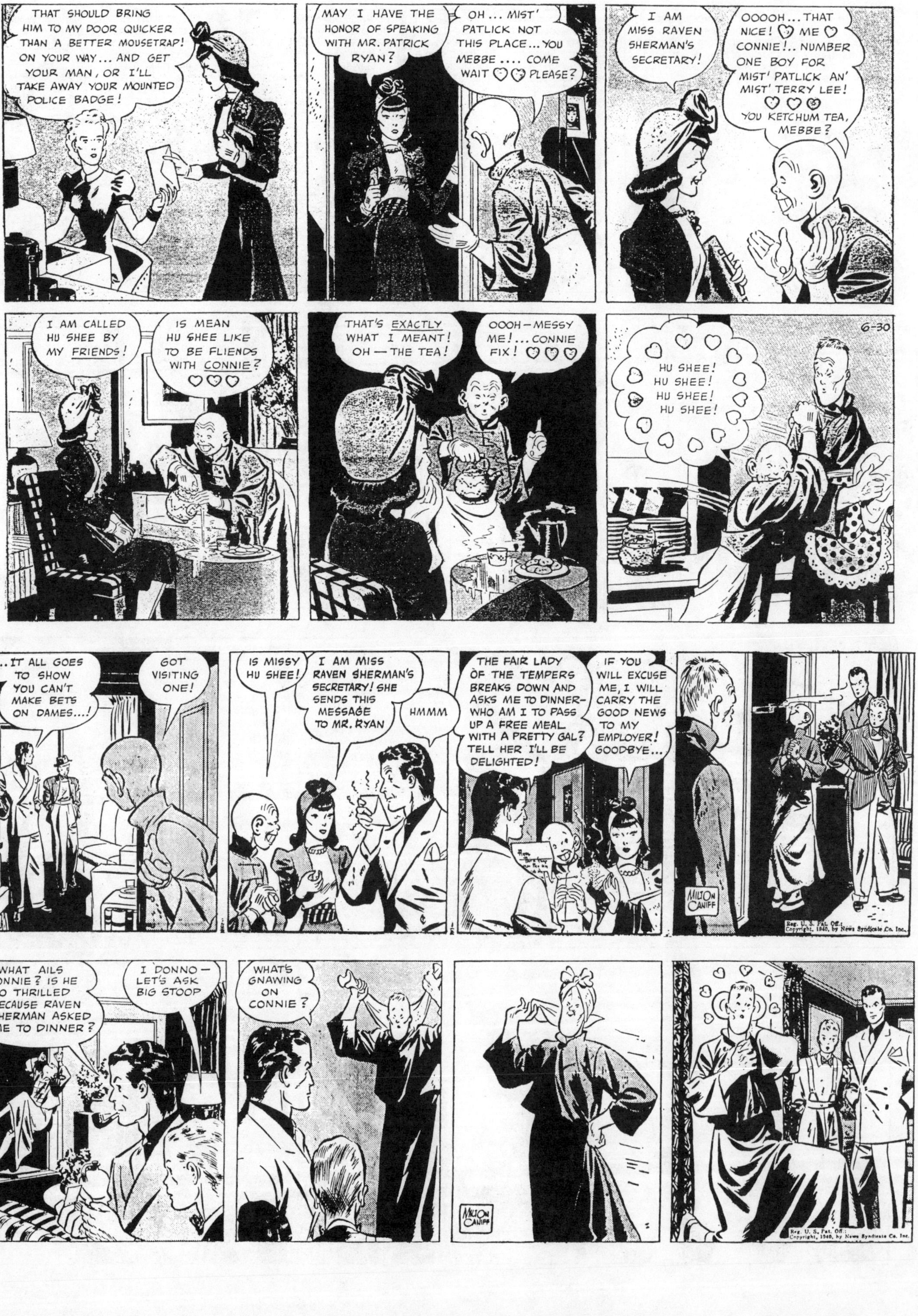

THAT SHOULD BRING HIM TO MY DOOR QUICKER THAN A BETTER MOUSETRAP! ON YOUR WAY... AND GET YOUR MAN, OR I'LL TAKE AWAY YOUR MOUNTED POLICE BADGE!
MAY I HAVE THE HONOR OF SPEAKING WITH MR. PATRICK RYAN?
OH... MIST' PATLICK NOT THIS PLACE... YOU MEBBE .... COME WAIT ♡♡ PLEASE?
I AM MISS RAVEN SHERMAN'S SECRETARY!
OOOOH... THAT NICE! ♡ ME ♡ CONNIE!.. NUMBER ONE BOY FOR MIST' PATLICK AN' MIST' TERRY LEE! ♡♡♡ YOU KETCHUM TEA, MEBBE?
I AM CALLED HU SHEE BY MY FRIENDS!
IS MEAN HU SHEE LIKE TO BE FLIENDS WITH CONNIE? ♡♡♡
THAT'S EXACTLY WHAT I MEANT! OH — THE TEA!
OOOH — MESSY ME!... CONNIE FIX! ♡♡♡
6-30
HU SHEE! HU SHEE! HU SHEE! HU SHEE!
7-1
...IT ALL GOES TO SHOW YOU CAN'T MAKE BETS ON DAMES...!
GOT VISITING ONE!
IS MISSY HU SHEE!
I AM MISS RAVEN SHERMAN'S SECRETARY! SHE SENDS THIS MESSAGE TO MR. RYAN
HMMM
THE FAIR LADY OF THE TEMPERS BREAKS DOWN AND ASKS ME TO DINNER — WHO AM I TO PASS UP A FREE MEAL WITH A PRETTY GAL? TELL HER I'LL BE DELIGHTED!
IF YOU WILL EXCUSE ME, I WILL CARRY THE GOOD NEWS TO MY EMPLOYER! GOODBYE...
MILTON CANIFF
Reg. U. S. Pat. Off.; Copyright, 1940, by News Syndicate Co. Inc.
7-2
WHAT AILS CONNIE? IS HE SO THRILLED BECAUSE RAVEN SHERMAN ASKED ME TO DINNER?
I DONNO — LET'S ASK BIG STOOP
WHAT'S GNAWING ON CONNIE?
MILTON CANIFF
Reg. U. S. Pat. Off.; Copyright, 1940, by News Syndicate Co. Inc.

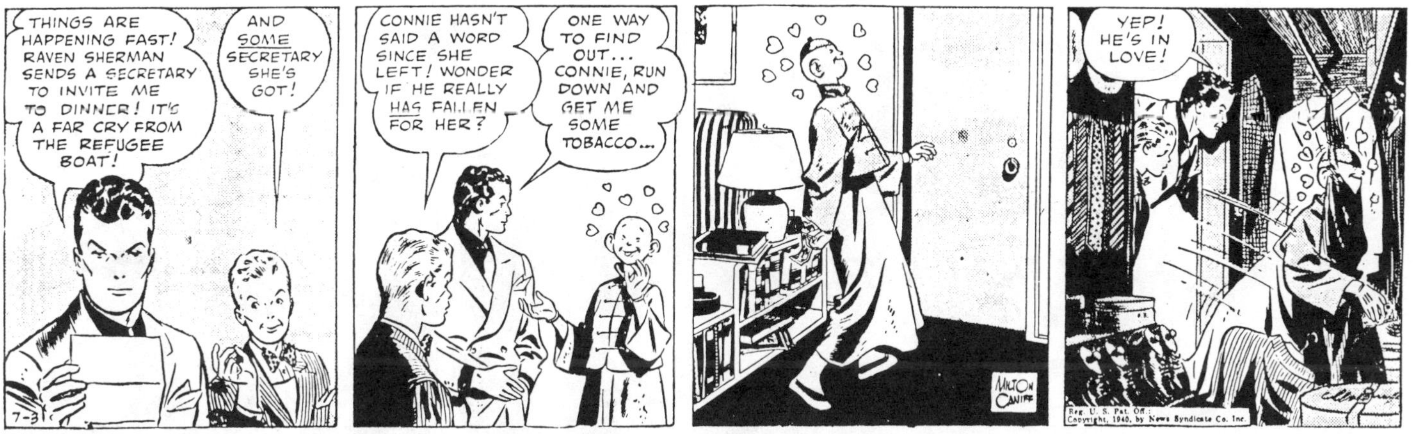
THINGS ARE HAPPENING FAST! RAVEN SHERMAN SENDS A SECRETARY TO INVITE ME TO DINNER! IT'S A FAR CRY FROM THE REFUGEE BOAT!
AND SOME SECRETARY SHE'S GOT!
CONNIE HASN'T SAID A WORD SINCE SHE LEFT! WONDER IF HE REALLY HAS FALLEN FOR HER?
ONE WAY TO FIND OUT... CONNIE, RUN DOWN AND GET ME SOME TOBACCO...
YEP! HE'S IN LOVE!
7-3
MILTON CANIFF
Reg. U. S. Pat. Off.: Copyright, 1940, by News Syndicate Co. Inc.

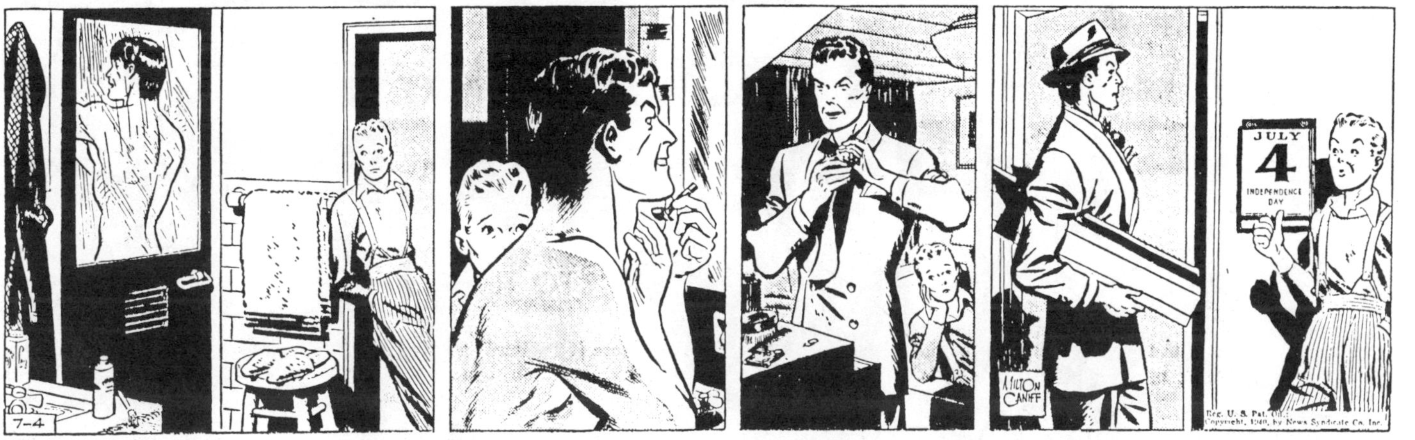
JULY
4
INDEPENDENCE DAY
7-4
MILTON CANIFF
Reg. U. S. Pat. Off.: Copyright, 1940, by News Syndicate Co. Inc.

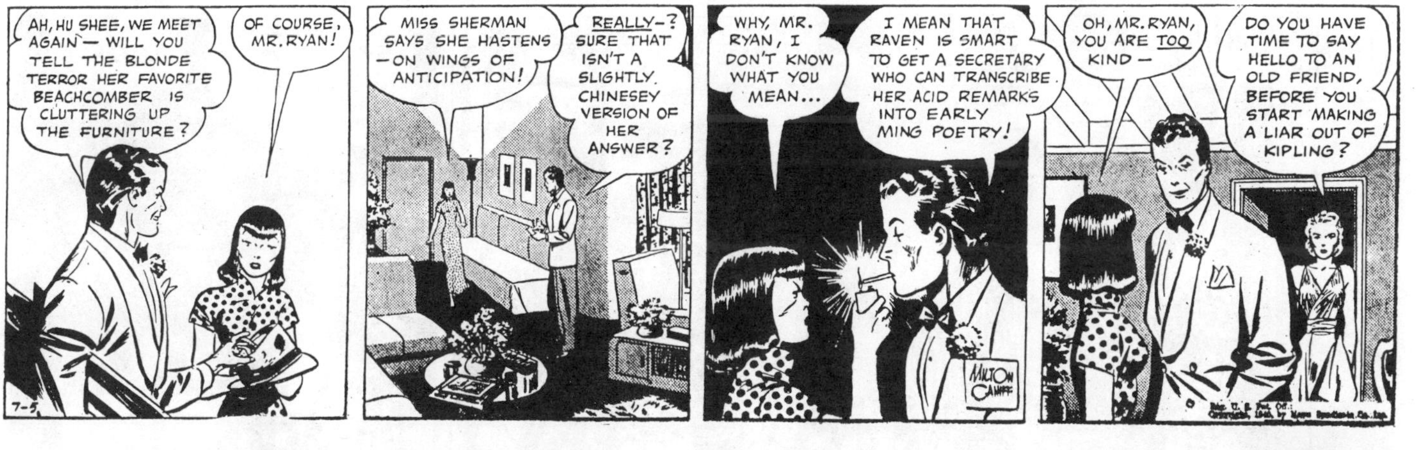
AH, HU SHEE, WE MEET AGAIN — WILL YOU TELL THE BLONDE TERROR HER FAVORITE BEACHCOMBER IS CLUTTERING UP THE FURNITURE?
OF COURSE, MR. RYAN!
MISS SHERMAN SAYS SHE HASTENS — ON WINGS OF ANTICIPATION!
REALLY—? SURE THAT ISN'T A SLIGHTLY CHINESEY VERSION OF HER ANSWER?
WHY, MR. RYAN, I DON'T KNOW WHAT YOU MEAN...
I MEAN THAT RAVEN IS SMART TO GET A SECRETARY WHO CAN TRANSCRIBE HER ACID REMARKS INTO EARLY MING POETRY!
OH, MR. RYAN, YOU ARE TOO KIND —
DO YOU HAVE TIME TO SAY HELLO TO AN OLD FRIEND, BEFORE YOU START MAKING A LIAR OUT OF KIPLING?
7-5
MILTON CANIFF

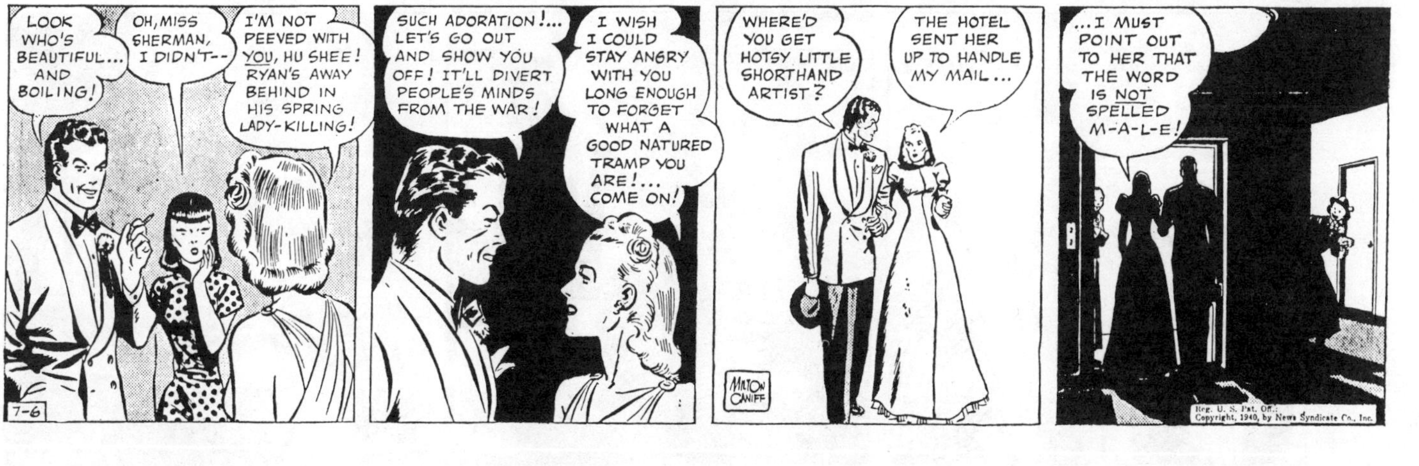
LOOK WHO'S BEAUTIFUL... AND BOILING!
OH, MISS SHERMAN, I DIDN'T--
I'M NOT PEEVED WITH YOU, HU SHEE! RYAN'S AWAY BEHIND IN HIS SPRING LADY-KILLING!
SUCH ADORATION!... LET'S GO OUT AND SHOW YOU OFF! IT'LL DIVERT PEOPLE'S MINDS FROM THE WAR!
I WISH I COULD STAY ANGRY WITH YOU LONG ENOUGH TO FORGET WHAT A GOOD NATURED TRAMP YOU ARE!... COME ON!
WHERE'D YOU GET HOTSY LITTLE SHORTHAND ARTIST?
THE HOTEL SENT HER UP TO HANDLE MY MAIL...
...I MUST POINT OUT TO HER THAT THE WORD IS NOT SPELLED M-A-L-E!
7-6
MILTON CANIFF
Reg. U. S. Pat. Off.: Copyright, 1940, by News Syndicate Co. Inc.

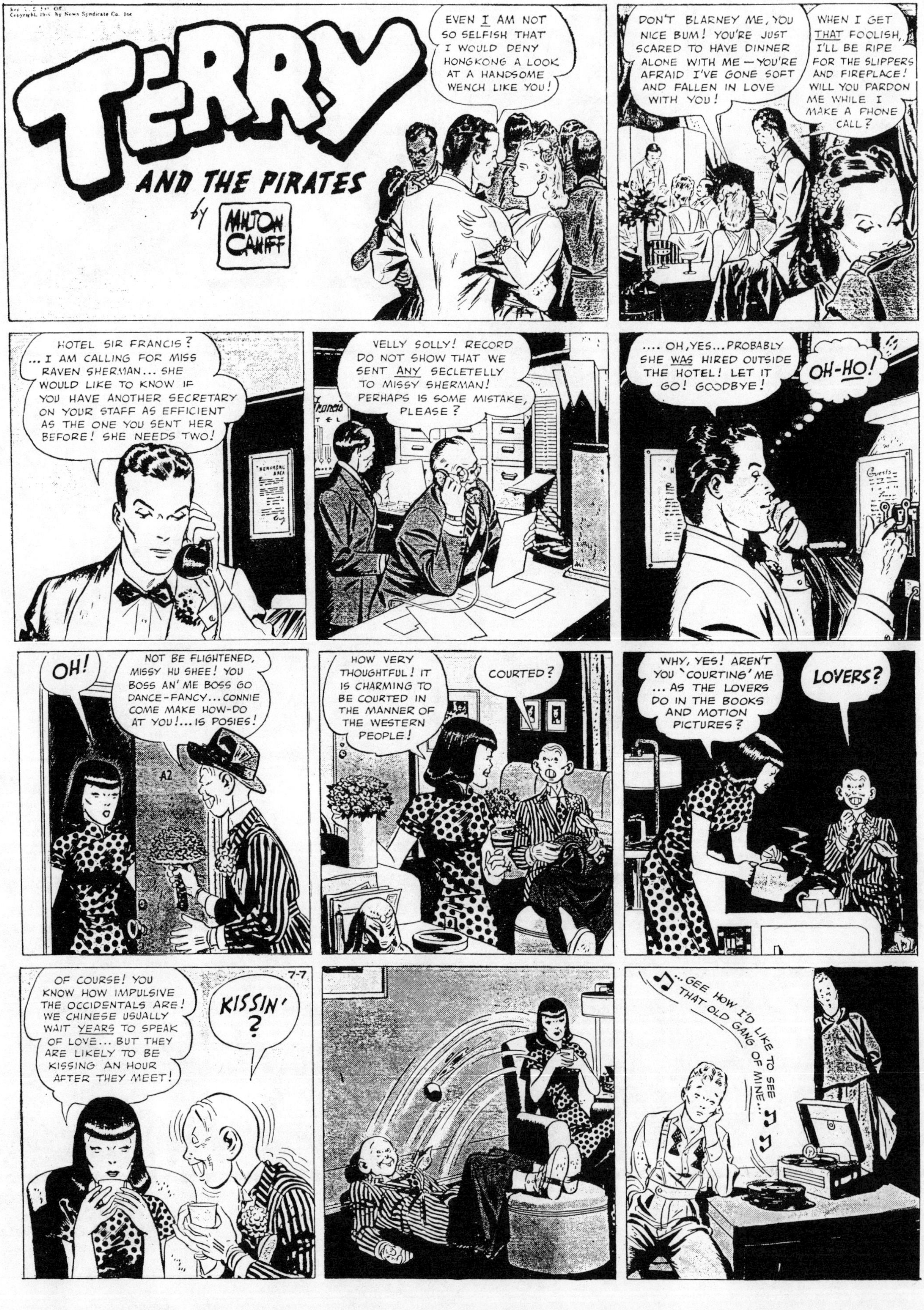
by News Syndicate Co. Inc.
TERRY AND THE PIRATES
by MILTON CANIFF
EVEN I AM NOT SO SELFISH THAT I WOULD DENY HONGKONG A LOOK AT A HANDSOME WENCH LIKE YOU!
DON'T BLARNEY ME, YOU NICE BUM! YOU'RE JUST SCARED TO HAVE DINNER ALONE WITH ME — YOU'RE AFRAID I'VE GONE SOFT AND FALLEN IN LOVE WITH YOU!
WHEN I GET THAT FOOLISH, I'LL BE RIPE FOR THE SLIPPERS AND FIREPLACE! WILL YOU PARDON ME WHILE I MAKE A PHONE CALL?
HOTEL SIR FRANCIS? ... I AM CALLING FOR MISS RAVEN SHERMAN... SHE WOULD LIKE TO KNOW IF YOU HAVE ANOTHER SECRETARY ON YOUR STAFF AS EFFICIENT AS THE ONE YOU SENT HER BEFORE! SHE NEEDS TWO!
VELLY SOLLY! RECORD DO NOT SHOW THAT WE SENT ANY SECLETELLY TO MISSY SHERMAN! PERHAPS IS SOME MISTAKE, PLEASE?
.... OH, YES... PROBABLY SHE WAS HIRED OUTSIDE THE HOTEL! LET IT GO! GOODBYE!
OH-HO!
OH!
NOT BE FLIGHTENED, MISSY HU SHEE! YOU BOSS AN' ME BOSS GO DANCE-FANCY... CONNIE COME MAKE HOW-DO AT YOU!... IS POSIES!
HOW VERY THOUGHTFUL! IT IS CHARMING TO BE COURTED IN THE MANNER OF THE WESTERN PEOPLE!
COURTED?
WHY, YES! AREN'T YOU 'COURTING' ME ... AS THE LOVERS DO IN THE BOOKS AND MOTION PICTURES?
LOVERS?
OF COURSE! YOU KNOW HOW IMPULSIVE THE OCCIDENTALS ARE! WE CHINESE USUALLY WAIT YEARS TO SPEAK OF LOVE... BUT THEY ARE LIKELY TO BE KISSING AN HOUR AFTER THEY MEET!
7-7
KISSIN' ?
... GEE HOW I'D LIKE TO SEE THAT OLD GANG OF MINE...

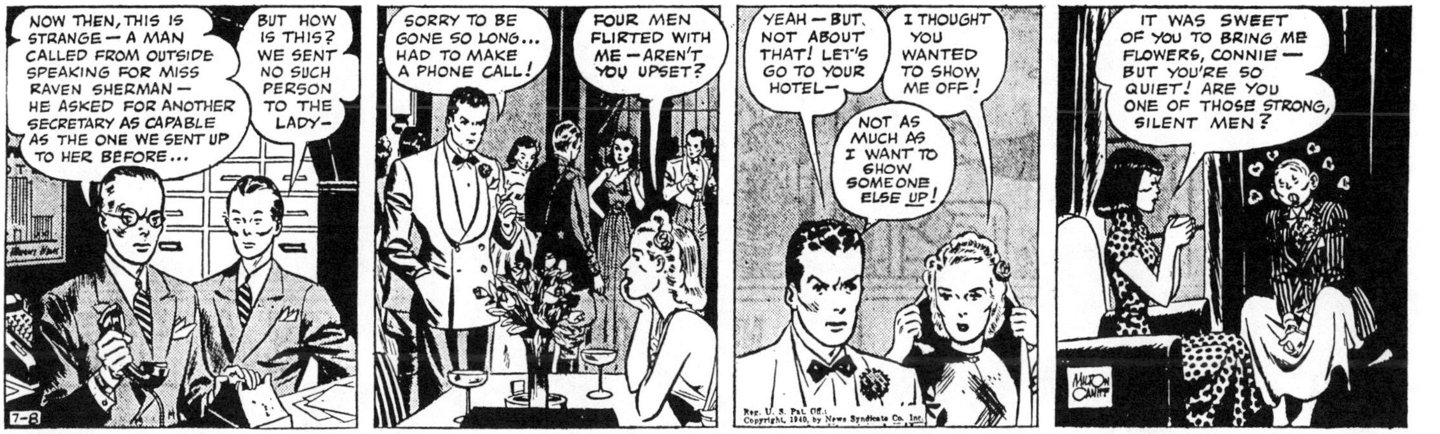
NOW THEN, THIS IS STRANGE — A MAN CALLED FROM OUTSIDE SPEAKING FOR MISS RAVEN SHERMAN — HE ASKED FOR ANOTHER SECRETARY AS CAPABLE AS THE ONE WE SENT UP TO HER BEFORE...
BUT HOW IS THIS? WE SENT NO SUCH PERSON TO THE LADY-
7-8
SORRY TO BE GONE SO LONG... HAD TO MAKE A PHONE CALL!
FOUR MEN FLIRTED WITH ME — AREN'T YOU UPSET?
YEAH — BUT NOT ABOUT THAT! LET'S GO TO YOUR HOTEL—
I THOUGHT YOU WANTED TO SHOW ME OFF!
NOT AS MUCH AS I WANT TO SHOW SOMEONE ELSE UP!
Reg. U. S. Pat. Off. Copyright, 1940, by News Syndicate Co. Inc.
IT WAS SWEET OF YOU TO BRING ME FLOWERS, CONNIE — BUT YOU'RE SO QUIET! ARE YOU ONE OF THOSE STRONG, SILENT MEN?
MILTON CANIFF

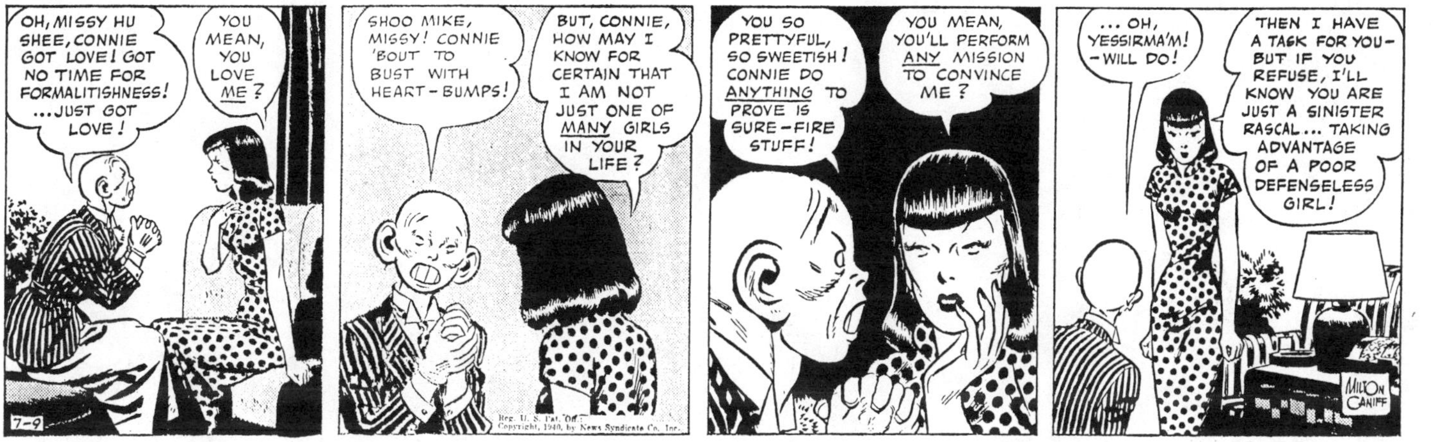
OH, MISSY HU SHEE, CONNIE GOT LOVE! GOT NO TIME FOR FORMALITISHNESS! ...JUST GOT LOVE!
YOU MEAN, YOU LOVE ME?
7-9
SHOO MIKE, MISSY! CONNIE 'BOUT TO BUST WITH HEART-BUMPS!
BUT, CONNIE, HOW MAY I KNOW FOR CERTAIN THAT I AM NOT JUST ONE OF MANY GIRLS IN YOUR LIFE?
YOU SO PRETTYFUL, SO SWEETISH! CONNIE DO ANYTHING TO PROVE IS SURE-FIRE STUFF!
YOU MEAN, YOU'LL PERFORM ANY MISSION TO CONVINCE ME?
...OH, YESSIRMA'M! -WILL DO!
THEN I HAVE A TASK FOR YOU- BUT IF YOU REFUSE, I'LL KNOW YOU ARE JUST A SINISTER RASCAL... TAKING ADVANTAGE OF A POOR DEFENSELESS GIRL!
MILTON CANIFF

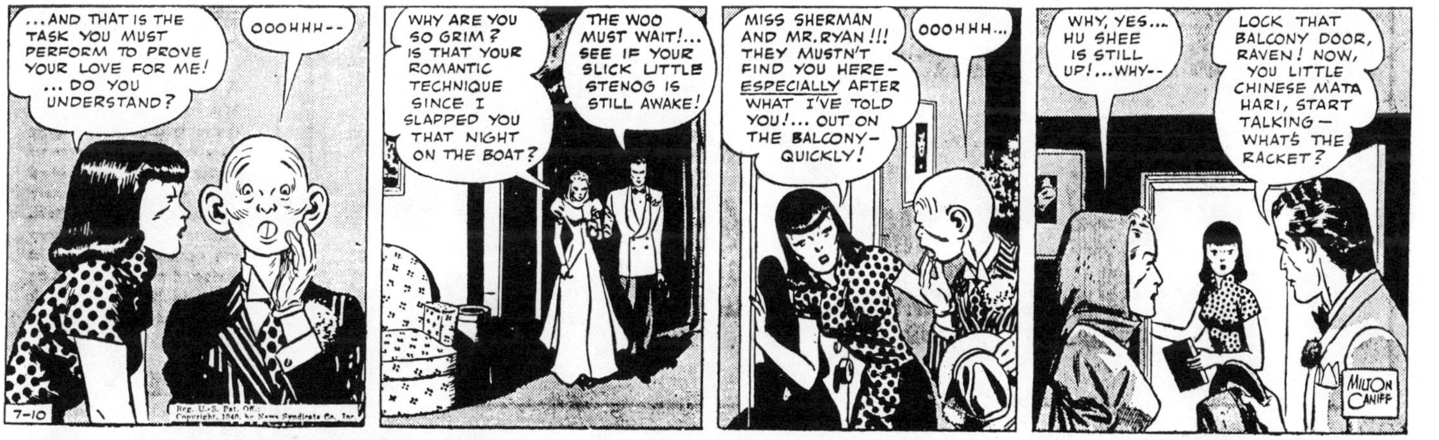
...AND THAT IS THE TASK YOU MUST PERFORM TO PROVE YOUR LOVE FOR ME! ...DO YOU UNDERSTAND?
OOOHHH--
7-10
WHY ARE YOU SO GRIM? IS THAT YOUR ROMANTIC TECHNIQUE SINCE I SLAPPED YOU THAT NIGHT ON THE BOAT?
THE WOO MUST WAIT!... SEE IF YOUR SLICK LITTLE STENOG IS STILL AWAKE!
MISS SHERMAN AND MR. RYAN!!! THEY MUSTN'T FIND YOU HERE- ESPECIALLY AFTER WHAT I'VE TOLD YOU!... OUT ON THE BALCONY- QUICKLY!
OOOHHH...
WHY, YES... HU SHEE IS STILL UP!... WHY--
LOCK THAT BALCONY DOOR, RAVEN! NOW, YOU LITTLE CHINESE MATA HARI, START TALKING — WHAT'S THE RACKET?
MILTON CANIFF

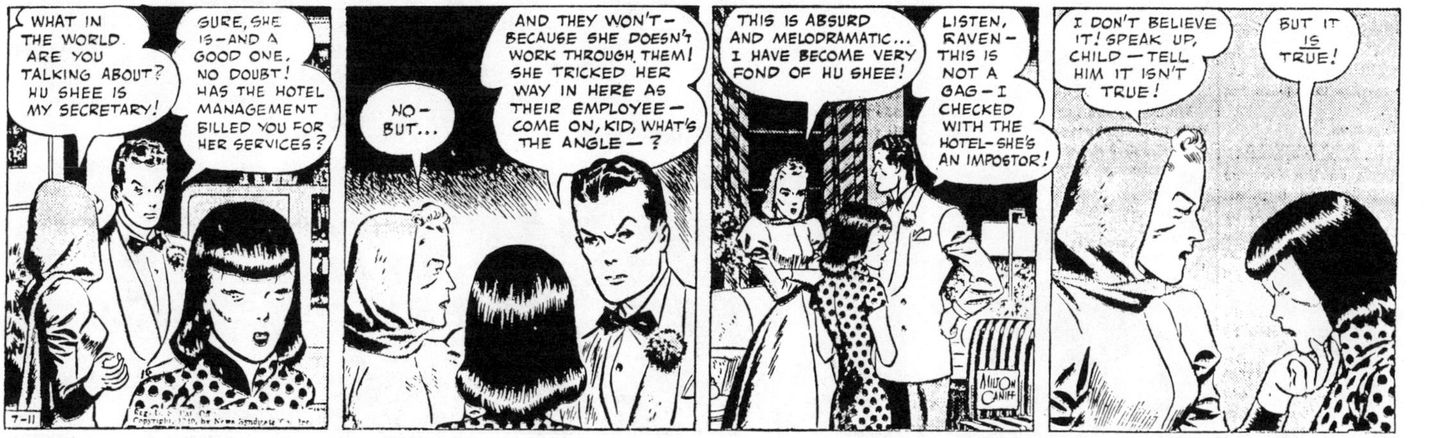
WHAT IN THE WORLD ARE YOU TALKING ABOUT? HU SHEE IS MY SECRETARY!
SURE, SHE IS — AND A GOOD ONE, NO DOUBT! HAS THE HOTEL MANAGEMENT BILLED YOU FOR HER SERVICES?
7-11
NO — BUT...
AND THEY WON'T — BECAUSE SHE DOESN'T WORK THROUGH THEM! SHE TRICKED HER WAY IN HERE AS THEIR EMPLOYEE — COME ON, KID, WHAT'S THE ANGLE — ?
THIS IS ABSURD AND MELODRAMATIC... I HAVE BECOME VERY FOND OF HU SHEE!
LISTEN, RAVEN — THIS IS NOT A GAG — I CHECKED WITH THE HOTEL — SHE'S AN IMPOSTOR!
MILTON CANIFF
I DON'T BELIEVE IT! SPEAK UP, CHILD — TELL HIM IT ISN'T TRUE!
BUT IT IS TRUE!

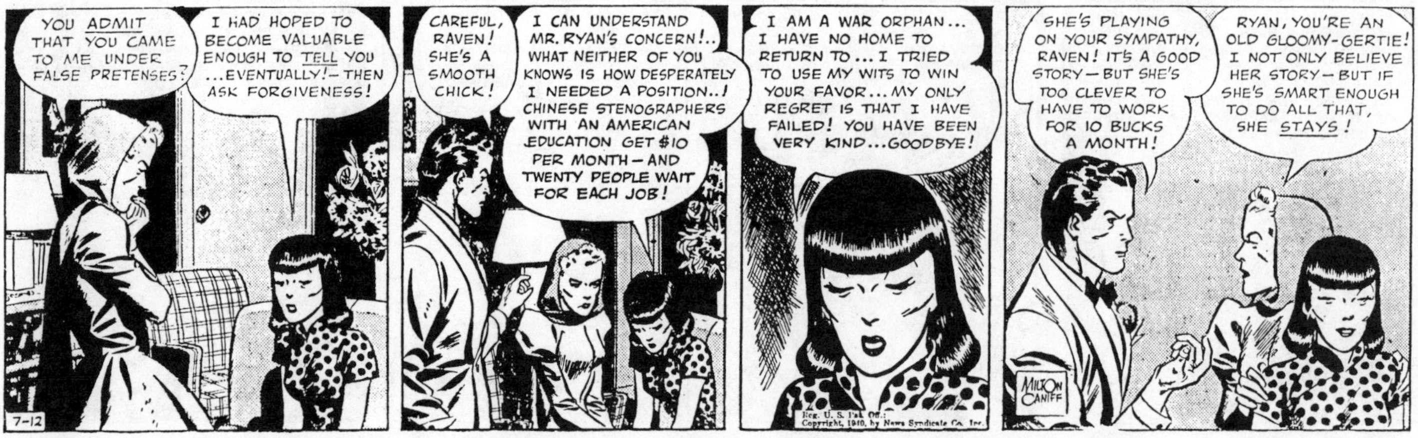
YOU ADMIT THAT YOU CAME TO ME UNDER FALSE PRETENSES?
I HAD HOPED TO BECOME VALUABLE ENOUGH TO TELL YOU ...EVENTUALLY!—THEN ASK FORGIVENESS!
7-12
CAREFUL, RAVEN! SHE'S A SMOOTH CHICK!
I CAN UNDERSTAND MR. RYAN'S CONCERN!.. WHAT NEITHER OF YOU KNOWS IS HOW DESPERATELY I NEEDED A POSITION..! CHINESE STENOGRAPHERS WITH AN AMERICAN EDUCATION GET $10 PER MONTH—AND TWENTY PEOPLE WAIT FOR EACH JOB!
I AM A WAR ORPHAN... I HAVE NO HOME TO RETURN TO... I TRIED TO USE MY WITS TO WIN YOUR FAVOR... MY ONLY REGRET IS THAT I HAVE FAILED! YOU HAVE BEEN VERY KIND... GOODBYE!
Reg. U. S. Pat. Off.: Copyright, 1940, by News Syndicate Co. Inc.
SHE'S PLAYING ON YOUR SYMPATHY, RAVEN! IT'S A GOOD STORY—BUT SHE'S TOO CLEVER TO HAVE TO WORK FOR 10 BUCKS A MONTH!
RYAN, YOU'RE AN OLD GLOOMY-GERTIE! I NOT ONLY BELIEVE HER STORY—BUT IF SHE'S SMART ENOUGH TO DO ALL THAT, SHE STAYS!
MILTON CANIFF

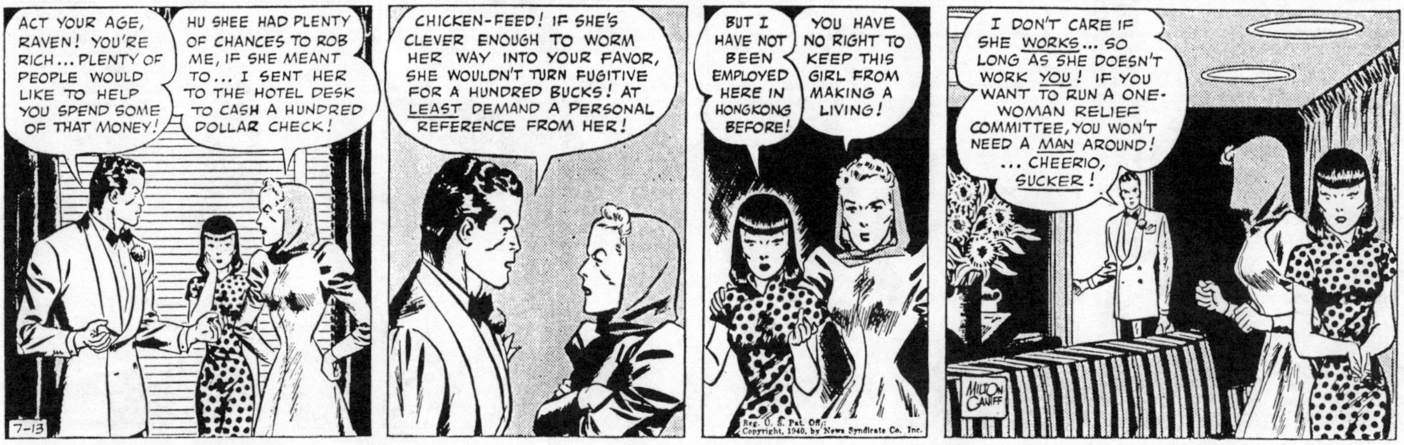
ACT YOUR AGE, RAVEN! YOU'RE RICH... PLENTY OF PEOPLE WOULD LIKE TO HELP YOU SPEND SOME OF THAT MONEY!
HU SHEE HAD PLENTY OF CHANCES TO ROB ME, IF SHE MEANT TO... I SENT HER TO THE HOTEL DESK TO CASH A HUNDRED DOLLAR CHECK!
7-13
CHICKEN-FEED! IF SHE'S CLEVER ENOUGH TO WORM HER WAY INTO YOUR FAVOR, SHE WOULDN'T TURN FUGITIVE FOR A HUNDRED BUCKS! AT LEAST DEMAND A PERSONAL REFERENCE FROM HER!
BUT I HAVE NOT BEEN EMPLOYED HERE IN HONGKONG BEFORE!
YOU HAVE NO RIGHT TO KEEP THIS GIRL FROM MAKING A LIVING!
Reg. U. S. Pat. Off.: Copyright, 1940, by News Syndicate Co. Inc.
I DON'T CARE IF SHE WORKS... SO LONG AS SHE DOESN'T WORK YOU! IF YOU WANT TO RUN A ONE-WOMAN RELIEF COMMITTEE, YOU WON'T NEED A MAN AROUND! ... CHEERIO, SUCKER!
MILTON CANIFF

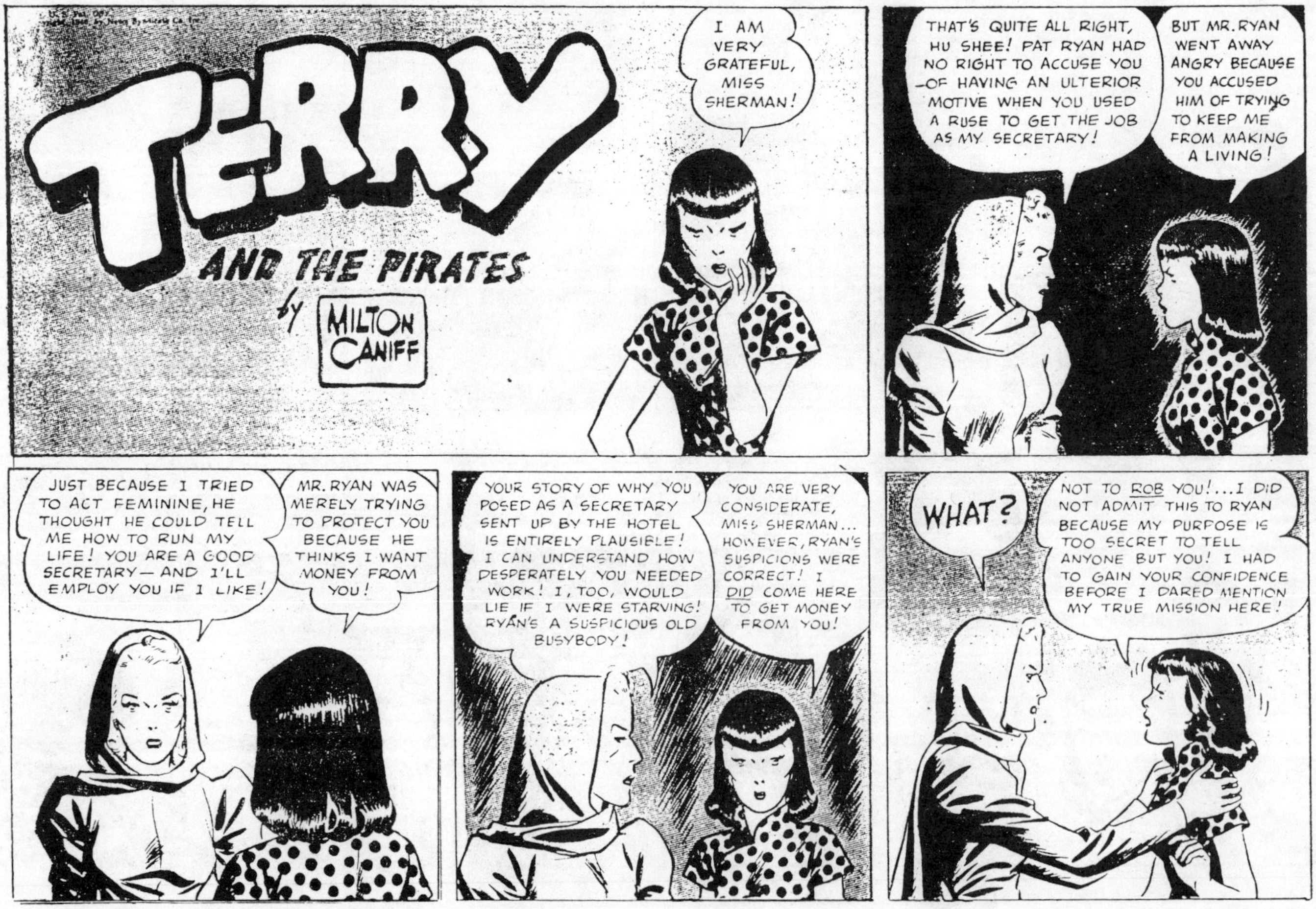
TERRY AND THE PIRATES
by MILTON CANIFF
I AM VERY GRATEFUL, MISS SHERMAN!
THAT'S QUITE ALL RIGHT, HU SHEE! PAT RYAN HAD NO RIGHT TO ACCUSE YOU OF HAVING AN ULTERIOR MOTIVE WHEN YOU USED A RUSE TO GET THE JOB AS MY SECRETARY!
BUT MR. RYAN WENT AWAY ANGRY BECAUSE YOU ACCUSED HIM OF TRYING TO KEEP ME FROM MAKING A LIVING!
JUST BECAUSE I TRIED TO ACT FEMININE, HE THOUGHT HE COULD TELL ME HOW TO RUN MY LIFE! YOU ARE A GOOD SECRETARY—AND I'LL EMPLOY YOU IF I LIKE!
MR. RYAN WAS MERELY TRYING TO PROTECT YOU BECAUSE HE THINKS I WANT MONEY FROM YOU!
YOUR STORY OF WHY YOU POSED AS A SECRETARY SENT UP BY THE HOTEL IS ENTIRELY PLAUSIBLE! I CAN UNDERSTAND HOW DESPERATELY YOU NEEDED WORK! I, TOO, WOULD LIE IF I WERE STARVING! RYAN'S A SUSPICIOUS OLD BUSYBODY!
YOU ARE VERY CONSIDERATE, MISS SHERMAN... HOWEVER, RYAN'S SUSPICIONS WERE CORRECT! I DID COME HERE TO GET MONEY FROM YOU!
WHAT?
NOT TO ROB YOU!... I DID NOT ADMIT THIS TO RYAN BECAUSE MY PURPOSE IS TOO SECRET TO TELL ANYONE BUT YOU! I HAD TO GAIN YOUR CONFIDENCE BEFORE I DARED MENTION MY TRUE MISSION HERE!

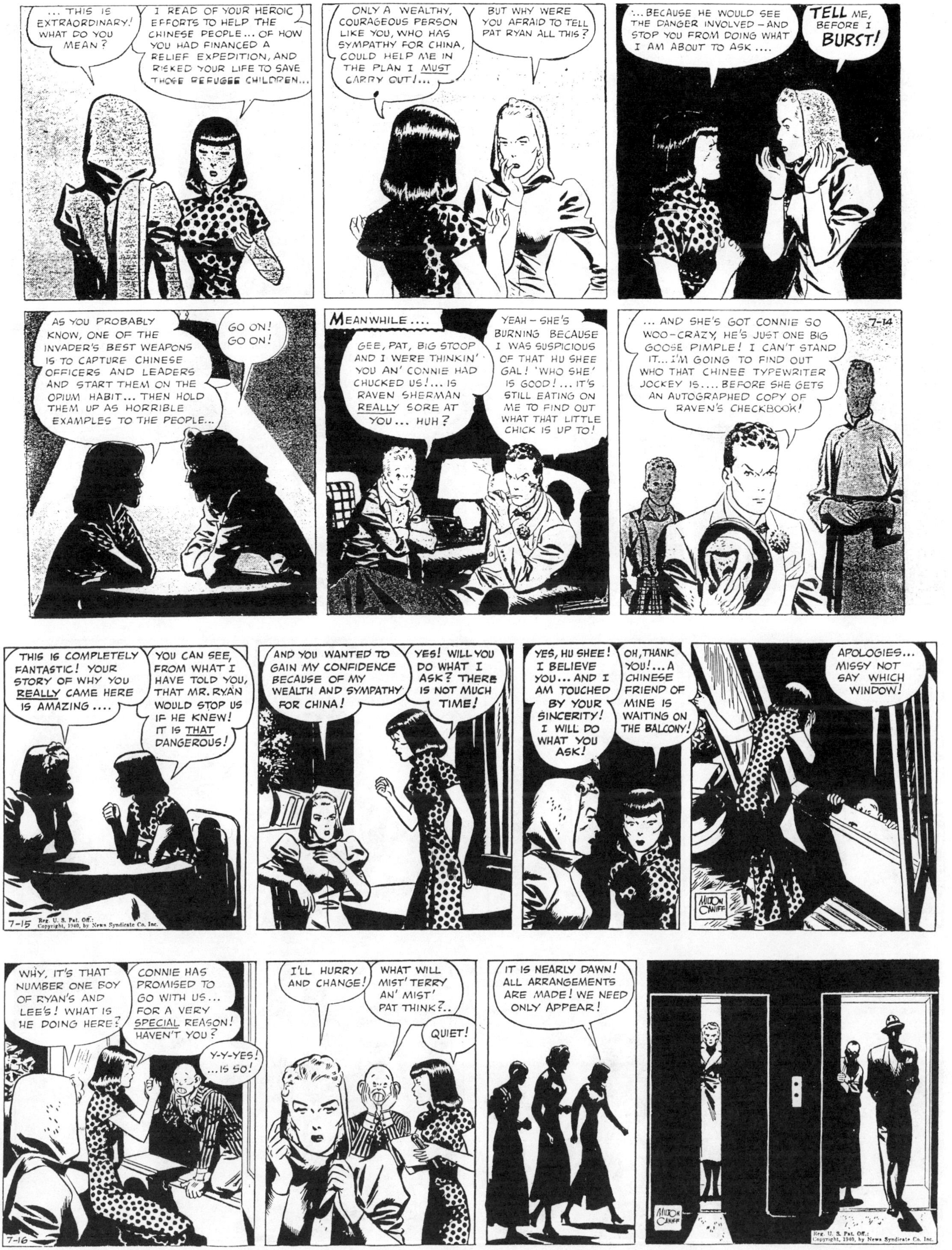
... THIS IS EXTRAORDINARY! WHAT DO YOU MEAN?
I READ OF YOUR HEROIC EFFORTS TO HELP THE CHINESE PEOPLE... OF HOW YOU HAD FINANCED A RELIEF EXPEDITION, AND RISKED YOUR LIFE TO SAVE THOSE REFUGEE CHILDREN...
ONLY A WEALTHY, COURAGEOUS PERSON LIKE YOU, WHO HAS SYMPATHY FOR CHINA, COULD HELP ME IN THE PLAN I MUST CARRY OUT!...
BUT WHY WERE YOU AFRAID TO TELL PAT RYAN ALL THIS?
...BECAUSE HE WOULD SEE THE DANGER INVOLVED – AND STOP YOU FROM DOING WHAT I AM ABOUT TO ASK....
TELL ME, BEFORE I BURST!
AS YOU PROBABLY KNOW, ONE OF THE INVADER'S BEST WEAPONS IS TO CAPTURE CHINESE OFFICERS AND LEADERS AND START THEM ON THE OPIUM HABIT... THEN HOLD THEM UP AS HORRIBLE EXAMPLES TO THE PEOPLE...
GO ON! GO ON!
MEANWHILE....
GEE, PAT, BIG STOOP AND I WERE THINKIN' YOU AN' CONNIE HAD CHUCKED US!... IS RAVEN SHERMAN REALLY SORE AT YOU... HUH?
YEAH – SHE'S BURNING BECAUSE I WAS SUSPICIOUS OF THAT HU SHEE GAL! 'WHO SHE' IS GOOD!... IT'S STILL EATING ON ME TO FIND OUT WHAT THAT LITTLE CHICK IS UP TO!
... AND SHE'S GOT CONNIE SO WOO-CRAZY, HE'S JUST ONE BIG GOOSE PIMPLE! I CAN'T STAND IT... I'M GOING TO FIND OUT WHO THAT CHINEE TYPEWRITER JOCKEY IS.... BEFORE SHE GETS AN AUTOGRAPHED COPY OF RAVEN'S CHECKBOOK!
7-14
THIS IS COMPLETELY FANTASTIC! YOUR STORY OF WHY YOU REALLY CAME HERE IS AMAZING....
YOU CAN SEE, FROM WHAT I HAVE TOLD YOU, THAT MR. RYAN WOULD STOP US IF HE KNEW! IT IS THAT DANGEROUS!
AND YOU WANTED TO GAIN MY CONFIDENCE BECAUSE OF MY WEALTH AND SYMPATHY FOR CHINA!
YES! WILL YOU DO WHAT I ASK? THERE IS NOT MUCH TIME!
YES, HU SHEE! I BELIEVE YOU... AND I AM TOUCHED BY YOUR SINCERITY! I WILL DO WHAT YOU ASK!
OH, THANK YOU!... A CHINESE FRIEND OF MINE IS WAITING ON THE BALCONY!
APOLOGIES... MISSY NOT SAY WHICH WINDOW!
MILTON CANIFF
7-15
Reg. U. S. Pat. Off.: Copyright, 1940, by News Syndicate Co. Inc.
WHY, IT'S THAT NUMBER ONE BOY OF RYAN'S AND LEE'S! WHAT IS HE DOING HERE?
CONNIE HAS PROMISED TO GO WITH US... FOR A VERY SPECIAL REASON! HAVEN'T YOU?
Y-Y-YES! ...IS SO!
I'LL HURRY AND CHANGE!
WHAT WILL MIST' TERRY AN' MIST' PAT THINK?..
QUIET!
IT IS NEARLY DAWN! ALL ARRANGEMENTS ARE MADE! WE NEED ONLY APPEAR!
MILTON CANIFF
7-16
Reg. U. S. Pat. Off.: Copyright, 1940, by News Syndicate Co. Inc.

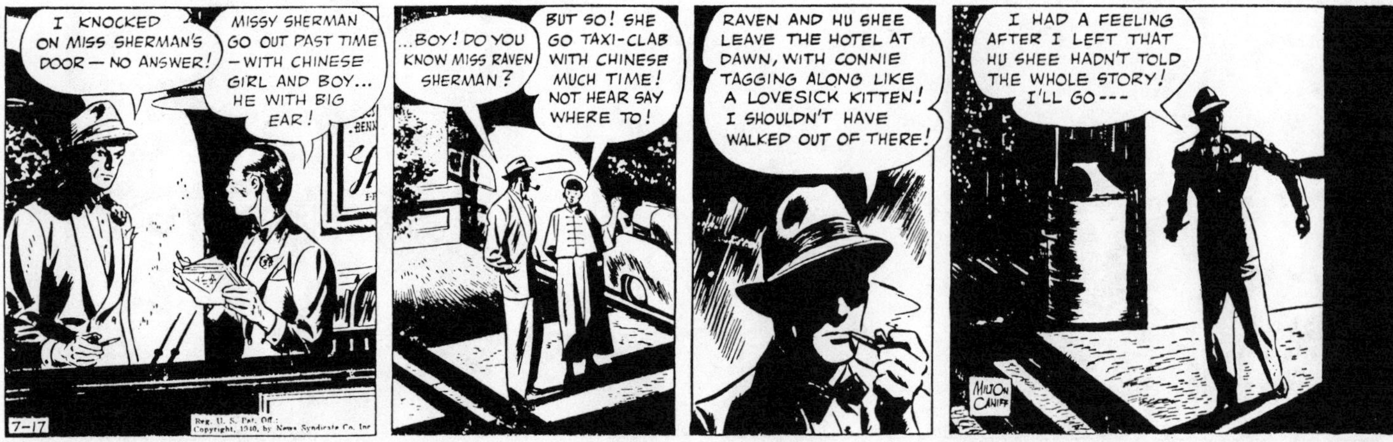
I KNOCKED ON MISS SHERMAN'S DOOR — NO ANSWER!
MISSY SHERMAN GO OUT PAST TIME — WITH CHINESE GIRL AND BOY... HE WITH BIG EAR!
...BOY! DO YOU KNOW MISS RAVEN SHERMAN?
BUT SO! SHE GO TAXI-CLAB WITH CHINESE MUCH TIME! NOT HEAR SAY WHERE TO!
RAVEN AND HU SHEE LEAVE THE HOTEL AT DAWN, WITH CONNIE TAGGING ALONG LIKE A LOVESICK KITTEN! I SHOULDN'T HAVE WALKED OUT OF THERE!
I HAD A FEELING AFTER I LEFT THAT HU SHEE HADN'T TOLD THE WHOLE STORY! I'LL GO---
MILTON CANIFF
7-17
Reg. U. S. Pat. Off.: Copyright, 1940, by News Syndicate Co. Inc.

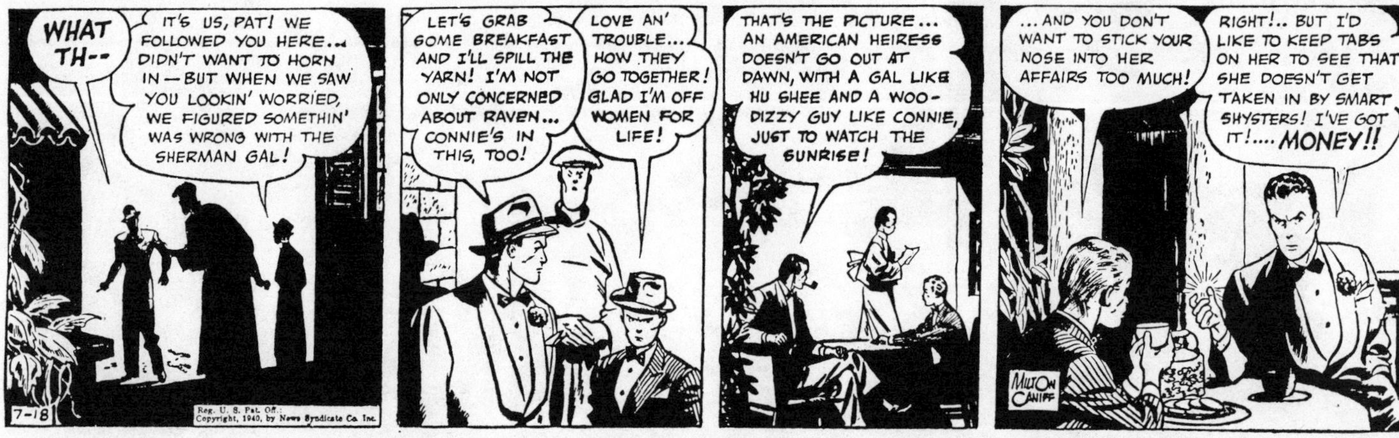
WHAT TH--
IT'S US, PAT! WE FOLLOWED YOU HERE... DIDN'T WANT TO HORN IN — BUT WHEN WE SAW YOU LOOKIN' WORRIED, WE FIGURED SOMETHIN' WAS WRONG WITH THE SHERMAN GAL!
LET'S GRAB SOME BREAKFAST AND I'LL SPILL THE YARN! I'M NOT ONLY CONCERNED ABOUT RAVEN... CONNIE'S IN THIS, TOO!
LOVE AN' TROUBLE... HOW THEY GO TOGETHER! GLAD I'M OFF WOMEN FOR LIFE!
THAT'S THE PICTURE... AN AMERICAN HEIRESS DOESN'T GO OUT AT DAWN, WITH A GAL LIKE HU SHEE AND A WOO-DIZZY GUY LIKE CONNIE, JUST TO WATCH THE SUNRISE!
...AND YOU DON'T WANT TO STICK YOUR NOSE INTO HER AFFAIRS TOO MUCH!
RIGHT!.. BUT I'D LIKE TO KEEP TABS ON HER TO SEE THAT SHE DOESN'T GET TAKEN IN BY SMART SHYSTERS! I'VE GOT IT!.... MONEY!!
MILTON CANIFF
7-18
Reg. U. S. Pat. Off.: Copyright, 1940, by News Syndicate Co. Inc.

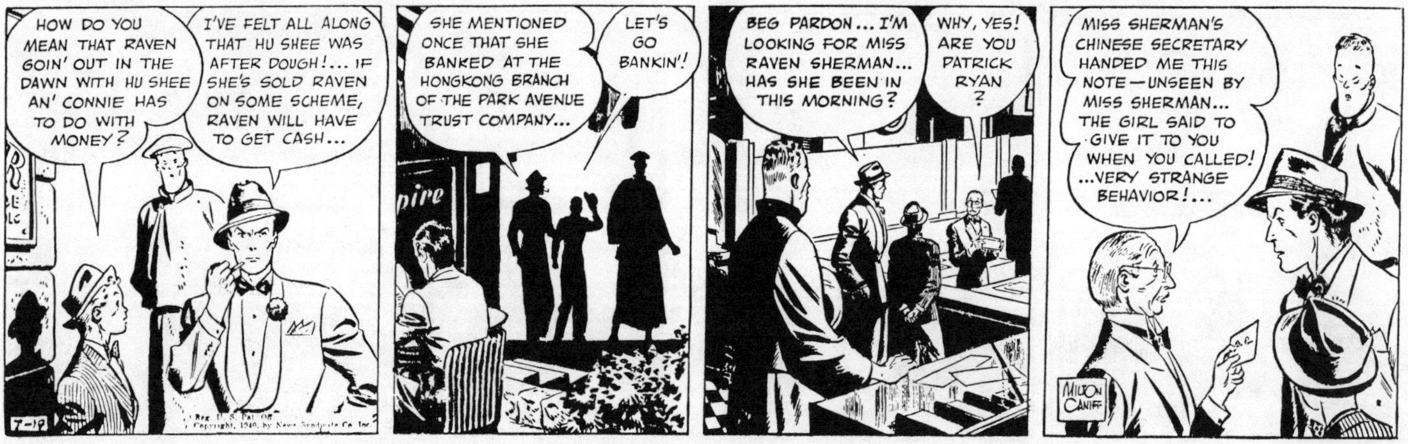
HOW DO YOU MEAN THAT RAVEN GOIN' OUT IN THE DAWN WITH HU SHEE AN' CONNIE HAS TO DO WITH MONEY?
I'VE FELT ALL ALONG THAT HU SHEE WAS AFTER DOUGH!... IF SHE'S SOLD RAVEN ON SOME SCHEME, RAVEN WILL HAVE TO GET CASH...
SHE MENTIONED ONCE THAT SHE BANKED AT THE HONGKONG BRANCH OF THE PARK AVENUE TRUST COMPANY...
LET'S GO BANKIN'!
BEG PARDON... I'M LOOKING FOR MISS RAVEN SHERMAN... HAS SHE BEEN IN THIS MORNING?
WHY, YES! ARE YOU PATRICK RYAN?
MISS SHERMAN'S CHINESE SECRETARY HANDED ME THIS NOTE — UNSEEN BY MISS SHERMAN... THE GIRL SAID TO GIVE IT TO YOU WHEN YOU CALLED! ...VERY STRANGE BEHAVIOR!...
MILTON CANIFF
7-19
Reg. U. S. Pat. Off.: Copyright, 1940, by News Syndicate Co. Inc.

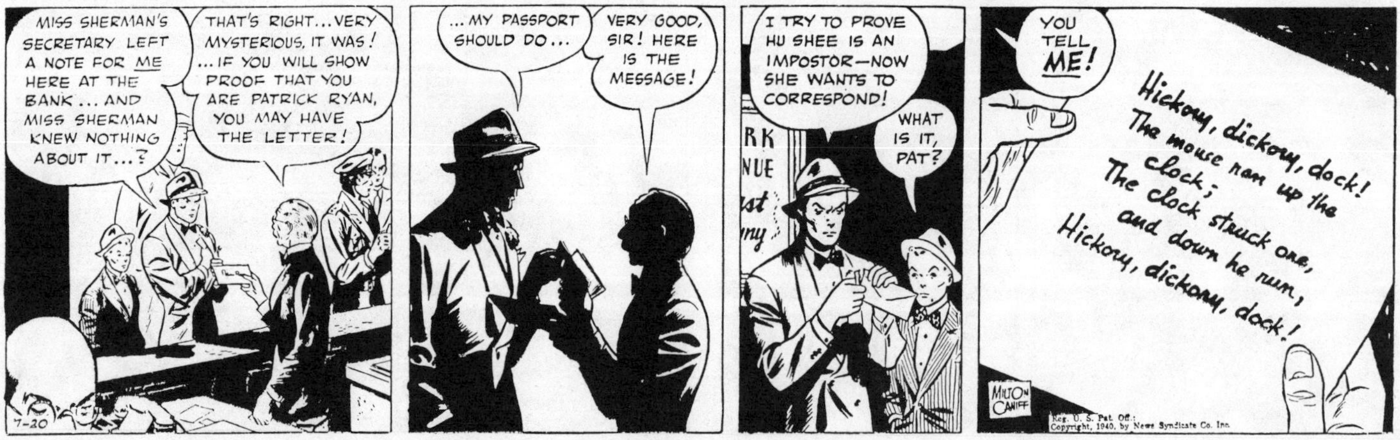
MISS SHERMAN'S SECRETARY LEFT A NOTE FOR ME HERE AT THE BANK... AND MISS SHERMAN KNEW NOTHING ABOUT IT...?
THAT'S RIGHT... VERY MYSTERIOUS, IT WAS! ...IF YOU WILL SHOW PROOF THAT YOU ARE PATRICK RYAN, YOU MAY HAVE THE LETTER!
...MY PASSPORT SHOULD DO...
VERY GOOD, SIR! HERE IS THE MESSAGE!
I TRY TO PROVE HU SHEE IS AN IMPOSTOR — NOW SHE WANTS TO CORRESPOND!
WHAT IS IT, PAT?
YOU TELL ME!
Hickory, dickory, dock! The mouse ran up the clock; The clock struck one, and down he run, Hickory, dickory, dock!
MILTON CANIFF
7-20
Reg. U. S. Pat. Off.: Copyright, 1940, by News Syndicate Co. Inc.

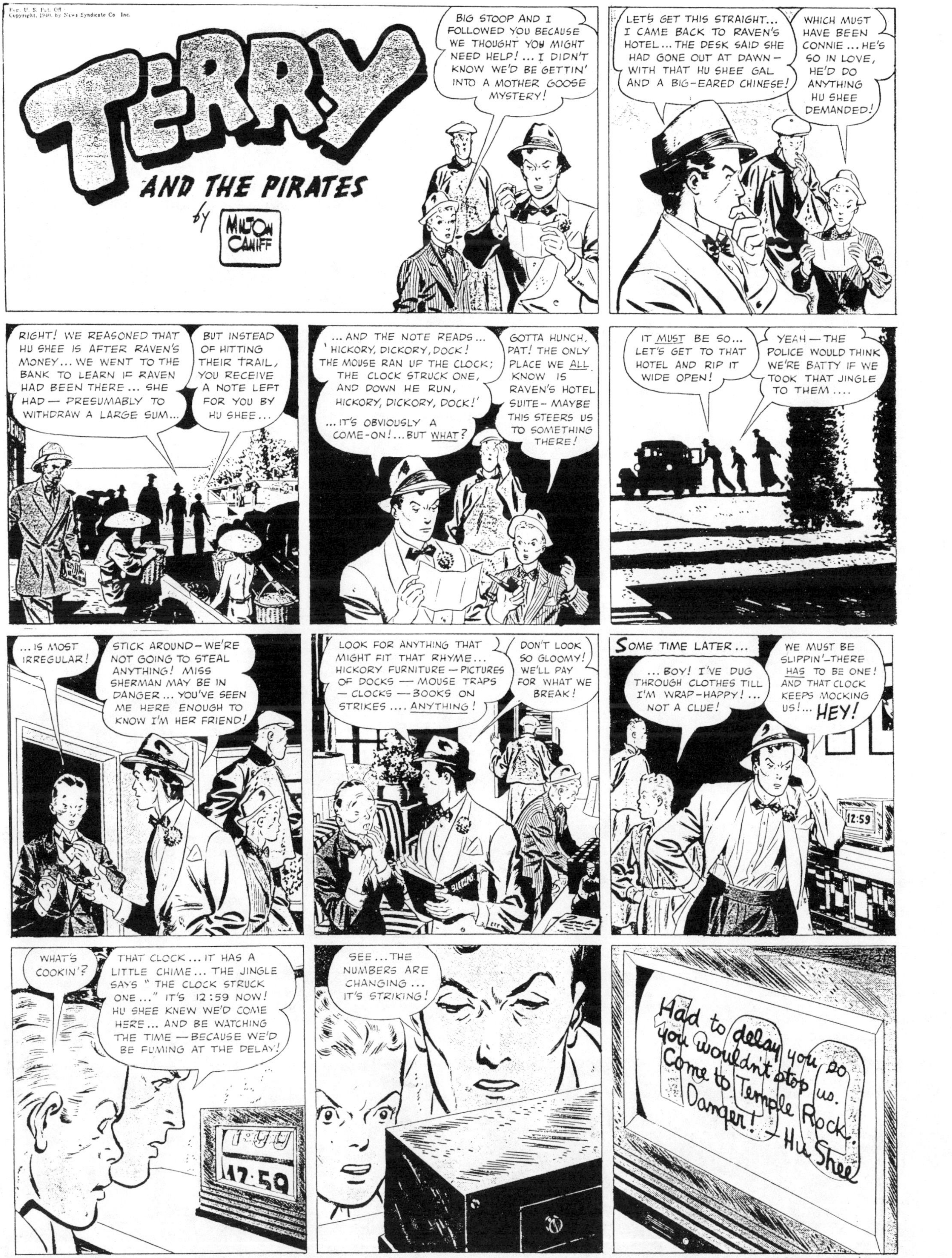
Reg. U. S. Pat. Off.
Copyright, 1940, by News Syndicate Co. Inc.
TERRY AND THE PIRATES
by MILTON CANIFF
BIG STOOP AND I FOLLOWED YOU BECAUSE WE THOUGHT YOU MIGHT NEED HELP! ... I DIDN'T KNOW WE'D BE GETTIN' INTO A MOTHER GOOSE MYSTERY!
LET'S GET THIS STRAIGHT... I CAME BACK TO RAVEN'S HOTEL... THE DESK SAID SHE HAD GONE OUT AT DAWN – WITH THAT HU SHEE GAL AND A BIG-EARED CHINESE!
WHICH MUST HAVE BEEN CONNIE... HE'S SO IN LOVE, HE'D DO ANYTHING HU SHEE DEMANDED!
RIGHT! WE REASONED THAT HU SHEE IS AFTER RAVEN'S MONEY... WE WENT TO THE BANK TO LEARN IF RAVEN HAD BEEN THERE... SHE HAD — PRESUMABLY TO WITHDRAW A LARGE SUM...
BUT INSTEAD OF HITTING THEIR TRAIL, YOU RECEIVE A NOTE LEFT FOR YOU BY HU SHEE...
... AND THE NOTE READS... 'HICKORY, DICKORY, DOCK! THE MOUSE RAN UP THE CLOCK; THE CLOCK STRUCK ONE, AND DOWN HE RUN, HICKORY, DICKORY, DOCK!' ... IT'S OBVIOUSLY A COME-ON! ... BUT WHAT?
GOTTA HUNCH, PAT! THE ONLY PLACE WE ALL KNOW IS RAVEN'S HOTEL SUITE – MAYBE THIS STEERS US TO SOMETHING THERE!
IT MUST BE SO... LET'S GET TO THAT HOTEL AND RIP IT WIDE OPEN!
YEAH — THE POLICE WOULD THINK WE'RE BATTY IF WE TOOK THAT JINGLE TO THEM....
... IS MOST IRREGULAR!
STICK AROUND – WE'RE NOT GOING TO STEAL ANYTHING! MISS SHERMAN MAY BE IN DANGER... YOU'VE SEEN ME HERE ENOUGH TO KNOW I'M HER FRIEND!
LOOK FOR ANYTHING THAT MIGHT FIT THAT RHYME... HICKORY FURNITURE — PICTURES OF DOCKS — MOUSE TRAPS — CLOCKS — BOOKS ON STRIKES.... ANYTHING!
DON'T LOOK SO GLOOMY! WE'LL PAY FOR WHAT WE BREAK!
SOME TIME LATER...
... BOY! I'VE DUG THROUGH CLOTHES TILL I'M WRAP-HAPPY! ... NOT A CLUE!
WE MUST BE SLIPPIN' – THERE HAS TO BE ONE! AND THAT CLOCK KEEPS MOCKING US! ... HEY!
12:59
WHAT'S COOKIN'?
THAT CLOCK... IT HAS A LITTLE CHIME... THE JINGLE SAYS "THE CLOCK STRUCK ONE..." IT'S 12:59 NOW! HU SHEE KNEW WE'D COME HERE... AND BE WATCHING THE TIME — BECAUSE WE'D BE FUMING AT THE DELAY!
12:59
SEE... THE NUMBERS ARE CHANGING... IT'S STRIKING!
Had to delay you so you wouldn't stop us. Come to Temple Rock. Danger! – Hu Shee

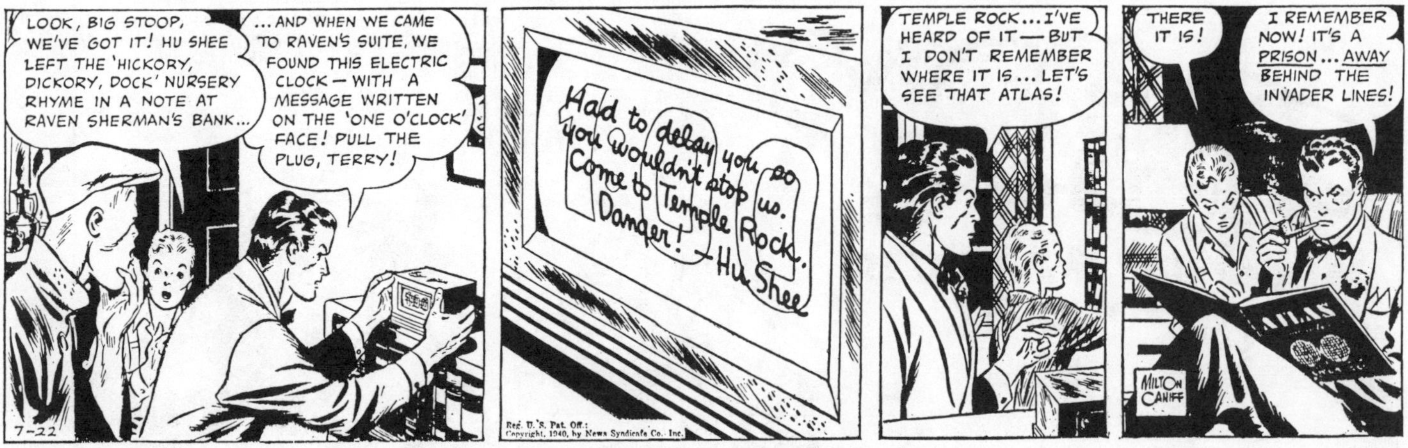

LOOK, BIG STOOP, WE'VE GOT IT! HU SHEE LEFT THE 'HICKORY, DICKORY, DOCK' NURSERY RHYME IN A NOTE AT RAVEN SHERMAN'S BANK...
...AND WHEN WE CAME TO RAVEN'S SUITE, WE FOUND THIS ELECTRIC CLOCK — WITH A MESSAGE WRITTEN ON THE 'ONE O'CLOCK' FACE! PULL THE PLUG, TERRY!
7-22
Had to delay you so you wouldn't stop us. Come to Temple Rock. Danger! — Hu Shee
Reg. U. S. Pat. Off.: Copyright, 1940, by News Syndicate Co. Inc.
TEMPLE ROCK... I'VE HEARD OF IT — BUT I DON'T REMEMBER WHERE IT IS... LET'S SEE THAT ATLAS!
THERE IT IS!
I REMEMBER NOW! IT'S A PRISON... AWAY BEHIND THE INVADER LINES!
ATLAS
MILTON CANIFF

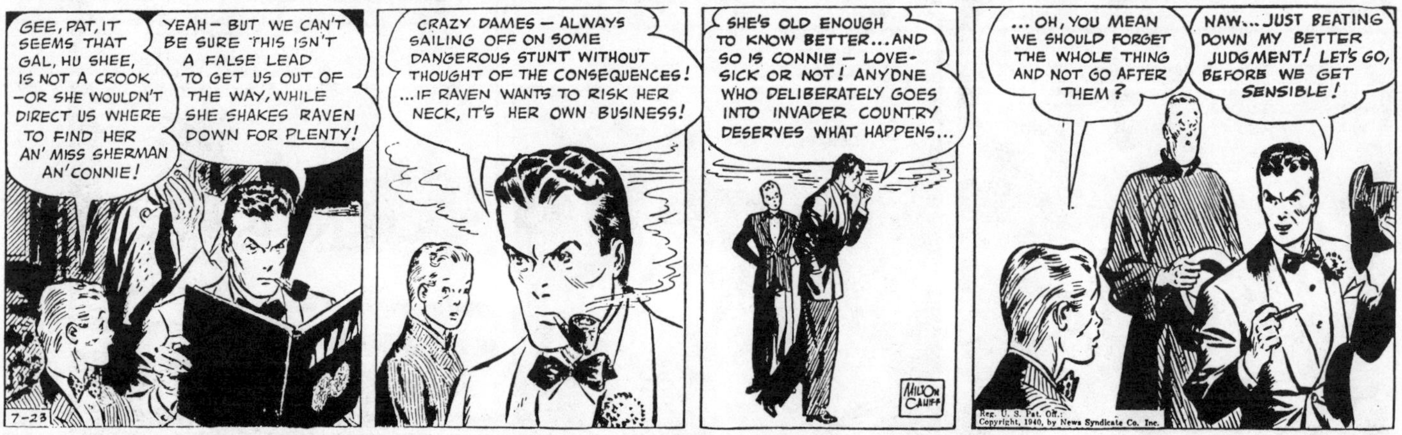

GEE, PAT, IT SEEMS THAT GAL, HU SHEE, IS NOT A CROOK —OR SHE WOULDN'T DIRECT US WHERE TO FIND HER AN' MISS SHERMAN AN' CONNIE!
YEAH — BUT WE CAN'T BE SURE THIS ISN'T A FALSE LEAD TO GET US OUT OF THE WAY, WHILE SHE SHAKES RAVEN DOWN FOR PLENTY!
7-23
CRAZY DAMES — ALWAYS SAILING OFF ON SOME DANGEROUS STUNT WITHOUT THOUGHT OF THE CONSEQUENCES! ...IF RAVEN WANTS TO RISK HER NECK, IT'S HER OWN BUSINESS!
SHE'S OLD ENOUGH TO KNOW BETTER... AND SO IS CONNIE — LOVE-SICK OR NOT! ANYONE WHO DELIBERATELY GOES INTO INVADER COUNTRY DESERVES WHAT HAPPENS...
MILTON CANIFF
...OH, YOU MEAN WE SHOULD FORGET THE WHOLE THING AND NOT GO AFTER THEM?
NAW... JUST BEATING DOWN MY BETTER JUDGMENT! LET'S GO, BEFORE WE GET SENSIBLE!
Reg. U. S. Pat. Off.: Copyright, 1940, by News Syndicate Co. Inc.

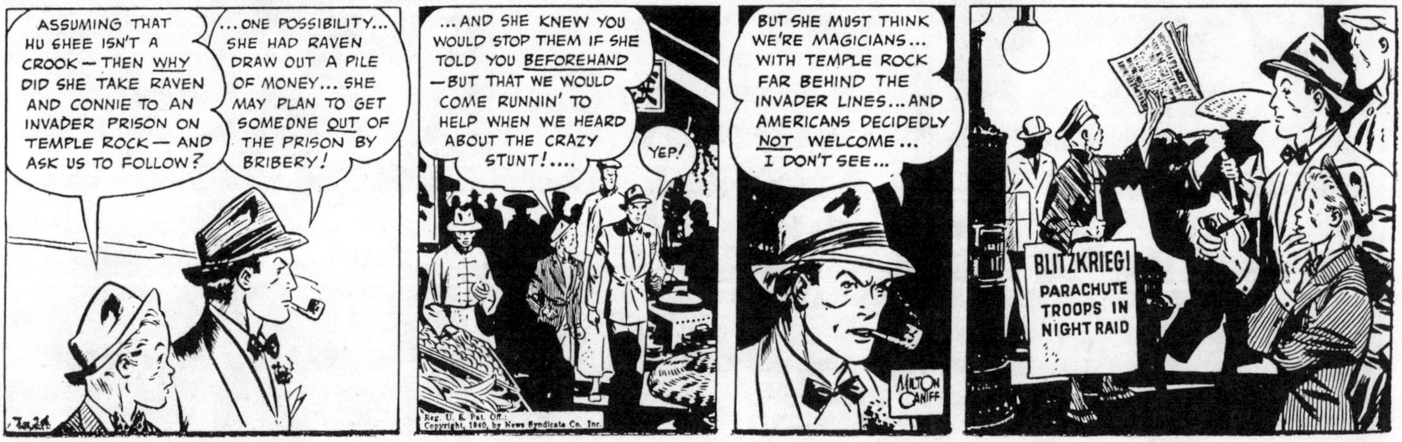

ASSUMING THAT HU SHEE ISN'T A CROOK — THEN WHY DID SHE TAKE RAVEN AND CONNIE TO AN INVADER PRISON ON TEMPLE ROCK — AND ASK US TO FOLLOW?
...ONE POSSIBILITY... SHE HAD RAVEN DRAW OUT A PILE OF MONEY... SHE MAY PLAN TO GET SOMEONE OUT OF THE PRISON BY BRIBERY!
7-24
...AND SHE KNEW YOU WOULD STOP THEM IF SHE TOLD YOU BEFOREHAND — BUT THAT WE WOULD COME RUNNIN' TO HELP WHEN WE HEARD ABOUT THE CRAZY STUNT!....
YEP!
Reg. U. S. Pat. Off.: Copyright, 1940, by News Syndicate Co. Inc.
BUT SHE MUST THINK WE'RE MAGICIANS... WITH TEMPLE ROCK FAR BEHIND THE INVADER LINES... AND AMERICANS DECIDEDLY NOT WELCOME... I DON'T SEE...
MILTON CANIFF
BLITZKRIEG!
PARACHUTE TROOPS IN NIGHT RAID

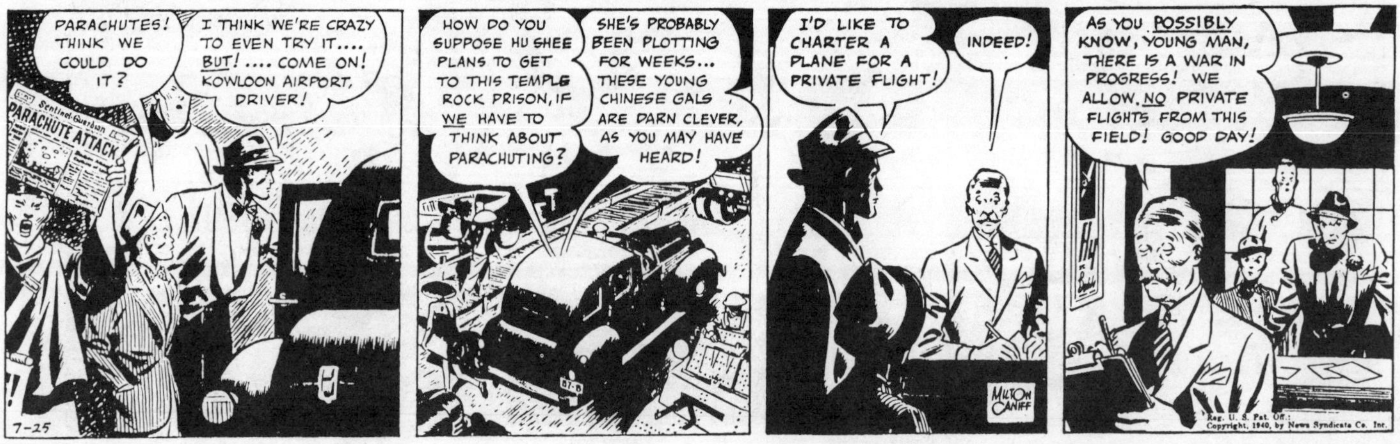

PARACHUTES! THINK WE COULD DO IT?
I THINK WE'RE CRAZY TO EVEN TRY IT.... BUT! .... COME ON! KOWLOON AIRPORT, DRIVER!
Sentinel-Guardian
PARACHUTE ATTACK
7-25
HOW DO YOU SUPPOSE HU SHEE PLANS TO GET TO THIS TEMPLE ROCK PRISON, IF WE HAVE TO THINK ABOUT PARACHUTING?
SHE'S PROBABLY BEEN PLOTTING FOR WEEKS... THESE YOUNG CHINESE GALS ARE DARN CLEVER, AS YOU MAY HAVE HEARD!
I'D LIKE TO CHARTER A PLANE FOR A PRIVATE FLIGHT!
INDEED!
MILTON CANIFF
AS YOU POSSIBLY KNOW, YOUNG MAN, THERE IS A WAR IN PROGRESS! WE ALLOW NO PRIVATE FLIGHTS FROM THIS FIELD! GOOD DAY!
Reg. U. S. Pat. Off.: Copyright, 1940, by News Syndicate Co. Inc.

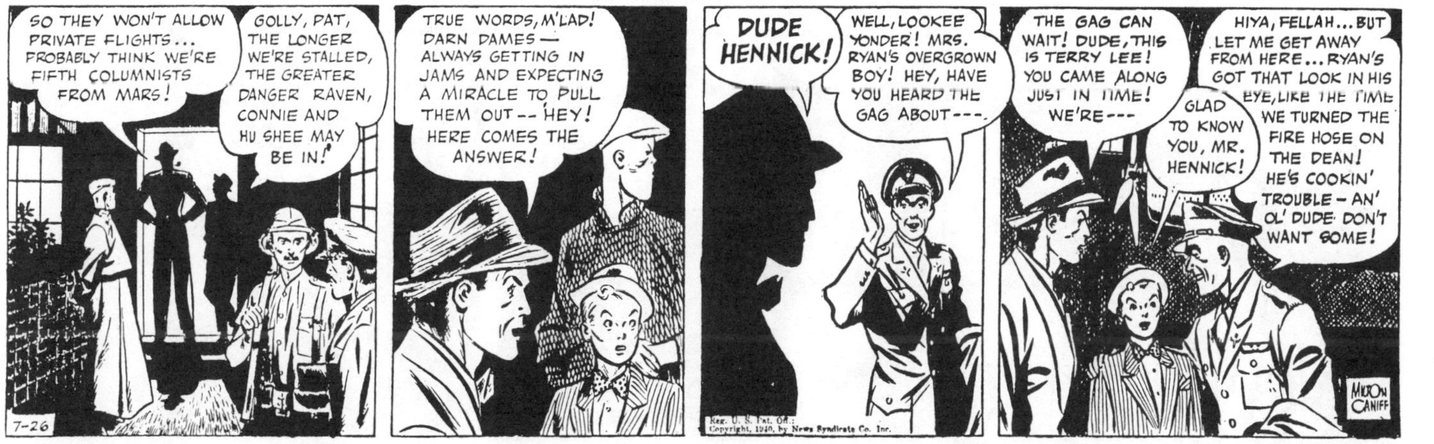
SO THEY WON'T ALLOW PRIVATE FLIGHTS... PROBABLY THINK WE'RE FIFTH COLUMNISTS FROM MARS!
GOLLY, PAT, THE LONGER WE'RE STALLED, THE GREATER DANGER RAVEN, CONNIE AND HU SHEE MAY BE IN!
7-26
TRUE WORDS, M'LAD! DARN DAMES — ALWAYS GETTING IN JAMS AND EXPECTING A MIRACLE TO PULL THEM OUT -- HEY! HERE COMES THE ANSWER!
DUDE HENNICK!
WELL, LOOKEE YONDER! MRS. RYAN'S OVERGROWN BOY! HEY, HAVE YOU HEARD THE GAG ABOUT---
Reg. U. S. Pat. Off.: Copyright, 1940, by News Syndicate Co. Inc.
THE GAG CAN WAIT! DUDE, THIS IS TERRY LEE! YOU CAME ALONG JUST IN TIME! WE'RE---
GLAD TO KNOW YOU, MR. HENNICK!
HIYA, FELLAH... BUT LET ME GET AWAY FROM HERE... RYAN'S GOT THAT LOOK IN HIS EYE, LIKE THE TIME WE TURNED THE FIRE HOSE ON THE DEAN! HE'S COOKIN' TROUBLE - AN' OL' DUDE DON'T WANT SOME!
MILTON CANIFF

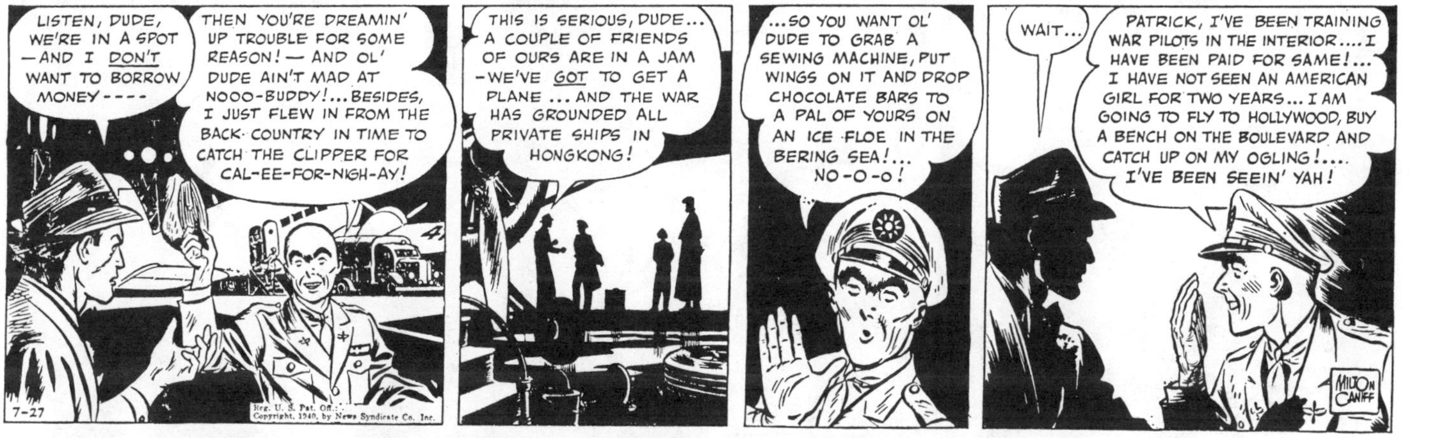
LISTEN, DUDE, WE'RE IN A SPOT — AND I DON'T WANT TO BORROW MONEY----
THEN YOU'RE DREAMIN' UP TROUBLE FOR SOME REASON! — AND OL' DUDE AIN'T MAD AT NOOO-BUDDY!... BESIDES, I JUST FLEW IN FROM THE BACK COUNTRY IN TIME TO CATCH THE CLIPPER FOR CAL-EE-FOR-NIGH-AY!
7-27
Reg. U. S. Pat. Off.: Copyright, 1940, by News Syndicate Co. Inc.
THIS IS SERIOUS, DUDE... A COUPLE OF FRIENDS OF OURS ARE IN A JAM - WE'VE GOT TO GET A PLANE ... AND THE WAR HAS GROUNDED ALL PRIVATE SHIPS IN HONGKONG!
...SO YOU WANT OL' DUDE TO GRAB A SEWING MACHINE, PUT WINGS ON IT AND DROP CHOCOLATE BARS TO A PAL OF YOURS ON AN ICE FLOE IN THE BERING SEA!... NO-O-O!
WAIT...
PATRICK, I'VE BEEN TRAINING WAR PILOTS IN THE INTERIOR.... I HAVE BEEN PAID FOR SAME!... I HAVE NOT SEEN AN AMERICAN GIRL FOR TWO YEARS... I AM GOING TO FLY TO HOLLYWOOD, BUY A BENCH ON THE BOULEVARD AND CATCH UP ON MY OGLING!.... I'VE BEEN SEEIN' YAH!
MILTON CANIFF

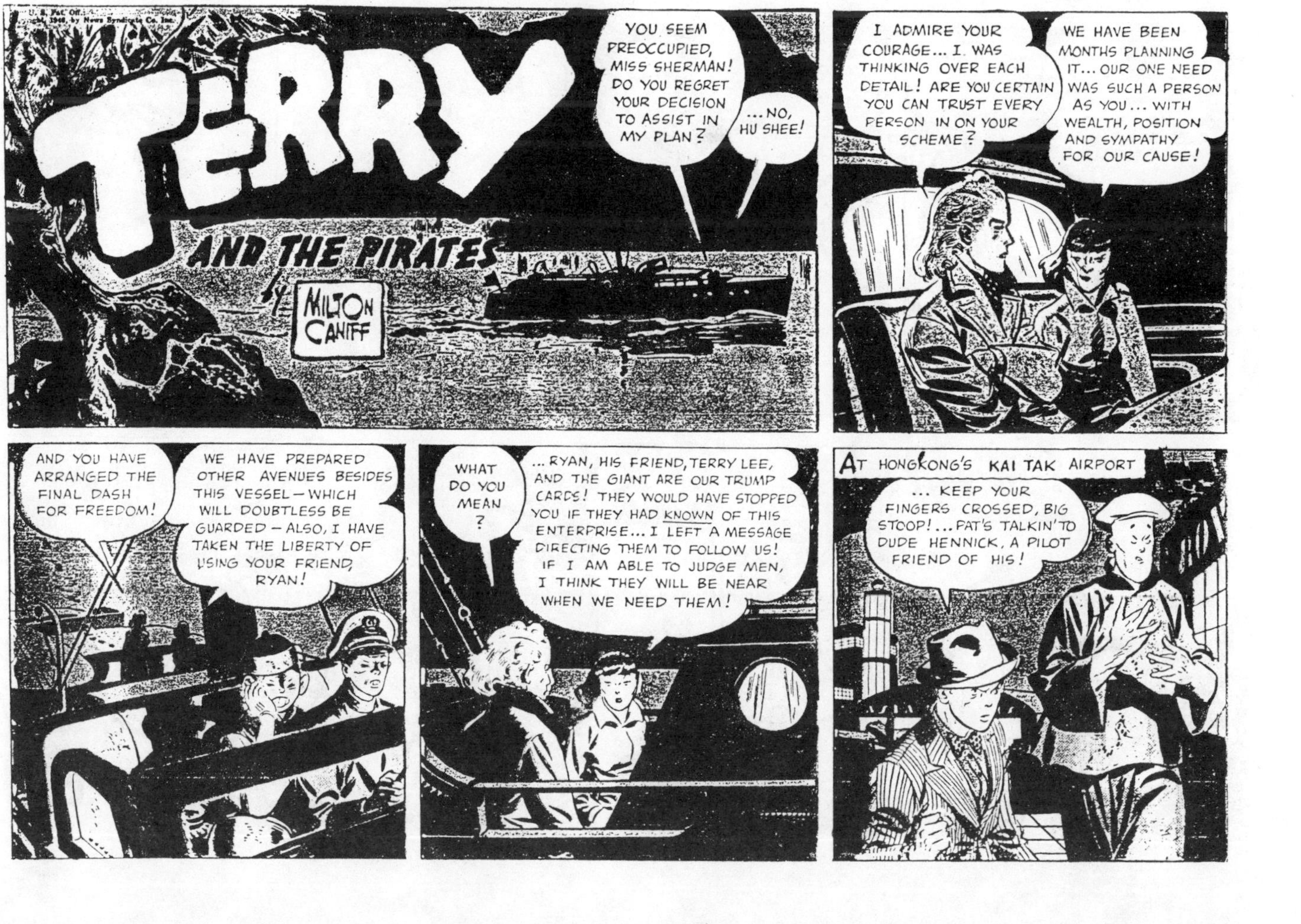
TERRY AND THE PIRATES by MILTON CANIFF
YOU SEEM PREOCCUPIED, MISS SHERMAN! DO YOU REGRET YOUR DECISION TO ASSIST IN MY PLAN?
...NO, HU SHEE!
I ADMIRE YOUR COURAGE... I WAS THINKING OVER EACH DETAIL! ARE YOU CERTAIN YOU CAN TRUST EVERY PERSON IN ON YOUR SCHEME?
WE HAVE BEEN MONTHS PLANNING IT... OUR ONE NEED WAS SUCH A PERSON AS YOU... WITH WEALTH, POSITION AND SYMPATHY FOR OUR CAUSE!
AND YOU HAVE ARRANGED THE FINAL DASH FOR FREEDOM!
WE HAVE PREPARED OTHER AVENUES BESIDES THIS VESSEL — WHICH WILL DOUBTLESS BE GUARDED — ALSO, I HAVE TAKEN THE LIBERTY OF USING YOUR FRIEND, RYAN!
WHAT DO YOU MEAN?
...RYAN, HIS FRIEND, TERRY LEE, AND THE GIANT ARE OUR TRUMP CARDS! THEY WOULD HAVE STOPPED YOU IF THEY HAD KNOWN OF THIS ENTERPRISE... I LEFT A MESSAGE DIRECTING THEM TO FOLLOW US! IF I AM ABLE TO JUDGE MEN, I THINK THEY WILL BE NEAR WHEN WE NEED THEM!
AT HONGKONG'S KAI TAK AIRPORT
... KEEP YOUR FINGERS CROSSED, BIG STOOP!... PAT'S TALKIN' TO DUDE HENNICK, A PILOT FRIEND OF HIS!

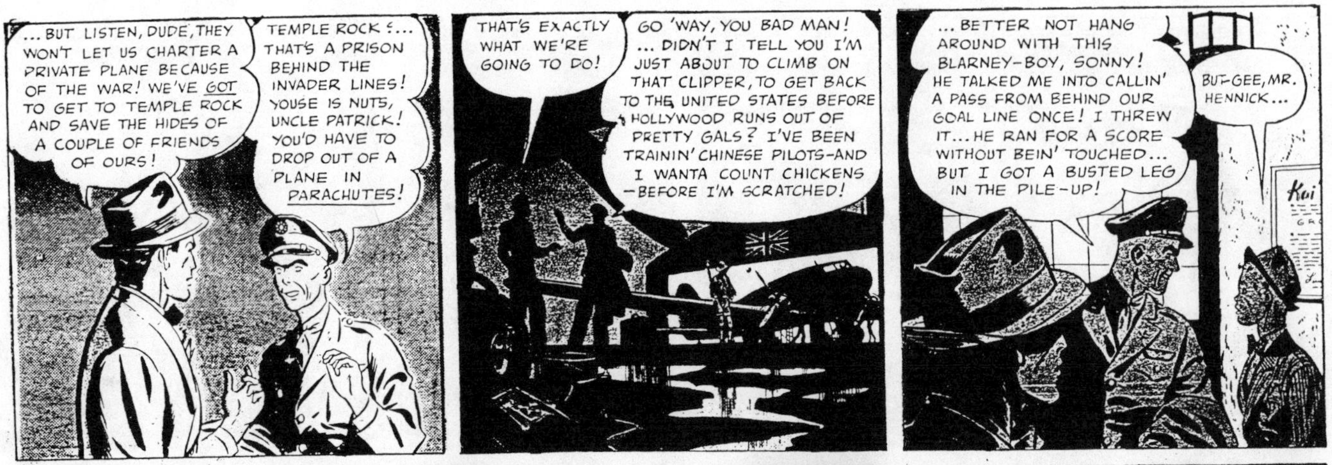
... BUT LISTEN, DUDE, THEY WON'T LET US CHARTER A PRIVATE PLANE BECAUSE OF THE WAR! WE'VE GOT TO GET TO TEMPLE ROCK AND SAVE THE HIDES OF A COUPLE OF FRIENDS OF OURS!
TEMPLE ROCK?... THAT'S A PRISON BEHIND THE INVADER LINES! YOUSE IS NUTS, UNCLE PATRICK! YOU'D HAVE TO DROP OUT OF A PLANE IN PARACHUTES!
THAT'S EXACTLY WHAT WE'RE GOING TO DO!
GO 'WAY, YOU BAD MAN! ... DIDN'T I TELL YOU I'M JUST ABOUT TO CLIMB ON THAT CLIPPER, TO GET BACK TO THE UNITED STATES BEFORE HOLLYWOOD RUNS OUT OF PRETTY GALS? I'VE BEEN TRAININ' CHINESE PILOTS—AND I WANTA COUNT CHICKENS —BEFORE I'M SCRATCHED!
... BETTER NOT HANG AROUND WITH THIS BLARNEY-BOY, SONNY! HE TALKED ME INTO CALLIN' A PASS FROM BEHIND OUR GOAL LINE ONCE! I THREW IT... HE RAN FOR A SCORE WITHOUT BEIN' TOUCHED... BUT I GOT A BUSTED LEG IN THE PILE-UP!
BUT-GEE, MR. HENNICK...

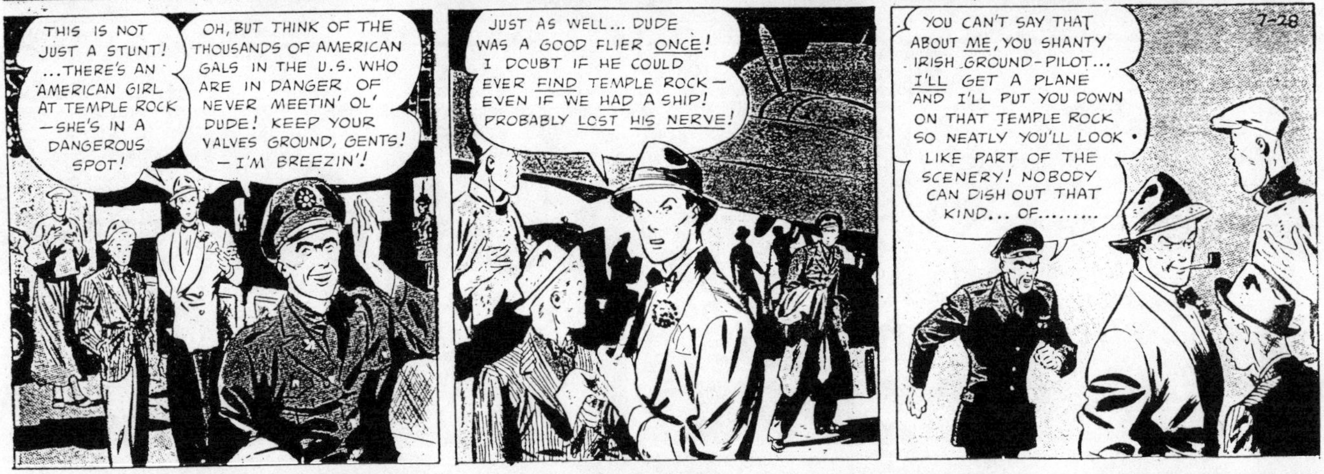
THIS IS NOT JUST A STUNT! ... THERE'S AN AMERICAN GIRL AT TEMPLE ROCK —SHE'S IN A DANGEROUS SPOT!
OH, BUT THINK OF THE THOUSANDS OF AMERICAN GALS IN THE U.S. WHO ARE IN DANGER OF NEVER MEETIN' OL' DUDE! KEEP YOUR VALVES GROUND, GENTS! —I'M BREEZIN'!
JUST AS WELL... DUDE WAS A GOOD FLIER ONCE! I DOUBT IF HE COULD EVER FIND TEMPLE ROCK— EVEN IF WE HAD A SHIP! PROBABLY LOST HIS NERVE!
7-28
YOU CAN'T SAY THAT ABOUT ME, YOU SHANTY IRISH GROUND-PILOT... I'LL GET A PLANE AND I'LL PUT YOU DOWN ON THAT TEMPLE ROCK SO NEATLY YOU'LL LOOK LIKE PART OF THE SCENERY! NOBODY CAN DISH OUT THAT KIND... OF........

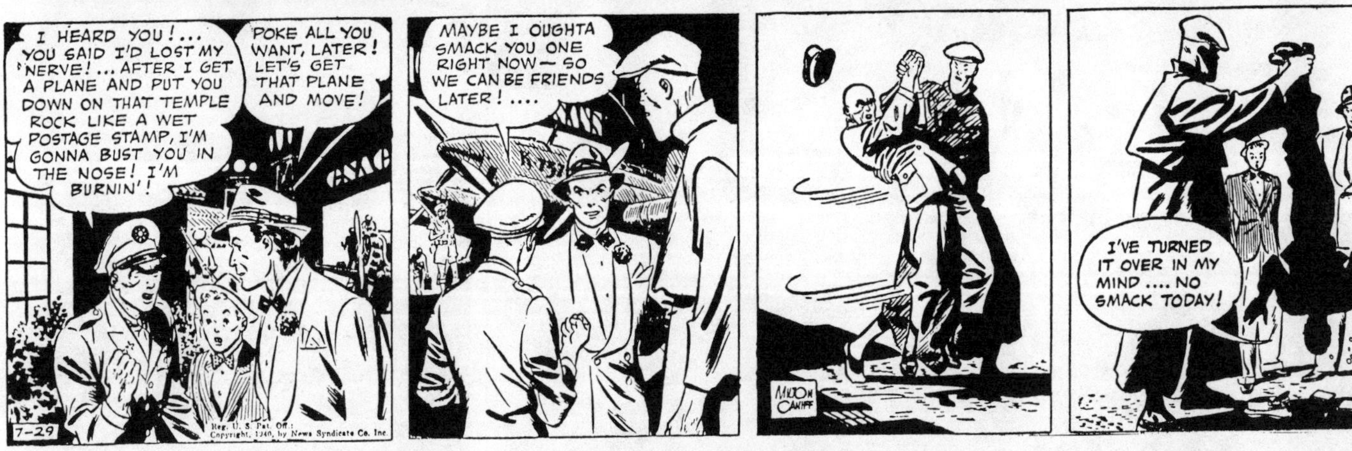
I HEARD YOU!... YOU SAID I'D LOST MY NERVE! ... AFTER I GET A PLANE AND PUT YOU DOWN ON THAT TEMPLE ROCK LIKE A WET POSTAGE STAMP, I'M GONNA BUST YOU IN THE NOSE! I'M BURNIN'!
POKE ALL YOU WANT, LATER! LET'S GET THAT PLANE AND MOVE!
7-29
Reg. U. S. Pat. Off.; Copyright, 1940, by News Syndicate Co. Inc.
MAYBE I OUGHTA SMACK YOU ONE RIGHT NOW— SO WE CAN BE FRIENDS LATER! ....
MILTON CANIFF
I'VE TURNED IT OVER IN MY MIND .... NO SMACK TODAY!

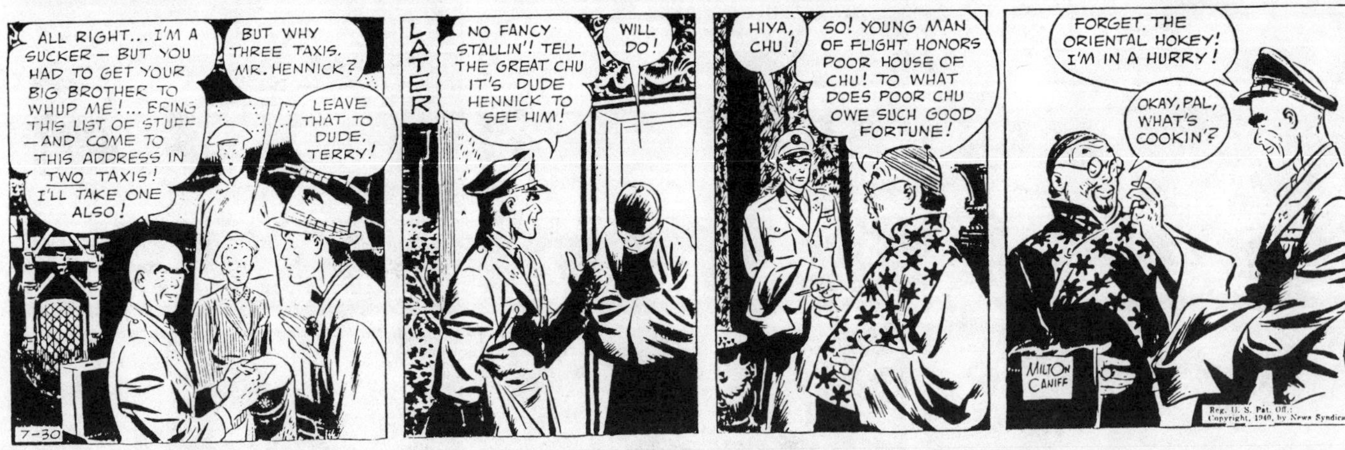
ALL RIGHT... I'M A SUCKER— BUT YOU HAD TO GET YOUR BIG BROTHER TO WHUP ME! ... BRING THIS LIST OF STUFF —AND COME TO THIS ADDRESS IN TWO TAXIS! I'LL TAKE ONE ALSO!
BUT WHY THREE TAXIS, MR. HENNICK?
LEAVE THAT TO DUDE, TERRY!
7-30
LATER
NO FANCY STALLIN'! TELL THE GREAT CHU IT'S DUDE HENNICK TO SEE HIM!
WILL DO!
HIYA, CHU!
SO! YOUNG MAN OF FLIGHT HONORS POOR HOUSE OF CHU! TO WHAT DOES POOR CHU OWE SUCH GOOD FORTUNE!
MILTON CANIFF
FORGET THE ORIENTAL HOKEY! I'M IN A HURRY!
OKAY, PAL, WHAT'S COOKIN'?
Reg. U. S. Pat. Off.; Copyright, 1940, by News Syndicate Co. Inc.

OTHER CANIFF BOOKS FROM NBM

TERRY & THE PIRATES "COLLECTORS ' EDITION"
12 288-320 page, hardbound, gold stamped books reprint the complete *TERRY*. Every daily and Sunday strip, many never before reprinted, is shown in full size. Write for more information.

MILTON CANIFF - REMBRANDT OF THE COMIC STRIP
The original version of this book appeared in 1946 as Caniff was finishing his work on *TERRY*. Comic historian Rick Marschall has updated this 1980 edition. There are many rare and beautiful illustrations and blowups of Caniff art. Paperback - $6.95.

KLANG THE WARLORD
TERRY
AND THE PIRATES
NO. 6
1938

MISSING ANY VOLUMES?
TERRY & THE PIRATES paperback
reprinting chronologically from the beginning. Issued quarterly. Each 64 pp., 81/2x11, color cover.

Vol. 1 Welcome to China (1934) $5.95
Vol. 2 Marooned with Burma (1935) $5.95
Vol. 3 Dragon Lady's Revenge (1936) $5.95
Vol. 4 Getting Snared (1936-1937) $5.95
Vol. 5 Shanghaied (1937) $5.95
Vol. 6 The Warlord Klang (1937-1938) $6.95
Vol. 7 The Hunter (1938) $6.95
Vol. 8 The Baron (1938-1939) $6.95
Vol. 9 Feminine Venom (1939) $6.95
Vol. 10 Network of Intrigue (1939-1940) $6.95

NOW AVAILABLE: SUBSCRIPTIONS!
You can subscribe to 4 starting with any volume: $25 (free P&H).

THE HUNTER
TERRY
AND THE PIRATES
NO. 7
1938

ALSO: HANDSOME SLIPCASED SETS
4 Volumes in each for a total of 256 pages of intense reading slipcased in beautiful leatherette, gold stamped.
Vols. 1-4: $27.50
Vols. 5-8: $29.50
slipcase alone: $7.50

THE BARON
TERRY
AND THE PIRATES
NO. 8
1938-1939

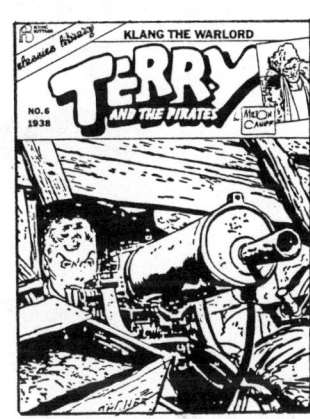

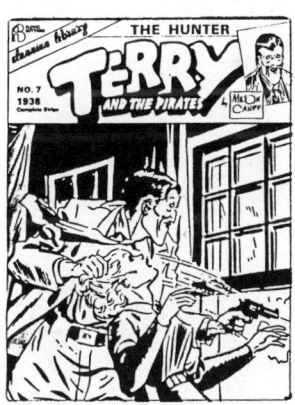

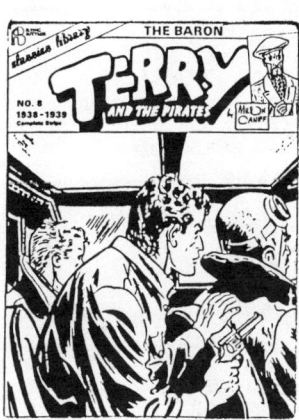

P&H: add $2 first item, $1 each addt'l.
Allow 6-8 weeks for delivery.

NBM
35-53 70th St.
Jackson Heights, NY 11372

Flying Buttress Classics Library

announces:

the complete

WASH TUBBS & CAPTAIN EASY by ROY CRANE

1924 - 1943

The Flying Buttress Classics Library, announces a new reprint: Roy Crane's classic WASH TUBBS (1924-1943). Wash Tubbs was Crane's first strip, and already with it he set the pace for future adventure strips to match, including Terry & The Pirates. Wash Tubbs exemplifies two-fisted adventure spiced with a good sense of humor. Wash and his pals, Gozzy Gallup and **Captain Easy**, battle arch villians Bull Dawson and Shanghai Slug in exotic locales on land and sea around the world.

Each volume of this quarterly **18** volume **complete reprint** will contain 192 pages of action. Like our recently completed Terry & The Pirates series, you can count on high quality and regular publishing schedules. Both hardcover and paperback will be available in a large but handy 11 by 8 1/2 format. Each volume will print approximately one year's worth of strips. Sundays are included.

PAPERBACK EDITION:
$16.95 each
(add $2.00 postage & handling)

HARDCOVER EDITION
$32.50 each
(add $2.00 postage & handling)

Vols. 1-6 available

SPECIAL OFFER:
Order your subscription to any 4 hardcover volumes and pay only $80! Also available: you can subscribe to the paperback edition for $50 for any four. (no p + h for subs)

NBM
35-53 70th St.
Jackson Heights, NY 11372